# Vore

Ariadne Pautina

**Vore** by Ariadne Pautina


ebook ISBN: 978-1-0687051-5-1
Paperback ISBN: 978-1-0687051-4-4



**The full list of content warnings are at the rear of the book.**

Where citations have been provided, these have been researched and clarified; however, should improvement or amendment be required, please make contact.

Find Ariadne here:
linktr.ee/ariadnepautina
www.ariadnepautina.com

**Also by Ariadne Pautina**

*The Elemental Pentology*
One: Alabaster
Two: Lacrymosa
Three: Torrefy
Four: Sempiternal
Five: And Let Time Stand, Still

The Menagerie

Path To The Dark Moon

*It’s only the dose which makes it poison;*
*so be a good boy, kneel, and consume every single drop*

# Vore

Ariadne Pautina

# One

Standing before the black wooden door, she hesitantly contemplated the store while trying to block the encroaching hum of foot traffic. Discordant shoes, voices, and distant music, mixing with the thrum of her heart, the vibrant pulse keeping eager pace in her ears.

Angrily, she wiped an errant tear from her cheek.

Exhaled.

Forced her body to calm.

Reseated the bag on her shoulder.

Her eyes lifting from the grey paving to the wide bay windows which overflowed with glass bottles and herbs. The enticing soft lights winding around the frames and over shelves. Her hazy gaze moving to the trio of women working within.

'Do you think she'll come in today?' Bryony asked, glancing up from the myrrh tumbling into a slim paper envelope; her slender sepia fingers tapping the base to ensure the contents settled. Beside her, a collection of differing jars formed an arc.

The granite worktop was graced with a precise scale, small weights, and instruction labels; the apothecary's bespoke design printed in tonal shades, conveying their mission in flowers, snakes, and wings. Services offered and quality strived for documented without words.

Though it was Anara Eden who had established this venture, who had built Erinyes despite personal sacrifice and adversity, each woman who worked for her shared their united purpose.

Resting the folded cloth on her thighs, Kerezen looked first to the street then her friend. On her knees, the polished parquet flooring below her and a caddy of cleaning materials to one side, she used her position near the window to assess the person loitering beyond.

'She'll come in when she's ready,' Anara remarked. On the sliding ladder affixed to shelves which spanned the back wall, she reached for one of the higher drawers. Fitted to the space, the old wooden shelving held a vast array of herbs, spices, and resins, with neatly typed cards on each. Some in vintage glass jars, some in clay, some in metal tins.

The rarer unlabelled and known only to the staff.

'I hope she doesn't leave it too late,' Kerezen said, pushing up from the floor and brushing stray auburn strands away from her face.

'That's for her to decide.' Anara, the desired item in her cotton apron pocket, returned to ground level. No malice in her tone, no cruelty in her words, only a simple truth.

Their offerings would be here, waiting.

They each knew how much courage it sometimes took to cross the threshold. Some visited for months before they dare enquire about what was whispered of. Others remained unaware of the full extent of support Erinyes could provide, and merely purchased herbs or tinctures, potions and spices, to utilise in their own ways.

Neither approach was wrong, and all were welcomed.

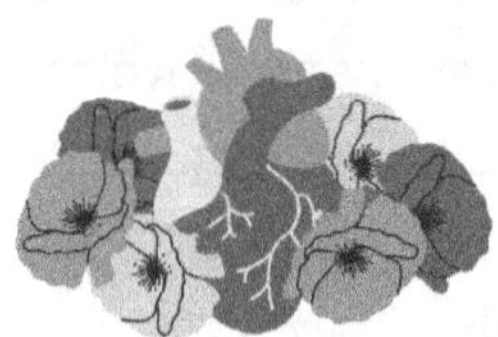

Methodically, Vadim buttoned the silk waistcoat. His dark eyes narrowed as he cast a critical gaze over his reflection; the dressing room's large mirror draped in shadow.

Behind him, tailored black suits hung above low cupboards. Sleek fabric framed him, shrouding him with familiar hue. Each identical layer caressing his statuesque figure, tonally complementary to his raven hair, to the stylish stubble across his strong jaw and full lips.

His focus shifted with the vibration of his phone.

Answering it, but remaining silent.

'It's done,' they confirmed.

Vadim disconnected the call, throwing the device to the upholstered black leather bench. He crossed to the dresser below the window, umber eyes quick to assess the visible grounds before falling to the drawer; a selection of blades glinting in the conflicting light.

Natural luminosity outside and diffused lamps within.

Sliding the смерш[1] combat knife from the custom-built cushion, he smiled. The sheath betrayed the years he had wielded the weapon, with creases in the leather and scuffs near the edges. A favourite, amongst so many he relied on.

With the trusted blade housed at his ankle, his Грач[2] and additional magazines in a shoulder holster, Vadimir Morozov felt ready to begin his day. Reaching for his jacket, he drew it over his broad shoulders, leaving it unbuttoned; dark material cut to accentuate his physique while hiding the weaponry at his side.

Content, he strode from the room, through the master suite, and to the spacious landing. The stairs. Arriving in the mostly open plan lower floor, he found a meal waiting for him in the kitchen; the plate warm and steam rising from the nutritious dish.

Vodka open beside it.

The sun was beginning to dip toward the tips of large trees along the boundary of his estate, with twilight devouring the sky. This was the time he felt most alive; the night his for conquering.

---

[1] смерш - Russian for 'SMERSH', an acronym meaning 'death to spies', a World War II Soviet counter-intelligence agency, and also the name of this Russian combat knife

[2] Грач - Russian for 'rook'. A high-capacity, double-action, semi-automatic 9mm pistol; Russian standard military-issue side arm, capable of firing armour-piercing bullets

Her hand curled around the cool steel, teeth chewing on her lip. She was more and more conscious of her surroundings, while simultaneously felt a greater detachment. Sound swollen and distorted. Her vision a mass of blurred shapes, of smeared colours. Pressure mounted in Sofiya's mind, in her muscles, her neck. Tension stiffening her limbs.

*Now or never*, she thought.

Soft music washed over her as she stepped inside; blended aromas soothing her body and soul. Sauntering with restraint, Sofiya browsed the shelves and saw nothing. The bottles and packets merging into a single row of hopes, of dreams, of potential. Remedies which could not deliver her from this silent nightmare.

The unspoken words and sleepless nights.

The duplicitous prayers and denied confessions.

Gripping her bag, Sofiya reached the counter and scanned the store again. Other than the three female staff, it was empty; it was why she had lingered. Why she had monitored it for the past few days.

'May I help?' Bryony Fournier asked, her lilac off-shoulder top partly hidden by the black apron; the Erinyes logo embroidered on the bib. She offered the woman a warm smile, her dark eyes creasing.

Sofiya's lips opened, her brow furrowing. Her gaze darted to the floor, to the shelves, to the door. Her tongue was dry, her throat sore. A slow bead of sweat rolled down her spine.

'Would you prefer to come into the consulting room?' Anara stood in the opening to the rear of the store; a private area which provided both stock and refuge.

She met the owner's welcoming face and nodded once.

Bryony, pushing her box braids over one shoulder, lifted the counter and opened the gated shelving to allow the woman through. She caught

Kerezen Appleton's hazel eyes and exchanged a knowing smile; heavy and sorrowful. Both women were cognisant of the likely discussion about to take place.

Anara guided the woman through to the room occupying the left side of the rectangular building. The front half dedicated to the public, and the back divided to suit their needs.

To the needs of those who needed them.

Nervously, Sofiya absorbed the large wooden table in the centre of the main space; a series of meticulous tools, evidence of how the stock was processed, placed at one end. Shelving housed pre-prepared items and raw materials. A small kitchen glimpsed near a door marked as a restroom. Two locked doors, one opposite the entry they had passed through and one at the farthest end, looked substantial. Sofiya assumed it would take them to the alley behind the row of shops.

Steering the guest through, Anara quietly shut the door. 'I can leave it open, if you'd prefer.'

Sofiya shook her head, the blonde ponytail whipping the air.

The room was simple. A desk in similar wood to the table they had walked by, cupboards, and two large armchairs. An examination table sat below the frosted glass of the window; the obscured surface disguised any possible view in or out. While a bright light remained off, it was ready and directed to the paper-covered surface. Otherwise, the ambience was peaceful, a softness which belied the brutality often discussed.

Anara strode to her usual chair, the suede moulding to her curves as she settled. The hem of her black trousers lifted to reveal the snowy skin of her long legs, the apron falling over her thighs. Tamed, most of her jet curls remained in the French twist created that morning.

She studied the woman, how uncertainly she held herself, how the knuckles of her entwined hands revealed her anxiety, how she trembled despite the warmth. Allowing the silence to speak, Anara waited.

'Are the adverts true?' Sofiya said hastily, her eyes anywhere but the woman. Roving the floorboards, the knots in the wood.

'Yes.'

Sofiya's breath stayed shallow; the answer allowing her to collapse into the vacant chair and risk raising her head. 'I need… I….'

'Take your time,' Anara said gently, when the woman's voice faded and her focus fell again. 'We don't need names or addresses, unless you feel comfortable to share; however, we do need some medical history so that we can keep you safe.'

Nodding, she closed her eyes. Exhaled. 'I'm okay. Sorry.'

'There's no need to apologise.'

'Sofiya.' She swallowed. Wondered if she should have provided an alternative name. Reassured herself with aspirational promises that they would never meet again. 'I've no allergies, no other meds.'

'Okay.' Anara smiled. 'Thank you, Sofiya.'

'I can't go to my doctor, because they can't help,' she said, urgency now driving her words, 'and I can't tell… him, because he… I can't do this, I can't. Not now.'

'It's okay.' Anara reached across, her hand lightly resting on Sofiya's knee and eyes searching for connection. Amber meeting azure.

'It's not.' A tear traced her flushed cheek. 'They'll know, I know they'll figure it out, and then… my Father… I'll be in so much trouble.'

She returned upright; chest tight and anger curtailed with purposeful breaths. Anara bit into her tongue, her jaw taut. Frustration bound her limbs, wrapped through each cell and roiled in her blood.

'Can you help me, please?' Sofiya turned watery eyes to her.

'Absolutely.' Anara stood and strode to the cupboard, pulling out a small bottle. 'This will help, but it won't be painless—'

'I don't deserve painless.'

'Sofiya,' she sighed, 'you do. But I can't give you that, I can only give you this, which will help your body find her rhythm once more.'

She chewed on her lower lip, rummaging in her bag for money.

'There's no charge, Sofiya.' Anara crouched before her. 'But before you take it, please let me check you over.'

Tears flowed unhindered; Anara's warmth, her assured poise and soft touch, drawing out the denied emotion from Sofiya's soul. She had fought for weeks, had pretended everything was normal, and continued to ignore the lingering possibility of discovery.

Of reality.

It was easier to live that way. Sofiya had struggled to accept things had changed, struggled to accept she needed to act. She knew there was no other way. No other route she could take.

Allowing this to continue was impossible.

'When you're ready, please get on the bed,' Anara coaxed, standing and placing the small bottle on the cupboard beside the exit. The green glass cast a mint shadow over the worn oak.

Bracing herself with the chair, Sofiya pushed herself up and moved to the bed in a daze. Part of her wondered if this was too easy; that she had been gifted a drug and would be free to leave. That she had no need to share any details. What she had volunteered the barest minimum to obtain what she wanted.

Perhaps this was a trap, a punishment.

'My shoes,' she muttered, sitting up from the paper.

'It's okay,' Anara said, one gloved hand resting on her shoulder to ease her back to the bed. She looked over the woman's petite form, how Sofiya's limbs still betrayed the unease in her system. 'I'm going to press on your lower abdomen, okay?'

Sofiya nodded, placing one forearm over her eyes and teeth digging into her lip. Her chest heaved with the swallowed sobs.

'Have you done any kind of pregnancy test?'

'Yes.' Sofiya's breath caught. 'Several.'

Each result unbelievable. Refused.

Anara continued to touch the woman's hard flesh. Evidence which supported the growth within. 'Take the tincture in one dose, today; you'll experience bleeding, abdominal pain and cramping, dizziness, nausea, lethargy, and an increased heart rate. Please see your doctor if—'

'I can't.'

'Sofiya, this tincture will help,' Anara said, stepping back, 'but the side effects are worthy of additional care, if you need to seek it. Please don't deny yourself the treatment you need.'

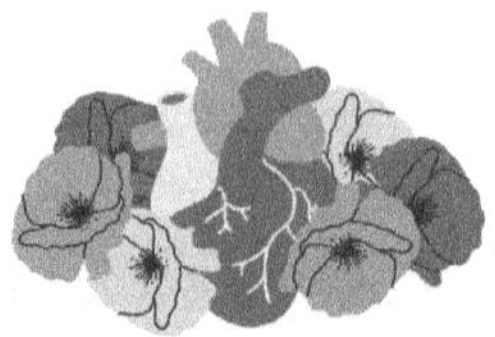

Exiting the sleek car, Vadim glanced instinctively around the remote yard before continuing toward the corrugated door. The spotlights surrounding the building were off, casting the expanse of concrete and asphalt in a myriad of shadow. In his black suit, Vadim melted into it, sliding from the evening moonlight to the warehouse's dark.

With a bloodied cloth in his hands, Artem Orlov wiped the crimson from his skin while offering a nod in greeting; the smears did nothing to disguise the heavily tattooed flesh. His light-brown eyes sought out the unexpected space behind the new arrival. 'Makari or Fyodor?'

'On his way,' Vadim replied, in matching Russian, slipping from his jacket and beginning to fold his sleeves; it was their natural language of choice. 'He needs to work on his driving.'

Artem chuckled, hearing the brakes and slam of the car door from beyond the slightly open entry. Hearing the rapid strike of heavy boots as the guard rushed inside.

Firearm drawn, and in black combat gear, Makari Komarov came to a rapid halt before the waiting men.

'So good of you to make it,' Artem remarked.

'Тёма[3],' Vadim warned playfully.

'What? You could've been attacked—'

'The day anyone fools you, is the day we're all dead,' Vadim stated while resting his hand on his advisor's shoulder. He had trusted this man for decades, had been provided with his support since childhood. Artem

[3] Тёма - Russian for 'Tyoma', the diminutive form of the name Artem

had been the first to show him how to live by the понятия[4], had been the first to sponsor his admittance into the fraternity. To recommend him for the title of вор[5]. It had been Artem who had shown Vadim how to shoot, how to use a knife, how to successfully run a business.

How to survive.

'You're too kind, пахан[6].' Artem gestured for the men to follow him further into the warehouse. He strode with purpose, confident the guard would defend their leader and certain he had already dealt with any risk ahead.

The aroma of acrid copper reached them before they heard the soft whimpers from the men tied in the centre of the empty chamber. What should have been row after row of product was a shell. Any and all trace of Morozov's operation moved the week before, leaving the building as a trap, a ruse, to ensnare their competition.

Waiting was something Artem was adept at; he had effectively lived in the warehouse, patiently prepared to act. His bespoke Lobaev rifle at his side, and an array of other weapons within reach.

The first of the intruders to fall had never seen the bullets coming, those who followed maimed, tortured, and secured.

Only two of the eight men were still alive. They were back to back and naked. Plastic ties bound their wrists and nails held their feet flush to the swept floor. Blood painted their skin, pooled around their limbs, and meandered closer to the bodies piled to one side; clothed and ready to be discovered.

Later.

'Did they give you anything?' Vadim asked, turning away from them to the bench. Along an unrolled length of leather lay a variety of knives and tools, some already decorated in a rich elixir.

'Not yet.'

---

[4] понятия - Russian for 'concepts', alternatively a code of conduct, which must be lived by prior to becoming accepted into the Russian Mafia (Bratva)

[5] вор - Russian for 'vor', a title awarded to men who embody the code

[6] пахан - Russian for 'pakhan', the title for a leader within the Bratva

'And did you give them anything?'

'Not yet.' Artem grinned, his eyes creasing. Beneath the harsh lights of the warehouse, his peppered hair seemed paler. His tattoos darker. As a veteran of the prison system, Artem's tattoos had a quality of their own with a mix of ink obtained behind bars and free. They mapped his life, the years dedicated to the вору[7], from recruitment in jail as a teenager and the ranks he moved through to become an advisor.

Vadim's eyes moved from the blades to Makari then Artem, shared understanding passing between them. 'Dimitri[8].'

Nodding, Makari spun and ran from the room.

Knife in hand, Vadim approached the captives, dragging a wooden chair behind him. The legs scraped over the concrete, a piercing scratch that purposefully echoed through the room. Reacting to his presence, his proximity, the men widened their eyes, bodies leaning. Sitting to their side and forcing them to rotate their heads, Vadim rested his forearms on his thighs and let the silence swell.

Approaching footsteps brought Makari back; a small box in his hand which he immediately presented to Artem. Vadim did not need to look to know his advisor would remove the drug, would prepare the syringe.

'We can't... tell... you any... thing,' one man spluttered, blood on his raw lips and tongue. Broken teeth in his gums.

The scent of burnt plastic overpowering the dripping wounds.

Vadim remained unmoved.

Observant, he tracked Artem's efficient location of a vein, of the swift injection of the chemical. One man then the other. Confident in the purity of their product, he knew it would not take long for the effects of the drug to be felt; intense distortions of colour and sound.

A kick in their blood which would spike their hearts, would bring an intoxicating nausea to their stomachs, while feeling unrooted in space, in time.

---

[7] вору - Russian for 'vory', part of the term вору в законе 'vory-v-zakone' which means 'thieves in law' or 'men who follow the code', the fraternity who are the Bratva

[8] Dimitri - a shortened name for the hallucinogenic dimethyltryptamine

Each man trying to balance imagination with reality. Overwhelming rivers of crimson and a choir of screams. The throbbing ache of the iron nails in their feet a source of pleasure they tried to reach for, confused by the way their limbs refused to comply.

Uncoordinated, each man trying to rip away from the other.

Vadim stood, circling them as the victims fell into oblivion. Noting the inked dragon on the men's flesh, the fear in their glazed eyes. A vibrant gleam shone from the knife in his hand as he twisted it from side to side, debating who he would target first.

'Kolya's sourced who ordered the job,' Makari stated, relaying the encrypted text delivered to his phone. None of the men needed to hear the confirmation of what they already knew.

'Time to play?' Artem met his leader's eyes.

'Time to play,' Vadim replied, settling the knife in his palm.

# Two

Prey was thriving. Each element symbiotically fuelling the other and fed by more. Underground gaming rooms, and a public bar and restaurant, had an electricity which other venues sought to emulate, but had failed to achieve. It was what kept their bookings vibrant and their accounts full. It also allowed them to launder their more illicit activities; the money which did not have such a transparent source.

Seated in his office, Vadim browsed the information Nikolai Kiselyov, his brigadier, had provided the night before. The large desk organised, a sleek series of leather and chrome, of technology and paper. Vadim had known the name Kolya would supply the moment he saw the tattooed flesh of the men Artem had nailed to the floor.

A Celtic dragon only meant one thing to them.

Vadim had expected Mace Kersey to make a play for his business at some point. Mace's trade was inferior, inconsistent, and irresponsible. A combination guaranteed to attract the wrong kind of attention.

Vadim Morozov also expected retaliation.

Mace would not permit the slaughter of his men without taking some form of vengeance against Vadim's organisation. But the loss of eight men would slow Septer's plans; Mace was poorly prepared and poorly resourced. A lack of intelligence had resulted in their defeat.

Vadim regularly moved his product. He had many warehouses and many decoys, a complex and varied schedule. The successful halting of Mace's attack would not change this.

Not now and, if Vadim retained control, not ever.

A chime drew his focus from his device to the monitor; notification of someone entering the outer corridor and approaching his office. Vadim overturned the tablet; facedown on this desk. His other hand dropping to the door's release button, ready to allow his restaurant manager through, his gaze following her progress. Watching her eyes lift to the concealed camera above the doorway. He shook his head, a wry smile forming, and unlocked the door.

'Is Makari not enough?' Ksenia remarked, in their usual Russian, walking straight toward the softly illuminated shelving; an array of vodkas and other spirits lined up above sparkling glasses.

Vadim did not answer. He trusted his guards, but he knew people had limits. Loyalty could be swayed, broken. He had not reached this point without paying heavy costs and making brutal choices.

Instead, he drained his glass and accepted a refill.

Settling into the black leather armchair, Ksenia Solovyova crossed her legs; towering heels supplemented her moderate height, elongated her frame. Her gold wedding ring struck the glass, the many diamonds glittering in the room's lighting. The ripple across the vodka's surface steadily dissipated in the low thud of music and laughter.

Leaning back, his eyes bore into hers, waiting for her to speak.

To explain the unscheduled interruption.

'There's disquiet in the kitchen,' Ksenia stated, refusing to allow his pressured attention to lower hers. She sipped her vodka, her iris-blue eyes focused on him, her powdered pale skin blush-free.

'Disquiet?'

'Chef tells me there's a human heart in the freezer,' she said with a barely disguised smirk, no trace of being intimidated. 'Wrapped securely or not, they're less than impressed about it.'

'Then they can speak to me.'

'I'm the manager—'

'They can speak to me.' He moved forward, his forearms folding and resting on the desk. Eyes never dropping.

She nodded. Ksenia swirled her drink once, brought it to her frosted pink lips, drained the glass. With a kiss left on the rim, she deposited it on the coffee table, smoothed down her fitted dress, and departed.

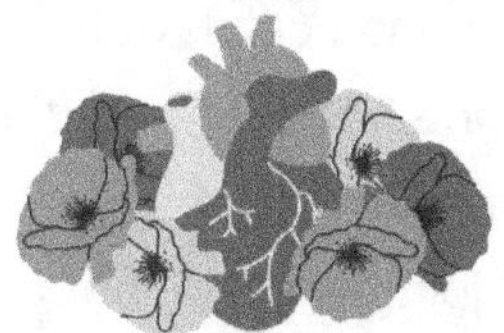

After a busy week, they were glad of this opportunity to gather, to eat, to enjoy time away from the store and relax. Something they had mutually agreed to do regularly; it provided the trio with chance to deepen their friendship. Their bond. It allowed them to operate with a greater sense of unity against the challenging moments they faced.

With the double doors opened by two men, handsomely suited in black, they paused in the entry. High ceilings, soft lighting, and opulent fixtures drew their focus in many directions; gliding over the rich velvets and dark granite, the mirrors and art. The large snake which wound from one end of the bar's shelves to the other.

'Wow,' Kerezen breathed, her freckled skin involuntarily developing bumps as she devoured Prey's interior.

'Told you it was gorgeous.' Bryony smiled, nudging her friend before leading the two women forward.

Angular and geometric, chrome trim marked the straight lines and curves, blended to perfect proportions. The Art Deco style suggesting a decadence echoed in the range of expensive spirits, in the leather stools which were spaced evenly along the marble bar. The sunburst tile of the floor encouraged patrons to draw closer, to sit, to drink while waiting for tables to empty.

For the restaurant to welcome them through into further luxury.

'It is beautiful,' Anara agreed.

'You don't look so sure,' Bryony said, analysing the frown that had appeared on her manager's brow. 'I imagine you'd prefer more flowers and herbs.'

Laughing, Anara ruefully shook her head.

'We don't believe you.' Kerezen's fingers anxiously spun her gold wedding band, loitering before a black leather stool. Accustomed to more natural surroundings, she found such lavish excess uncomfortable.

Sitting, Anara rested one hand on Kerezen's upper arm and met her eyes with kindness. A reassurance which provided sufficient coaxing to release some tension and join her at the bar.

Though Bryony and Kerezen had partners, it had been established that these evenings would be just for them. To give each woman a space away from the obligations of family. Anara was not so deluded to believe they did not create these nights as an intervention; both women tried to coax Anara out more, making this weekly event more potent.

Anara entertained it with grace. She had no plans to alter her status, nor seek a relationship. Her last connection had not ended amicably after they discovered how she utilised her business.

'Good evening,' Anoushka said warmly, her dark-brown hair pulled back, away from her peach skin. Alert, her eyes drifted to the door briefly before returning to the women to take their orders, registering the men striding in.

Men who continued, confidently, toward the other end of the bar. An assertiveness to their stance when they paused before Ksenia, who had arrived downstairs. Their voices hushed. Their black suits tailored to their muscular bodies. Their delay short before moving to the privately marked door, passing Ksenia with barely a glance.

The knock, though expected, caused Vadim to flinch. So absorbed in the feed from the bar, he had not checked the corridor. The chime ignored, almost unheard, as he tried to reconcile what was on the screen. Tried to decipher what he felt. He had failed to notice the trio ascending the stairs after greeting Makari at the base.

'Everything okay, Vadya[9]?' Artem asked, reflexes fuelling his pacing of his pakhan's office to determine if anything was wrong.

'Yes.' Vadim did not wish to elaborate. His inattentiveness had been uncharacteristic, but admitting to the cause would only have fed rumour and brought questions. Questions he could not answer.

Artem's eyes narrowed, but he remained quiet.

The images on Vadim's monitor sufficient to offer a range of possible causes; ones Artem intended to explore later. Trust between the two men worked both ways. Artem Orlov knew enough of his leader's secrets to know when he was deflecting.

'What do you make of the intel?' Nikolai asked, settling into the chair Ksenia had recently departed. He accepted a drink from Pavel; cubes of ice in the bath of vodka.

Vadim turned his attention to his two brigadiers. Nikolai Kiselyov and Pavel Solovyov had served him loyally for several years, and both had been recommended by Artem. Both men were in their forties, but Nikolai had remained single. Though their paths had been different, they had devoted decades to the fraternity, and had the scars to chart every single sacrifice they had made.

'Thorough, as always, Kolya[10],' Vadim stated, his dark eyes resting on Nikolai's light-brown. 'Mace will be out for blood—'

'We've increased patrols,' Artem interjected, perching on the edge of the oak desk. His black suit draped to effectively camouflage the rig that held his firearm and ammunition; the leather shoulder holster balanced and snug to his dark-grey shirt.

---

[9] Vadya - the diminutive form of the name Vadim
[10] Kolya - the diminutive form of the name Nikolai

In his fifties, Artem had begun his life for the vory from prison; his many tattoos reflected the choices he had made. The lives he had taken. Knife or gun, rifle or hand, he was competent but knew his limits. Years of discipline were reflected in his every move, in how he stood, in how he spoke. He had earned the respect he was afforded.

Nodding, Vadim acknowledged his advisor's words.

'Do we change the timetable?' Pavel asked, his right hand rubbing through his short brown hair. Bruises stained his knuckles, healed scars mixed amongst more recent slashes on the back of his hand; the colour caught the light. 'If they know about that warehouse—'

'We won't use that one again.' Vadim stood, crossing to the row of spirits to pour fresh vodka. Neat. No ice.

There was no requirement to share the plans for that location; the united understanding that the warehouse would be ash by the end of the night unspoken.

'I can find new options,' Pavel offered. 'My team are already looking out for suitable trade and product.'

'Have them report to Kolya,' Vadim instructed, returning to his black leather chair, 'who can compile them into a hierarchy; I need to know which will offer the best yield and security. I refuse to allow Mace to get this close again.'

Pavel gritted his teeth and nodded; he could already hear Ksenia's scathing comments about the decision. He had made a proposal, and yet it was Nikolai who would get the opportunity. Though he was happy serving Vadim Morozov as a brigadier, his wife saw a different future for him, which would not be achieved by such choices.

'What about the… other thing?' Nikolai glanced around the room, his weight shifting as he leaned forward.

'The other thing?' Vadim, momentarily distracted by movement on the camera feed, frowned, his eyes following the activity.

Artem stifled a chuckle, watching Vadim reclaim his focus.

'The unknown supplier?' Vadim clarified.

Control of himself reasserted.

'Yeah.' Nikolai's eyes darted between the two more senior men, his own frown digging into his brow as he tried to understand what the cause of the humour was. Why his pakhan was inattentive.

'They're not encroaching on our sales,' Pavel stated.

'No,' Nikolai agreed, turning slightly to catch his eye, 'but they're not afraid to kill anyone either, Pasha[11]. I'd rather not have to worry about another group encroaching on our territory.'

'Is there any evidence it is another group?' Artem straightened, his mirth restrained and mind calculating.

'There's no evidence it's not.'

'It's only men, yes?' Vadim leaned forward; arms resting on the desk and gaze tracking around his office. 'It's only men who've been targeted and they've all been poisoned, nothing more violent?'

Nikolai shrugged. 'Yeah, I guess.'

'Poison seems violent to me,' Pavel muttered. Cleared his throat. 'If it's a rogue product,' he said, 'then that could make people more hesitant to buy ours.'

'Pasha, find out exactly what's killing these men,' Vadim stated, a slight narrowing of his eyes betraying the frustration which began to eat through his veins. 'I want to know if we need to be concerned.'

'If it's Mace?'

'Their product is inferior,' Vadim stated, standing. 'I understand that the victims aren't associated with us either, which makes me think he's not involved, especially as he's lost men.'

'So, we do nothing?' Pavel laced his fingers together, stretching his arms; the bruises aching with the effort.

'For now.'

Artem moved to stand beside his leader, observing how Vadim slid his attention to the camera feed. How he then grimaced, shook his head slightly, and drew the holster over his muscular shoulders. Pulled on his

---

[11] Pasha - the diminutive form of the name Pavel

suit jacket. The others readied themselves to leave, their drinks drained, their clothes straightened.

Expectant.

'Go enjoy the tables,' Vadim suggested, 'have some drinks; I'm sure Ksenia will make sure you're taken care of.'

He knew they would follow him to the bar, but he hoped once they reached it, the others would continue down to the hidden casino. Another exclusive avenue for laundering their money and building connections. It offered an escape and an opportunity; somewhere people could gather and feel worthy, feel powerful.

Even if they were not.

Vadim set a quick pace to the door, the corridor, the stairs. His tall frame and bespoke tailoring allowing effortless manoeuvrability as he ate up the distance. A quick smile formed to greet Makari in the lobby, eyes conveying the intent to leave.

The guard fell in step with the four men, opening the heavy wooden door before permitting them through. Conversation and music swelled as they entered the bar, the gentle chimes of glassware weaving through in a tender lullaby. Below soft lighting, the glass shelves and fluted marble looked almost ethereal; part sin, part divine.

An exquisite blend enhanced by the winding snake.

Pausing, Vadim drank it in.

Tables in the bar area were full, stools claimed, people standing as they waited to be served. To his right, a guarded door allowed access to the basement gaming rooms. At the far end of the bar, open double doors offered access to the restaurant; Ksenia hovered by the entrance, guiding patrons to eat, to pay.

Tonight would be a good night; a night where Prey's books could be more easily manipulated. A night where the earnings from their other ventures could be integrated with less required creativity.

'You only need to call,' Pavel stated, resting one hand on Vadim's shoulder before gesturing for Nikolai to walk with him.

'Who is she?' Artem asked quietly, leaning in; unnecessary as it was unlikely anyone around them would understand. Though close to Vadim, his focus stayed on the people in the bar, on the foot traffic beyond the large windows, the discreet presence of Makari just behind them.

Exhaling, Vadim turned his attention to his advisor. The amber flecks in his eyes shone brighter in the bar's lights, adding a greater depth to the menace in his stare.

'I can get you girls,' Artem continued, undeterred.

He shook his head, stepping toward a newly vacated stool closer to the restaurant; Makari and Artem following him without hesitation.

'It's been a while.'

'Tyoma,' he exclaimed in a low hiss, 'leave it.' Vadim did not need to signal for a drink; Anoushka arrived with a sealed bottle of vodka and a glass the moment he took the seat.

'You spend too much time alone,' Artem remarked, watching Makari take up a new position near the wall with a good vantage point. 'There's more to life than business; you're not getting any younger.'

Vadim's grip tightened on his glass.

'Vadya—'

'You won't get any older if you continue,' Vadim interrupted, the crisp remark delivered with venom. Advisor or not, history or not, enough was enough. His right hand dropped to his side, moving under his jacket without shifting his gaze from Artem.

'I taught you well.' His smirk did not fall, his eyes glinting. 'I'm going to gamble and fuck.' Artem nodded to Makari, assessed those loitering in the bar, then headed to the basement.

Leaning against the marble, Vadim twisted and returned to the view of the restaurant; his attention drawn to her. To the woman he had seen on the camera feed the moment she walked into Prey. The woman who had ordered a drink but been slow to smile. The woman who had kept a distance from those who approached her and her friends.

He assumed friends; they appeared connected.

She had not paid for her drink, so he could not track her from card details. But, she would have to pay for her meal. He would ensure she had to provide something, some way to trace who she was.

Each bite she took brought new tension to his skin. The drag of her full, blood-red lips over the tines of the fork caught his breath. The curl of her snowy fingers around the knife made him want to sigh. Made him roll his tongue over his lip.

His glass abandoned mid-way to his mouth.

'You okay, pakhan?' Makari asked, tentative, after a discreet cough failed to get his leader's focus. He had stepped forward, his booted steps dulled by surrounding noise and years of training.

'Of course.' Vadim took a drink, welcoming the vodka's warmth in his throat. 'Have Ksenia come over.'

The unknown woman moved her hand through her long curls.

Raven hair he envisaged wrapping around his fist. Her neck. Vadim swallowed, forcing himself to turn to the bar and pour more vodka into his glass. To drain it and replenish it once more.

'Vadim?' Ksenia's concern dripped through the word.

'The women at table seven,' he responded, slow to bring his eyes to the manager, 'I need you to get their details.'

'Their details?'

'Their details.' He could request Nikolai or Makari find them, her, but he would prefer to do this himself. And if he had something more than a photograph pulled from their security feed, then that would narrow down the search. Would provide him with a quicker result.

He could be a very patient man when he needed to be.

But now, Vadim felt patience begin to slip.

# Three

The groan echoed through the room, the pressure becoming unbearable even as he fought against it. Pleasure radiating and bringing a tightness to his muscles, an electricity to his flesh. Mace increased the grip in the man's hair, forcing his head to change rhythm; delaying Mace's descent over the edge.

'Fuck,' Mace growled out, his eyes on the man below him.

His tongue slowly drifted over Mace's shaft, breath as erratic as the man seated above him. His lingering kiss on the tip delivered a shudder, a sigh. He spread his fingers, running them over the top of Mace's thighs before taking his cock in his mouth again. The swirl of his tongue around the head slow, wet.

Taking him deep and moaning.

'You're such a good boy,' Mace Kersey muttered, brown eyes on the man kneeling between his legs. Hips thrusting up from the chair to set the tempo he desired, pushing further into the man's throat.

He smiled, one hand daring to roam Mace's abdomen, to flick the small, hard nipples on his chest. The touch timed with a soft hum, heated breath vibrating over Mace's cock. His tongue stroking the root, a flat lick to the head. Lapping against the underside.

Control was disintegrating.

Waves of pleasured ecstasy with slow caresses and slick spit, with tongue and hand, mouth. Chasing the release which teased the base of Mace's bucking spine. He trusted in this man to deliver the distraction he sweetly pursued.

Eye contact brought a guttural moan from Mace's throat.

Denying the man his own relief increased the satisfaction Mace knew would come. He could see, through his hooded gaze, the way the man's erection pressed against his jeans, saw the damp stain betraying his arousal.

Domineering power rushed through, fuelling a sharp shiver. Mace's erratic pace shuddered with the twisting tongue and deep, dripping, suck being given. He barely registered the man's hand dropping, one finger sliding inside; the internal manipulation combined with a low vibration in the man's throat signalling finality.

Mace's roar fracturing.

The man's swallow done without lowering his eyes. A connection to intensify the moment, to suggest it could be repeated. The torturously sedate retreat, tongue dragged over brutally sensitive skin, caused Mace to whimper.

A weakness he would never allow at any other time.

Settling, Mace rubbed his hand down his face, shifting to cup his trim beard, eyes closing. The man's careful attention a distant sensation as the afterglow wrapped his body, his mind. A numb awareness of how he took his cock and licked it clean, returned it behind the zip. The man's gentle touch offered reverently.

Eye contact burning between them.

'Leave,' Mace instructed, his voice rasping.

The man stood, using the desk for support. His body aching from the duration he had spent on his knees. From unreciprocated pressure in his cock. From a burn in his jaw.

'There's cash on the table.' He blinked, watching the man hesitate, a coy look in his hopeful gaze. 'I'll call if I need—'

'That'd be good,' he interrupted. His lips parted, swollen and red, but fresh words failed. Spinning toward the door, the man snatched up the thick tan envelope before bolting out.

Bracing himself, Mace drew closer to his cluttered desk.

Though the interruption had been welcome, the delay had impacted the funeral arrangements he needed to finalise. Discovering eight of their men slaughtered had infuriated all members of Septer, and Mace Kersey intended to seek vengeance. The warehouse belonged to Morozov, and the bodies discarded within it bore the Bratva's touch.

Six with gunshot wounds.

Two with restrained violence; drugged, tortured, bled empty. Naked, the men had torn their feet from barbed coffin nails protruding from the concrete floor. Eyes gouged and hair unrooted; vitreous fluid fused with blood on their fingers. Vomit crusted on sliced flesh.

Care had been taken to extract pain, to deliver punishment.

And Mace was furious.

Lifting his brown eyes to the door, he watched his advisor stride in, a box in both hands. Mace frowned, chilled anxiety beginning to creep over his tattooed spine. 'Aeron?'

'Boss.' Aeron Barnes placed the cardboard in the centre of the desk and stepped back. The seal broken. His ruddy skin pallid, but his blue eyes remained vibrant below his blonde hair; undercut and braided. The same rage Septer felt coursed through Aeron's veins, nourished with this delivery. 'You need to see this.'

Tipping his body forward, he curled his pale fingers around the edge of the reinforced cardboard. Sliding the box closer, his eyes widened in disbelief. A pronounced swallow betraying the kick of nausea clawing at his stomach.

Centrally, amongst black paper and felt, lay a heart.

A human heart.

It shone under the office lighting; gleaming tissue and muscle which had once beaten. Had once flooded a body with blood. With life. Instead it lay static, broken. A discarded organ of no further value. Only to send a message in the lost beats. In the precise cuts which had severed it from the body it had been stolen from.

With gritted teeth, Mace pushed the box back and met his advisor's gaze. Poison soaked his mouth, ire burning over his bones. He believed he was furious before, now he was incandescent.

Aeron reflected similar intent.

'Who?' he snarled.

'One of the scouts,' Aeron offered, handing over a file containing the meagre details. With so many men, boys, used on the streets, they each struggled to keep track. Faces, yes. Names, no.

'That fucker!' He leapt up from the chair, slamming his palm against the desk. Mace shook his head, the wrath branding his flesh in a heated glow. 'The audacity of this fucking man!'

Aeron watched his leader stride from one side of the modest office to the other, incredibly aware of the significance of Vadim's actions. Of how their violent need to assert Septer's dominance invariably resulted in lower ranks becoming trapped. Lost. It was a risk each person knew before they agreed to any association, but that did not make it easier, nor more palatable, to accept.

Pausing, Mace released his fists and slid both hands over his hair; part-braided, part-shaved, dark-brown strands. Letting them cradle the nape, he exhaled heavily. 'Fuck!'

'What's the plan, boss?'

'I want their territory, and I want them dead—'

'We both want that,' Aeron agreed, 'but perhaps we need to bury our men first?' He held his leader's stare.

'And let that fucker think he's won?'

'Never.' Aeron perched on the desk, folding the box lid closed. 'But we need to play this smart, and launching another attack now, before we've thought things through, won't work.'

'So, what do you suggest?' Mace forced himself to sit down.

'We gather our trusted guards and our trusted soldiers,' he said, a measured calm soothing his tone, 'and we strategise.'

Reaching for his phone, Mace began to type; a message composed and delivered to those very names neither needed to speak. Those who had been the most loyal, the most valuable, to his organisation since they joined. Who would remain by Mace's side until death.

'First we hold the funerals for our men—'

'All of them,' Mace interjected. Reluctance still soured his voice, the rage yet to be assuaged by his advisor's honey.

'All of them,' he echoed. 'Then, then we need to get product onto the streets, especially *their* streets. We're going to need to sell cheap for a while, but we can cut the product more—'

'We'll need higher quality to get them hooked.'

'It'll work,' he asserted. 'Give the right people the best, and what we sell to the others won't matter. It'll bring them to us. Vadim'll be begging for us to take the business in no time.'

Mace narrowed his eyes. 'I can't wait that long. We're losing people almost every week, if it's not a direct attack like this, then it's the random men being poisoned.'

'Boss, it's the nature of the game.' Aeron smiled, refusing to glance at the cardboard box. 'We tried to get their product, and they were one fucking step ahead and emptied the place, and our men paid for that. But the others, yeah, that's… that's just the streets.'

Neither man believed those words. The growing number of men who were being found dead, in their homes or in social spaces, who showed traces of poison, who appeared to have overdosed, was unsettling. It was a trend which ate into their confidence, it made them question their tactics, but it had yet to destroy their thirst for victory.

At the head of the table, Vadim Morozov looked over those he had asked to attend. His advisor, Artem Orlov, and brigadiers Nikolai Kiselyov and Pavel Solovyov. To his right, Makari Komarov watched the almost empty dining room.

Instead of the usual kitchen staff, three of their foot soldiers were working the restaurant floor. There were several hours before Prey would open for the evening, allowing them this opportunity to talk; to discuss possible avenues for expansion, possible repercussions for the attack on the warehouse, possible deployment of resources.

Vadim had heard, but found it challenging to listen. His umber eyes drawn to table seven, his mind consumed by memories. The research he had begun the night before was burning in his veins, talons scoring his flesh; he wanted nothing more than to retreat to his study and devour it.

To continue the work he had begun.

Not sit here and conduct business.

The crunching kick to his shin brought him back to the moment.

'Vadya,' Artem hissed, 'what's got into you?'

He clenched his teeth and slowly turned to face him; defiance added darkness to his gaze. 'Don't.'

'This isn't like you,' Artem continued, his voice low, mouth almost on his pakhan's lobe. He had raised one hand, concealing his tense words further. 'You're distracted; that's when mistakes get made.'

'You underestimate me.'

Pyotr and Ilya quietly brought out plates of food, Maksim bottles of vodka. The men placing the items before their leaders before returning to the kitchen.

'Pasha,' Vadim stated, sliding his knife through the tender meat, 'tell me what you've discovered about the poisoned men.'

'There's not much to tell,' Pavel replied. 'According to my contact, there's very little to connect the guys who've died, other than the poison itself.' He skewered some vegetables with his fork.

'And that is what?' Vadim gestured with his knife.

'They're not sure,' Pavel said, chewing hastily. 'Doctors say it's some kind of herbal mix.'

'So, what, they're accidental?' Artem replenished his vodka.

'Not what I've heard,' he said. The desire to be valued festered on his tongue, desperate to offer something useful to the conversation, even if only anecdotally.

'And what've you heard?' Vadim sensed something deep in his mind snap, something he felt he should be connecting. Something taunting his thoughts, his synapses.

'Only that the men who died weren't the most… kind.' Pavel's mouth tipped into a smirk, very aware of who he was talking with and what their reputations were. 'None of the grieving widows were particularly… upset about the loss.'

'Even my women would miss me,' Artem joked, his glass raised and eyes glinting with mirth. 'And I'm a cruel fucker.'

'In every sense of the word,' Nikolai muttered, laughing.

'Damn right.' Artem's grin was wide. 'At least that means Vadya will be safe from this… herb.'

Vadim's eyes darted to his advisor; head quick and hand quicker to locate the knife in his boot. He dragged the Smersh from its sheath, the point placed below Artem's chin. 'Say that again.'

'I'm only suggesting you've lately not had any… liaisons,' Artem said with no sign of unease. The glint still in his eyes. 'Women are there for you to use, Vadya, and you're not—'

Vadim exhaled heavily, flipping the knife in his hand before sinking it into the table. The action smooth. Definite.

'Fuck!' Artem shook his head. 'Now we've a table to fix.'

Vadim ignored the comment and took another bite of his meal. 'Tell me about new business prospects.'

With a surreptitious glance around him, Nikolai cleared his throat. 'I managed to narrow a few options down; my personal preference are the ones closest to our established sites—'

'I want to make our position clear,' Vadim stated calmly, his eyes on his brigadier. 'If that means taking territory from Septer, I want to take it. They don't get to attack and go unpunished.'

'You killed—'

'And I'll kill more.' Vadim put down his cutlery softly, his focus on his advisor. 'I will pick them off one by one if that's what I need to do.'

'They're recruiting more,' Pavel said.

'Then we've more to take.'

'What about expanding into other trades?' Nikolai gathered the last remnants of his meal onto his fork. The idea was not a new one; under Vadim's leadership, the group had excelled. They had an array of plans and schemes which had increased their wealth, which had increased the contributions they made to the communal fund.

'I'm happy with our choices,' Vadim said, finality in his tone.

Since becoming vor, Vadim had developed his own preferences and style. He had never fallen from the laws, never betrayed the rules, but he did bend them to suit his own tastes. As such, Vadim had angered some of his old fraternity through omission of more traditional options.

Those days had been decisive.

A rebellion he had effectively, and swiftly, defeated. His actions had secured his seniority, had allowed him to obtain territory and business. It had proved his ruthless nature and demonstrated his skills. He was cold-hearted, efficient, and refused to compromise. The number of dead still entirely unknown, yet whispered of, admired.

For Vadim, it had been necessary.

It was why he maintained a closer role than was usual for a pakhan, determined to forge his own path.

And it had ensured he could steer this group, his group, toward the avenues he wished to pursue. Cyber crime, money laundering, casinos, and drugs. Extortion and intimidation. Strategic and cross-border. They were reliably lucrative and Vadim's team were acutely aware of how vital each strand was to the whole.

Diversify too greatly and it becomes a weakness.

A risk.

Attracting the wrong kind of attention.

'There's a place selling herbs,' Pavel suggested. An anxious tension clung to his spine, an urge to please his wife feeding the words as they spilled from his mouth. Pavel would not admit to being intimidated by Ksenia, but she had such confidence in him it was hard not to be swayed to her desires. To her ideas.

'Herbs?' Artem frowned, his eyes sliding to his pakhan before they returned to the brigadier. The change in direction tenuous, but welcome to dissipate any lingering hostility; advisor and pakhan knew each other too well for their words to truly wound.

'Yeah,' Pavel stated, reaching for his glass. 'Maybe the owner could be persuaded to expand into other things; growing opium or khat for us and distributing product, perhaps.'

Vadim swallowed. 'Erinyes?'

Pavel nodded, his smile wavering slightly at the wary expression on his pakhan's face. Something hesitant in his gaze. A chill dragged over Pavel's skin. He reached for his vodka and drained the glass, letting the burn refresh his dry throat.

'Isn't that the—'

'Kolya,' Vadim interjected, his jaw tight. 'I'll look into it.'

# Four

With no plans to leave the grounds, Fyodor Zhukov had dressed in all black combat gear. It was how he felt most comfortable. There was more space for his weapons and it enabled him to move more easily. He had trained for years to become the proficient guard Vadim demanded, his journey from prison recruited foot solider chronicled in the vibrant tattoos which he wore with pride.

Leaning back, his eyes scanned the wall of monitors. After the failed attempt to steal from them, and the deaths of Mace Kersey's men, the whole team were expecting retaliation.

Though Vadim refused any additional guards, he had accepted an increase in the number patrolling the estate, and in their warehouses. It was a compromise Fyodor did not feel wholly comfortable with, but he had learned, many years earlier, to trust in Vadim's instincts.

They had yet to be proved significantly wrong.

Behind him, the one-way glass provided a view of the expansive driveway and large building, where Fyodor lived. Two apartments above the spacious garage provided both he and Makari with a home, allowing them to be nearby even when off shift. Alongside more money he could ever spend, the free accommodation was an extra incentive to be readily available.

Not that Fyodor, nor Makari, required persuading.

They would both happily place their lives in the line of fire for their pakhan. That was the law. That was the deal. And it was one they would choose time and again.

'Fedya[12],' Vadim stated, opening the door which connected his study to the surveillance suite, 'our guests are getting restless.'

With a grin spreading over his face, Fyodor stood. His tongue swept over his lower lip before the flesh was captured by his teeth, hazel eyes on the image of the men in their cells. He stretched his arms upward, his fingers lacing, as he rolled his head from side to side.

'If you could remind them of our hospitality,' Vadim added, waiting for his guard to stride over.

'How deeply would you like them to be reminded?' Fyodor took one final look over the screens, patting his colleague on the shoulder, and left the room.

A biometric lock sealing the reinforced door.

'I'd prefer they remained guests for a little longer.' Vadim was happy to visit the cells in person, but he had learned to save such punishments for when a message needed to be delivered. And, now, the message did not need to be handled in person.

Forcing them to wait for an audience held more power.

Both for the men screaming below the house in the soundproofed compartments and, if Vadim decided to allow them to leave, for the tales they would convey to their leader.

With a nod, Fyodor crossed to the corner cupboard; an innocent oak full-height door amongst the panelling which lined the study. Behind it, a spiral wrought-iron staircase would take him to the basement, a series of rooms which covered the same area as the home above.

Hearing the steps retreat, the cupboard door close, Vadim exhaled and returned to his desk, facing the library. The study was a room of camouflaged entrances and exits, with one-way glass windows.

---

12 Fedya - the diminutive form of the name Fyodor

Leaning back in his leather chair, he closed his eyes.

This was becoming a problem.

He shook his head. Sat more upright and drew himself closer to the large desk; dark wood polished smooth. Void of anything but the devices Vadim utilised each day and a lamp.

With Fyodor gone, Vadim retrieved the documents he found difficult to either dispose of or admit to. Images pulled from the cameras in Prey. Images pulled from online sources. Her professional profile, compiled by Nikolai in confidence, pored over in detail.

The scant personal information dissected.

Anara Eden, owner of Erinyes Apothecary.

And woman he could not remove from his head. She consumed his every thought. He could not escape her when he slept; those limited hours of slumber broken with her smile. With how he wished to use her and to be used. To learn how she breathed, learn how she moaned. How she would writhe below him, his knife.

How she would taste.

How she would bleed.

Discovering her name from Ksenia had only enabled him to speed up the process, enabled him to locate her and learn. Vadim had hoped he would find something to make him stop.

Something to make him back off.

But all he found made him want to know more. Which was a risk; he loved his life, he revelled in his role as pakhan, and he could not afford to be this distracted.

Not with Septer's threat.

'Ебать[13],' he breathed, dropping his head into his hands; elbows on the papers. Eyes closed. Slowly, Vadim raked his fingers through his raven hair, measuring each breath even as she devoured it. Her face all he found in his mind, her name all he desired to scream. Her body all he wanted to claim.

---

[13] Ебать - Russian for 'fuck'

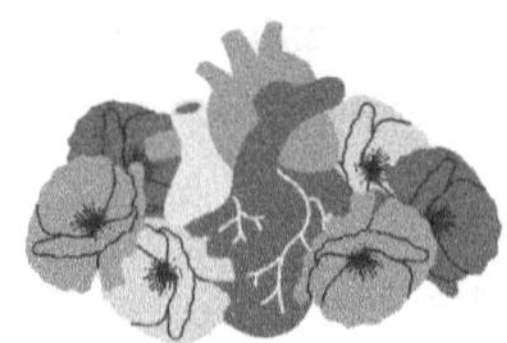

It had been a slow day, one where they had used the time to undertake a thorough inventory of the herbs, spices, and resins kept in the towering shelving and drawers. The items carefully catalogued and a list prepared to ensure stock remained plentiful. They each knew how vital every part was, how every individual ingredient worked with another.

'He's there again,' Kerezen said, turning from the window.

At the counter, Anara glanced up but kept her gaze on her colleague rather than the street. Her peripheral vision enough to confirm the man who loitered outside was the same one they had each seen throughout the week.

He was discreet, certainly.

Hovering with a coffee. Taking a call. At the same time, every day, he would pause, would linger. In a black suit, dark jacket, his brown hair undercut and braided. He moved easily, with a confidence they had each witnessed.

Something Anara could read.

'Do you think he's sussed out what we're doing?' Bryony asked, her voice carrying from the back room; preparing herbal tea.

'If he has, then he should have the guts to come in,' Anara said with greater defiance than she felt. Every nerve was on fire, chasing over her skin and cautioning her to be wary. 'I'm not changing a thing about what we do, not for one man.'

'Or any man.' Kerezen smiled, her back straightening.

'Damn right,' Bryony echoed. She brought the three mugs through and placed them on the counter; steam coiling in the afternoon light. The gentle aroma of lemon and ginger mingled with the cacophony of other scents within the store. A unique and complementary fragrance which merged with the soft music.

'If he's here because he's scared,' Anara continued, 'then he only has himself to blame.' She curled her hands into fists, hidden within the pocket of her black apron. Her eyes remained fixed on her friends, a firm refusal to acknowledge the stranger.

Bryony and Kerezen exchanged quick glances, seeing the tension in their boss and hearing the venom in her tone. Anara preferred to keep her past her own, and had chosen not to share exactly what inspired her to build this business; Erinyes both public and supplementary.

The actions taken in private.

Each of the three women were readily complicit in the criminal acts they undertook. The remedies offered, the cures provided. The results of both deadly. It was a decision they had each made peace with; a pact, a condition of employment. One with a verbal affirmation of compliance.

No paperwork.

No liability.

Anara insisted that should they be discovered, she would be the one to take accountability. It was why she was the one to speak to the clients alone, in the consulting room, out of sight. It was why she was the one to manufacture those tinctures and blends.

There was deniability.

There was confidence and strength.

It was a weapon they could wield, silently and with subversion. Their actions taking place in a store which appeared peaceful. A tranquil slice of nature amongst stone, amongst modern conveniences and daily life. It was a dichotomy Anara relied on. Her advertising subtle but sufficient to share what could be administered within her paradise.

The very name of the store a code, for those who understood.

Underlined with the logo of snakes and wings.

With the trio of women who diligently served.

'What if he's pissed about his girl making choices without him?' With a slight widening of her eyes, Kerezen's question was clear. Even if she did not specifically voice it.

'Then that's his problem, not ours.' Anara unhooked her apron from her neck, dragged it from her waist. She laid it on the granite and began to move toward the counter's hatch, only for Bryony to grab her arm.

Shake her head. 'He's not worth it.'

Anara's chest heaved with the restriction of her breath. The fight to confront and the instinct to hide. She swallowed down the history which taught her to do neither; to fawn and please. To placate. To avoid conflict and pain. Slow, she exhaled. 'I wasn't—'

'Oh, okay.' Bryony released her arm, a flush of heat rushing over her skin and awkward grimace curling her lips. Lining her brow.

'Don't worry.' Anara smiled; glad she could reassure her friend. Even if it was not entirely truthful. The conclusion of her internal debate would only have been made once she reached the door. To continue out onto the street, to the man, or to return to her colleagues, safe. 'I appreciate you looking out for me.'

'Will you be alright?' Kerezen asked, her mug cradled in both hands and green eyes on her boss.

'Absolutely.'

Bryony chewed the inside of her mouth, her gaze wandering. 'If I didn't have plans with the kids—'

'I'll be fine!' Anara collected her own tea, taking a soothing sip. 'He's not tried anything, and I've good locks.'

'Are you sure you don't want to come stay with us?'

'You and Willow have your own lives,' she countered kindly, her eyes creasing. 'I'm sure your wife wants you to herself, not having me sleep on your couch.'

'But—'

'Enough.' There was soft authority in her tone, a chastisement which was delivered with love. 'I'll be perfectly fine. He's a pathetic man who's done nothing but watch, he hasn't even dared to come into the store. It's a public space, and he's frightened.'

'Or he's biding his time.'

'Bry, I'll be okay,' Anara said, solace in her eyes. 'I'll make sure the store is secured and alarmed, I'll set my apartment's alarm, lock every door and window, and slide every bolt. I promise, I'll be okay.'

'We just worry, with you being on your own,' Kerezen said.

'It'd take more than one man to scare me.'

Bryony and Kerezen's shared uncertainty was barely veiled.

An uncertainty Anara felt; one she was determined to ignore.

Wiping blood from his hand, Fyodor's tattoo shone. Smeared in red, the black inked cat marking him as one of the vory had faded. His dedication had not. With his sleeves rolled back, his thick forearms glistened with slick crimson; roses which surrounded the cat in the hat, before climbing to his elbow, speckled by hot spray.

Every pass with the dermatome had removed another layer; slow and precise, Fyodor had drawn the surgical device over, and under, the man's quivering skin. A well-practised strip separated from deep tissue as piercing wails echoed around the room.

Each oscillation of the blade harvesting flesh.

Uniform lengths coiled in a steel dish on top of the cart.

Lowering the cloth, he meandered to the small lever protruding from the stone. Stretching up he pulled it down, a blast of glacial water falling rapidly over the man.

The screams almost inaudible; so high, so sharp.

Raw, debrided skin, shrinking away from the cold, powerful, liquid; a fierce and burning ache which catapulted over each cut site, spreading further until the man believed his whole body was in flames.

He flicked off the shower, returning to collect the shallow dish. Each sliver of the victim's skin confirmation of Fyodor's skill, his cruelty. He did not know exactly when he learned of this preference, did not recall when brutality became salvation. All he knew was the elation which came from the application of such skill; his tongue on his lips, mouth desperate to taste the results of his tortures, and cock hard.

Standing before the wounded man, Fyodor's fingers dipped into the warm dermis. Sifted through stolen flesh to select a piece. He kept his eyes on the prisoner, bringing one length to his teeth. Bit. A low groan of pleasure vibrating through his throat.

The man wretched, bringing nothing but bile to his lips.

Laughing, he dropped the remaining half back into the bowl before temptation encouraged him to devour it all. Fyodor intended to save the delicacies for later, to steam these strips alongside whatever other body parts he could convince Vadim to release.

His hazel eyes assessed the captive.

Manacled, the man's arms were limp, his body sagging between the two iron chains hanging from the stone ceiling. Rivulets meandered over his naked flesh, a blend of sweat and blood, of urine, toward the drain in the floor.

Though underground, there was no damp. No stagnation. A network of ducts filtered air, kept the cells ambient. Pipes kept them clean. There were several enclosures, distributed along the length of the house, each with a solid steel door. An impressive storeroom and chamber filled the remaining space, with a wide doorway leading to a tunnel. A tunnel large enough to easily accommodate a van, allowing them to transport their victims from the garage directly into the cellar.

It was how this man had been delivered. His body deposited into the vehicle then thrown into his new abode. One of many guests currently languishing below ground, with walls sufficiently thick to subdue voices and screams.

Prayers.

The scrape of the door brought a rapid turn to Fyodor's body; alert, his hand dropped to his side. Fingers curling around his knife. Tension which dissipated quickly as he met Vadim's gaze.

'Is our guest tired?' Vadim asked, umber eyes critically moving over the inert body swaying in the centre of the room. Witnessing the pattern of persuasion over the exposed skin.

'Very.' Fyodor's mouth widened, his smile creasing his skin. 'But not very talkative, despite my best attention.'

'Perhaps you were too… attentive.' Vadim walked toward the cart, a bespoke wheeled store for a range of devices they employed with their visitors. Every item Fyodor had used returned to the allotted home, blood dripping over the metal.

Fyodor's smile fell a little.

'You do go too far, sometimes,' Vadim continued softly, his fingertips dancing over the handles of differing knives; size and curvature.

The guard's eyes narrowed, tracking his pakhan's actions with keen interest. Though his face remained calm, his pulse began to quicken. His mouth drying.

'It's why I like you, Fedya.' He rounded the cart, selecting one of the smaller blades and contemplating it. Balancing it on his palm. Placing it back in the cart.

Some of Fyodor's disquiet shifted.

Vadim glanced up, eyes moving to his guard then the captive. He had not expected this scout to offer anything of value. Snatching him from within Septer's boundary was message enough. How he would be returned would send another. 'I've got it from here.'

'Sure, pakhan,' he replied. Hesitated. 'May I—'

'I'll call you when I'm done,' Vadim stated, a wry smile on his lips to confirm their mutual understanding. 'He'll be all yours.'

Fyodor grinned and nodded, retreating to the coolness of the outer chamber; his sturdy combat boots resounding in the hallway toward the basement's showers.

Opening one swollen eye, the prisoner gauged his position; the man who stood with his back to him, the steel door only partially closed, the drifting sounds from beyond his confinement.

Vadim reprioritised his attention.

'How would you prefer this to end?' Vadim asked; methodically, one slow turn at a time, he folded back the sleeves of his black shirt. He kept his gaze fixed on the victim, breathing steady, anticipation surging in his veins.

'Fuck… you,' the man spat; slurred through missing teeth.

Bleeding gums.

'We're not that friendly,' he said. Vadim stood beyond the reach of the chains, beyond where the man could kick. Incessant desperation fed the need for violence in the pakhan's blood.

He needed the distraction.

Needed to channel the obsessive hours, the building pressure, into something familiar. To release the sweet desire coaxing him to leave the house, to track her down, devour her. A craving slowly overpowering his reputation. His monstrous side not deserving of such beauty, of the purity he saw in her approach to life.

No, Vadim had to focus on this conflict. On the attempts Septer was making to take his territory. On the business commitments he had made and intended to honour. There were many families who depended on the transactions Vadim undertook every day. He must ensure those people were cared for, were safe.

And if that meant he became a martyr to his heart, then Vadim had learned to accept that. At this point, he believed whatever remained of the muscle in his chest offered little but pain. Solitude. Ice.

'Just… kill… me,' the man whimpered; broken ribs sharp, rattling as he forced each breath. With shreds of defiance he raised his head, the controlled gashes on his chest pulling.

Bleeding.

'There's no rush.' Vadim collected the knife once more, his polished boots sticking to the drying ichor. He circled the man, studying the work his guard had completed.

Satisfaction blended with pride.

He had trained Fyodor well.

The wounds were varied and raw, coloured with bruises and stained with sweat. With earlier scabs ripped off to re-open tender flesh. Nails missing. A finger taken.

The man had not been the sole focus of their attention. There were other cells, other prisoners. When not hanging for such treatment, they were permitted to rest; a hard bench available, bolted to the wall.

This man would not need the bench again.

Vadim scratched the tip of the blade across the man's shoulders, the touch light. Almost above the skin. A graze of pearls blooming the only real evidence of the intimate act. Adding more pressure, he stroked the knife along the same path, opening the cut a little deeper each time.

Until the man was wailing.

Begging.

Screaming for Vadim to stop.

The grating scrape of the metal on bone the moment the prisoner lost consciousness; succumbing to the agony. Water from the overhead shower forcing him to wake once more.

'I'd hoped you'd not be so weak,' Vadim remarked calmly, flicking the lever off and returning to stand before the scout.

The man trembled, watching Vadim. There was only blood left in the man's mouth, but he swallowed it down as he tried to shuffle away from the approaching pakhan.

'I wanted a man with a better heart,' he continued, his head slightly tilted as he brought the knife's tip to the man's chest. 'But I'll work with what I've got.'

Despite the ache, the man widened his one functional eye, straining to see what fresh torture the Russian planned. He was no longer sure of how long he had been trapped, no longer cognisant of time.

All he knew was fear, dread.

He had spilled everything he knew the moment the guard had pulled his first fingernail from the bed. Every single shred of information yelled over and again until the words became a confused and incoherent mass of broken phrases, punctuated with pleas for clemency, for release.

For death.

He knew he would not leave this cell any other way.

Vadim pressed the knife deeper, through already fractured skin and tissue, to create an incision above the sternum. Swapping the blade for a retractor, he efficiently split the ribs, sensing the victim's consciousness lapse. With the chest open, he further admired Fyodor's work.

Internal bleeding and splintered bone.

With no concern over keeping the man alive, there was no need to act quickly. No need to divert blood flow or preserve organs. All Vadim required was to remove the heart. To channel the frustration he felt into every slice, every cut.

Throwing the heart into another steel dish, Vadim felt no relief.

The tension which caged his broad shoulders remained; a restraint unwelcome and unfamiliar. This intervention designed to provide respite from the images which toyed with Vadim's mind, a visit which had been engineered to alleviate the lust which heated his blood.

But they remained, as strong and tempting as before.

Her body an altar for him to worship, her image the icon he wished to kneel for. Her blood to drink, her flesh to taste, her quim to lick, to be consumed by.

With a loud groan, Vadim plunged his knife into the man's bleeding shoulder and split the skin to the wrist. Jagged. Raw. 'Fuck!'

# Five

Whoever the man was who had loitered outside Erinyes, he had gone by the time they closed. Despite this, both Bryony and Kerezen had tried to persuade Anara to come with one of them, reluctant to leave. The dark skies and chilled air adding to the ominous nature of the unknown, a tool used to argue against Anara.

It was an argument the two women lost.

Her compelling words resulting in solitude.

Anara had ensured the store was locked before retreating into the storage area behind the counter. Here, opposite the consultation room, a robust door provided entrance to a small windowless lobby and the stairs to her apartment.

She checked both the external door and the internal one were safely bolted before climbing up to her home. There was no additional block to the open plan living area, a space decorated in a similar style to the shop below. Flowing shapes, diverse textures, white walls concealed by dark bookshelves and thriving plants.

Sensible enough to consider the possibility the man had waited out of sight, she crossed to the three large windows; the curtains drawn on both sides of the room. Only then did she switch on a lamp, the soft glow illuminating her mismatched furniture.

Determined not to allow past ghosts to ruin her evening, she made her way to the kitchen to prepare a meal. Fresh ingredients flavoured with spices, with herbs; each aromatic addition savoured, inhaled. A spell cast as she combined and cooked. The wine sipped as she set the table for herself. Her book ready on the bespoke stand so she could read as she ate. Habitual and instinctive.

It was as music drifted, warm water on her hands as she cleaned the dishes, that ire began to simmer in her veins. Anara had let the man affect her more than she had hoped.

She had considered confronting him.

Had considered leaving the store and accusing him.

Of what, she was still uncertain.

But Anara had been prepared to set aside years of well-practiced and safe submission in favour of conflict. Of retaliation. At the time she had convinced herself it was so she could protect her colleagues; a way to prevent them experiencing harm.

Yet, as she tidied her kitchen, Anara knew she was refusing the truth of her decision, the root of her cautious choices.

She wanted revenge.

She wanted to avenge the life she had lost.

If that man was truly someone who could cause them trouble, then he needed to be dealt with. And she was comfortable with that. She had resigned herself to her role, one carved from her ruins. Fragments which had taught her the skills she required to survive, to live.

She resolved to review the security feed in the morning, to research who this man was. If he was a threat. If she needed to do more to keep her colleagues protected. Until then, Anara needed to prove she did not need to hide, that she deserved to thrive.

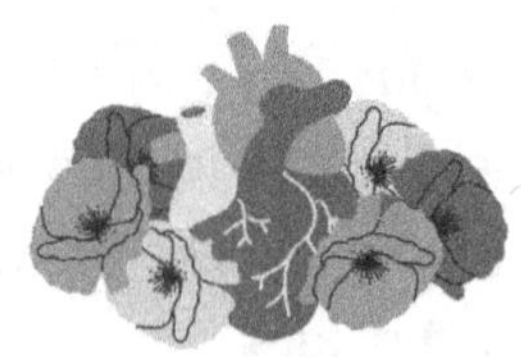

Returning to Prey had not been Anara's intention. She had removed the simple trousers and shirt she had worked in and slid into a fitted black dress. She had redone her make-up, had called a taxi. It had been so long since she last ventured out for pleasure she had been unsure of where to go.

Hesitation made her pause on the threshold; the two men either side of the doors waiting for her to pass through. Their gloved hands securely gripping the chrome Art Deco hardware. She inhaled deeply, raised her head a little higher and continued into the inviting heat. Crossed over the sunburst tile toward the bar.

Marble, leather, and glass offered a delicately balanced glamour. A sense of opulence softly lit. Enticing. Gentle music did not compete with the chimes of glasses, the hum of conversation, but enriched it. Patrons convinced to partake of the expensive spirits, to consume the delicacies offered in the adjoining restaurant.

Provided with the opportunity to pause time.

Slipping off her coat, Anara took up residence on a leather stool; she recognised the woman working behind the geometrically curving slab of marble. Her eyes followed the efficient way she selected bottles from the shelves, grabbed a glass to decant the measure.

'Good evening,' Anoushka said, 'what can I get for you?'

Anara chewed on her lower lip, the red wine from dinner still flowing in her veins. 'Do you have any green chartreuse?'

'Yeah.' She nodded, her mind automatically filtering options, where the stock was, what blends she could offer.

'Then a verdant muse, please.' Anara smiled. Her mouth anticipating the complex flavours of the cocktail and if this establishment could make it as she remembered.

'Sure,' she confirmed, turning to her colleague. 'Nadia, I need some basil from the kitchen; I'll just be a minute.'

Glancing toward the other woman working behind the bar, Anara felt colour blossom over her face. *Perhaps*, she thought, *wine was the better option*. She almost opened her mouth to suggest a change to her order but swallowed it down.

She had not been deterred by the man loitering outside her store.

She would not be deterred by a drink request.

Anara had set out with the intent on reclaiming herself, her life, her passion. She had spent too long with the fury, the anger, the hate. And while she would continue to use the pain from the past, would continue to provide help to those who needed it, she could no longer lock herself away. She deserved to use the strength she had forged; she would not waste the time and energy she had spent in healing.

She placed her hands on the marble; the titanium bridal set shone in the ambient lighting. Her eyes fell to it, her chest tightening. Despite the assertion she could move on, she still relied on old tools.

Slipped on before she left the apartment.

An automatic action.

Wedding ring, engagement ring, eternity ring; symbols of a marriage she had never had. A symbol to keep unwanted attention away. A symbol of something Anara was unsure she would ever have.

Unsure if she even wanted it.

She had been alone for years. Something incredibly positive would be needed to change that. Someone who would enhance her life.

She shook her head, dismissing the thought. *Perhaps this token of my defence should be removed.* Her fingers curled around the metal, feeling the smooth and the sharp; angular emerald cut of diamonds and sleek titanium. She spun them lazily around the digit before exhaling, her decision quick to pull them from her left hand to her right.

Anara was still staring at them when her drink arrived; chilled coupe glass garnished with oval leaves. It looked divine. 'Thank you.'

'Enjoy.' Anoushka smiled, turning away to tend to another customer who sought her attention. Prey's trade had been steady as the weekday evening turned to night, allowing time to chat with Nadia, alongside the other tasks which kept the drinks flowing.

The first sip rushed over her tongue and reassured Anara she had made the correct choice to come out, to come here. She let the cocktail sit in her mouth for a moment, savouring the flavour; the blended green chartreuse, lime juice, basil, and syrup. Richly herbaceous and chilled by the ice it had been shaken with.

Finally swallowing, she closed her eyes.

Allowing the taste, the ambience, the music of her surroundings to wind around her. Visiting the bar with her colleagues, Anara had thought Prey to be too decadent for her to feel comfortable, but, as the meal had progressed, she had relaxed. The food had been delicious, the service impeccable.

Whatever had brought her back did not disappoint.

Perhaps it was the two female servers behind the bar, or the woman who ran the restaurant. Perhaps it was the surreptitiously placed security men who integrated with the background; men she had taken note of the moment she arrived.

Placing down the glass, she exhaled. Smiled. Shoulders releasing some of the tension Anara had unwittingly carried into her evening, after the unsettling appearance outside the store.

'Surely a sweet thing like you isn't drinking alone?'

The tension immediately clawed through her body, taking root in her every muscle, every cell. Resolutely facing the bar, she inwardly cursed the decision to swap her rings.

Kassian sat on the neighbouring stool and gestured for service. He tilted toward her; jean-covered knee knocking her thigh with deliberate force. 'Hey, sweet thing, you listening?'

'What can I get you?' Nadia interjected, her blue eyes quick to scope the dynamic between the two seated patrons. Her gaze lingered a little longer than needed on the woman, but struggled to read her.

'Rum,' Kassian answered, 'and another of those.' He nodded toward the cocktail Anara held.

Her knuckles turning to chalk with the grip on the stem.

‘A verdant muse, yeah?’ Nadia hesitated, hoping there would be a sign, something to help her gauge if help was needed.

‘There’s no need to buy me a—’

‘Rum, and a verdant muse,’ Kassian stated.

Nadia pressed her lips together and bit her tongue.

Turning to the shelves, she pulled her phone from her pocket and sent a text to those in the surveillance team; this guest was one they would need to monitor. If they did not, then she would be happy to deal with him, later.

Once her shift was over.

‘So, you do listen,’ Kassian remarked, drumming his fingers on the marble. His hazel eyes drifted over her, his lips parting. The sleeves of his light-grey shirt had been rolled up, revealing the dragon tattoo which began at his wrist, meandering, unseen, to coil around his chest. ‘Care to provide your name, sweetheart?’

Anara closed her eyes and inhaled.

Slowly, he brushed his hand over her arm.

She dodged away, her focus snapping to him, eyes narrowed. Deep furrow on her brow. Fury in her gaze.

‘Only trying to get your attention, sweetheart,’ he said, a smirk on his lips and glint in his eyes, ‘seeing as how you’re not talking to me.’

‘Perhaps I’ve nothing to say.’

‘Prefer to scream it, instead.’ He winked.

Anara’s nails dug deeper into her palms.

‘I see no ring on your finger,’ he said, ‘and you’re here alone. That says looking for a good time, or trying to forget someone. And I can help with both of those things.’

She shook her head, returning to her drink and draining the glass. A rush of chilled liquid soothing the raw exasperation in her body.

‘You see, sweetheart, you need that fresh cocktail now.’ He rested his cheek in his upturned palm with a satisfied smile.

‘Which I’m more than capable of paying for myself.’

'Never said you weren't.' His fingers began to tap a steady rhythm against his cheekbone, bringing a flush rose to his skin.

'Do you want me to add this to your husband's bill?' Nadia asked, a direct stare trying to convey her idea as she placed the verdant muse in front of Anara.

'She's no ring, honey, so I think you're trying to prevent me making a connection,' Kassian said with low menace, his torso twisting to face her while his leg remained in contact with the woman beside him.

Between the hard marble of the bar and the man's denim, Anara had little room to move without walking away. And, as much as she felt uncomfortable and ready to depart, she also knew better than to bait him or make a scene. That was a lesson she learned a long time ago.

'She does.' Nadia's smile did not fade. 'Right hand.'

'Wrong hand,' Kassian argued.

Nadia leant on the bar, her spine dipping slightly. 'Russian.'

Anara's frown reappeared, watching the interaction before dropping her gaze to her hands. She had no reason to doubt what the server had said, but she wondered if that could be enough to deter the advances the man was making.

'This ain't Russia, sweetheart.' Kassian took the shot, grimacing as he tipped the contents into his mouth and swallowed.

Nadia stepped back. She knew all she had to do was utter one word and the security Prey employed would come running. And that one word would be in Russian. Looking over the man, registering the braided hair above the shaved section, and the dragon tattoo, Nadia guessed he was part of Mace's crew.

Which meant he should know better than to be here.

But she was confident he would not be here long.

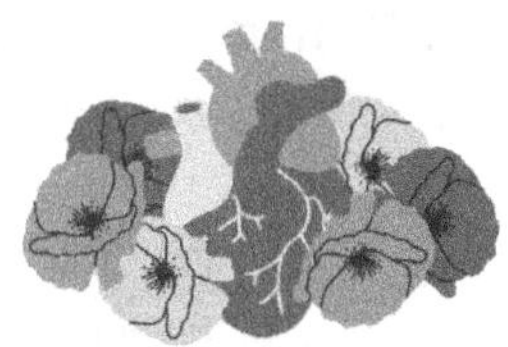

Striding through the double doors, Vadim paused. His dark eyes instantly on her, the umber reduced to slivers as the jet grew. His body alive with desire. With hunger. It rolled off him with an intensity that those close to him mistook for anger, for danger.

There was elements of each in his blood.

The moment one of the soldiers, posted at the bar, alerted him to Anara's arrival at Prey, Vadim had left. The afternoon's work in the cells resigned to memory, shed with each stroke across his pool. He trusted Fyodor to deal with the body; however he saw fit.

Vadim had long since learned to allow Fyodor his vices.

Any relaxation he had conjured from his swim, his meal, fled when he stepped inside. Thick tension clung to his flesh, pulsed under his skin. His jaw ticking with restrained vexation as he watched the man crowding her. The impulse to draw his weapon coiled through his veins. A plea to drag his knife through the man's throat.

'Pakhan?' Makari spoke softly, eyes scanning the bar, the patrons, to discover what had caused the spike in his leader.

*Mine*, Vadim thought, *that fucker has the audacity to try and claim what's mine*. His fists curled at his sides, his chest heaving with a deep inhale. For all his attempts to deflect his interest in Anara, his arguments to leave her alone, to not drag her into his life, here he was. Standing in his bar ready to come to her rescue.

Whether she wanted him to or not.

Everything he had learned about Anara suggested she would refuse his assistance. But it did not prevent him placing one booted foot after the other to stride across the tiles. Each step a calculation, determining what he would do. The scraps of conversation steering his plans. All he observed confirming his choice.

'I'm sorry I'm late крошка[14],' he announced, taking a position beside her and facing the man with a firm stare.

---

[14] крошка - Russian for 'kroshka' - a term of endearment, meaning a small crumb of bread or biscuit, something tiny

A stare which normally resulted in capitulation, in cowed pleading and prayers. Yet this man remained, his attention still fixed on Anara with barely veiled lust.

Vadim could understand it.

He felt similar attraction growing; her black dress was tight enough to suggest what lay below, the red of her full lips an invitation to kiss. To bite. Her long curls begged for him to wind them around his fist and drag her head back. To conquer her mouth, her throat, her body. To have her moan around his cock as she consumed him.

Twisting to see who spoke, further heat climbed Anara's spine. A sense of incredulity digging into her flesh and increasing the frustration which had already taken root.

This new man was standing too close.

His assertion causing her lips to part in confused anger.

Leaning against the rear counter, Nadia observed the development and folded her arms; a bemused smile creasing her blue eyes. This was unexpected, but she was enjoying the spectacle.

'Wife, please,' Vadim said smoothly, his tone seductive and gaze a promise. A chaste request she accept his words, his actions, to willingly participate in this ruse. 'I'm sorry you had to endure such unwelcome company, let me make it up to you.'

*Definitely unexpected*, Nadia thought. One eyebrow lifted. Glancing to Anoushka she inclined her head slightly to direct her colleague toward the trio at the bar. To witness the interaction.

Slowly rolling her tongue over her lips, Anara studied him. Noticed that despite his proximity, he did not touch her. He was close enough to suggest his words were real, but distant enough to be respectful. To give her a choice. She could walk away, never see either of them again.

Or she could participate in the game.

Take the risk.

It is what she had promised herself, when she left her apartment in a defiant gesture to the universe. That she live life. That she take chances when they presented themselves. It is what fuelled her decision to place a hand on his forearm and meet his dark eyes. 'You have much to make up for, husband,' she replied.

The slow curl of his fingers over her hand sent a shiver, electric and urgent, spiralling from the contact. Branching under her snowy skin to set her body on fire. Their eyes hooked into each other. Pupils blown black and devouring the person before them, surroundings melting; sound and image blurred to a kaleidoscope of interference neither Vadim nor Anara wished to entertain.

'Makari,' Vadim said with a rasp, 'I think our guest has had enough for tonight.' He did not shift his attention from Anara, studying every small change in her expression. How her parted lips released shallow breath, how her teeth caught on her lip, how her gaze moved from his eyes to his mouth.

And how she shielded the reaction and locked the desire away. The way she denied the sensation he was sure she felt. It was rapidly eating through his blood, choking his heart, his mind. The touch only confirming why he was so drawn to her.

Why he could not forget her.

'You don't need to—'

'I do.' Vadim stepped back, conscious of his audience; the way his staff had begun to gather. To whisper. He trusted his guard to escort the man from the bar, but Vadim was cognisant of the need to retain his own reputation. His glacial approach to life.

If she could shut him out, then he could do the same.

'Hey,' Kassian objected as he stumbled from the stool, 'I was only talking—'

'And now you're leaving.' Vadim turned to him, blocking Anara from the man's line of sight. His eyes roamed Prey, grateful that most patrons continued to enjoy their evening regardless; oblivious to the events by the bar. Grateful for the subtle actions being taken by his security team who blended so effortlessly.

Kassian shrugged Makari's touch from his shoulder, neck snapping toward him and eyes narrowing. 'Hands off,' he hissed.

'I'm sure he'll leave without any trouble,' Vadim stated, measured, a calm tone undercut with venom. His right hand moved to his suit jacket with a slight flick, a gesture understood between the two men.

Kassian's throat drying. He swallowed. His eyes met Anara's as she shifted behind the broad frame of her protector. Kassian scoffed before turning, stalking out; resolving not to allow this sour development to deter his pursuit.

# Six

'I'm not your wife,' Anara announced, after Kassian had unceremoniously left; glass doors firmly closed behind him. Her blunt tone coupled with a straightening of her spine. A smoothing of her dress. Her eyes resolutely on the glass before her, guarding her breath.

'No, if you were you'd have a better ring.' He took the vacated stool beside her. A bottle of vodka and glass ready waiting; Vadim poured and drank swiftly. The spirit doing little to quell the sparks burning his blood, the raw hunger which begged for sustenance.

She frowned, exhaling heavily, risking a slide of her gaze to the man beside her. 'And I didn't need rescued.'

'I know.' He poured another drink.

'Do you do this for all your customers?' she asked when Nadia drew closer, the lines on her brow growing deeper.

'No.' Nadia looked from the woman to her boss, the bemused smile returning. 'And I didn't do anything. I mean, I alerted security about him, but I—'

'So, what, you didn't do this?' Anara gestured toward the man, her confusion tightening her shoulders and creating a crack in her voice. She had, albeit in a strange way, dispatched of one unwanted admirer, only to attract another.

Vadim's eyes remained focused on pouring, on drinking, to avoid the temptation devouring his control. Her presence claiming his body with taunting hooks. All he needed to do was shift slightly and he would be able to touch, to reignite the fire which clawed through his skin. To feed the way she consumed his entire being.

'No.' Nadia shook her head. 'This was… chance?'

He placed down his glass and tilted his head toward her. It was all he dare do. 'Vadimir Morozov, owner of Prey.'

'And do *you* do this for all your customers?' Anara met his gaze for a moment, then dropped her focus to the dark marble. Her body too readily reactive; a fierce heat which continued to bite at her core.

'No, kroshka, I do not.' He risked a smile; seeing how it brought a mellowing in her defences eased some of his own tension. 'But, for you, I made an exception.'

She considered his words, debating what they could mean. What he wanted. Slow, Anara licked the tip of her tongue over her lips, resisting a smile when she registered the pained expression ghost his face when her teeth caught the lower one.

He twisted back to replenish his vodka, willing the pulse in his cock to fade. Willing the erratic beat in his heart to settle.

'You shouldn't have.'

Vadim clenched his jaw, fingers pressing more firmly on the glass as his eyes briefly closed. He inhaled. *This woman*, he thought, *will test the limit of my patience and control*.

'I'm more than capable of arranging my own social calendar,' she continued, 'and if I'd wanted to see Kassian again, then that would be my choice—'

'He's wildly unsuitable for you.'

'That's not for you to decide,' she retorted. 'You don't even know me, so how can you possibly make such a statement?'

He bit into his tongue, letting the copper mix with the vodka. 'I know him, kroshka; he's not someone you want to associate with.'

'And you are?'

Vadim wanted to say yes.

He wanted to say he was the only man worthy of her, that she was the only woman he had wanted in years, maybe the only woman he had ever wanted, that she was the woman he would protect, worship. Love. That Anara had invaded his every waking moment, and every sleeping thought. That she was a woman he could admire, could support.

With disciplined precision he turned to face her, careful to avoid his leg making contact with hers. He met her fiery gaze, conscious of every single breath. Aware of every single person in the room. The insistent yearning of his heart. 'No.'

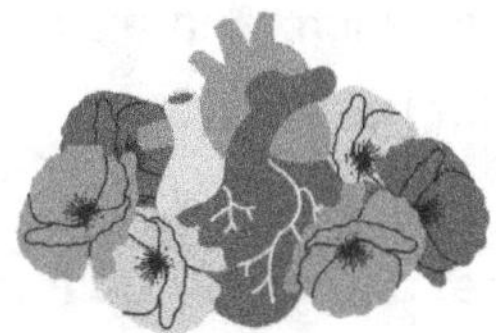

Anara was furious. And confused. The frustration had lingered, invading her attempts to sleep and leaving her even more annoyed. She rejected allowing someone she had only just met influence her in this way, yet the continued replaying of the conversation failed to leave her mind.

Something about Vadimir Morozov had taken root in her soul.

Though she had been the one to leave Prey, the verdant muse lining her veins, she felt abandoned. Vadim's dismissal of her, delivered with iced cruelty, had hurt more than she had cared to admit.

Even if she had gone out with no intention of making any sort of connection, the ease with which Vadim had removed Kassian only to also remove himself infuriated her. Even if they had physically sat side by side for some time, the walls he put up were impenetrable. Anara could have stayed until the bar staff threw her out, and she doubted she would have got another word from the owner.

He had not moved when she got up to leave.

He certainly was not looking in her direction when she glanced back, foolishly, on reaching the doors.

'For fuck's sake,' she muttered, pausing the video. She had not seen the last fifteen minutes of it, her mind wandering, hands stroking over her skin. Checking the time, she grimaced.

The shop would need opening in another half hour.

Deciding Bryony or Kerezen were more than capable, she rewound the surveillance footage and pressed play. Accommodating the pressure of the morning, she did concede to move the speed to double. All Anara needed was a clean shot of the man loitering outside Erinyes. From that, she could track him down.

And once found, he could be dealt with.

Though, strictly to their code, he had yet to be labelled as a threat to a customer, nor identified as such, Anara's instincts suggested he could be. And that was enough, for her, to act.

The others would not need to know.

She had done it before, and would do it again. Her conscience was clean; every one of her targets had sufficient evidence against them to ensure their demise was necessary. Anara would not take a life if there was inadequate harm to warrant it.

*Perhaps*, she thought, *Vadimir should be a target.*

'Get out of my fucking head!' Anara tilted her head back, her eyes on the ceiling. Her sigh fracturing with a half-hearted scream.

He turned his collar up, hazel eyes studying the window display. A focus on checking for security while appearing to review merchandise. His soft gaze floating over shelves while studying who was inside. Seeing the woman from Prey the night before lifted his eyebrows, before he quickly masked the surprise.

Kassian had hoped to find her again, but not like this.

This made it awkward.

However, he could work with this development. Their prior encounter may make it easier, or at least enable him to get something out of it.

He had been reluctant to be the one sent to monitor Erinyes; head foggy with a hangover. He had suggested Logan, as the more senior, be dispatched to resume the observations, after already being posted there the last few days.

Yet, now, Kassian was pleased he was forced to wander the streets surrounding the apothecary. Pausing by the display of herbs, he sought to understand the dynamic of the trio of women inside. They each wore an apron, which suggested they all worked there. But he could not quite determine who was in charge.

If any of them were.

Deciding to utilise his advantage, he pushed his shoulders back and fixed a smile, strolling to the door. Kassian stepped inside to the melodic chime of a bell and gentle music, alongside an aromatic blend of herbs, spices, and resins, which wrapped his limbs. After loitering in the damp this warmth was welcome.

'Kassian,' Anara stated, her eyes narrowing slightly.

Bryony and Kerezen shared glances, curious. They had noted their leader's uncharacteristic lack of patience earlier but had not pushed for clarity. On seeing the man walk in, and be recognised, the two women's concern wrestled with inquisitiveness.

'She speaks,' he remarked with a smirk, approaching the counter. A low laugh echoed from his chest while his eyes raked over her body. 'Not married today, sweet thing?'

'I don't wear jewellery to work,' Anara said. The heat which dragged over her spine was unwelcome. She had been dodging her emotions all morning, and now she was defending a stranger's actions.

A stranger who should mean nothing.

She should feel absolutely no obligation to maintain a ruse she had no part in creating.

And yet, the words slipped from her tongue with little pause.

In the periphery of her vision she observed her colleagues and their increasing confusion. The atmosphere of the store had been tense since she arrived downstairs, and this was not helping diffuse things. Anara needed him to leave, so she could explain.

Ideally before they said something to contradict her.

'This your place?' Kassian picked up a small glass jar, throwing it up before catching it in his open palm.

'What can I help you with, Kassian?' Anara felt every nerve spark; a warning which licked over her bones. She had found him distasteful the night before, and the sourness had quickly reappeared. His attitude, and his misguided sense of entitlement, did nothing but bring back memories she wished to forget.

Kassian threw the jaw toward the beams of the ceiling again, hazel eyes tracking the ascent. The descent. Mind working through the options available. He could lay the groundwork for Mace, could even get the win Septer needed; those would likely earn him promotion. He could also try and knock down the defences she had erected to keep him at bay.

Snatching the jar from the air, on the third throw, Anara slammed it down on the granite counter.

The glass cracked.

'Someone didn't get any last night,' Kassian quipped; impressed and shocked in equal measure by her skilled speed. 'Clearly that husband of yours isn't paying you the right kind of attention.'

'Husband?' Bryony mouthed to Kerezen.

Kerezen's brow furrowed with her raised eyebrows.

Folding her arms, Anara exhaled. 'What can I help you with?'

'That depends.'

Anara waited, her eyes boring into his. The scent of rosemary began to coil between them, escaping from the broken jar.

'Who owns this place?'

'I do.'

'So, you make the decisions?' he asked, slow, deliberate.

'Yes.'

'You didn't last night.' He winked.

'Is everything okay, Anara?' Kerezen asked, walking over to the pair by the counter. She remained on the store side of it, not wanting to lift the barrier, nor wanting to leave.

'Fine,' she replied, lips tight.

'Anara,' he said, a crooked smile revealing his teeth. He stroked one hand over the braid at the top of his scalp.

One barrier, down.

The sound of her name in his mouth made Anara shudder.

'Where do you source your herbs, Anara?'

'Why?' She placed both hands on the counter.

'Maybe I have a business proposition for—'

'We're happy with our supplier,' she interjected, her voice firm.

Gaze unwavering.

She pressed her fingertips into the granite, inhaling.

'I wasn't suggesting supply,' he argued. 'Well, not that kind of supply, I guess. More… growth.'

'Just say what you want.'

'Anara, sweet thing, I'm your customer—'

'We both know you're not.'

'But I could be,' Kassian took a step closer, leaning into the counter and placing his hands either side of hers. Almost touching. 'We could have a wonderful relationship, working or otherwise.'

She refused to move back, but his presence was oppressive. Each exhale brushed over her skin, each word ate into her resolve.

Her patience on the verge of collapse.

'As Anara explained,' Bryony said firmly, 'we're very happy with the arrangements we have and don't have any plans to expand.'

'So, you're not the owner?' He did not move from his stance, eyes hooked into Anara. 'You lied? That makes me think maybe, Anara, you're lying about other things too.'

'I am the owner,' she asserted.

'But we also make decisions together,' Kerezen added.

'I've not had three women at once,' he said, 'but, for you I'm willing to give it a go.'

'That's enough.' Anara's fingers curled into her palms, the fists tight on the granite. 'You need to leave.'

'Your husband isn't here, sweetheart.'

'Kassian—'

'Okay, okay.' He pushed up from the counter, eyes taking one last sweep of her body while licking his lips. 'I'll be in touch.'

'There's no need—'

'Oh, you think this is a negotiation?' His grin was accompanied by a slow laugh, by his hand stroking over his jaw. 'I've barely started, sweet thing, and you'll much prefer dealing with me than my boss.'

She bit her tongue, waiting for him to walk away. Her knuckles bone as her nails dug perfect crescent moons into her palms with each heave of her chest. Her amber eyes following his tall frame across the store; a renewed sense of vengeance swirling in her blood.

'We need to talk,' Bryony stated, her arms folded, after the door had closed. She glanced to Kerezen, seeing the support in her colleague for the conversation which was needed.

'I'll make tea.' She passed through to the rear.

'You've got until she comes back,' Bryony stated, her eyes firmly on Anara, 'to decide what you've got to say.'

Pacing, Anara considered how she could explain, how the mistrust which gnawed her bones had only developed more bite the longer he had spoken. What had been an easily deflected interaction at Prey had become a challenge, a problem. Something that she would need to deal with. Alone. Protecting her colleagues from the consequences.

The music, usually a gentle backdrop to their work, seemed to swell and join with the pulse of her heart. Clash with the conversation filtering from the street.

She channelled the energy into cleaning up the broken glass, her eyes on the flecks in the granite. On her slender fingers, void of any of the rings which had been her rescue the night before. Her head shook as a wry smile formed; she was so tired of needing to defend herself.

'Anara,' Kerezen said, placing a mug down, 'what's going on?'

'Nothing I can't handle.'

'We know that.' Bryony walked to the door, turning the lock and the sign; intent on no interruption to this discussion. 'But you don't have to handle it on your own.'

# Seven

The timber and glass of the large summer house, where the pool's water shimmered, was visible from the window. Surrounding it, and along every wall from floor to ceiling, were books. Varied in age and topic. Below the frame was a padded seat, set into the shelves to create a comfortable space to read.

It was one of Vadim's favourite places in his home.

Disguised by the wooden shelving, laden with books, the tall double doors to his study were usually kept closed. With only staff expected in the house that day, he had propped them open. It had provided him with an unencumbered gaze to his gardens as he plotted.

As he researched.

The encounter at Prey haunted him; body and soul. He regretted the negative response he had delivered to Anara, had regretted it the very moment it left his lips. He had been a fool to deny her, had been a fool to deny what he felt in his heart.

He continued to pirouette his knife into the stack of papers to his right. The hole digging into the layers, evidence of how long Vadim had duelled with his thoughts. The desire to change his mind, to pursue her, at odds to the rational knowledge he could not drag someone like Anara into his world.

She was too pure for it, too kind, too sweet.

A woman who ran an apothecary, who dealt with herbal remedies, was not someone who would feel at ease in the Bratva. His world was too cold, too violent, too cruel.

The click of the door behind him had him rearranging the handle, the tip repositioned as he spun toward the sound.

'Pakhan,' Fyodor announced, appearing in the doorway; the hum of the surveillance screens following him, 'Artem's here.'

Vadim nodded, swiftly tidying the papers and placing the stack into a drawer. Locking it as he slid the knife into his boot's sheath. Beckoning Fyodor through, the door sealed in an almost invisible join amongst the panelling, he gestured for his guard to follow.

'Ilya confirmed he's alone,' Fyodor added, closing the study's doors behind them as they crossed into the library; assuming Vadim would not want to conduct the unexpected meeting there.

'Okay.' He considered why his advisor had not called ahead, phone dragged from his pocket to check if he had missed something. With no messages of note, Vadim's eyes narrowed. Confident the gatehouse would not have permitted anyone unauthorised through, he continued to stroll toward the open plan living space.

'Where do you want me?' Fyodor's black-clad silhouette was stark before the white walls, the minimalist décor. He remained at the foot of the sweeping staircase, back to the open library door.

'Check in with the patrols,' Vadim stated, striding to the front of the property, 'and then be ready should I call.'

Fyodor turned back to the library, his words delivered softly into the communication system to request updates. He collected a book, settled into one of the library's armchairs, and waited.

Patient, Vadim studied the paved driveway, watching Artem's car navigate the centrally planted trees. He knew he was fortunate to live so well, to have the estate he did, have such comfort. It had, however, come at great cost, with the loss of his parents many years earlier. The family home had been demolished, been rebuilt to his taste. But there were still memories in the stone, still old laughter in the flowers which reappeared each season.

Still tears in the worn wood.

With the kettle on the stove, he retraced his steps, veering off to the front door to meet his guest. His kind dismissal of the housekeeper made with a smile. With a promise not to mess up the kitchen.

Greetings offered as he ushered Artem into the lounge area.

As he prepared coffee.

'I hear one of Mace's soldiers appeared at Prey last night.' He stood before the wide hearth, his back to the mantle, and observed his leader approach. Watching for his reaction.

'Correct.' Vadim offered him the mug; he waved it away, leaving the pakhan to place it on the low table. 'I handled it.'

Artem's head cocked to one side. 'That's one term for it.'

He settled into the sofa, black shirt blending with black leather, as he waited for Artem to disclose the reason for his visit. The appearance of Kassian at Prey was notable, but insufficient to warrant this. Vadim's arm rested on the back of the sofa, one ankle propped on his knee.

'Married, Vadya? You told him you were married?'

*There it is*, he thought. His lips curled into a smile. 'It seemed like a good idea at the time.'

'It was a reckless idea!' Artem sighed, crossing the room and heavily falling into one of the armchairs. His head shaking. 'Not only did you fail to introduce her to the group, you failed to meet with Father Matvey, or even do this in church—'

'It's not real, Tyoma.' Vadim's fingers moved against the leather; an enduring debate continuing within about whether he wished it was.

'Then you've put a target on a woman who shouldn't have one,' he snapped. 'And made yourself look like a fool.'

He bit his tongue.

'You've made us look weak—'

'For defending a woman?' Vadim did not shout, his tone glacial and wrapped in venom. 'Have we fallen so far from the code?'

'Dedication to one woman is detrimental,' Artem argued, 'it suggests you're no longer as committed to the fraternity.'

'It's not real.' His jaw barely moved; tension gnawing his veins. 'And if it was, then I'm quite capable of being dedicated to both. I welcome all and any attempts to overthrow me.'

Artem did not drop his gaze as their eyes met; a fierce challenge in them. 'My job is to advise you, pakhan; I am merely explaining potential consequences for your actions. You know I'd never doubt your loyalty, to our group and the vory as a whole.'

Vadim nodded, his shoulders relaxing slightly.

'Who was she?' Artem ran a hand over his peppered hair, his eyes softening. He determined he had said what he needed to, the chastising done, and now he could be the friend. The man who had known Vadim for decades and helped steer his progression from probationary member to pakhan.

The man who saw how lonely it was to live the way Vadim did.

He shifted in his seat, dropping his foot to the floor so he could lean forward and rest his forearms on his thighs. As soon as Vadim spoke her name it would condemn her. Condemn him. He knew this. Not because she would be removed from his life, no Artem was not so cruel. But he knew confessing who she was would bring additional pressure.

'Vadya,' he prompted.

'Anara Eden.'

'Owner of that herbal place we've been looking into?' Artem's head tilted, interest piqued.

He nodded. Once.

'Perhaps you should stay married, then.' Artem laughed, his chest vibrating with the sound.

Vadim remained quiet, his eyes on his coffee. The black liquid on his tongue welcomed, the heat soothing as it slipped down his throat.

'Do you think Kassian was trying to connect with her,' Artem said, a sombre note to his words, 'or the shop?'

'Neither will be successful.'

'Of course.'

'I'll remove him from the equation—'

'No, Vadya, no.' Artem shook his head.

His eyes narrowed, quick to find his advisor's.

'Let's see how it plays out.' Artem reached for his coffee. 'It seems Mace is looking to expand, and he thinks he can use her shop; if he's still only sending soldiers, then he hasn't got far, yet.'

'I don't want him to get anywhere.' Vadim was unsure exactly what he meant by that; if it was purely in relation to business or if it included getting close to Anara.

He did not feel comfortable with either.

Kassian, and by extension Mace, did not deserve her.

But, Vadim was unsure if he did either.

'And we won't let him win,' Artem stated. 'We continue our approach and we see what his play is going to be. If we move too soon, then we show our hand, we show our own interest in Erinyes. There's no value in escalating this until we need to.'

'You're ducking from the fight, Tyoma?'

'No, merely waiting until it's going to be more worthwhile.' The grin met his eyes, creating creases. Artem stroked his hand over his jaw, the cat in the hat tattoo on the back of it faded from the years of hard work undertaken for the Bratva.

Vadim took another drink, letting the coffee slide deeper, letting the heat quell the confusion which continued to develop.

He wanted to deal with Kassian, to remove the threat, before Anara was compromised, was hurt. He wanted to show Mace that attempting to use Erinyes was futile.

He wanted to claim both for his own use.

But exactly how that would look, Vadim remained uncertain.

Though Mace believed his bar was a worthy rival to Prey, his faith was regularly undermined by the meagre patrons who chose to frequent the establishment. He had tried offering food, but it had failed. So, he stuck with alcohol, music, and illicit drugs, to keep Iðun operating as one of the ways he laundered Septer's trafficking money.

Narrowing his brown eyes slightly, he reviewed the camera feeds; a critical glance over the public area of his business and the hidden cellar beneath. Vibrant lighting, conversation, and laughter, above the shadows and cages where naked women cowered beneath.

'How's it looking?' Aeron asked, slowly rolling thin paper between his fingers before sealing the joint; his lighter clicking to bring flame, to fuel his deep inhale. The marijuana smoke held on his tongue, his mouth, for a moment. Eyes closing. A slow exhale releasing vapour which clouded the office in aromatic sweet musk.

'There's some good prospects.' Mace swung the monitor around to his advisor. 'Get Jarah on her.'

'Good choice.' Holding the joint between his lips, Aeron patted his pockets, searching for his phone. The device shuffled from his jacket and message sent to one of their soldiers in the bar.

'You want to sample her?' Mace leaned back, arms folding.

'Be my pleasure, boss.' He grinned. It had been a while, and his wife was being difficult; constantly requesting his money before squandering it on lavish trinkets and jewellery. Aeron sighed, taking another drag.

'Consider it done.'

The knock on the door was brief; Logan Pottinger entering, closing it behind him. 'The movement's gonna have to be delayed.'

'The fuck?' Mace leapt up from his chair, his fists slamming onto the desk; white dust motes spiralled.

'We've had reliable word Morozov's on his way.' Logan, his black combat gear wrapping his muscular frame, folded his arms. Legs apart and stance emphasising his status as the key guard within Septer.

'Tonight?' Aeron's blue eyes roved the men, one hand rubbing over the braided strands of his blond hair, lower over the undercut to his ruddy neck. Resting above the collar of his shirt.

Logan nodded.

'Get the word out,' Mace instructed, his jaw tight and mouth sour. 'I want a new date scheduled within the fucking hour.'

'I'm on it,' he said, turning, ready to leave.

'Logan—'

'Yeah boss.' He pivoted back, already pulling his phone from the leg pocket of his trousers.

'Try find out what this fucker's visiting for,' Mace said, his jacket slid from his shoulders and holster rig slid on. The firearm on the desk tucked inside with ammunition added as a counter-weight opposite. 'No-one's to take any fucking chances, but if the opportunity presents itself, then that fucker's mine.'

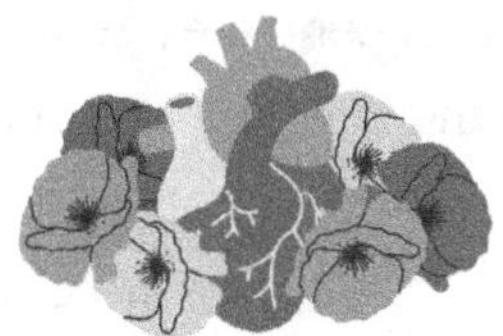

Oblivious to the developments and discussions, solider Jarah Malinowski gestured for another drink. Two drinks. He winked at the man preparing them, his head slightly inclining to confirm his intent. The bartender gave a brief nod, reaching below the steel to the innocuous tin containing a range of different options.

Different strengths.

Different presentations.

Different formulations.

But all some form of benzodiazepine. The bartender had taken note of the woman Jarah was now sitting beside so had an idea of what would be most effective. He dropped a tablet into the vodka soda and stirred, the ice rattling against the tall glass.

'You here alone, sweetie?' Jarah asked, his voice honey. The Celtic dragon tattooed sleeve, seen below his white short-sleeved t-shirt, was a visible confirmation of his allegiance to Septer. His cropped afro different to others in Mace's group who opted to mimic the Norse style; instead, Jarah had silver runic beads in his beard.

She turned to face him, eyes widening as she looked over the young man, her smile steadily matching his. The initial caution fading with the appreciation of his presence. The lack of threat in his words, in how he had spoken but not touched. 'Yeah… my friends—'

'Are stupid.' Jarah acknowledged the arrival of the drinks, his thanks offered with warmth. 'For you… what's your name?'

'Candy.' She looked at the drink, a quick frown ghosting her brow.

'I can get him to make you another, if you're concerned.'

'No… sorry,' Candy said hastily. Her hand went to her mouth, teeth biting her nails as her skin flushed with embarrassed heat. 'God, I'm just so… you hear so many horror stories.'

'I know,' he agreed. 'My sisters, they keep me honest.'

Candy exhaled, her hand lowering and curling tentatively around the cool sides of the glass. It looked the same, tasted the same. The small sip slipping over tastebuds dulled from the others she had imbibed over the course of the evening. 'Thank you.'

'No worries.' He smiled.

'So, you know people here?' Her nails tapped against the glass. Her attention on him and missing the way her coat, slung over the back of the bar stool, fell to the floor.

'Yeah,' Jarah confirmed; he flipped between truth and lie so often he was adept at either. 'It's home from home.'

'But you're here alone?' Candy's blue eyes roamed the bar, seeking any kind of connection to the man, searching for anyone watching their interaction.

'I was.' Jarah's focus dropped to his watch; an analogue piece on the wrist of his corded forearm. 'Now I'm not; I couldn't've left a gorgeous woman sitting on her own.'

'Smooth.' She laughed, taking another, larger, drink.

Jarah joined with her laughter, finally relenting to collect his whiskey from the bar and take a sip. Only a sip. From what he had heard from the scouts, he would need to stay alert.

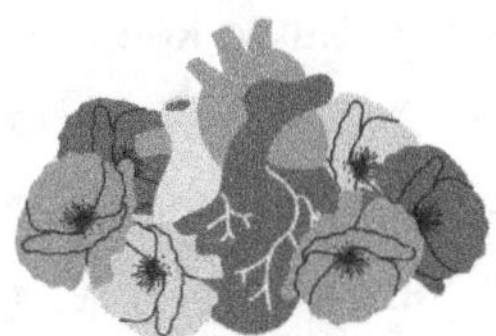

The trip down the poorly lit stairs was one Aeron Barnes had taken many times before; stocky yet trim he navigated with relative ease. The thud of music, the scrape of stools, the irregular steps, fading the deeper into the structure he travelled. The large cellar divided into storage for every type of contraband Septer trafficked, including people.

Their bodies housed in make-shift cages or crammed inside small windowless rooms, with barely sufficient facilities to share. Mattresses thin and blankets rare, bodies stripped and usually left in darkness.

'You're here?' Jarah remarked, turning to face Aeron. 'I'd've thought the boss'd kept you with him.'

'The bastard ain't here yet,' he stated, eyes voraciously moving over Candy. 'I'm not wasting my night or a chance to fuck.' Aeron was already removing his jacket, unbuttoning his shirt.

Jarah smiled, acknowledging his words.

'Where am I?' Candy slurred, leaning into Jarah with drooping eyes and weak limbs. Her head struggled to remain upright, jaw-length blonde strands making it even more difficult to see as she swayed.

Taking the sequinned clutch bag from her loose grip, Jarah tossed it over to one of the scouts loitering in the corner of the only presentable room the basement's warren offered. A bed, an armchair, an en-suite shower, and a range of clothes and toiletries utilised by both members of

Septer and those looking to buy. Whether for an hour, a day, a night, or for longer, Mace prided himself in permitting a taste of the property he made available.

'Make sure that ends up a long way from here,' Aeron instructed, his hands on his belt. His boot on the door to kick it shut after the youngster had run into the hallway.

'You want me to undress her?' Jarah held the petite woman against his side, one arm around her chest to keep her from falling. The sedative had worked quickly, combining with the alcohol, enabling him to steer her from the bar with another wink to the bartender. 'Cuff her?'

Licking his lips, Aeron took a step forward. He tipped her chin up to face him, seeing her glassy eyes as her head involuntarily weaved in an unsteady rhythm. 'Nah… this doll won't fight.'

Candy stumbled forward, released from Jarah, only to be flung back onto the bed. She bounced against the fabric, her limbs liquid, her mind uncertain of what had happened. The room cloudy. Noise muffled. Those crowding her only shapes. Shadows. Touch not quite registering, ghosts on her skin. The slam of the door a whisper.

'Such a sweet little doll,' Aeron crooned, one hand on her throat as the other dragged a knife through her dress; fabric tearing to reveal the lace beneath.

She tried to reply, but her tongue was sticky.

Her mouth dry.

Her words only faint sounds.

Using his knees, he kept her legs apart. The knife twisted in Aeron's hand to ensure the blade could clip through the front of her bra. Tatters of material which would be incinerated before the sun rose. Shuddering below the gliding metal, Candy was unaware of how Aeron smiled, how he ached. The final barrier cut away with a deft flick of the knife.

Her whimpering scream smothered by his palm.

# Eight

He had been ushered through the bar with little ceremony, vigilant eyes on the three members of the Bratva permitted entry to Iðun. Vadim's strides ate up the space, forcing their hosts to work to his schedule, his speed. A pressure inflicted without words, without violence.

Artem critically assessed the bar; for both quality and risk. 'Perhaps we should've chosen a neutral—'

'I want to see his face,' Vadim interjected in the same hushed tones, his focus never shifting from Logan, leading them to the stairs.

The Russian advisor's chuckle was soft, earning him a quick smile from Makari; the pair following behind their leader. Their weapons taken before they could step inside, they would rely on their strengths. And the overlooked knives hidden in their boots.

Makari clutched the box they had insisted should not be searched. A concession made to keep the peace. Even if the trio knew it would break the moment it was opened.

The haze of smoke drifted along the corridor, wrapping their suited bodies, coiling in their hair. Vadim's eyes devoured every part of the worn walls, the scuffed floor, the closed doors and crooked artwork. Details he chronicled, absorbed, considered. Exits mapped, attacks formed, in each minute aspect of the space.

It was as natural as breathing for him.

He had only reached his position as pakhan by being this way.

And he would be damned if an inferior organisation would end him.

'Boss,' Logan stated, entering the office.

Looking up from his desk, Mace met Vadim's piercing gaze with an attempt of his own. Failing. His eyes returning to the wooden surface and range of drug paraphernalia. A large knife taunting each man present in the now crowded room; evidence of superiority.

Vadim almost laughed, amused by Mace's need to prove himself.

'You wanted to meet?' Septer's boss said.

Behind Vadim, advisor and guard remained standing, watching as their leader sat and placed one ankle on the opposite knee. Knife in easy reach. Taller than any of the others in the room, Makari remained straight and alert; brown eyes shrewdly calculating.

'So?' Mace had not stood when they arrived, had tried to project an aura of poised calm. The silence was beginning to undermine his plan to retain control. His fingers itched to swipe the gun from the cluttered desk, to request Logan engage. He curled his hands into fists, hidden; rested them on his thighs.

Biting his tongue, Vadim fought a similar urge. From the angle of his chair, he could see the monitor Mace had forgotten to turn. It allowed him to witness the row after row of cages, the naked flesh, the man walking away from a clearly unconscious woman on a disheveled bed. He could take Mace now, certain Logan would be dealt with by Artem or Makari; a change in plan, but maybe a change that was needed.

Or, he rationalised, Mace had left the screen visible intentionally; his attempt at appearing stronger, more dangerous.

He bit his tongue more firmly.

'Your hospitality is rather disappointing,' Vadim stated, leaving it up to Mace how he interpreted it; his cells or his lack of courtesy. 'Any guest of mine would've had drinks by now.'

'I... I—'

Logan took a step toward the closed door.

'We won't be here long.' Vadim paused. 'We're here to remind you of our boundaries, and how important it is to respect them.'

'Хотя любому умнику напоминание и не понадобится[15],' Artem muttered, face turned to Makari with a wry smile.

'We've not broken any of the accords,' he objected, a frown creating deep grooves across his brow.

'And yet you're attempting to take what's mine.' Vadim retained his dark eyes on Septer's leader, seeking any indication he was aware of Kassian's presence in Prey, Kassian's flirtation with Anara.

'I assure you, we're not.'

He smiled. 'Then, let this be merely a friendly piece of advice; stay away from Erinyes, and stay away from my wife.'

'You got married?' Mace leaned forward, his elbows landing on the desk and creating a disturbance in the dust. In the corridor, approaching footsteps indicated Aeron was finally on his way; knowledge which aided his bravado.

By the door, Logan's eyes widened; this changed things. She would provide them with leverage, a target, someone they could utilise if Vadim ever tried to damage Septer.

'That's a reckless thing to do in our profession,' Mace continued, his lips quirking into a smile as Aeron strode through.

The lingering scent of sex following him as he made his way to the rear of the room. Poured a glass of whiskey. Conscious of Vadim's eyes on him, tracking his movements, Aeron scoffed and downed the contents before refreshing the glass. Turned his focus to the screen to see Jarah dragging the woman to the shower.

'It's only reckless if you're incapable to defending her.'

'And you believe you can keep your wife safe?' Mace settled back in his leather chair, the mechanism creaking.

---

[15] Хотя любому умнику напоминание и не понадобится - Russian for 'Though any smart fucker wouldn't need a reminder'

'Would I have done this otherwise?'

Vadim had faith in the words, even as doubt clawed at his soul. The very idea his actions could place Anara at risk causing a shard of ice to scrape over his spine. She had no knowledge of the steps he had taken, no knowledge of his brutal nature, no knowledge of his life. She would recoil at his truth, too fragile to survive it.

'Are you sure you can even control a wife?' Aeron nursed the glass in his hand, the amber liquid rocking with his shifting stance, moving to perch on the edge of the desk.

'Say that again,' Vadim hissed, 'I dare you.'

'And what? You'll throw a fucking punch?'

'Aeron,' Mace warned.

Flicking open his jacket, Logan rested his hand on his gun.

The atmosphere seemed to pause, the air still, even breath caught in the descending tension. Each man watching, waiting.

Vadim measured his pulse, using each beat to stretch the time, to weave his patience and prevent his instincts from releasing his knife. His desire to snap their necks.

'What's your interest in Erinyes?' Mace asked.

'It's in our territory,' he replied, 'and I'm aware you've sent scouts to check the store over.'

'We'd never—'

Makari took a step, placing the wooden box on the desk. Silent, his boots made barely a whisper as he resumed the defensive guard behind his leader.

'What the fuck's that?' Mace looked to Logan, to Aeron, before his attention landed on the rectangular object. The grain sanded smooth, the ash unmarked, a simple cut to delineate the way the lid could be prised from the base.

'Confirmation of your dishonesty.' Vadim's hand drifted to his calf, his focus on the men behind the desk, trusting Makari and Artem would stay attentive to any movement from Logan.

‘It’ll be nothing,’ Aeron said dismissively, ‘they were searched.’

‘Not that.’ Logan felt uneasy, his fingers flexing by his weapon.

‘I’ll kill the fucker who let them through without checking,’ Aeron spat as he slammed his glass down. His palms either side, he leaned over the desk and studied the creamy wooden box.

‘You can open it,’ Vadim suggested, ‘it won’t bite.’

‘Но это может сломить их дух[16],’ Artem quipped.

‘You think you’re fucking smart, I get it,’ Mace said, his eyes hooked on the box. ‘You make it known you’re coming here, then you fucking act like you’re invincible, talk knowing we won’t understand—’

‘I’m more than happy to translate,’ Vadim interjected, fingers edging closer to his ankle.

Swallowing nothing but air, his throat dry, Mace spun the box toward him with the lightest of touches. No rattle. No tick. Not that he expected it to be a bomb; *Vadim would never be so stupid*, he thought.

‘You can touch it,’ Vadim said, ‘it won’t hurt you.’

‘He probably has to say that to his *wife*.’ Aeron chuckled, the roll of his eyes halted when the blade speared through his hand.

His howl guttural as it echoed in the office.

‘I did warn you,’ Vadim stated calmly, standing before them with a cold glare, daring them to retaliate. Daring them to escalate this feud into a war. Whatever they opted to do, he was ready.

Artem by his side.

Makari facing the door, his back almost touching Vadim’s. The trio prepared to act, but finding it to be unnecessary. Though his hand had been poised above his firearm, Logan had frozen with uncertainty. Mace had only sought to grip his advisor’s arm. The lack of a command loud in its absence.

With a grunt, Aeron pulled the knife from his hand, blood leaking from the wound and smearing the dust. Dripping onto the vinyl floor. He flung the weapon aside, the metal sliding across the table.

---

[16] Но это может сломить их дух - Russian for ‘But it may break their spirits’

Vadim caught it.

Settled it in his grip. His eyes lifting. 'Stay away from Erinyes, and stay away from my wife.'

'Agreed,' Mace said faintly.

'And you stay away from me, fucker,' Aeron said, winding a length of fabric awkwardly around his palm. The scrap found after digging through his leader's drawer. It was floral satin, meaning the scarf slipped and the blood kept flowing even as he tried to staunch it.

'Happily.' Vadim wiped the blade on his trouser leg before returning it to the sheath in his boot. His gaze fell to the unopened box. 'If you stick to your word, then this'll be the last gift I need to deliver.'

'The address to locate the rest of your scout,' Artem added, 'is in the box.' He nodded toward it, underlining his words. Observing Vadim's turn from the desk and clear intent to depart, he fell in step. Trusting Makari would follow, and that they would meet no resistance.

No attack.

Should anyone move, should an instruction be voiced, the brigade of soldiers, with Nikolai, outside Iðun would massacre the entire bar, a member of Mace's crew or not.

The trio did not look back after leaving the stifling room, listening to the opening of the box and the curses uttered by each man left behind. It only brought a smile to the Russian men as they walked, knowing they had made the point they had intended, and delivered the threat without further bloodshed.

For now.

None of the men assumed this would be enough.

By the door, hands by his sides, Logan watched numbly as an idea formed; Mace was weak. Aeron was brittle. And, perhaps, Septer needed a more assertive direction which he believed he could offer.

# Nine

In Vadim's office, above Prey's bar, the men had gathered, following the visit to Septer. With vodka poured conversation flowed, allowing them to determine how to progress. The exchange of observations conducted in the car paused with their arrival, with their navigation through the patrons intent on enjoying every minute of the bar's service.

'Perhaps the long game isn't working,' Artem suggested, returning to his chair with a fresh bottle, placing it in the centre of the table.

With Makari standing guard on the corridor, beyond the closed door, they were each relaxed. The relative safety of their space enabling any lingering tension to dissipate. Once the music died below, indicating the emptying of Prey, they would find even greater freedom. Until then, they spoke and drank with weapons in easy reach.

'What makes you think that?' Vadim retained a calm gaze, slow to move over each of the other three men. Assessing.

'If they're growing bold enough to try and take control of a property in our territory,' Artem stated, 'then what's to stop them mounting any other kind of attack?'

'We both know how that would work out.'

'Yes, Vadya,' he said. 'But the strike on the warehouse should never have reached that point. Previously, Mace'd never dare—'

'Septer isn't our only problem,' Vadim interjected with precision, with a sharpness belied by the soft timbre of his tone. 'Or have you forgotten about the random poisonings?'

'So far, they haven't targeted anyone in our fraternity,' Pavel offered while shifting forward to replenish his drink.

'That doesn't mean they won't.' Vadim rubbed his hand over his dark hair, mussing the strands. 'I need to understand exactly what this thing is Pasha.'

'Maybe you could ask your *wife*.' Artem laughed, his eyes creasing even as he watched his leader's jaw tighten.

'Tyoma,' Vadim said with a sigh, shaking his head. 'I'm not bringing her into this. Considering how Septer treat women, these poisonings are more a threat to them, and I refuse to take the blame for anyone targeted by this killer.'

'Considering how we deal with Mace's crew,' Nikolai said, 'I think the poisoner may be on our side.'

'Yeah, poisoning is a bit subtle compared to delivering a heart.'

'You think I can't do subtle, Pasha?' Vadim's lips formed a wry smile, his chest shuddering with gentle laughter.

Pavel's neck warmed, his cheeks flushing with heat.

'He's got a point,' Artem said. 'You didn't name Anara, only Erinyes, and you never mentioned Kassian's presence here or—'

'Mace doesn't need to know.'

'But, Vadya, how're they going to know who to keep away from, if you don't give them the details?'

'They know I'm married.' Vadim kept his focus on Artem, all humour lost. 'They should respect our lives and respect the store. That should be enough; they can do their own research.'

'Yeah, research.' Nikolai winked. His light-brown eyes narrowing with mirth as he sipped on his vodka.

'Kolya?' Artem asked. 'What've you done?'

He opened his mouth to reply, only for Vadim to shake his head.

'If Mace doesn't know about Kassian,' Vadim said, 'which from how he reacted suggests he doesn't, then I'd rather keep that information to ourselves. It's something we can maybe use.'

'You think Septer is fracturing?' Smoothing over his black suit jacket, Artem sensed the opportunity to hunt, to destroy. It brought a wicked grin to his lips, a sparkle to his eyes.

'I think they're stretching themselves too thin,' Vadim explained. 'You saw the place tonight, it's in dire need of renovation, and they're already cutting their product with inferior shit.'

'That doesn't mean they're falling apart as a unit—'

'But Logan never moved,' Vadim continued, eyes on his advisor. 'If it was me who had a knife slammed into my hand, you'd have slaughtered everyone in the fucking room.'

Acknowledging the point with an incline of his head, Artem dwelled on the events in Mace's office. In how Logan had held back. In how they appeared unfocused and uncoordinated. Despite the prior notice he had issued about their intention to visit, as requested by Vadim.

'Kolya, what do you know about their trafficking?'

'Only a little, pakhan,' he replied, 'but I can find more.'

'Do it.' Vadim's jaw ticked. 'What I saw in their basement… if I ever hear of any fucking one of you treating women the way I saw them treat that woman, I'll remove your fucking skin.'

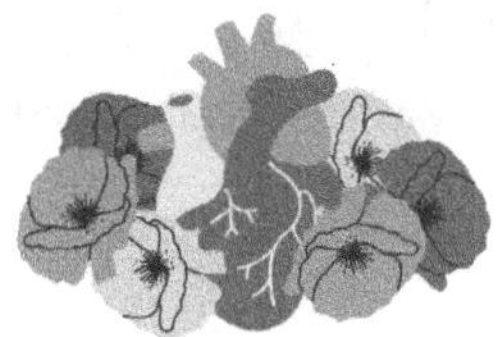

Accustomed to late nights, and late mornings, Ksenia Solovyova's offer of vodka was not unusual. Their arrival home from Prey at two together was; their lives diverted with her management of the restaurant and his varied assignments often resulting in staggered proximity. Her regular work conflicting with Pavel's commitment to Vadim, to the Bratva.

A commitment accepted as part of their marriage.

But one she wished to change.

Draining the glass, Pavel accepted another before navigating to the armchair and making himself comfortable. Suit jacket unbuttoned and boots kicked off.

'What does he expect, Pasha? You can't make a pattern from these random attacks,' she stated, her weight shifting to one hip, as she stood over him. 'Asking you to find who's killing these men is doomed to fail, you'll never earn any promotion—'

'Маленькая птичка[17], I'm happy as I am.' He stroked his palm over his brown hair, his musculature evident in how the fabric of his clothing tightened. 'I've no desire to do any more than run a team.'

'But you can do more, you deserve more.' She sighed, dropping into the chair opposite and sliding her heels from aching feet.

'For who? For you?' His eyebrows rose; this argument one they had often. This life was all they had; with no children, it was their work and their marriage which consumed them. Happily.

'You're getting older, Pasha, and I don't want you to get hurt,' she admitted, her blue eyes lifting to find his gaze. In the earlier years of their partnership, the days they courted and sought each other out before they stood at the altar, she had encouraged him and supported him; moving from prison-recruited solider to brigadier.

Yet, Ksenia still believed he could do more.

Could be in a safer position.

'You don't have to worry about that,' Pavel said with warmth, with a wry smile. 'I've plenty of fight left.'

'But—'

'Vadim is happy with me, Kolya and I work well together, my team are efficient and we're bringing in revenue,' he said, his eyes on his wife and compassion evident in his tone. 'This fascination with these deaths, these poisonings… it'll pass.'

'I don't want you to fail.'

---

[17] Маленькая птичка - Russian for 'Little bird' - a term of endearment

‘I won’t fail.’ He had not achieved all he had by failing. Even as a boy there had been conviction in his words, his actions. Pavel Solovyov was not made to quit.

When his time came, he would die with fury, not silence.

The task to discover the random poisonings was nothing more than an exercise in fantasy. Something Vadim had got his teeth into but which would ultimately decay, his interest waning and Pavel instructed to move onto another, new, scheme.

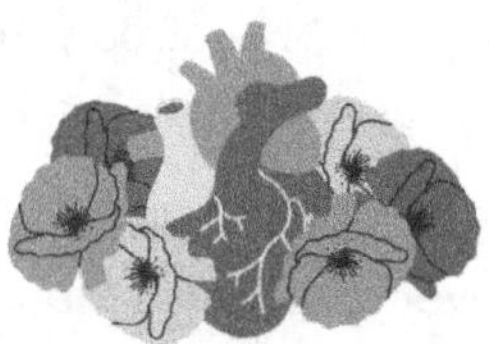

Though Maksim had tried, his gentle drawing back of the duvet and quiet shuffling into bed, did not prevent Yeva waking. She welcomed his return home, relieved her husband appeared identical to his departure, even if the bedside lighting created shadows. In his absence, slumber struggled to claim her, waiting for some notification of his status.

Alive or dead.

In the city or sent away.

And what that would then mean. For her. For their children. For how life would continue without his presence. If Yeva would have to collect as many possessions as she could and run, or if she would die defending those she loved.

Such thoughts plagued her as she tried to settle beside him, as she softly slid away to shower, to dress, to prepare breakfast for their young children. Their voices hushed with a forced smile, her mask of joy. Any trace of anxious weariness hidden with well-practiced skill. The two boys watching her before dashing outside to play.

‘I want out,’ she stated, turning from the window to face Maksim.

‘Morning to you too.’ He frowned, continuing toward the stove as he rubbed the heel of his palm into his eye. The hours ahead promised to be as long as the day before.

'Maksim, I won't have our boys live this life.' Yeva's hands turned in front of her stomach, her gaze clouded with heated moisture.

'It's a good life, золотце[18],' he said, stifling a yawn. 'Look around, all we have is because of this life and how hard—'

'How much use is it if you're dead? If someone kills you while you're out on the street?' Yeva's fingers untangled, moving to grip the orthodox cross around her neck. 'What if Pasha or Kolya decide you're no longer worth keeping on the team? What happens then?'

'That's not going to happen.' He strode from the simmering kettle to enfold her in his arms; the fabric of his pyjamas and gown soft against her warm cheeks. The tears finally breaking as she sobbed. 'You and our boys are everything; I'd never jeopardise that.'

'Please, Maks, please let us leave,' she mumbled into his chest.

His eyes closed as he clenched his jaw. His head tilting up toward the ceiling as the sound of hissing water merged with the almost silent weeping of his wife, the carefree laughter of their boys in the garden. It was almost enough to make him agree.

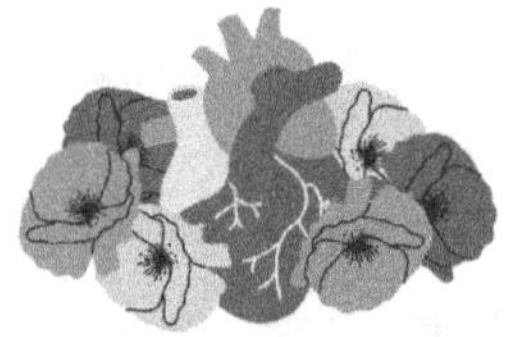

Behind them, the body remained limply suspended from iron hooks, the manacles resting against bone and chains stained with ichor. Groans still hummed, low, from the man's chest. Remnants of a dragon tattoo visible on the flayed skin of his arm. Evidence of where a dermatome had been used, where knives had sliced, where rope had been tightened, formed a map of pain.

Of torture.

The chains breaking through flesh as his weight dragged him lower with each shuddering attempt to dodge incisions. His toes too far above

[18] золотце - a Russian term of endearment, rooted in the word 'золото' which means gold, suggesting the person is precious

the stone floor to feel, achingly close but unreachable. A prone position which had steadily forced his shoulders to dislocate with the release of an agonised scream.

'Please,' he slurred, swollen eyes following the blurred images of the men. Registering the way one pulled an arm back, a long leather whip in his hand. 'Please.'

'I think our guest is ready to talk,' Vadim said. His black shirt sleeves were rolled to the elbow, his clothes marked in crimson. Blood formed sticky rivers to his boots. Any exposed skin mottled with colour. In the shrouded lighting of the cell, his dark hair looked darker still.

'Shame.' Fyodor dropped his arm, the thinner end of the whip coiling by his combat boots.

'I... I...,' he croaked. Swallowed. Cut lips and a fractured jaw making it difficult. The effort to lift his head felt impossible, the pressure on every joint, every muscle, wailing through his veins.

Fyodor flicked the whip against the stone; the sound cracked around the enclosure with deafening precision.

'They drug them.' The words were raw, scraping over his tongue and broken teeth, delivered with defeat in every breath.

'Two days, and that's all he can tell us.' Fyodor sighed. 'Either I'm no longer any good at this, or this fucker is a waste of our time, pakhan.'

'To be fair,' he said with a wry smile, 'you only started asking about the human trafficking this morning.' Vadim doubted this scout would have much to share; the man had been picked up easily enough, discovered lurking around Prey, but that only confirmed how little they would likely know about Septer's operations.

'All I'm hearing is I need to try harder.' He began to wind the whip around his hand, loose, the worn leather stained red. Fyodor's wide grin bringing creases to his hazel eyes.

Vadim rested his hand on his guard's muscular shoulder. 'If you try any harder, there'd be nothing left for me.'

Fyodor chuckled, tossing the whip to the floor.

Striding to the cart, Vadim assessed the blades, the knives, the tools which they used effectively. Lengths of the man's debrided flesh lay in a stainless steel bowl on the top shelf, viscous fluid and blood leaking. He shook his head, eyes glancing to Fyodor briefly.

The guard swept one strip from the bowl, his tongue out to receive the delicacy; the skin folding as it dropped.

With a moan, the tortured man wretched air.

'When do I get to play with Mace?' Fyodor asked, strolling toward the wall then leaning against it; one foot flat to the stone, knee bent.

'Not yet.' Vadim weighed a knife in his palm, debating it that would be the one he used. The man was young, the flesh elastic.

'But he's letting his advisor fuck unconscious women—'

'Fedya.' His jaw tightened, the tick evidence of the tension creeping through his body. The uncertainty surrounding exactly how Septer was finding the women, housing them, using them, made it difficult to know how to approach the destruction of it.

*Was it only women? Was it children? Was it men? Did he keep them on his property, or move them on? Did he have more locations?*

Vadim did not want to strike, only to find he had played his hand too soon, or spoiled the opportunity to remove their den entirely. He detested that he felt so weak. So disadvantaged.

'What's Kolya found out?' Fyodor asked; he had known Vadim for long enough to know when it was best to leave a thread stitched, leave an argument unspoken.

'Not enough.' Vadim gripped the hilt of a каратель[19]; a curving blade glinting in the overhead light, the black grooved handle secure.

'Do you think it's linked to the poisonings?' He licked his lips, blood smeared his chin. He used his thumb to swipe it into his mouth.

'I doubt it,' he replied. 'From what Pasha's said, the poisonings are sporadic and targeted on men like Septer.'

---

[19] каратель - Russian for 'karatel', which means 'punisher / chastener', a series of knives developed for the FSB

'So, they're an ally?' Fyodor's eyebrows raised, his tattooed hand rubbing his neck before tilting his head side to side. Ready to step in and assist with this next stage of their routine. Keen to explore this victim alone. Unaware Nikolai had expressed similar sentiments.

Vadim released a breathy laugh, his head shaking. 'If this poisoner is, then they're going to need to reach out and talk soon, otherwise they'll find themselves heartless.'

Turning to their victim, his aim was sure. Sinking the blade deep into the man's chest and slicing upwards along his sternum. Leaving it buried in his throat. Just enough to keep him alive. Vadim held out his hand, the retractor readily provided by his guard. Spreading the ribs, he dragged the knife through the pulmonary artery, curling lower.

The organ ripped from the cavity.

Hot, cloying, slick.

'He's all yours,' Vadim stated, stalking away with the muscle in his palm, the knife thrown onto the cart. He preferred to prepare the hearts he took with different tools. To ensure it conveyed the message intended when it arrived with the person responsible for such violence.

# Ten

The vibration of his phone brought the device from his pocket. Kassian's eyes quick to scan the words; the warning to stay away from Erinyes and Vadim Morozov's wife blunt.

He shrugged.

Kassian's focus lifting to the building before him, the painted black door and soft lighting. The rows of apothecary jars, herbs, flowers.

About to return his phone when it began to vibrate again.

'Boss,' he said, answering the call with a frown.

'You seen the text?' Logan asked.

'Yeah.'

'Where are you?' He paused, listening to the sound of shoppers and music. Referring to the schedule, their arrangements; placing what was heard with what he knew. 'Erinyes?'

'Maybe.' Kassian kicked at the pavement, his boot scuffing at loose grit. Eyes following the movement. 'What if I am?'

'Keep at it,' Logan instructed.

'But, the text—'

'Mace wants to keep people away, so it was sent to everyone,' he continued. 'I want you to keep up the surveillance.'

'Okay.' He smiled. 'The view sure is worth keeping up.'

Logan chuckled. 'I bet.'

'The things I'd get her to do, fuck,' he said with a breathy sigh. 'Her mouth, those lips—'

'You're checking out the shop, not her.'

'She's fair game, boss.' Kassian may have been kicked out of Prey and received poorly last time he saw her in Erinyes, but he had not yet reached the limit of his options. He still had methods to try. Still had ways he could convince her to agree to his ideas.

And if that got him her store too, then that would be a win which would make Mace notice his value as a member of Septer.

'Just don't ruin our chances of getting our product in there with your games,' Logan warned.

'I won't.' He grinned.

Kassian watched Anara climb the ladder at the rear of the store, her lithe body clad in black and hair pulled high. Perfect for him to hold from behind, to push her onto her knees. Kassian plunged one hand into his pocket to adjust his cock as it began to harden.

He barely heard Logan's closing words, the line disconnected as he opened the door. The aromatic warmth wrapping him as he crossed the threshold. Eyes darting around the store, quick to place where Kerezen and Bryony were.

'Happy Valentine's Day, sweet thing,' he called out, approaching the counter and watching how the apron's bow framed her waist.

Facing the shelves, Anara closed her eyes, bit her tongue. A wash of acrid copper bursting over the muscle before she swallowed. The open drawer of herbs a temptation, an urge to pull more nightshade than was needed from the wooden tray. Inhaling deeply, she slammed it shut, and began to climb down to the shop's floor.

'May I help you?' Her spine was straight, her amber eyes on him.

Kassian leant forward, his chin on his upturned palm and elbow on the granite countertop. His eyes tracked her body, no attempt to hide his interest. 'That depends, you want to invite me back—'

'Kassian,' she interjected. 'You've got to stop doing this.'

'It's just to talk, sweetheart.' He winked. 'Like I tried to explain last time, I've got a great business opportunity for you.'

'And I told you we're happy with things as they are.' Anara kept her eyes on him, noting the movement of her friends in the periphery. Both women walking closer to the counter to offer support.

'You've not let me explain what I'm—'

'Kassian, no.' She curled her hands into fists, hidden in the pocket of her apron. 'Please leave.'

'You're making a mistake, sweet thing.' He stood, his tongue slow to trace over his lips as he made another overt sweep of her form. 'You and I could be so good together.'

Anara's teeth clenched tightly.

'Relax,' he crooned, 'or let me come help you relieve the tension.'

'That's enough,' Kerezen said. 'You need to leave, now, before I get the police—'

'Fuck off,' he scoffed. 'There's no need for that. I'm going, okay.' He strolled leisurely toward the door, turning up the collar of his jacket. With a brief pause, he twisted to look over the three women.

Standing, united, their eyes filled with venom.

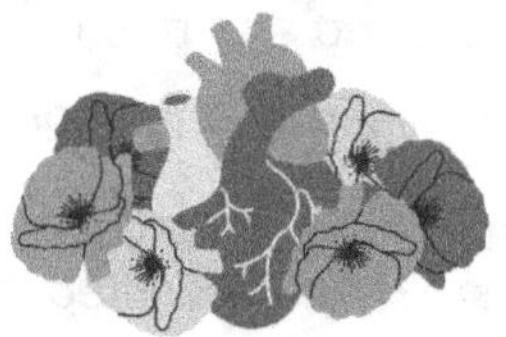

Shrugging her bag further up on her shoulder, Yeva Zaitseva looked from one side to the other. She had been cautious on her way to Erinyes, but habits were hard to break. All her planning could unravel if she made the wrong move now, made the wrong choice, said the wrong thing.

Her brown eyes returned to the black paint of the door. The gently lit bay windows. She exhaled slowly, one hand falling to spin her wedding band around her finger.

It felt like a manacle.

With one further deep exhale, the briefest closure of her eyes, Yeva pushed down the handle and crossed over the threshold. Forcing herself to walk slowly, she tried to browse the shelves. Her eyes unseeing and senses alert; listening for any steps, any shouts, any attempt to grab her and drag her back into the street.

The chime of the door remained silent.

The low melody and fragrances blending around her.

Yet through it all, her heart pounded a brutal warning which drowned all else. It threatened to swallow her whole. Her fingers drifted to her dry throat, fumbling with the gold orthodox cross which sat below her coat. A smooth reminder of duty.

Of consequence.

'Are you okay?' Anara asked softly. She had watched the woman as she wandered; the likely intention betrayed by the pensive lines on the customer's brow. The expression one Anara had witnessed more times than she would like to admit.

Startled, Yeva clutched the cross more tightly. Her eyes wide before darting behind her.

'Would you prefer to come through to our lounge?' Anara glanced over to her colleagues. 'It's more private.'

With a swallow, Yeva nodded and pushed her shoulders back.

Followed after one last lingering check of the windows.

Only relaxing when the consulting room door was closed.

'May I get you some tea?' Anara waited, hovering by the cupboards and observing Yeva's analysis of the space they had arrived in.

She shook her head.

Anara gestured for her guest to sit, as she settled into her usual armchair. Her posture one of openness, of amiable calm.

The diffused light from the frosted glass window fought with the overhead fixtures, making the oak and suede seem more pale. More fragile. Even the floral arrangement in the corner appeared brittle in the February light.

'Sofiya told me I could trust you,' Yeva managed, voice scratching over her tongue. Raw and broken.

Knowing better than to confirm or deny any past interactions, Anara remained unmoved by the words. Her face unreadable. Her body static as she waited for the woman to elaborate.

'I need help,' Yeva admitted. 'Not like Sofiya… different. I—'

'Anything discussed here is confidential,' Anara interjected kindly, 'so I can't say who may have been here, or what—'

'Of course.' Yeva's peach skin darkened; heat sweeping through her blood. The anxious sweat on her back increasing.

'That means whatever you tell me, if you feel able to,' Anara said, 'I'll keep completely between us. I don't keep records, I don't need names, I only ask that if there's any medical history I *need* to know, that you tell me so I can keep you safe.'

'It's not for me,' Yeva said hastily. 'I mean, it is… sorry.'

'There's no need to apologise.' Anara smiled. Seeing the tears begin to gather in the woman's eyes, she twisted to collect the box of tissues from the counter and pass them over.

'I need to get out,' Yeva explained after wiping her cheeks; fresh salt tracing them with quiet determination. A mourning with each word she delivered. 'I love my husband, I love my children, but I can't stay in this life anymore. I need to get out. I need to get my children out.'

Anara's chest tightened. She felt comfortable supporting women with herbal remedies to rid them of unwanted pregnancies, of unwanted men. She had long since reconciled those choices. But to agree to kill a child once they were outside the womb felt a step too far.

Her lips opened, ready to object.

'The only way I can think,' Yeva continued huskily, sobbing, 'is to kill my husband. That way we can leave.'

'Is he preventing you leaving?' Anara's voice was tentative, the grip on her chest yet to abate. Caution gnawing at her bones. The removal of the children from the request doing little to abate her concern.

'No… not him.' She sniffed, grabbing another tissue to replace the sodden one in her hand. 'It's just… it's just the way our life is. We can't get out, not while he's working there. And… the only way we get out is if he's dead. And I don't want him to die, I really don't… I love Maksim, but I don't know any other way.' Yeva closed her eyes, inwardly cursing her lack of discretion; she had not meant to give his name.

Any name.

Silent, Anara's mind digested the options. The possibilities. This felt too much. Too difficult to rationalise or justify.

'Please,' Yeva whispered, 'it's for my children.'

'My remedies aren't for this.' Anara spoke carefully, gently, her eyes on the woman who continued to crumble before her.

She wanted to obtain more information, was eager to know why there was such pressure on this family, why they could not leave the life they had. Maksim. Sofiya. Those names she could, maybe, use to dig a little deeper.

She could use the surveillance images and search.

'Please.' Her voice fractured. 'He's dead, one way or another, he'll end up dead and I'll be a widow. I'd rather it be on my terms.'

Anara's jaw tightened as she drew on the resolve in her core. 'I have strict rules about how I do my business—'

'I understand that, but Sofiya… but, I need help.' Yeva's hands went to her hair, dragging through the shoulder-length strands before her head tipped forward. Her body dropping to the floor, heavily on her knees. She crawled over to Anara, her fingers laced and stained face up.

'Does your husband hurt you?'

One hand uncoiled, moving to grip her cross, the chain pulled tight around her neck. She shook her head, deep lines creasing her brow. For all the brutality of life in the Bratva, Maksim was a loving husband, and a doting father to their children. She could not lie.

Even for this.

'Then, I'm sorry,' Anara said with compassion, 'truly.'

Yeva's heart shattered, her body folding in on herself as she sunk to the hardwood floor. Hope had gone, as lost as she felt. All she knew, for certain, was that Maksim would be taken from them, but now she had no control over when.

# Eleven

The decision to kill Kassian Garner had not required much thought. Any complex emotion which should have made the choice difficult had been slow to arrive and quick to dispatch. While the other man who appeared on the security feed remained someone who would need to be dealt with, Anara knew Kassian was the more concerning.

Concerning enough to put aside her curiosity about the woman who visited earlier that day. That was a situation she intended to return to, at some point, to determine if there was more she could do.

More she could offer.

Curled on her small sofa, above Erinyes, she mentally considered the options for Kassian. Something quick or something slow. Something she could administer at a distance or something which would require her to meet and be more intimate.

She shuddered.

Stretching, Anara unfolded her limbs, stood. Crossing to the kitchen, toward the rear of the apartment, she poured a generous glass of wine from the open bottle of Cadão.

Collected her laptop from the table.

Anara was careful. Life had taught her to be cautious, had taught her that being reckless brought consequences which hurt. It was why her devices had sophisticated encryption and she was deliberate about what she searched for and when, about what could generate suspicion.

Reviewing her own store's security recordings was one thing.

Sourcing a person's information was another.

She had obtained the name of the man who had loitered outside Erinyes; her laptop had scoured multiple online avenues while Anara worked. Further research on Logan Pottinger could wait.

Kassian could not.

She could create a profile for him, she could determine his routines and connections. Devise a strategy, plan a way to remove him from her life, before he did something neither of them would survive. If he struck first, if he tried again, she vowed to take him down with her.

She doubted Vadim would be her saviour a second time.

Back on the sofa and tucking her legs below her, she balanced the device above crossed limbs. Navigating swiftly to her secure account, the screen shifted to display what she needed.

Anara hesitated. Tempted to type *Vadim Morozov*. To discover more about the enigmatic bar owner who had swept in to rescue her from such unwanted attention, only to then dismiss her himself. Frustration pulsed in her blood. She should not want to have him.

Either of them.

She had gone out for a drink, to relax and enjoy an evening beyond these walls. There had been no other expectation; the swapping of her rings was not a signal. It had not been intended to portray availability nor commitment. It had not been a plea, nor a hope.

Yet, the ease with which Vadim had both made a connection then broken it consumed her. In her dreams, he devoured her. In her store, Anara caught herself desiring his appearance. In the quiet moments at home, she found herself imagining his presence. He had set her body on fire, then stepped away to let her burn.

He infuriated her.

She infuriated herself.

Vadim was the sweet possibility of something stolen before it could become more, a prayer fading in daylight. He was something she had not considered and had not sought. Yet, her mind was alive with every potential future, with every way he could manipulate her pulse.

Anara should not be grieving a man she had never met before that night, and should not mourn a relationship which did not exist. Yet, her body felt the tension of loss. Felt the ache of betrayal.

The sorrow of rejection.

*Am I not good enough?* Anara thought.

Draining half the glass, she let the rich red wine coat her tongue. Let it snake down her throat. The warmth crept through her veins, bringing a boldness to her thoughts and a tightness to her jaw.

'Fuck you, Vadim,' she muttered, typing his name with fury.

*Perhaps Kassian could wait*, she considered.

Her heart thrummed loud as images and text began to populate the screen. Her amber eyes widening as fury was replaced by wrath.

'*Fuck. You.*' Anara's tone was venomous, her grip on the wine glass threatening to snap the stem.

She had forgotten how to blink, grit and heat gathering in her gaze as her breath shuddered.

Line after line, picture after picture.

Vadim Morozov, his new *wife* Anara Eden.

Their businesses, their lives.

Their secret romance which resulted in a secret wedding; their love eating away hesitation. A fierce love consuming all doubt until they could do nothing but scream of their union. Dedicated to each other, navigating this new development. Nurturing their commitment.

Black began to encroach her vision the longer she stared.

The photos looked real. Whoever had created these articles, crafted the candid images, had done exceptional work. She had to admit that, it was incredibly polished. If it was not for the fact she had never been in any of them, Anara would have believed every single pixel.

Inhaling deeply, she forced her eyes to close. To locate a crumb of calm amongst the gripping tension. Confusion duelled with rage. Vadim had dismissed her, told her he was not an appropriate companion, let her walk away. And now, this?

*Was this a game?*

Anara's mind was drowning in theories, each one craving further exploration, further understanding. She brought her glass to her lips and swallowed what remained of the wine. With determined precision she leaned forward and placed the empty glass on the low table.

Which is when her phone vibrated.

An unknown number.

Anara's eyes narrowed, ignoring the device, turning to the larger screen, where the message was replicated.

The apartment was locked. The curtains were closed. The laptop camera was off. Her home should be her sanctuary; she had fought hard for it to be. The notification eroded her sense of peace. If she opened the text, then her carefully constructed security would shatter.

If she acknowledged it, then they would know.

Anara was confident the message came from Vadim; it had to be. It felt far beyond Kassian's skill, Kassian's knowledge, from what she had gleaned in the short time he attempted to charm her.

Anara

That was all it said.

No more.

No less.

The word made her heart hot, made her blood ice. It snaked through her veins with an expectant threat; death whispered in the text's simple characters. Destruction in the glowing icon.

The timing felt too coincidental for it to be anyone but Vadim.

But how had he known she searched for him? How had he known she had discovered his tricks? How he had used her? These questions eluded Anara's understanding. As did her comprehension of the purpose behind Vadim's continuation of this ruse.

He had categorically stated he was not a suitable person for her to associate with. He had been clear. Now, now Anara's mind was a fog of disorder and bitterness.

Her fingers hovered on the keys, tempted to reply. To call. To ensure he was aware of her frustration. Anara had been manipulated before and she refused to allow herself to be played this way again. For him to make such an assumption, and use her without warning, screamed of Vadim's arrogance. His lack of decency or respect for her. For women.

Vadim was correct.

He was absolutely *not* someone she wished to associate with.

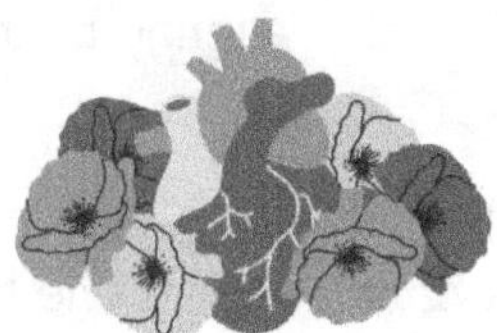

Below the wrought iron streetlight, Kassian assessed the dark windows of Erinyes. The shop front a ghost of merchandise disguised by shutters and promises of their return the following day. The floor above shrouded with drawn curtains which betrayed occasional shadows.

Though he doubted Anara would peel back the fabric, he hoped. He had given up trying to be inconspicuous far earlier, instead his eyes were trained on the midnight glass. Searching for any small glimpse. Any hint of her frame. Any slight possibility she would leave her apartment for the night. Any sign of the husband she proclaimed to have.

So far, he had been disappointed; the briefest movement confirming she was inside but nothing further. He had shifted his surveillance to the rear of the shop once the shutters fell, allowing him to be sure no other person had entered the apartment either.

Kassian debated knocking on the door. If Anara would not come out, then he would make an opportunity for himself. It would be far easier to convince her to allow him in than it would to trail her to another, unknown location. And, he reasoned, if Anara tried to close the door he had other means of persuasion. Or brute force.

Turning his wrist, he checked the time on the large dial. 'Thirty more minutes sweet thing,' he muttered, 'then I'm coming for you.'

A strike of stone resounded along the pavement.

Kassian grimaced before pivoting to face his direct supervisor.

'You're not supposed to be here,' Logan stated. His hands slid into the pockets of his thick coat; nights remained cold. A small cloud of white vapour fell from his lips as he spoke.

His hazel eyes met Logan's brown, confidence in his stance. With a grin, Kassian shrugged. 'Just checking things out.'

'Those weren't your orders.'

'No, boss,' he said, his smile faltering a little, 'but I thought you'd like the initiative.'

'Nothing to do with the other night then?' Logan dug his lighter and pack of cigarettes from his coat, cupping one hand to hide the spark. His inhale deep. Letting the smoke sit on his tongue, he looked over one of the soldiers he used. Kassian had promise, and was disciplined enough to forge a decent career in Septer.

He just needed a bit more guidance; sometimes his temper flared too quickly and his mind seemed more intent on women than the job.

Logan knew he could direct this energy, push Kassian into actions of benefit to him. To them both. 'I get she's stunning, but you also said she was married—'

'Like that's an issue.'

'Could be.' Logan's exhale misted the air between them.

'I'm being careful.'

'By standing outside her apartment in the dark?' Logan's eyebrows rose, the pale skin of his brow creasing. Like others in Septer, he wore his brown hair in an undercut Norse style; braided over the crown of his scalp. And like other members, when out on operations, he wore black tactical gear; boots, combat trousers, quilted jacket.

It was comfortable, warm, and hid weapons effectively.

'Only checking on our possible investment.' Kassian's grin returned, his eyes glinting in the ivory pool overhead.

'Mace hasn't decided to pursue this yet—'

'But it's likely.' Kassian paused, gaze darting to the store then back to his boss. 'It's only Aeron who's hesitating.'

'True.' Logan nodded, taking another drag of nicotine. Pleased his soldier had noticed who had become the one to delay progress where this venture was concerned.

'I don't get why we're waiting,' Kassian remarked, gauging his words would be well received. 'This is the ideal set up.'

Logan slowly licked his lips, ran his thumb along the lower, taking a breath. 'You're right. If we can convince her to grow what we need, the store's also the perfect cover to sell, too.'

Tension slipped from Kassian's shoulders; relief unknotting unseen anxiety. The thought he had made a mistake, that arriving here to watch Anara could be misjudged. Misinterpreted. His motives undermined by his desire. 'That's what I'm working on, boss.'

'Good.' Logan's focus shifted to the store. To the secured doors and blink of the alarm. The security camera which they believed did not quite reach their position on the street.

He had been about to shower when the notification sounded. Sufficient to halt the removal of his soaked clothes, insufficient to stop rinsing most of the blood from his hands. His knuckles thick with crimson, the black of his tattoos disguised by varying shades of burgundy. Under his nails, the evidence of his ruthless interrogation lingered.

Quick to check his phone, Vadim smiled.

Bit back laughter.

He watched her scroll through the images, the articles, meticulously created by himself and Nikolai. Guessed how incredulous she would be with each one she found. Seeing how she utilised encrypted methods to access online information intrigued him.

Made him wonder if there was more to Anara Eden.

Vadim's fingertips drummed the side of his device, resisting the urge to acknowledge her discovery, trying to understand why she needed to take such precautions. His umber eyes closed for a prolonged moment, a silent plea for restraint.

A vow to wait.

Which crumbled the instant his gaze returned to the suite of security images he could also access, thanks to Nikolai's assistance. Seeing two of Mace's men on the street outside her apartment brought a gritting of his teeth, a violent tightening of his jaw.

He typed her name; intending to explain once she responded to his opening message. Depending how she reacted.

If she replied.

'Fuck,' he hissed, 'what is this woman doing to me?'

Bracing his palms on the countertop, his gaze roved his reflection; a slow tracking of his narrow waist, broad chest. The black fabric glistened under the bathroom lights, the blood steadily drying. His usually styled hair was matted with it.

*I should stop*, he thought.

Vadim had meant what he said in Prey, even as it broke the remains of his heart. A heart adept at death. The man he saw before him should reinforce the choice to step away.

But something kept pulling him back to her.

A: So now I can be associated with you?

He shook his head at her message, his smile broadening. She had remembered their conversation; the more he struggled against this, the harder the hook embedded in his flesh.

V: We are married.

Vadim replied before beginning to unbutton his black shirt. Dragging it from the waistband of his trousers. Peeling it from his limbs to reveal his sculpted torso, his tattooed muscular arms. A further larger blackwork piece covered his back and part of his chest.

No reply. He grimaced slightly, eyes flitting back to the surveillance feed to check on Mace's men. They were still standing near the lamp, a cigarette glowing in the night air.

Sliding the belt from the loops, he assessed it before deciding it was past saving; the leather slashed by the knife hurled in his direction, and blood staining the grain. He tossed it to the tiled floor before pushing his remaining clothes to the growing pile to be burned.

His shower flicked on.

Vadim was beginning to wonder if he should have added cameras to the inside of Erinyes, and Anara's apartment. The delay needling his skin and gnawing his pulse. Tempted to pick up his phone again.

A: Our wedding night was uneventful; I can't even remember it.

Her words sent blood to his cock. Sent a cascade of images to his mind which consumed every breath, every beat of his heart. The idea of the things they could have done permeating. He groaned.

V: Perhaps I should remind you.

The text sent instinctively, a flare of sensation rushing over his skin. Shrouding him.

A: In your dreams.

V: The real thing is always better, kroshka.

His fingers curled around his cock, a steady rhythm stroking from root to tip, as he crossed to the expansive shower. Resolved to make her wait for any reply. The speed with which he responded making him feel weak.

Chasing after a girl he desired.

But, Anara was so much more.

She was a woman he wanted to devour. To worship and feast on every night. Every day. To claim her. To prove to her how delicious their union could be.

He was confident she would come to realise this.

Until then, Vadim would continue with the façade of their marriage, despite how he had dismissed her originally. The regret of that one word echoed in his mind. The weight of it dragging his soul, creating an ire he found hard to accommodate.

The fury had driven his attack that evening. His blade put to work as his firearm languished. Vadim had struck over and over, until the man's body was beyond recognisable, until Artem had to pull him away.

But he still felt angry.

He felt conflicted.

With each tight slide of his palm over his cock, with each image that ate into his synapses, Vadim felt his conflict duel with his lust.

Anara was too pure, too kind, for his world, it was cruel to continue this association. Yet, he could not end the ruse, could not prevent how his skin heated with the thought of her, how his blood ran warm, how his breath caught.

And seeing how she compartmentalised her life, how she kept so many barriers to who she was, and how she teased in her texts, this only intrigued him more. There was something about this woman he did not understand, and he wanted to.

She was a challenge, a dichotomy, a temptress.

He wanted to dig into her and discover her bones.

Her tissue.

Her cells.

Every single part.

He wanted to dismantle her, to slice through every defence she had constructed, to ruin every attempt to keep him out. He wanted to swallow every part of her.

To wrench open his flesh and let her nestle within.

Wanted to run the tip of his tongue over every inch of her skin, to dip inside her, to chase his mouth with his hands. To taste her nipples, her quim, her lips. To wind her hair around her throat and capture her breath as she screamed for him to fuck her. To be surrounded by her. A sheath to his cock, a home for his soul.

Not just a physical consumption, but a spiritual one.

Where she would reciprocate his worship with her own; his body a meal for her to crave. For her fingers to trace his flesh, for her hands to stroke and twist, for her mouth to suck him dry. Her tongue to lick and teeth to bite. For her to drink the blood he offered as wine.

For her to take his heart and devour it.

As water meandered over his skin, as crimson was diluted from his flesh and bled into the shower's river, Vadim's mind was lost. Lost to all he planned to do, lost to all he envisaged her to be. Imagination creating a banquet of her body. Snowy skin marked by his blade, blushing under his gaze, bruised by his teeth.

Each vibrant image increasing the pressure, each expression of his desire barely relieved by his own touch; pursuing his climax to growled sighs and yearning breath. Vadim needed more. He needed her.

Every single part.

# Twelve

Pausing outside of the temporary fence, Anara looked to her colleagues and their families. The excited anticipation which rolled off the six people should have encouraged her own, yet she felt empty of it. Her heart only harboured frustration. Long after she should have succumbed to slumber she had found only fantasies, nightmares.

Vadim had succeeded in keeping her awake.

Her hands delivering on what she imagined he would do.

But her body had remained tense.

Her mind wired.

The diagnostics she ran on both her own and the store's systems revealed nothing of note, which also concerned her. Enhanced the level of vigilance she usually displayed to a higher state.

'You'll feel better if you relax,' Kerezen stated, leaning into her boss while her arm stayed hooked through her wife Willow's. Together for over twenty-five years, the two women also practiced witchcraft in unison. It was rare they were apart, aside from work.

'She's right. You've been on edge all day,' Bryony added, narrowing her eyes when she caught the glint of Anara's rings.

Noticing her colleague's focus, she quickly folded her arms, tucking her hands into the thick fabric of her padded coat.

'You're wearing them.' Bryony's voice had become softer, her tone conspiratorial. 'I thought you'd decided not to.'

Anara chewed on her lower lip, uncertain. She doubted they would have found the information online about her fictitious status; if either of them had seen the articles, they would have challenged her by now. She also did not trust herself to talk about it. How could she explain the text exchange with Vadim, the way his words had made her feel, the debt she felt obliged to pay.

If wearing a ring for a while was required, then so be it.

'Has something changed?' Kerezen asked, observing the hushed discussion; her own disquiet creating lines across her brow.

They shuffled forward as the queue grew closer to the entrance, the brightly lit ticket booth steadily allowing people inside. Their focus shifted to ensure they maintained a respectful distance from those ahead of them. Neither woman registering the man approaching.

'If you were my wife, I'd not let you out of my sight,' Kassian said, his arm draping around Anara's shoulders.

She ducked, twisting to face him.

Bryony instantly checked on her husband, their young twins; Omer understood her expression and gripped Juniper and Rue more tightly. By their side, Kerezen laced her fingers into Willow's. The strained incident in Erinyes remained very vibrant in their minds.

'Which is why I'd never be your wife,' Anara retorted. She removed her right hand, purposefully drifting it over her hair.

'Still on the wrong hand, sweetheart.'

'And you're still wasting your time.'

'There's a really easy way to fix that,' Kassian said, taking a stride with the septet closer to the gates.

Anara did not answer. Her attention caught by a blur of movement from within the carnival ground; black clad men who forged an easy path through the crowd. One veering off before the gates, leaving two to pass the ticket booth and onto the street.

She gritted her teeth, closed her eyes.

And willed her body to cool.

'This time you're late, kroshka,' Vadim said with a wry smile.

'I'm not—'

'I've been waiting by the carousel, as we agreed.' His chest ached, a claw which sliced into his heart. The desire to eat the distance between them, to ferociously kiss her full lips, to bite into her tongue, roared in his blood. Instead, he offered his hand, palm up. His umber eyes willing her to take it.

'That was before you fucked up,' Anara hissed.

'I fucked up?'

'You know what you did.' She kept her eyes on his, despite the blaze it sparked; her body a mass of ravenous energy.

'Let me make amends,' he said, sincere. His extended hand had yet to drop, yet to even tremble, as it waited for Anara to slide her skin over his. 'Come.'

She swallowed; attention broken only momentarily by the slightest of movements by the man behind Vadim. Anara used the break to breathe, to inhale deeply, find calm. Her senses overwhelmed with the aromas of popcorn, doughnuts, and candy floss. Of the sound of the carnival.

'Kroshka,' Vadim coaxed.

Slow, her eyes fell to his hand. Right hand. And that was when she noticed he also wore a ring. Her breath caught and ripped something open in her chest. A surge of questions, of confusion, fuelling the steady placement of her hand in his.

The instant their fingers touched, Anara felt her core weep. Felt her body growl for more. *Fuck this man*, she thought.

Even as she allowed him to twist their connection so his hand was dominant, to pull her closer to his side. To move her away from Kassian and hide the subtle command he made to have one of his men deal with Septer's solider. Another black-clad man appearing from the gathered people waiting to enter the ground.

'If you harass my wife again,' Vadim said with crisp precision, 'there will be consequences.'

Shrewd, Kassian's eyes moved over the pair. There was something about the man that suggested he should be wary. He had barely studied him when they were in Prey, his focus Anara, but now he wondered if he had underestimated his opponent.

Behind the couple, Kerezen and Bryony exchanged glances; the word *wife* causing their heads to turn. Their mouths to gape.

'It's not harassment,' Kassian objected, stepping forward a little, 'just an opportunity she'll benefit—'

'Are you with this party?' Pyotr asked, his stocky build covered by a borrowed jacket; hiding his black tactical gear with a coat from one of the carnival employees.

'No, he's not,' Bryony stated, leaning into her husband.

'Then you'll need to move to the back of the line.' Pyotr raised his arm, pointing along the pavement. His brown eyes never left Kassian as he waited for the man to move.

'I'll come chat with you later, sweet thing,' he called out, tripping, his feet misjudging the kerb. Kassian managed to find his balance, cursed, and strode away, digging his phone from his pocket.

With a nod to Vadim, Pyotr melted back into the queue, sliding the jacket from his shoulders.

'Let's enjoy the carnival, kroshka,' Vadim said, resisting the urge to bring her hand to his lips. Instead, he tightened his grip while balling his free hand into a fist by his thigh.

'My friends—'

'Them too.' He began to walk, Makari following discreetly to one side as they neared the ticket booth.

'The line is—'

'For other people.' Vadim smiled.

'I'm guessing that man always gets what he wants,' Bryony said in muted tones, her lips near Kerezen's ear.

'Looking like that, even I'd entertain him,' she whispered in reply, her wife's elbow nudging her ribs. 'What? He looks like a god.'

Being only just ahead of the women, Vadim's lips quirked higher on hearing the poorly hidden words. His gaze flitted briefly to Makari, finding a similar bemused expression on his guard's face.

'I'm worried about Anara,' Bryony admitted, covering her mouth and speaking more quietly still. 'What's he got on her to force her into this? I hope it's nothing to do with the store.'

Kerezen shook her head, but the thought chilled her. A rapid series of bumps chasing the ice which dragged over her skin.

'Ilya,' Vadim said, at the gate, 'please look after my wife's colleagues and their families. I don't want them to have to pay for a thing; anything they want, they get.'

'There's no need—'

'Bryony, it's my pleasure.' Vadim smiled. Turned back to the solider who would be their guide. 'Anything they want, they get.'

'Sure.' Ilya's hazel eyes quickly worked their way over the group, his youthful smile warm. 'If you'd like to follow me.'

Anara took one step, only to be pulled back. She whipped her head to Vadim, frowning. 'What?'

'You're with me.'

Pausing just past the gates, Kerezen rested her hand on Bryony, a concerned gaze ghosting her eyes. 'You're not coming with us?'

'My wife tells me I've got some making up to do,' Vadim answered with an indulgent smile. It would be a torturous delight to spend more time with her, but he intended to discover more about Anara, especially after the night before.

Just thinking of their interaction hardened his cock.

Being so close to her, being able to feel her flesh against his, being able to inhale her intoxicating scent, only increased the desire which ate through his veins.

'I'll be fine, you go enjoy yourselves,' Anara said calmly.

Even though her body was anything but. Every nerve was urgently crying for her to run. Every sense was telling her to scream. To attack. To unleash the fury which heated her blood. Which sang through every cell but died on her tongue.

'Have you been to the carnival before, kroshka?' Vadim protectively guided her through the initial stalls.

'Every year.' She kept her eyes ahead, sweeping over the raucous children and laughing adults who were oblivious to the strange energy he exuded. Noting the presence of the man with Vadim, remaining one short pace behind them, added to her unease. As did quick glimpses of other similarly dressed men loitering through the grounds.

'Tell me about your favourite attraction.'

Anara exhaled, halting and allowing their arms to stretch before he turned back. The speed with which she was steered between two tents, to the soft canvas of a vendor, widened her eyes. Shadows fell over his face, but did little to hide the jet of his gaze, the set of his jaw.

'Don't fight me,' he said with soft menace, standing close, 'you won't win.' His breath fell over her skin. Vadim regretted the intimacy of their location; all he could see was her framed against the fabric, illuminated by a kaleidoscope of colours. She was radiant. Her lips full and parting as she looked up to him.

'I don't even know what I'm fighting against; you need to explain the rules.' Anara's arms burned from the grip he had on them; his hold was not tight but it promised restriction. It promised strength and control. The padding of her jacket did little to dull the electricity which webbed through her skin.

She could hardly breathe.

'I'm not sure we're there yet, kroshka.'

Her brow furrowed.

'Unless you want to be.' Vadim's head dipped forward slightly, desire unwittingly bringing his lips closer to hers.

'Bite me,' she retorted.

'Don't tempt me,' he said, caging laughter while drawing back, 'don't make promises you can't keep.'

His intense presence was becoming oppressive; she fought to break the suffocating connection. She slid her eyes toward the light of the main fairground. The man who had followed them now faced away, watching the excited crowd. 'Who is that?'

Vadim stepped back, reclaiming her hand and leading her out from between the booths. 'Meet Makari Komarov, my guard.'

'Guard?' Anara's frown reappeared.

He looked to Vadim before nodding.

'And do you talk?' Her eyes tracked him from his combat boots, over black clothes, the brown eyes and buzz cut.

Makari grinned. 'Yes, Anara Morozova, I talk.'

Her heart skipped.

'Осторожно, следите за тем, что говорите[20],' Vadim warned.

Makari's pale skin flushed. 'Да, пахан[21].'

Watching the exchange, their unknown words bringing heat, she took the momentary shift in focus to try and process what had occurred since they met in Prey, since they arrived at the carnival.

Since he had manipulated her into pretending to be his wife.

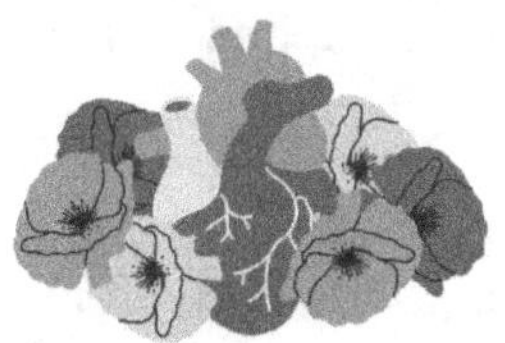

Moving under the cone of amber light from the overhead lamp, shrugging the backpack from his shoulder, Kassian strode with purpose toward the rear door of Erinyes. He knew his plan was reckless. Knew it would bring consequences which would be difficult to navigate.

But he was humiliated.

Angry.

---

[20] Осторожно, следите за тем, что говорите - Russian for 'Careful, watch what you say'
[21] Да, пахан - Russian for 'yes, pakhan'

He dug into the pocket of his trousers, dragging out his set of pick keys and spinning them in his hand. His hazel eyes narrowing, selecting which of the two doors he would target. The store's reinforced with metal bars, a gate proud of the architrave. The other more simple. Black paint gleaming, obscure glass, and chrome fixtures.

It did not take long for him to work the lock free, his hand pausing on the lever to check for any noise. He knew there was an alarm, and yet he heard no siren, no warning, no indication he had to rush.

*Perhaps she only set it when she was home*, he thought.

Reasoning the store and the apartment had two separate systems, Kassian stepped inside and closed the door. Silence remained. From the hallway, he ascended in darkness toward her apartment.

The space revealed itself steadily. His greedy touch tracing over her furniture, her walls. Kassian dropped his backpack by the sofa to allow more freedom of movement, to allow him to explore. Light from the fridge illuminating his braided hair, the undercut. The glint in his eyes. He took a bottle of soda from the shelf and snapped it open.

Sharp and sweet, it dripped over his tongue.

Ignoring her bathroom, he crossed to the bedroom. The bed's dark wooden frame draped in flowers and lights; still extinguished. A stack of books cluttered the bedside table, beside a lamp, a carafe of water. Even in the gloom, he could make out the richness of the fabrics. Soft below his fingers.

He sat down heavily onto the bed, draining the bottle before tossing it to the hardwood floor. Reclining, Kassian closed his eyes. Breathing in Anara's lingering fragrance, he groaned.

It was glorious.

Forcing himself up, he moved to the wardrobe, her drawers, hunting for her clothes. Her lingerie. Anything he could take as a memento, as a token he could keep. Any evidence she was married. So far, all he had found proved his suspicions.

She was lying.

He was lying.

Grasping lace, he brought the fabric to his face. Eyes closing once more as he imagined Anara dressed for him. Imagined removing every barrier to discover her snowy flesh beneath for him to mark. He shoved the lingerie into his pocket before collecting more and retreating to the bed's thick blankets.

Removing his jacket, unbuckling his belt. Kassian lay back against the pillows and pulled his erect cock free. The sweep of his hand languid at first, twisting silk over his flesh as his head tipped back. An increased pace soon developing with the closure of his eyes and ideas playing in the hollows of his mind.

Her body bound to the bed by the lights she found so pretty.

Her mouth taking his cock, her body at his mercy, her skin a map of his palms, his strikes bringing a blush he could bite. Her hair wound tight around her neck as he fucked her to his own satisfaction.

That fake wedding band ripped from her finger.

He would show her how a real man could treat her; teach her how to obey his instructions and meekly submit. Anara would be on her knees when he returned home, would be ready whenever and however he wanted her to be.

Kassian would claim every part of her.

Whether she wished it or not.

The thought of how she would learn to offer herself to him, bowing before him as he drove repeatedly into her, brought a husky cry from his throat and slick pulses from his cock.

Soaking into her silk which wrapped him.

'Fuck,' he breathed, his head tilting into the pillow. Neck arching and chest heaving. He cleaned himself up, tossing the fabric aside, before standing and reclaiming his jacket.

Strolling back to the living space to collect his backpack.

The pleasurable part of the evening was done.

Now, now came her pain.

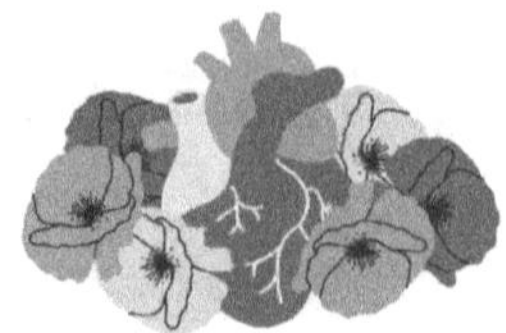

Strolling through the crowd, Anara continued to marvel at how easily they navigated the space. People moved. Without word, without any apparent action, without any gesture. She had never felt so much power, despite the continued sense of oppression. Choice stolen.

Her status changed without ceremony.

Without any courtship, any consent.

Anara may have been preparing to consider dating again, when she ventured into Prey and swapped the rings to her right hand, but she had not decided. Nor had Vadim done anything but assume. And, considering Makari's casual use of a surname she had not agreed to, it was common knowledge amongst his staff.

She slid her eyes to him, finding him looking at her. Instantly, her body flushed with lust. Arousal pulsing in her core, her blood. Her heart beating loud in her ears, drowning out the surrounding noise.

'You never told me what your favourite carnival attraction is,' Vadim remarked, fighting the distortion of the stalls, the definition fading until all he saw was her.

'I don't particularly have one.' Her voice was huskier than it normally sounded, and Anara inwardly cursed the timbre. The last thing this man needed was to know he was affecting her; she had resolved to resist and to discover why he had continued with this game.

'Then we'll try them all until we find one.' He tightened his grip of her hand, bringing it almost to his lips only to pause.

She tensed. Her gaze widening as she digested the entwined digits, the spark of her rings, the shine of his. The black ink on the back of his hand contrasting with the pale emptiness of hers. Her lips parted and her breath seemed to choke her throat.

Vadim lowered their hands, breaking the moment.

'Why are you doing this?' she asked faintly.

'You're my wife, Anara,' he replied with a smile, 'it's important I know what you like.'

'I don't mean the fair, I mean… this.' She used her free hand to point from her to him, to how they remained connected.

'Let's enjoy the evening.' He steered them toward the wide booth for the shooting gallery. A series of coloured lights beat a vivid sequence above the red and white striped canvas marquee. 'We can discuss our relationship later.'

Her eyebrows rose and she stopped walking.

'Later, kroshka.' He pulled her to him, catching her as she stumbled and drawing her to his chest. This close, the scent of her hair consumed him and he almost dropped his chin to kiss her crown.

This close, Anara could feel that her attraction to Vadim was not unrequited. She was grateful he could not see her face, certain it burned with desire, with intrigue. If she was not so conflicted, so annoyed with his behaviour and presumptions about her, she would have ground her hips against his hard cock and made him as frustrated as she felt.

Reluctant, he released her.

Stepped back and turned to the game, discreetly adjusting himself as he resumed their journey. The chained weapons loaded by the girl behind the cloth-covered table without question, without requesting any payment. Vadim's nod of gratitude earning a shy smile.

'Here,' he stated, passing the weapon over.

'You trust me with a gun?' She took it, her hand strangely cold after being held for so long. 'After what you've done?'

His eyes reflected the overhead lighting, the revolving colour. 'That depends on how good a shot you are.'

Anara laughed lightly, before steadying herself. Raising the barrel, her eyes tracked the staggering targets moving across the mechanical track near the rear of the booth. Varying sized metal discs painted with chipped numbers on springs and hinges.

Her first shot clipped the edge of one, but did not tip it over.

'I think I'm safe,' he quipped.

Anara's head twisted to him, jaw tight. Spine straight. 'Don't be so certain; women have relied on other methods for far longer than such weapons have existed.'

His head slowly shook, a smile genuinely creasing his eyes; if he was attracted to her before, her words only deepened the sensations which flared through his blood. Vadim drunk in the determined fire in her gaze and wondered if there was truth behind her statement. If there was some threat behind her tone. 'Other methods?'

She remained quiet, watching the ghost of concern dance with the suggestion of hunger in his stare. In how the pale skin of his face, his neck, grew a little darker. *Interesting*, she thought.

Vadim readied the rifle in his hand, dragging his focus to the targets continually cycling across the canvas backdrop. Confident, he squeezed the trigger and heard the satisfying chime of the metal disc succumbing to contact. And another. And again as he emptied the weapon.

*Why does that excite me?* Anara's mind fought against the carnal heat pooling at the apex of her thighs. Perhaps it was the precision of his execution, the clinical way he assessed and dispatched. The way he so nonchalantly fired and forgot. It was aspirational. It was how Anara sought to conduct her own business.

Her own treatment of those who hurt women.

Inhaling, Anara gripped the rifle's stock more tightly and suppressed the tremor in her hands. She blinked. Attention on the blurring discs. Her ears muffled with distorted melodies and the thrum of her pulse.

Every shot missed.

'Yeah, I think I'm safe,' Vadim remarked, jovial.

'From a firearm, maybe,' she muttered. She set the rifle down on the table, the chain spooling beside it. Embarrassment glazing her eyes.

'You get any of the top row.'

Vadim turned to the girl, his brow momentarily knitted.

'You won.' She shrugged.

'I'll let my wife choose.' He wrapped his arm around Anara.

'I get to choose?'

'Of course.' Vadim bit his tongue, knowing the question carried other meaning. Resolute to avoid dealing with the answer.

Anara surveyed the options, her lips forming a wide smile when she saw the white plush, dotted with silver, to create a shimmering, frost-like polar bear. She nodded to the girl who pointed to the toy, confirming her decision. Offered her thanks when it was granted.

'Why the polar bear?' Vadim asked as they walked away.

'Your surname—'

'Our surname,' he interjected, weaving their hands together.

'Your surname,' she repeated.

'So you did some research?' Vadim smirked. He knew she had, had been alerted to her attempts to find him. Knew she had returned to the images he had altered. But it was pleasing to hear her admit it.

She elbowed him, only to hit solid muscle.

'There you are,' Kerezen said, seeing the pair of them grow closer to the carousel. Noting how relaxed her boss appeared, despite the initial hesitation to leave them. 'You okay?'

'Yeah.' Anara's reply was honest, instant.

Leaning on the painted railings, Willow watched Bryony, her family, ride the horses; music and lights accompanying their circular journey. An occasional wave made to them as they passed. To one side, Ilya stood in an alert state of attention.

'We'll be heading home soon,' Kerezen explained, resting her hand on Willow's back, 'but we can stay longer, if you need—'

'No, no,' Anara said gently, 'please; I'm sorry I got... ambushed. But, I'll see you at work tomorrow.'

'Don't let that handsome *husband* of yours keep you out too late.' A slight rise of her eyebrows emphasised the title, their eyes conveying an unspoken understanding.

A collusion in the game.

Even if neither woman comprehended the rules.

'I'll get her home safely,' Vadim asserted, placing his right hand on his chest. In the carousel's illumination, his titanium band shone. 'Would you like to ride the horses, or take a spin on the wheel, kroshka?'

She considered the options, and which would offer more opportunity to talk. If her colleagues, her friends, were going to leave, that gave her greater flexibility. While they remained, she felt responsible. Even if they were not with her, even if they were being escorted by Ilya; another of his guards, she assumed.

Which only added to the questions she had.

'The wheel.'

He bowed slightly. 'Kerezen, Willow, please pass on my farewells to Bryony and her family. Ilya will make sure you're taken care of until you decide to leave.'

'Мне позвонить тебе, если Септер появится[22]?' Ilya asked, eyes moving from Makari to Vadim, voice low.

Vadim nodded once, trusting that was sufficient.

Though Kassian had been dealt with earlier, the Bratva presence at the carnival made it unlikely any of Mace's crime group would appear. It would be suicide for them to venture onto Vadim's territory, especially on a night where Vadim had his soldiers and apprentices selling to revellers intent on pursing excess.

This city fair, held in the week when Lent began, was an event they regularly attended. It was an opportunity to celebrate, to draw out those who sought to enhance the feelings of celebration. To consume drugs which increased the euphoria found in winning card tricks, or games of chance, feats of skill. To take chemicals which exacerbated the fleeting connections made amongst groups moving to the beat, experiencing the attractions.

---

[22] Мне позвонить тебе, если Септер появится? - Russian for 'Do I call you if Septer turn up?'

It was the ideal time to increase revenue.

A time of sanctioned indulgence which overlapped, slightly, the initial days of penance. The beginning of those forty-eight days which some of Vadim's team observed, to one degree or another.

Such restraint acknowledged by Vadim but not always followed; his primal longing, his hunger for the raw violence of life, often overtaking the obligations of faith. Renouncing his intrinsic nature too challenging a transformation when temptation and ruthless power remained.

They walked in silence, arriving at the head of the line for the wheel without any need for debate. The operator simply allowed them through as soon as the next cabin rolled to the ground.

Vadim gesturing for Anara to enter first, his eyes meeting Makari's.

The guard nodded before sauntering to the railings to wait.

'What do you get out of this?' Anara asked as she sat on the worn wooden bench. The surrounding distractions, the music, the lights, all dampened by the barrier of the secured door.

'Out of what?'

'This. This… fake marriage.' She held up her hand, the three rings highlighting her point.

He did not answer, could not answer.

Vadim was still uncertain why he was continuing this façade. The argument Artem had made returned to his mind; keeping Anara as a wife may make it easier to use Erinyes for growing or moving product. But, that felt sour. Almost as sour as the thought he did not deserve her. That his rejection of her was the correct reaction, that he should have stuck to what he said in Prey.

'Vadim, what—'

'Vadya,' he interjected, 'you should call me Vadya.'

She frowned, confusion etching into her skin.

'Vadim is too formal, for my wife to use.' A wry smile formed.

'But I'm not your wife.'

'Yet.'

She exhaled heavily, holding the polar bear more tightly to her chest in attempts to find calm. 'You make a lot of assumptions… you assume I'll play along, you assume I'm happy with how you've publicly claimed me, you assume I'm unaware of how you've manipulated me—'

'I'm only protecting you,' he argued, 'from someone you don't want to be associated with.'

'You said the same about yourself,' she retorted.

'Kroshka, while you're attached to me, publicly, you're safe.' Vadim hoped the pledge was true. He hoped he had not put a target on her by creating the images of her online, by being seen with her.

'I can look after myself.' Anara had learned to; she had adapted, she had carved out the skills she needed. But she was tired.

Vadim lifted his hand, relieved she did not flinch away as he stroked it over the silken curls of her hair. Did not pull back when he cupped her face. 'I don't doubt that, kroshka, but I know Kassian. He will destroy you so he can prove capable of being your hero.'

Her throat was dry, her quim soaked. Her skin flames. Trying to find any moisture, she licked her lips, the tip of her tongue slow to move over soft flesh. Each drifting exhale he made sent a cascade of sparks, made her vision blur, made her heart hungry. The frustrations with his actions had melted into the frustrated arousal which pulsed in her core.

It would be so easy to lean into him.

To feel his lips on hers.

Her darkly lined eyes dropped from his gaze to his mouth.

So easy.

She swallowed, chest heaving.

Halted by the vibration of her phone.

# Thirteen

She was furious. Devastated. Though she was grateful Vadim offered to drive her home, arriving to the wild inferno and cracking glass almost brought Anara to her knees. His arms forming a secure chain around her torso when she tried to run toward the carnage. Her heart breaking with every fresh plume of smoke, every splintered jar and aromatic scent.

She refused to allow him to see her cry.

Refused to allow him to see her weak.

Instead she wanted to free herself from his embrace and stride over to the officers who appeared to be in charge. The journey to Erinyes had been conducted with speed, but Vadim had done nothing but scour his phone and bark instructions in, she presumed, Russian. She had been too intent on maintaining a stoic expression to really listen or take note of his actions.

His words.

The moment Makari cut the engine, she and Vadim had exited the car. And that was when her world crumbled. Everything she had worked for was burning. Ash floating, mocking her as it fell. And while Anara wished to be separated from the pressure of his body behind hers, she knew if Vadim released her, she would fall.

Her struggles futile.

'Kroshka, let me handle this,' he said, a loud whisper, a vow, made directly against her ear. A plea dripping with venom. With vengeance and a craving for excess; it screamed for liberation.

The security feed he checked as Makari drove sufficient to warrant Kassian Garner's death. A break in. A prolonged stay. The exit before the first flames began to lick across the glass. If it was not for needing to be here for Anara, Kassian would already be in Vadim's cells. Would already be bleeding.

Begging for his life.

'I can deal with this myself.' Her voice was raw.

'You don't have to.' Vadim spun her around, bringing her to his chest and stroking one hand repeatedly along her spine.

'This isn't real, Vadim—'

He sighed. Shifting to hold her upper arms, he leant back and found her dark eyes; red from the smoke, hollow from denied tears. 'You are so unbelievably stubborn. Kroshka, you're my wife—'

'I—'

'You. Are. My. Wife.' His eyes were wide, black blown. His veins ate the vision of her flesh, consumed the way she was framed by the amber heat as the midnight sky drowned in vapour. If this was not her store, her home, if Vadim had been the one to set the blaze, he would have fucked her there and then.

Either to punish her for being so unwilling to allow him to help.

Or reward her for such determination.

Vadim was unsure.

The only thing he was certain of was that the façade was done. The game over. The ruse crumbled. He would win her, would prove he could be worthy of someone as pure as Anara Eden.

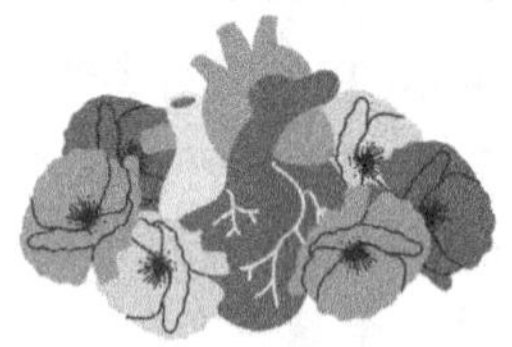

Arriving at the scene, Maksim Zaitsev glanced first to the passenger seat, then the rearview mirror. Maksim, recruited into the Bratva while in prison, had the evidence of his past tattooed on his flesh. In the flickering light from the fire, the emergency vehicles, the black ink was testimony to his life.

Despite the years he had spent serving the fraternity, his position as a solider remained one he was both proud of and content with. Loyal to Vadim, to the crime group, Maksim had reacted swiftly to the request he collect brigadiers Nikolai Kiselyov and Pavel Solovyov.

The trio walking to great Vadim and Makari on the edge of the tape barricade. The purpose of their presence a question, but the urgency in Vadim's command had kept it unvoiced.

'This was Kassian, and by extension Septer,' Vadim stated bitterly after their greetings. Conversing in hushed, clipped, Russian. 'Whether Mace knew about this attack or not, I'm no longer prepared to allow him to act so fucking recklessly with what's mine.'

'Pakhan, I thought we hadn't got the store yet?' Pavel frowned, his brown eyes moving over the men to the continued efforts to dampen the flames. Ash was making their hair gritty, greasy, as it settled. The smoke thick and fuelled by the resins and herbs within.

Strange fragrant colours in the fire's tongues.

'We hadn't secured it, no.' Vadim's jaw was tight.

'Then, why—?'

'His wife,' Nikolai interjected.

'That's real?' Maksim asked, then grimaced with embarrassment.

'As far as they know, it's real,' Nikolai explained. He had seen how passionately Vadim threw himself into the work they completed to create the online confirmation of the relationship. He had seen how Vadim was certain it would protect Anara. And, by extension, Artem believed it would allow them more time to claim Erinyes.

'So, they've attacked her, and the store,' Pavel said, working through the sequence of events. The potential consequences.

‘They’ve signed their deaths.’ Vadim’s fists were by his thighs, nails cutting into his palms. ‘Every fucking one of them; I want them hunted, I want them served to Mace one by one.’

‘Wouldn’t it make more sense to just walk away,’ Pavel argued. ‘We didn’t get the store, but they won’t either—’

‘I will not be seen as weak,’ Vadim hissed, stepping closer to Pavel and holding eye contact. Fury rolled off him. ‘I will not allow that fucker to take what’s mine.’

‘Yes, pakhan.’ Pavel swallowed. He cleared his throat, dispelling the chill which climbed his spine.

‘She’s coming over,’ Makari warned.

Vadim pivoted to face her, seeing the anguish she masked. The way her stoicism formed with each step closer. The briefest of frowns when Anara registered the additional men standing with him. He could see the calculations she was making; trying to place who they were. What their connection to him was.

‘They’ve said it’s likely arson,’ she said, her throat sore from being so close to the smoke. From the increase in volume required to be heard over the raging heat and spitting glass. ‘Everything’s gone.’

‘Kroshka, I’m sorry.’ He meant it. Vadim felt responsible.

It had been him to approach her in Prey. Him to warn Kassian off. It had been him who continued this ruse and forced Kassian to react. Mace may yet be unaware of the actions Kassian had taken; though they had fought over territory for years, this was the first time a personal strike had been made on a location neither had a business established in.

She shook her head, gripping her phone more tightly. ‘I’m going to call Kerezen, see if I can crash on their—’

‘You’ll come home with me.’

Anara’s breath caught, her lungs emptying.

Vadim steered her away from the others, his palm on the dip of her lower back. Even with ash clinging to her curls she was beautiful. Raw and vulnerable, and still reluctant to accept help.

She infuriated him.

'I can't stay with you, I don't even know you,' she argued.

'You can and you will.' Vadim tipped her chin up, maintaining contact with her eyes. The desire to capture her lips clawing at his heart. 'Let me take care of you, kroshka.'

'And what do you expect from me in return?' Anara wanted to agree to the offer, wanted to let him take over so she could collapse. So she could scream, cry, grieve. But old habits were difficult to escape and they whispered in her blood. 'If you think this means I owe you sex—'

'No!' He frowned deeply, shoulders rounding slightly at the thought she would believe he could be so malicious. 'I would never…, you'd have your own rooms.'

'Oh, okay.' She tried to pull her gaze away, but somehow feeling the intensity of his eyes kept her upright. Kept her from succumbing to the loss which cracked behind her. 'I don't know how I can repay you—'

'You don't.' Vadim's hand slid lower, cupping her neck, his fingertips on the nape. 'You're my wife, what's mine is yours.'

She laughed at the ridiculous words, which transformed into tears. A shuddering change even as she tried to retain her smile. Anara did not prevent him folding her into his chest, her tears salting the ash which coated his jacket.

'It's okay,' he soothed. 'Let me take you home. I'll make sure you've clothes… whatever you need… kroshka, I've got you.'

She believed him. His kindness only brought fresh sobs; the robust defences she had carved devoured with each stroke of his hand.

'Do you need to contact Kerezen, or Bryony?' Vadim gestured for Makari to come over; his guard responding immediately.

Anara shook her head, then nodded. Her forehead etched with deep lines as the amount of things to deal with grew. Hearing the approaching footsteps, she tried to compose herself. Tried to extricate herself from his arms, wipe the tears from her face; neither successful.

'Get the housekeeper to find Anara some things for tonight.'

'She's staying—?'

Vadim's eyes met his guard's in warning. 'Ensure she has a suite made available, and she's added to the security system; I want Anara to feel at home.'

Makari nodded, the ball of his boot grating as he spun in return to the other men. Phone already pulled from his pocket and dialling. His leader's precise instruction ready to be followed, with a little extra detail added. Reading between the lines Vadim set.

The security system had many layers.

Anara did not need to be given access to all of them.

'I don't want to cause any problems,' she muttered, pushing on his chest and finding only unyielding muscle.

'You're not.' He permitted her to move back, his thumb stroking over her cheeks to remove the tears, which had slowed but continued to drift down streaked flesh. 'Anything you need, you ask for. I'll do all I can to provide what you require—'

'You can't, this is… it's too much.'

'It's not.' His hands settled on her neck, the pads of his thumbs tilting her chin up so he could look her in her swollen eyes. 'I have the time and the resources to help, and as far as the world knows you're my wife. It's normal for me to be here and to help.'

'But—'

'Stop fighting me, kroshka.' He smiled. 'You won't win.'

Anara was finally coming to understand he may be correct.

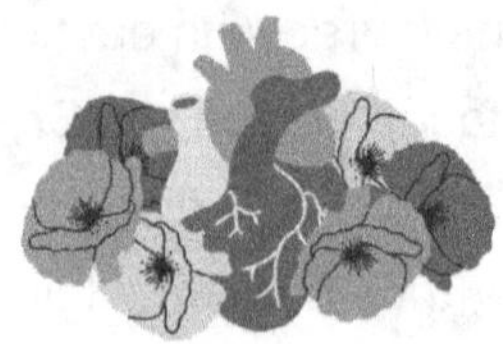

She was numb. Her eyes unseeing, even as the lights began to thin and greater space appeared between the houses they passed. In the rear of his expensive car, she tried to relax. Tried to rationalise the decision she had made to join him.

Her phone continued to vibrate.

A series of messages, of missed calls, which she resolved to handle in the morning. It was too late. She was too tired.

Part of her believed if she slept, when she woke it would no longer be real. That the business Anara had poured every single asset, every single moment into would still be as she had left it earlier that evening. That her home would still be there. That she would be able to curl into the secure haven she had crafted from the ruins of her past, and still be ready to assist other women in need.

Her breath misted the window when she exhaled.

'We'll rebuild,' Vadim stated softly. Tempted to rest his hand on her shaking knee. The walk to the car had broken whatever connection they had found in the firelight. Now he felt unsure.

Not of his decision to fight for her.

But of if she was open to it.

Their time at the carnival felt like a beginning; the start of something sweet, something delicious, something he could savour. Something he could almost taste. Now, a barrier had descended between them.

Weary, Anara twisted to face him. Offered a slight smile.

'Anything you need, kroshka,' he pledged.

Cautious, she placed her hand on his.

The spark branching despite her sorrow, his uncertainty. Vadim was relieved to witness the blush snake up her neck. A signal she may still be the woman who almost kissed him, may still be willing to see where this could lead.

He filed the thought away; tonight was not the night for that.

The car slowed, allowing time for the metal gates to slide open.

Anara's attention drawn to the towering trees flanking the entrance, a small stone building steadily revealed. Watched a black-clad man step out from the circular structure; his nod offered to Vadim as they drove past. Makari's leisurely speed taking them along the tree-lined driveway, passing immaculate gardens subtly lit with evenly spaced lanterns.

Her sore eyes widening as the paving split to accommodate more established trees, neatly clipped shrubs. The home beyond the sweeping arch of grey paving causing her head to shake in disbelief.

'Who are you?' she remarked.

His eyes creased with mirth. 'Your husband.'

Anara exhaled, resisting the urge to roll her eyes.

Keeping the engine idling, Makari waited before the imposing double doors to the house. The car faced the garage, an outbuilding that easily stored the multiple vehicles Vadim had access to, below the apartments where the guards lived independently. It also hid the tunnel's entrance which led, underground and large enough for a van, to the cellars.

'Welcome home.' Vadim had sufficient time to stride around to the passenger side, to open the car's door.

She was frozen. Stunned. Still sitting, contemplating the structure; a blend of stone and glass which had her greedily tracing each pristine line and curve. His words barely registering in her stupor. In the emotional toll of the evening, the aftermath finally settling in her bones.

'Anara,' he coaxed, hand outstretched, waiting for her.

Taking a deep breath, she met his gaze and accepted the support to leave the warmth of the cabin. Though spring was steadily staking her claim, winter remained reluctant to depart; there was almost a month left until the seasons turned. It made the nights cold. And any lingering heat from the fire, from the carnival, from travel, was quick to dissipate.

She shivered, pulling her coat tighter.

The realisation she was standing on the driveway of someone she barely knew, wearing all she owned, almost dropped Anara to the hard ground. Her body emptying of all fight.

All hope.

Her eyes closed. A lone tear wrestling from her long, dark lashes to scratch through the soot, the ash. She tasted it; salt leaking between her lips, soaking into her tongue. Anara felt his arms surround her as though she was no longer present in the moment.

No longer cognisant of what she needed to do.

'I'll happily carry you inside,' Vadim whispered, his eyes tracing the double doors. 'You'd look beautiful in red.'

She blinked, straightened her spine, mind spiralling through what his words could mean. 'I'm okay.'

And she felt those words in her soul. Somehow, despite how fragile, how vulnerable, the situation was, Anara felt safe. From the moment he had appeared at Prey to rescue her from Kassian, Vadim had given her space to decide. He had made an offer, but he had never forced her into this deception.

She was the one who participated, she was the one who agreed to play his wife, she was the one who allowed this to continue.

Altered online photographs aside, Anara had willingly matched him step for step. She had done her own research, had contemplated her own resolution to the circumstances.

But through it all, she did feel safe.

It would take time to rebuild her business, but it could be done.

The click of the opening door brought an increasing wash of light over them, forcing her to turn her head. Her body tensing when she saw a familiar woman in the entryway. Jaw clenching. The recognition in her gaze quickly hidden. Not quick enough; his torso close and sensing the sudden flinch in her limbs.

'What's wrong, kroshka?'

Anara shook her head, beginning to walk toward the door, relieved he had released her. She kept her eyes ahead, kept her head up, and hoped she was not finding errors when there were none.

This woman was in Vadim's house. This woman had visited Erinyes with an unwanted pregnancy. Sofiya had got the help she needed, and Anara was happy to see her looking so well.

But, if this woman was in Vadim's house, then Anara's sense of safety was built on dust.

On the ash of her business.

'Kroshka?' Vadim's strides easily caught up.

'Nothing, I just… it's a strange night.'

He could hear the hesitant catch in her voice, heard the wariness which had begun to creep into Anara's posture, her face. Something was wrong, but he could not place what.

'The front suite's ready,' Sofiya confirmed, pushing the door closed behind the pair; hiding the tremble which had begun to spiral from her chest the instant she saw Anara.

Fear she was about to be discovered screamed.

'Thank you, Sofiya.' Vadim slid his hand into Anara's, relieved she did not shake it off. 'Anara, this is one of my housekeepers.'

Heat crept over her back. 'Oh, okay.'

'Ilya's still at the carnival,' he explained to Sofiya, 'but I imagine he'll be back soon to collect you.'

She nodded, not trusting herself to speak.

'I've got it from here.' He smiled, eyes moving between the women and trying to determine what had triggered the glacial atmosphere.

'He's your partner?' Anara asked tentatively. 'Ilya?'

'Yeah.' Sofiya's smile was weak. She swallowed, mouth dry. 'Do you want me to take your coat?'

Anara began to reach for the zip, her attention finally moving to track the spacious hallway, the open concept living area. The wide stairs and double-height entry. Closed doors and pathways. It was exquisite.

And entirely opposed to the vibrant and cluttered home she had created for herself.

Which was now destroyed.

'They'll need thoroughly laundered,' Vadim stated. 'The smoke's got into everything. Do you want a drink? Food?'

'No, I… I'm okay.'

'Then I'll take you up to your suite; if you leave your clothes outside the door, I'll get them sorted while you shower.' He began to lead her to the staircase. 'Sofiya, did you buy her some clothes?'

'Yes, some pyjamas,' Sofiya said, 'and something for tomorrow, like Makari asked. If anything's not right—'

'I'm sure they'll be perfect.' Anara met her blue eyes, saw the peony blush on Sofiya's skin, petite frame clad in black. 'Thank you.'

'Come.' He coaxed her to keep moving, to follow him up. Watching as she drank in the white walls, the modern artwork, the large windows framed with thick fabrics, closed blinds. 'I'll give you the tour tomorrow, after you've got some rest.'

'I bet you say that to all the girls,' she retorted, without as much bite as she would normally use; he was correct, she was tired. She needed to let the day catch up with her and sleep.

Or at least try to.

'No other girls, kroshka.' He resisted bringing their entwined hands to his lips, even as each step brought them closer to the room he really wanted her in. Each step confirming how natural it felt for him to be with her in this space. 'Only you.'

She chewed on her lip, shaking her head.

'Anara, I mean it.' Vadim stopped them on the landing, shifting so he could grip her upper arms. 'There's no-one else. And I had to ask Sofiya to buy you clothes because I don't have anything for you, I don't have any reason to keep anything here for women—'

'You don't need to explain.'

'I do.' His brow creased, his eyes on hers. 'I didn't presume to buy you lots of things you may not want, so I only requested enough for one night, for one day. Tomorrow, tomorrow we can buy more.'

'That's not necessary, Vadim… Vadya.' She could not help but mirror his smile when he reacted to her use of the less formal name. 'I can buy my own things.'

'You've just lost everything, kroshka,' he reminded her gently, 'let me help you.' His thumb brushed over the greasy fabric of her coat, his eyes imploring her to acquiesce to his wishes.

Slow, she nodded; resolved to object after she had slept.

# Fourteen

Tipping his chair forward, Mace Kersey scanned the split-screen before him; his desk cluttered with remnants of a heavy night. A drained bottle of whiskey, a light coating of powder over several surfaces, and smeared with evidence of sex. The woman he had used now languishing, naked, in one of the cages in the basement.

He watched her, still sleeping curled on the thin mattress.

*She'll fetch a decent price*, he thought, releasing the pause so the images could cycle through the other storerooms. The other women. The men he intended to sell. The trusted members of his team counting their takings, bagging their product.

The brief knock on the door, followed by the immediate entry of one of his soldiers, brought his eyes from the monitor. Weary tension gripping his limbs. His jaw. 'What the fuck were you thinking?' he shouted.

Kassian shrugged, sauntering to one of the chairs. Comfortable, he rested one ankle on the opposite knee and met the furious brown eyes of Septer's leader.

'I should get Logan to teach you a fucking lesson—'

'It'll all work out, boss,' Kassian said smoothly, his lips quirking into a smile. 'You'll see. This is the push she needs.'

'She's married to—'

'Nah, she ain't married.'

Swift, Mace drew his firearm from the desk, pointing it directly at the man's head. 'Interrupt me again, and you'll never speak again.'

A chill crept over his back as he nodded. Contrite. He knew how to play the game, when it was required. But Kassian also knew setting the apothecary alight had been the right call at the time. It would be the only way to get Anara to comply.

'What makes you think she's not married?' Mace asked, lowering the weapon. Picking up his phone, typing in some details.

'That apartment is hers, no trace of any husband. It's a sham.'

Mace grimaced, shaking his head. He turned the phone around and showed Kassian the images which flooded the screen; scrolling through it as proof. 'She's married to Vadim fucking Morozov.'

His throat dried. That was unexpected. Inwardly cursing himself for not recognising the leader of the local Bratva, Kassian felt hollow. A cool blade sliding through his stomach. A rush of pins over his skin.

'Burning Erinyes to the ground… a place I wanted us to take, was a monumental fuck up,' Mace continued, slamming his phone down. 'You fucking cunt, you've escalated the fucking war.'

'She ain't married, I assure you.' Kassian's vision had tunnelled, the black dots on the periphery thickening as he tried to spin his role in this development. 'That place was hers, only hers.'

'Maybe she stayed there sometimes—'

'Or perhaps….' Kassian stopped himself, wincing at the knowledge he had interrupted. His gaze fell to Mace's hand, beside the gun, which had not moved.

'Perhaps what?' *One last chance.*

'Perhaps this is Vadim fucking with us,' Kassian said. 'Maybe he's trying to stake a claim on Erinyes through her, and put out those images to fool us and keep us from taking it.'

Mace leaned back, rubbing his jaw with his palm, digging his fingers into the bristle of his beard. Contemplating the soldier's words.

'Now he ain't got a chance to take it,' Kassian continued. 'I've sorted it; he can't use that place for his product and he can't get her.'

He waved his hand, dismissing the last part of Kassian's statement as the fanciful dreams of youth; Anara was never going to entertain his solider, Mace knew that. But he also acknowledged that Kassian had a point. 'So, you're suggesting we use this to our advantage?'

'Yeah, boss.' He dropped his foot to the floor, leaning both elbows on his thighs as he bent closer to the desk. 'Now we can build with Anara from scratch and get it how we want it.'

'Convince her to stock our product and grow what we need,' Mace added, picking up the idea.

'Yeah.' He nodded, relief slowly warming the lingering anxiety.

'What made you act?'

The anxiety reclaimed any heat, glacial branches clawing through each cell. 'I... I saw her at the carnival so knew she wouldn't be at the store... felt right to do it when she was out.'

Mace nodded. 'What did Logan say about it?'

'I didn't... I didn't tell him.' Kassian's brow creased. His hands laced together, knuckles tight.

'Initiative... I like that.' Mace grinned. 'Thinking one step ahead.'

Surreptitious, Kassian exhaled. Tension slipping from his shoulders and eyes lifting to meet his leader's welcoming gaze.

'Perhaps you've served your time in this current position.' He licked his lips, drummed his fingers on the desk. 'I'll let you know.'

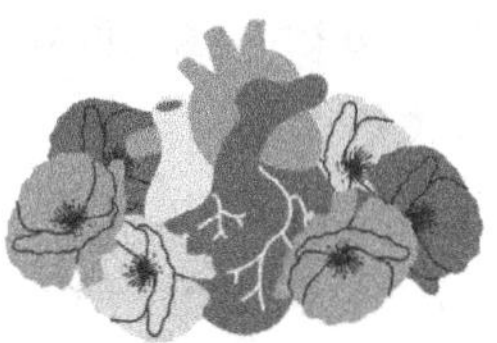

For one more blissful moment, Anara forgot what had happened. Where she lay. The incredibly comfortable bed a cocoon which could convince her everything was alright.

That she had not lost all she owned.

All she had built.

That her evening shower had not drowned the sobs which forced her to her knees on the tiles. Body curled in on herself, until she felt even emptier.

Vadim had been correct.

The shower had helped, it had removed the ashy grit from her hair and washed the aroma of the fire away. Even if the memory lingered. It had fought against the weariness of her body when she slipped into the pyjamas and under the thick duvet.

Waking, she found the room ambiently lit by weak morning sunlight filtering through the closed curtains. It felt late. Her phone screen dark and unresponsive. Falling back into the soft fabrics, she found the polar bear sitting on the neighbouring pillow. Anara was confident it had not been there when she left the en-suite to climb into bed.

Which meant someone entered the room as she slept.

Her body tensed, her eyes searching her surroundings with greater scrutiny, fiercer attention. The white walls held a few pieces of art, the pieces of furniture were black, the chairs leather. An iron bed frame was clothed in luxurious white sheets. The dark wooden floor led to closed doors; the bathroom, the dressing room, the landing.

And all her remaining possessions were on the bedside table.

A phone, her keys, her purse.

Refusing to cry any more, knowing she had to address the damage inflicted the night before, Anara forced herself to stand. To make herself presentable; staring into the bathroom mirror as she brushed her teeth and feeling gratitude heat her eyes.

Finding a robe hanging in the bathroom, she drew it on and knotted it before cautiously opening the bedroom door. There were soft sounds of life below her, leading her to peer over the landing's balustrade into the hallway but seeing no-one. Anara exhaled, eyes moving to the wall of glass which faced the driveway, the trees. Even in late winter, it looked impressive; branches and buds piercing the sky.

*There are worse places to have to stay*, she thought, beginning to descend, her knuckles almost bone with the grip on the handrail.

The staircase wound down at the rear of the house, with another large window providing further glimpses of the estate. A wide paved area flanked the property, with a stone path leading to what appeared to be a summer house, and more pristinely planted gardens and old trees.

Reaching the ground floor, Anara discovered most of the wall to be a folding door; spotless glass panels with blinds between the panes. She paused, her eyes caught on movement from outside.

Though the summer house was almost entirely made of glass and timber, and the pool within shimmered, she had not noticed anyone had been inside it when she glanced over the view. Now, however, she could not drag her eyes away.

Strolling toward her, was a barefoot and barely dressed Vadimir Morozov, skin glistening with water. His swim shorts tight; low on his hips and high on his thighs. Every tattoo and muscle was readily visible; his torso smooth, and lean. Statuesque. Stubble graced his jaw, his raven hair slicked back from his swim.

Anara's mouth opened as heat flooded her veins, hunger mewled in her core, arousal warming her flesh. Thighs involuntarily sliding together to find some pressure. Her tongue rolling over her lower lip before she caught it with her teeth; biting into the flesh.

The need to rake her fingers over his iliac furrows, to draw blood, an incessant pulse within her. Some innate urge to claim him.

'Fuck,' she breathed. Her left hand found her right, twisting the rings around her finger. She swallowed, trying to steady her erratic heart, the keening plea in her body to submit.

# Fifteen

Tucked in the corner of the coffee shop, the women spoke softly, each complimentary voice layering with other conversation, with the chime of cutlery on plates, slices of spoons through beverages. Orders taken and fulfilled, with payments made.

Kerezen insisted on picking up the bill for their lunch.

In unfamiliar clothes, Anara surveyed the patrons laughing, enjoying a relaxed break in their day, with caution. After finally charging her phone that morning, she had found a staggering amount of messages and missed calls. Returning one from the detective assigned to her case had confirmed the original summation. Arson. The thought someone wished to destroy her business, and possibly her, ate into her bones.

She caught the eye of Pyotr Melnik and offered a weary smile; her eyes closing. *Perhaps Vadim was right to have sent someone to watch over me, considering the circumstances*, she thought.

'Who's that?' Bryony asked, twisting to find where Anara's focus had moved to. 'Haven't we seen him before?'

Kerezen assessed the black-clad man. 'The carnival. He was one of the staff, I think, got Kassian to leave.'

'Oh yeah.' Bryony nodded, turning back to Anara. 'But why's he here and staring at us?'

Anara exhaled. 'He's… with me.'

Both women raised their eyebrows, leaning closer.

'Vadya requested I have someone… guard me.' Anara's pale skin flushed with heat. 'I tried to explain it was unnecessary, but—'

'You have a bodyguard?' Bryony rested her head on one palm, her manicured nails tapping on her cheek. 'And, Vadya?'

'Vadim.'

'Ah, the *husband*,' Kerezen said with light mirth.

She shook her head, chewing on her lip. 'It's just… I don't know how things have got so… messy.' Anara frowned, sighing. 'It's hard enough trying to convince Vadya not to buy me everything I've lost; relenting to Pyotr being here seemed the best compromise I could make.'

'Excuse me?' Kerezen put down her mug, the sip she was about to take forgotten. 'Buy you *everything* you've lost?'

The heat snaked higher, burning deeper, as Anara dodged the eyes of her colleagues. She knew she would have to explain more details at some point, but she had hoped to avoid it today. Had hoped to deal with other matters and return to her strange relationship later; if relationship was what she could call it. The words to explain how Vadim's offer felt overwhelmingly *right* difficult to convey.

'Anara, where'd you stay last night?' Bryony asked gently, her gaze flitting between the two women.

Her tongue traced the seam of her full lips, the truth strangled in her throat. Eyes falling to the aromatic herbal tea and sandwich in the hoop of her arms.

'You're staying with him.' It was not a question, nor an accusation. A statement requiring confirmation, words Kerezen offered in her quest for clarity, for peace. Hope that, if correct, perhaps Vadim could provide her boss, her friend, with the support she usually denied.

'You and Willow don't have room,' Anara argued, 'and Bryony, you, Omer, and the kids, don't need me crashing on your couch either. I've nowhere else to go, nothing—'

'And what does he get,' Bryony interjected, 'in return for this act of benevolent generosity?'

Fierce, Anara's eyes lifted from the table to meet her gaze. 'He gets my agreement to wear this ring and be his plus one at any of the events he has to attend.'

'That's where it starts,' Bryony said. 'Then, he'll expect more.'

'And if that happens, I'll be at your door, and we'll be making one of our signature blends,' she retorted.

The words easily delivered but without substance. The more Anara saw of Vadim, the less he fit the parameters they set for removal. He had been nothing but kind, nothing but generous, and had kept every single vow he had made… so far.

Yes, Vadim was an adept and dangerous flirt, who seemed to know more about Anara than she cared to admit. And yes, he had manipulated her into this situation. But he had also rescued her without hesitation and without expectation of any reward; his appearance at Prey, his arrival at the carnival, removing Kassian for her.

All done without any pressure.

He held her hand, offered an embrace, but had done nothing more, despite their proximity. Their moments of solitude. Even as she slept, she had felt safe.

The polar bear being on her bed when she woke had been easily explained, and she trusted his answer. Sofiya ensuring she had the items from her coat, and bringing the toy at the same time. Something the housekeeper had volunteered with an apology for intruding when she was providing breakfast.

Even if Sofiya's presence was a hurdle.

And something which required further discreet investigation.

'That may be a little tricky,' Kerezen ventured; hesitant to dampen the moment, but they were each acutely aware of their loss.

Anara shook her head. 'I had an email from Origins,' she said, 'and it was… that's kinda why I wanted to get you all here. The owner of Origins has offered to cover all our costs until we rebuild; so salaries, materials, or whatever we need.'

Bryony's eyes instantly misted, her hands reaching to grip Kerezen and Anara across the table. 'Fuck, really?'

'I'm not going to pretend I'm not relieved by that,' Kerezen said, 'it'd be so difficult without my wage coming in.'

Anara smiled. 'I'd planned to pay you anyway; I'd some savings and the insurance—'

'You would absolutely not use your savings on us!' Kerezen looked to Bryony, seeing the agreeing nod.

'Vadya's also insisting on helping me, too.' Anara's admittance was barely audible, but she knew she had to be honest. These women were family, they had been there through those initial years crafting Erinyes into what the store had become.

'I bet he is.' Bryony laughed.

'Maybe you need to be open to this,' Kerezen added, a gentleness to her tone and warmth in her hazel eyes. 'Even if he's gone about things in an unconventional way.'

'Maybe.' Anara's eyes dodged the intensity of her colleagues, her hands curling around the mug. Allowing the heat to deflect from swiftly returning arousal; the memory of the morning flooding her.

How the sight of his sculpted body had almost broken her resolve.

A desire flaring.

She had unknotted her robe by the time he arrived at the door, one hand stroking her neck imagining it was his lips. It had only been the blast of February air which snapped her from the fantasy.

His prompt disappearance a relief.

'What's his place like?' Bryony asked.

'Immaculate, and huge.'

'That's a great combination.' She smirked, winking.

'Even I'd admit that.' Kerezen chuckled. 'But, seriously, Anara, are you safe there?'

'I feel very safe,' Anara confided. 'Which is strange.' She inhaled for a beat, settling her racing heart. 'I've always felt safe with him, and he's been nothing but a gentleman; my room is my own. The only thing... the housekeeper—'

'The housekeeper?' Bryony shook her head. 'First it's a bodyguard, then he's wealthy enough to replace *everything* you've lost, and now a housekeeper. Who is this guy?'

'I'm still figuring that out, believe me.' Anara took a sip of tea. 'The thing is, though, we know the housekeeper.'

'We know them?' Kerezen's eyes darted to Bryony, finding her friend already turning with matched concern.

'She came to Erinyes.' Anara paused. 'For help.'

Though the words had been barely audible, barely above a whisper, they roared through the women with shared understanding.

'You don't think...,' Kerezen's voice faded, not wanting to suggest it was Vadim who had caused the woman to require their services.

'He says not.' Anara sighed, gathered her thoughts. 'I've not asked him, obviously, but he noticed I kinda tensed when I saw her, because she was there when I arrived last night.'

'Then how did he know to deny it?'

'He doesn't,' Anara continued, meeting Bryony's gaze. 'He asked me if I was jealous this morning, when he saw me watching her.'

'And are you?'

'No.' The heat crept rapidly back up her spine, undermining the force of her reply. 'He told me he's very strict on boundaries with staff. She's also... you remember the guy who looked after you, at the carnival?'

The women nodded.

'That's her partner.' Anara would not usually share so much about the clients who came to her, but she knew this was an unusual situation which would require careful navigation. She did not want her friends to be compromised, should they visit; presuming she could have visitors at Vadim's house.

That had yet to be discussed.

But the last thing Anara wanted was to put Sofiya at risk.

Or her friends.

'I mean, it sounds reasonable,' Kerezen said.

'As long as you're being cautious.' Bryony curled both hands around her mug, glancing between the two women.

'I am, Bry.' Anara smiled, nodded. 'Thank you.'

'Have you reached out to—'

'No.' Anara's weary eyes seemed to grow darker, her expression a mask of composed determination. She knew what Kerezen was about to suggest, and it would never happen. 'They've not bothered to contact me in years, and I'd rather keep it that way; they know where I am, I'm done chasing. I can resolve this myself.'

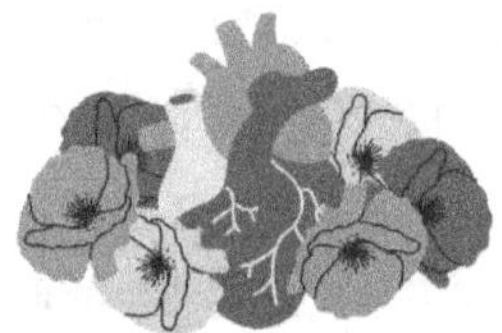

It had been bittersweet watching Anara leave. Returning from the pool to find her by the stairs, her skin flushed and pupils blown out, had heated his blood. Had made it imperative to stride past her and to his suite; his body too readily responding to her presence. Desire screamed at him to pause.

To kiss her, claim her, fuck her.

Love her.

A natural Anara, in her pyjamas and robe, was as arousing as when he first saw her dressed meticulously for a night out. Her beauty was luminous, a pure delight. Raven curls and pale skin, full lips and amber eyes, curves he longed to trail with his tongue.

It had taken every shred of his discipline to calm his cock, to throw on some clothes, and return downstairs ready to talk. To argue. Ensuring she was safe, and would be okay.

Which had taken time and persuasion; skills Vadim excelled in.

With Pyotr driving her to the coffee shop and instructions to bring her straight back afterward. By which time, some of the items he had ordered for her would also have arrived.

Vadim was meticulously analysing the footage of Erinyes when he received notification of Artem's car entering the estate. Standing, closing the laptop, he strode from his desk to one of the cupboards; inside a well stocked bar lit up. He poured out vodka and drained the glass. He had a feeling he would need it.

Pulling the study door closed, he moved to the hallway to wait.

'Have you gone mad?' Artem stated, skipping straight over greetings as he marched into the house. 'You bring her here?'

'She'll be safe—'

'Safe!? Vadya, she's living above our cells—'

'Which she'll never know about.' Vadim clenched his jaw. Gestured for his advisor to follow him into the library. 'She's involved in this, like it or not. She owned Erinyes, and she's linked to me.'

'Another of your crazy ideas.' Artem shook his head. 'I told Kolya to talk you out of creating that online connection.'

'And I told him to ignore you.' He held his advisor's stare. Vadim was getting close to digging the knife from his boot, to reinforcing his decision with blood.

Head tilting, Artem's eyes narrowed as he leaned back.

'Kassian destroyed Erinyes,' Vadim stated, 'which means it's Septer and this is all linked. Anara being here doesn't change that.'

'Vadya—'

'It doesn't fucking change anything.'

'It already has.' Artem ran his hand over his peppered hair. 'You've sent one of our soldiers with her, taking him away from the schedule. If we're going to remove Septer, we need all our people working.'

'What makes you think we'll fail?' He shifted in the armchair, placing one ankle on the opposite knee. The boot more accessible. Vadim knew Artem was astute enough to notice the action.

What it meant.

'I don't.' He paused. Sighed heavily. 'But you're distracted. You need to stay focused on our organisation, our objectives.'

'And here I was thinking you believed I needed to get laid, and was spending too much time alone.' He raised one eyebrow.

'Yeah, and looking at you, you still need to do that.' Artem laughed, the tension breaking in the room even as it clung to Vadim's frame. The tight shoulders and jaw evident to the advisor. 'Have you finally found a woman immune to your charms?'

Vadim exhaled, shaking his head. 'She deserves better,' he softly muttered. For all his longing to take Anara to his bed, to make that ring on her finger real, he also knew he could not entangle her in his world.

It was too dark.

Too violent.

Too brutal.

The things he had seen, the things he must do, had done, were not for her to experience. Vadim preferred to protect her from them no matter the cost to his heart.

'Remember that when all this comes crashing down.' Artem leaned forward, keeping his eyes on his leader. 'You brought her into this, and you marked her as yours the moment you said you were her husband. I get why you did it, she's fucking gorgeous—'

'Tyoma,' Vadim warned.

'—and it was a decent ruse to protect our claim on Erinyes. But the store's gone, Vadya, so cut her loose.'

'No.' Vadim shook his head. 'I've promised to help her rebuild—'

'Fuck!' Artem's laugh betrayed his bewilderment.

'Even if I kicked her out, even if I didn't help her with the apothecary, she's still linked to me,' he argued. 'So I may as well pursue this and see what happens. And, maybe, rebuilding gives us leverage.' Vadim knew those words were meaningless even as they left his mouth.

Any plans for Erinyes discarded the moment he met Anara.

He would not allow her to be used in such a way.

Contemplating possibilities, Artem slowly nodded, seeing how they could use the involvement to their advantage. 'It would seriously piss off Mace, that's for sure.'

'Yeah.' A beat. 'But it doesn't halt my intention to destroy Kassian; I want him in my cells and I want his heart.'

'That's more like it.' Artem smiled broadly, rubbing his hand over his jaw; the tattooed skin, inked in prison, from his fingers to his wrist faded and blurred with time.

'I want to know if Mace knew,' Vadim continued, 'or if Kassian was acting alone when he destroyed my wife's home.'

'Careful.' Artem's smile shrank. 'You're believing your own lies.'

Vadim's hand shifted, resting lower on his calf. The suggestion of his blade being drawn readily conveyed.

'It's not just Septer we need to watch, Vadya,' Artem said, changing the focus of the discussion. 'I had a report of Yeva visiting Erinyes.'

'Shopping?' Vadim shrugged.

'She left with nothing, and they said she'd been taken into the back of the store.'

'Did Pasha send her?' He ran through options, considering why the woman would visit, and why she would not remain in the main body of the apothecary. 'He's been trying to track down the poisoner, perhaps he sent Yeva to herbalists?'

'He says not,' Artem confirmed. 'I asked him for a status update; only sent out шестерка[23] to dig up information from the street.'

'Has Maksim said anything about it?'

Artem shook his head. 'As far as he knows, that day Yeva was home with the kids.'

'Which makes it even more curious.' Vadim dug his phone from his pocket, sending a text to Pavel. He needed to increase the pressure on his brigadier and get some progress on this poisoner.

---

[23] шестерка - Russian for 'sixes', the errand boys who are probationary Bratva members

He needed to know if this killer was a threat, or a glitch; a hobbyist who held grudges or someone out to disrupt their business. If someone felt it was acceptable to kill men with herbal poisons, that may also put their drug trade at risk.

*Perhaps it was something to ask Anara*, he thought.

# Sixteen

She had caught the earliest direct flight. Her departure from her home in Žďár nad Sázavou made in darkness, and arriving, via London, before the tall imposing gates of Vadim Morozov's estate by early afternoon. As the engine of the taxi faded, Kasdeya assessed the entry; tracking both cameras and people.

She refused to allow how impressed she was show.

Accustomed with travelling, Kasdeya had learned to pack lightly and this visit was no exception. She did not intend to be here long, and only had one neatly stocked bag with her. Most of the contents would also not be returning with her.

Running thin fingers over the slicked back jet ponytail, she began to walk to the intercom. Her umber eyes were heavily lined in kohl, and she kept her gaze hooked on the camera, sharp teeth biting into her darkly painted lower lip. In towering heeled boots, pencil skirt, and fitted jacket, Kasdeya knew she appeared divine.

The slit almost to her hip revealing incredibly pale skin.

Her impact evident in the husky and stilted greeting made when she pressed the button for admittance. 'I'm here to see Anara Morozova.' The words were more breathed than spoken.

'Who?'

'Your pakhan's wife.' Kasdeya had been tempted to avoid using the fake surname, his title, but assumed it was more likely she would be permitted inside if she proved her knowledge.

The silence was punctuated by her throaty laughter. A sound quickly hidden behind her hand, swallowed with a forced cough and a smile. The eventual soft slide of the smaller, pedestrian, gate's mechanism barely audible over the low hum of distant traffic and bird song.

'Before you're allowed up,' Maksim Zaitsev explained, 'we need to search your bags.' He gestured for her to wait.

'Bag.' She handed it over, holding his stare.

Maksim flushed, the heat coiling over his skin and bringing colour to his face. Dressed in black, with short brown hair, his athletic form easily moved back inside the guardhouse. Placed the bag onto the counter. On the surveillance monitors he could see the other soldiers employed to patrol the grounds, saw Fyodor leaving the main control room.

'Do you have some identification?' Maksim called, unzipping the bag and beginning to decant the items. Confusion creasing his brow.

Kasdeya stepped closer. 'Side pocket.'

He nodded, moving to locate the slender wallet. To check the photo matched the woman standing before him. 'Origins Research Group?'

'Yeah.' She paused. 'I'm one of Anara's suppliers.'

'Drugs?'

'Herbs, spices, and resins,' she corrected. 'Though I guess they're all the same thing, if you use them with the appropriate intent.'

Drowning under her gaze, Maksim forced himself to return to the bag's contents. 'What is all this stuff?'

'Nothing for you to worry about.'

'That won't get you to the house.' He dared to raise his eyes to her once more. With rumours of someone targeting men with poisons, this bag screamed caution. The large book appeared innocuous enough, but the tins, strange aromatic leaves, and oils were suspicious.

Maksim refused to be responsible for any casualties.

'That's not for *you* to worry about.' Kasdeya smiled. 'I'm sure there's someone on their way here to escort me up to Anara, who's confirmed who I am by now.'

'How did…,' he began. Then stopped himself. He knew there was no way she could see the camera feed from her position, so presumed she may have been guessing.

'If you could put those items back carefully, I'd appreciate it; I'd like to give them to Anara in good condition.' Her smile remained, enjoying how he became more uncomfortable under her scrutiny. She may need to play their game, but she could still play it her way.

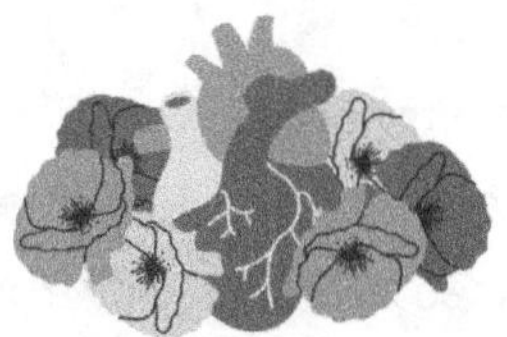

While she acknowledged that she required support, the quantity of it was becoming difficult to accept. Returning from the café to find Vadim eager and waiting to bring her to the generously provided bedroom had made her instantly cautious. But on discovering why, Anara had felt her caution turn to ire; his decisions directly opposed to their agreement.

'This is ridiculous,' she exclaimed with exasperation. 'We had a deal and this is *not* it.'

'I said I'd ensure you had everything you need.'

'Need, yes,' she retorted. 'This is far more than I could possibly ever need. I appreciate it, truly, Vadya, but this is too much.'

'Kroshka—'

'And what does that mean?' She spun to face him, her back to the extravagant amount of clothing hanging in the dressing room. She had not yet dared to open the drawers, nor looked in the en-suite, expecting to discover more items she would enjoy but had not requested.

Vadim smirked, low laughter in this throat. 'You're not ready for that, wife,' he said, 'but I assure you, it's nothing bad.'

She narrowed her eyes.

'You're only angry because you don't want to admit I'm right,' Vadim stated. 'You need this help, and I've told you I'm happy to provide it, so, please, accept my support.'

'There's support and support.' She sighed. 'This is not support, this is lavish and wasteful.'

'How?' He leaned against the doorframe, scanning the items he had chosen, items he had bought. Every single one he imagined draping her limbs, every single one he imagined removing.

'They… they probably won't even fit.' She risked taking a step closer to the exquisitely dark fabrics. 'And I've yet to see a tag.'

'They'll fit.' He folded his arms.

She tilted her head to him, eyebrows raised.

'Sofiya's mother is a seamstress, and she's never once fucked up a sizing on anyone.' He paused. 'Even if only from a photo.'

'This is still more than I need,' she said. 'When I leave—'

'You won't be.'

'When I leave, I can't take them.' She fought the erratic surge in her heart at his words, denying how she wished to stay; if only to figure out who this man was and why he had so rapidly broken through each of her established defences. 'I won't take them.'

Vadim was about to argue when he heard footsteps on the stairs, on the landing. The knock made quickly before Fyodor entered.

'Are we having a party in here too?' Anara looked to both men, her eyes conveying the frustration. Even if they failed to share the raw carnal source of it which thrummed in her blood.

'У ворот стоит женщина[24],' Fyodor said softly, glancing toward her but focusing on Vadim; his expression displaying concern.

'Кто она[25]?' Vadim felt confident their hushed conversation was not something Anara would understand.

His research diligent, and showing no Russian comprehension.

---

[24] У ворот стоит женщина - Russian for 'There's a woman at the gatehouse'
[25] Кто она - Russian for 'Who is she?'

'Она говорит, что знает Анару и что ты пахан[26].'

Vadim's hands became fists, a chill snaking over his spine; hidden behind his composed features and steady gaze. *This was a problem*, he thought. 'Как ее зовут[27]?'

The guard hesitated. 'Kasdeya.'

'Kas is here?' Anara frowned.

'You know her?' Vadim felt some of the chill retreat, a slight release of the tension in his fingers. The fact this woman knew his status, even if Anara did know her, was still a problem.

'Yeah, she's my supplier.' Anara dug into her coat pocket; the freshly laundered scent lingered after whatever magic Sofiya had worked on her ashy clothes. Pulling out her phone, her frown deepened. 'It's weird she hasn't sent a text though.'

'Supplier?'

'Vadya, you've invited someone you barely know to live here,' she replied with a slightly wicked curl to her lips.

'Kroshka,' he warned, taking a step toward her.

Behind him, Fyodor stepped out into the main room; satisfied the link had been confirmed, he returned downstairs in readiness to meet the guest by the gate and escort her. Whether to his leader or the cells.

'My business supplier,' she said, relenting to the heavy questioning of Vadim's stare. 'Kas works for Origins, they provide most of the herbs, spices, and things for Erinyes.'

'And she knew you were here?'

'I notified Origins about what happened,' she explained. 'They said they'd cover my costs, for rebuilding and salaries—'

'You said.' The dressing room was not as spacious as his own; he was almost touching her, subconsciously backing her toward the rail.

She forced herself to keep her eyes on his, even as she struggled to control her breath. 'I never gave them your address.'

---

[26] Она говорит, что знает Анару и что ты пахан - Russian for 'She says she knows Anara, and that you're the pakhan'
[27] Как ее зовут - Russian for 'Her name?'

'So, why did she know to come here?'

'I don't know.' The words were a husky whisper, her breath shallow and rapid. There was danger in his eyes, an intensity consuming her with his every exhale. And she was addicted. Anara could not look away even if she had wanted to, could not do anything but stand there, wishing he would grip her neck and kiss her.

'Is she trustworthy?' His voice was as low, as rough. This close all he could feel was her heat, all he could inhale was her fragrance. She was intoxicating and he wished to feast on her. Yearned to drag her from the hanging silks and throw her on the bed, to gorge on her.

'Yes.' She closed her eyes for a moment trying to locate some calm, to gather her thoughts. 'Maybe she saw… your online posts… and made the connection about where… I'd be.'

Vadim hummed an acknowledgement, tearing himself away before the urge to act overwhelmed him. When the time came to worship Anara, he intended to do so completely. It would not be rushed. It would not be on a whim. And she would be begging for him to take her, not meekly waiting but actively requesting to be conquered.

It would happen.

He was certain of it.

And involuntarily manoeuvring her to the edge of the dressing room was not how his feast would begin. No matter how his cock ached.

'Then we better get ready to greet our guest, wife.' He turned from her, discreetly adjusting himself before taking his phone and sending a message to Fyodor; Kasdeya was permitted access.

'You want me to act—'

'It'll be good practice, kroshka,' he confirmed, holding his hand out for her to take; his titanium ring glinting in the soft light.

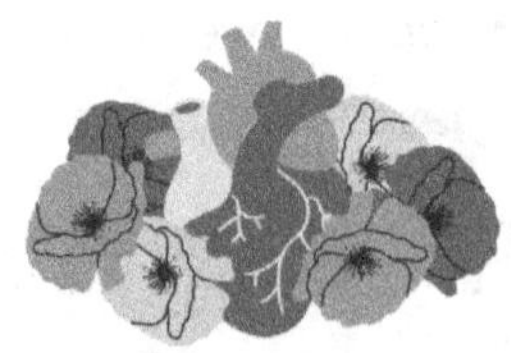

It had been surprisingly easy. Almost effortless. Though initially awkward, Anara soon found sitting beside Vadim felt normal, but not comfortable. A constant purr of desire continued to pulse under her skin, distracted her from the conversation, the events occurring around her. It was devouring every remaining barrier she had built; from the first moment Vadim stood behind her in Prey, he had steadily consumed her.

And she liked it. Welcomed it.

'Your house is beautiful, Vadimir,' Kasdeya said, leaning forward to collect the glass of black tea from the low table.

'Our house,' he corrected.

She smiled, inclining her head slightly. Their eyes met, her tongue slowly rolling over her lips. 'It's very monochrome, for a woman who had such an eclectic apartment, красный угол[28] aside.'

Anara blinked, the unfamiliar words slicing through her imagination and the heat slithering up her spine.

'Though I'm sure it'll take time for your tastes to align,' Kasdeya said with a prolonged look over her hosts; seated together on the sofa. There was barely a gap between them.

'You speak Russian?' Vadim asked. He shifted his arm, laying it on top of the sofa's back, so he could caress Anara's neck, fingers sinking into her curls. Relieved she did not flinch.

'I speak many languages,' she replied. 'Origins is an… international group, so we ensure we can converse wherever we are.'

'And what exactly does Origins do?' There had been no opportunity to research Kasdeya, nor the company, prior to her being brought into his home; Fyodor by her side. Vadim felt at a disadvantage, and it was only because Anara felt happy to meet her he had allowed Kasdeya to be seated opposite them now.

'We do many things.' She took a sip of tea, closing her dark eyes as the taste settled on her tongue.

---

[28] красный угол - Russian for 'red corner' or 'beautiful corner', a space usually on the east / right side of the main room near a window where religious icons are displayed

'That's hardly an answer—'

'Vadya,' Anara interjected softly.

'My apologies.'

Kasdeya met his gaze and smiled. 'I'm sure you understand, when organisations have wide portfolios, it's hard to then quantify exactly what a business does.'

He swallowed; being cognisant of his title, he should have guessed Kasdeya would hint at it, or at the very least the nature of his work. But he intended to protect Anara from his truth for as long as he could. 'Very true. Either way, I'm glad Anara has your support.'

'The work she does is incredibly valuable; we don't want her to face any challenges or disruption to that,' Kasdeya said, turning her attention to her client. It was evident both of those seated before her were hiding their true natures from each other. Now was not the time to expose them, nor to force what she could see was obvious attraction.

'I'd no idea you'd be coming to see me.'

'I got on the very first flight.'

'You're not based here?' Vadim picked up Anara's cup and handed it to her, before returning to collect his own. The amber liquid still steamed, and the central plate of cubed honey cake remained untouched. Today's housekeeper had served them then retreated to other tasks.

'No.' She paused, rationalising there was very little they could do if they knew more. 'I travelled from my home near Prague; I'll be returning as soon as we're done here.'

'Do Origins do this for all their clients?'

'It depends.' She smiled.

'That must keep you busy.' Vadim was intrigued, he could not deny that. Not by Kasdeya as a person, beautiful as she was, she was nothing compared to the woman sitting beside him.

He was confident Kasdeya was accustomed to using her looks, her guarded remarks, to gain the advantage when it came to making deals, to business. The long legs, the virtually skin-tight black clothing, the dark make-up, and straight hair pulled back smoothly, all conveyed power. It was an ensemble designed to intimidate and to ensure those she spoke with obeyed.

Vadim was unimpressed.

But he understood the purpose and admired the attempt.

'There's more than just me who works for Origins.' Kasdeya's smile broadened, her tongue tip resting on her lip for a prolonged beat; she would have enjoyed playing with this couple.

But now was not the time.

And it was not what her creator requested for this visit.

'Where is Origins based? I've never heard of them before—'

'We've been around a very long time.' She re-crossed her legs, the slit of her skirt falling and ignored. 'Yekaterinburg, primarily, now.'

His head tilted slightly; intent on investigating further. His curiosity a gnawing ache which he itched to depart and research. This group, this representative, screamed potential, screamed prestige, profit. To send someone immediately after an arson attack, on a property they supplied items to, seemed an incredibly extravagant approach to running any kind of business. Which meant either Anara did more than she said, which he doubted, or Origins was as valuable an asset as he believed it could be for his organisation.

'Anara, do we have somewhere we could talk?' Kasdeya placed her empty glass down, taking a square of honey cake and releasing a low moan as she bit into it. 'This is delicious.'

'I'll pass on the compliments to my housekeeper.' Vadim smiled. 'I've some work to attend to, please, stay and chat here.'

Anara's eyes closed briefly at the removal of his presence; the brush of his arm against hers sending a shiver of sparks through her skin. To her core. His retreating footsteps almost soundless as he headed toward the front door, phone to his ear, followed by Fyodor.

'Are you okay?' Kasdeya asked, leaning forward.

'Yeah.' She met the woman's gaze, seeing the concern.

'You sure? He's not got you—'

'It's all fine, I'm here by choice,' she said. 'I mean, obviously, it's a bit of a weird situation, and I hadn't planned on being here, but—'

'Even though you're married?' Kasdeya's eyes burned into Anara, a mischievous glint in them, daring her to confirm or deny the truth of the circumstances.

Anara's throat dried, reaching for her tea she drained the glass.

'Don't worry, Anara, everything works out, in the end.' She stood and collected the bag, crossed to sit on the sofa beside her host. 'Inside here is all you need to continue your work—'

'But, I can't possibly—'

'Your work is important.' Kasdeya rested her hand on Anara's thigh, her eyes level. 'We don't want you to be compromised, or for any woman to be without the support they may need.'

She shook her head, released a slow breath.

'Will these items be safe if I pass them to you now?'

'Yeah.' She nodded. 'Yeah, I've my own room.'

'Of course you have.' She laughed, watching as Anara's skin flushed a deep peony. 'Here, these are all the herbs you'll need, and some of the tinctures and resins which may be useful.'

'Thank you.' Anara's eyes veiled with warmth, her hands trembling as they accepted the large box.

'And here's a grimoire to replace the one you lost.'

'No,' she said huskily, her voice breaking.

'It's full of useful… recipes you may wish to employ.' Kasdeya could feel the gratitude roll off Anara's body, even as the woman tried to hide the emotion. To deny the relief which flooded her.

The leaders of Origins knew Anara Eden would be very reluctant to accept help, and they knew this would be a way to teach her it was okay to be the one receiving support sometimes. Being strong, being eternally the woman helping everyone else, was not infinitely sustainable when a carefully crafted life began to crumble.

'There are enough materials for you to create several remedies,' she continued. 'And I can send more, so you can help—'

'Thank you, but I can't.' Anara raised her head, fingers brushing the salt water from her cheekbones. 'The fire—'

'Here's a replacement laptop,' Kasdeya stated, ducking to obtain the last item she had to deliver. 'It's encrypted, and we've ensured you've the very best software installed to enable you to continue your work.'

'How can I ever repay you for this?' Anara was bewildered, shock a slowly progressing series of knives climbing her limbs, searing her vision with patches of black. *This was too much, all too much*, she thought.

'You don't.' Kasdeya stood gracefully, slender hands smoothing over her precisely tailored suit. The bag refastened, much lighter now only her return travel items remained within. 'We are very alike. We thrive using what our beautiful earth provides; she gives us all we need. And though I may utilise things a little differently, we have the same goal.'

'Origins does this too?' Anara frowned slightly, considering how a global organisation could conduct this and not have been caught. She reasoned that utilising many smaller businesses to complete the tasks could avoid detection.

'Haven't all women done this,' she replied, 'one way or another, over the eons we've had to face such difficulties?' Kasdeya, as a Goddess of Poisons, would forever rely on the ingredients hidden in plants, found in the earth, to both excite and subdue. She honoured her creator every time she worshipped or destroyed.

'Yeah, I guess.' She chewed on her lip, slowly digesting the words Kasdeya had delivered and the potential in them. The concept of female unity and strength straightening her spine with empowerment.

With a chance to begin again.

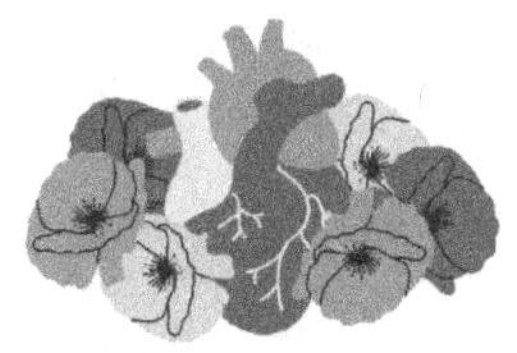

Relieved, Anara leant against the solid wood of her bedroom door. There was a raw ache in her body which only seemed to grow. Grief for all she had lost slowly being replaced with an unspoken desire to retain these new developments. Every moment spent in Vadim's company nurturing the possibility of surrender, of submission.

Not of who she was, nor of what she could achieve.

But a moment to rest, to allow someone else to care for her, ensure she had all she required. Anara could not recall when she had last felt such attentive kindness as she was being shown.

Provision without obligation.

It was rare, was genuine, and developed her sense of trust. Which scared her. After all Anara witnessed within Erinyes, she should be alert and cautious, should be concerned Vadim was manipulating her. She should be investigating him to prevent her heart being broken, to prevent her world shattering.

There was only so much someone could take.

And Anara was overwhelmed. Vadim. Kasdeya. Her friends, Bryony and Kerezen. They had all been so generous, not only materially but with their understanding, their time.

The debt was increasing and Anara felt the weight of it as her steps brought her from her dressing room to the small table and chairs near the window. While she had eaten dinner with Vadim, Sofiya had been in to close the curtains, to refill the carafe by the bed, provide fresh linens. Anara had carefully stored the laptop, the herbs and grimoire; buried beneath clothes in one of the drawers of her dressing room.

It was all exactly as she had left it.

Opening the device, it chimed to life after a moment and requested the biometric unlock. The screen filtering to display the settings she had established in the hours since Kasdeya departed. Typing Vadim's name done without further thought.

The results a series of images and text which made her heart erratic and breath shallow.

Quick.

Logic screamed that the information was too clean, too sanitised for it to be real. The links too direct and too precise. As though someone had scrubbed the reality of Vadim from any possible search. A familiar pretence in the presentation.

Anara was too far gone for logic. Her mind too consumed by visions of his virtually naked body slick with water from the pool, of his hand reaching for hers, of his eyes blown out with lust.

Imagined lust.

A belief he felt the same as she did.

Such thoughts altered how she perceived the screen before her; her slender fingers reaching out to touch the photo of them together. Even though she knew it was fake, it looked real.

'Anara?'

Jolting, her hand dropped hastily to the circular table. She twisted toward her locked door. 'Yeah,' she replied, husky.

'You okay?' Vadim asked.

'Yeah.' Stronger, less rough.

A pause.

Anara watched him move; the shadow beneath the door shifting as he debated what to do. She wondered if she wanted him to knock. Or to tear the door from the hinges and dominate her.

She swallowed.

'I'm going out,' he said, finally, 'but if you need m… anything, call.'

'Okay.' Her eyes remained fixed on the door, waiting. Unsure what she was hoping, praying for. Every nerve alight. Each inhale dragging his scent closer, into her lungs, her veins.

The retreating sound of his footsteps became the click of the front door, the growl of the car's engine fading as it drove toward the gate.

Only when the roar of her pulse was the last remaining sound did she consciously exhale and return to the screen.

The range of images bringing an instant kick to her quim.

'I should've asked for a vibrator,' she muttered.

Laughed.

Her hand covering her mouth, fingertips falling to trace her lips. Dark eyes closing with a low sigh. The heat at the apex of her thighs made her thighs clench; the bite of her teeth into her lower lip increased the hunger in her descending touch. Fingers splayed to move down the curving arc of her neck.

Reaching the swell of her breasts she paused. Caution forcing her eyes open, hand snatching at the laptop to push the lid down. She did not require the digital image when his every feature was engrained in her mind, the warmth of his touch remembered on her skin. The sound of his voice an echo.

She wanted to make him scream.

Wanted to make him groan with her name on his lips. On his tongue. Drenched with her, them. Their unified taste dripping over their flesh. It was an ache which made her mouth open, her chest heave.

'Fuck,' she breathed.

Standing, she began stripping the clothes from her frame; they felt too restrictive. Too oppressive. She needed to feel, to explore, to devour. To crawl over her skin and provide Vadim with a map, a whisper of where he could feast.

Collapsing onto the thick fabrics of the bed, she could barely prevent the moan escaping. Anara's hands split between her pebbled nipples and her trembling stomach. Dipping lower, to the glistening heat, to the pressure of her clit. Her back bowed with the pinch of her fingers on both, her hand kneading her breasts before sliding to her throat.

A cage around her neck she envisaged he made.

His conquering of her, bringing her to her knees so she could take him in her mouth. Swallow him. Lick and taste, drink him down, before bringing him entirely inside her body. Her heart. Her soul.

To relish his flesh, indulge on it.

To present her own as a banquet for him to graze on.

She wanted him to eat her, consume her. To worship her in the ways she had only dreamed of; Anara's desires always unfulfilled. Leaving her empty, starving for true affection, true connection.

Swirling her fingers over her clit, she choked on the mewl, holding her breath. Prolonging the agony. Closed eyes seeing Vadim crawling up her legs, his tongue sweeping over, strong arms holding him above. A controlled lowering of his skin to hers. The swift entrance of her fingers to her cunt timed with the belief he used his cock to stretch her.

Fill her.

The moan no longer held, Anara bit into her lower lip.

Her body a mass of tremors as her fingers curled, her thumb slid; a blend fuelled by her imagination and the intensity of her desire. Devotion weeping from her every pore, his movements restrained, designed for delivery of her pleasure, not his. Every withdrawal, every forceful return, bringing her closer to the precipice.

It felt real.

So very real.

Her muscles tensing with the coiling symphony waiting to sing. Tight breath, famished thoughts, Anara's hand gripped the bars of the bed and used the conflicting chill to push herself over the edge.

# Seventeen

In sporadic street lighting, the occupants of the car were illuminated then forced into shadow. The cabin quiet, tense. An unspoken focus which they had honed in the years they had conducted such operations. Each car in the convoy sleek, black, with plates which would never connect the vehicles to Vadim, or anyone with their group.

Three cars.

Twelve men. All eager to remind Septer that their attempts to take Bratva territory would fail. In the rear of the central car, Vadim glanced to Artem; his advisor's usual tailored suit swapped for combat gear.

'It's your call, pakhan,' Artem stated.

He turned back. 'Kolya, the research?'

Twisting from the passenger seat, the brigadier looked over the two men. 'Since your call earlier? I'm good… but not *that* good.'

'I didn't mean Origins—'

'What's this?' Artem interjected, a slight frown appearing. Creasing the pale skin below peppered hair.

'Later,' Vadim said, focus darting from Nikolai to Artem. 'This club, it's definitely one of Mace's?'

'Yeah.' Kolya nodded.

'Then we strike.' He settled back into the leather, jaw set.

'How much longer?' Artem asked.

'About another twenty,' Makari confirmed, eyes shifting to the mirror and meeting the advisor's gaze.

'Then you've time to tell me about this… what, Origins?'

Vadim sighed, his exhale heavy; he preferred to work nights like this through silently. To sit and contemplate each move he intended to make in reflective peace. His advisor knew this. Everyone knew this.

'Vadya,' Artem prompted, fist lightly punching his pakhan's arm.

'Anya had a visitor today—'

'At the house?' He opted to ignore the affectionate term his leader used to refer to Anara.

Vadim nodded. 'A rep from Origins Research Group, who supplied the apothecary; flew out especially to check in with her.'

'Okay.' Artem's brown eyes were fixed on his leader, his lips curling into a bemused smile; the frustration in Vadim's face betraying how such a lack of control ate into his blood. 'So, your *wife* prefers women; that could work in your favour.'

'Tyoma,' Vadim warned, mouth tight.

'Then why so concerned?' His frown reappeared. 'Do you think this rep's a threat? Or the group… you think they're trying to get product over here from… where'd she fly from?' His mind hunted for clarity.

'She flew from Prague,' he explained, 'but the group is international, based in Russia.'

Artem's eyes narrowed, his arms folding across his broad chest.

'She knew who I was.' Vadim's jaw ticked.

'What, the whole fake marriage thing?'

'That too,' he muttered. 'No, she called me pakhan.'

'Fuck.' Artem shook his head. 'Everything we've put online, there's no way anyone—'

'Exactly.' He paused. 'Unless they're operating in similar circles as us, but I can't see Anara involved in that.'

'No, I agree,' Artem said. 'She's too… sweet.'

'Careful, Tyoma,' he retorted, a wry smile finally breaking the tension in his face, 'I'd hate to have to kill you.'

Artem chuckled, rubbing his hand over his face; the tattoos dark in the flickering neon of shop displays.

'Kolya, what've you got on Origins and Kasdeya so far?'

'I got her image from the gatehouse,' he confirmed, twisting toward the rear of the cabin again. 'Running image searches only delivered the official Origin's online pages, nothing personal. It did confirm an address in Žďár nad Sázavou, which I'm looking into—'

'So, she's who she said she was?'

'Looks that way.' Nikolai shrugged. 'In terms of the organisation, it's all very professional and clean. Pretty much an entirely female staff and they do operate all over the world.'

'Doing what?'

'That's what's tricky,' he said cautiously.

'Tricky?' Vadim felt chilled knives eat into his spine.

'Why don't you just ask Anara?' Artem asked, eyebrows raised. The mischievous smile only enlarging when his leader narrowed his gaze and shook his head.

'Anya's confirmed Origins supplies her herbs—'

'And just those?'

'Yes.' He clenched his teeth. 'Kolya, continue digging into this, I want to know more. I need to know how she knew who I am.'

Nikolai nodded once, precise and firm.

'Five minutes,' Makari stated, the timing echoing through the convoy as they neared the club. The stretch of closed stores thinning out until a large illuminated sign indicated the forecourt; cycling images of a woman dancing on a bar and the establishment's name.

'We wait until they close,' Vadim confirmed. 'The target is their staff, only Septer.'

Acknowledgements repeated through the earpieces they wore, the words reinforcing the determination forming in their blood.

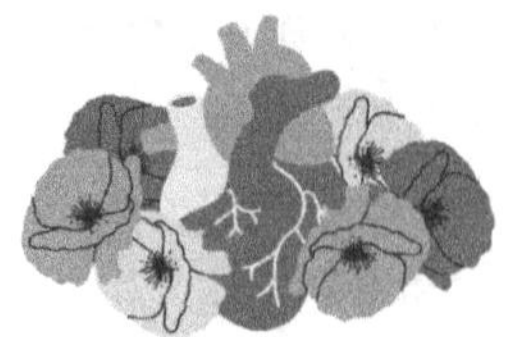

Pacing, Logan Pottinger could scarcely contain the frustration. The brittle fury. Every step matched the muffled beat from the club overhead. His neck flushed with the fury he tried to quell, his undercut betraying the depth of his anger. Every muscle of his tall frame rippled with it. Poison wrapping every hollow cell.

Seated, Kassian's hazel eyes tracked the guard, his body relaxed; a gentle smile on his full lips. His ankle was propped on the opposite knee with one hand resting on his thigh.

'What the fuck were you thinking?'

'You said to keep watching her, so I kept watching—'

'And clearly saw nothing,' he spat. 'Married to Morozov, you stupid fucking cunt; you've put a target on all of us, Kass.'

'Mace thinks—'

'I don't give a fuck.' He spun, gripping the arms of the chair, face low to almost touch the soldier's. Breath falling erratically over his skin, his knuckles chalk. 'I don't give a fuck.'

The music died.

A hush swelled between them, the small office without windows, a room tucked in the corner of the sprawling basement. It was somewhere Logan regularly retreated to, able to survey the dance floor and bar, able to direct the soldiers toward women he thought would be appropriate to seduce. To capture.

To claim.

'This way, we get her to work with us,' Kassian explained, cool and meeting the man's stare. 'She'll want to rebuild the store, and we offer to help her.'

'She's married to—'

'Look, Mace may buy your bullshit,' he stated, 'but I'm not.'

Logan pushed away from him, folding his arms and perching on the edge of the desk. His back to the monitors, which faced the chair he had rapidly left when Kassian appeared.

The incursion of men, dressed primarily in combat-gear, unseen and unheard until the screaming began. Rapid footsteps followed by distant thuds. A crack of a gunshot. Shouts which became wails of agony hastily quietened.

The two men's eyes met.

'Fuck,' Logan breathed, reaching for the firearm at his side.

Kassian was on his feet immediately, his weapon drawn, running toward the door. His finger rested above the trigger, ready, his head tilted to listen for any sound of the intruders approaching. The complex maze of corridors and rooms of the lower level working in their favour.

'Slow,' Logan warned.

'I'm not fucking stupid,' he hissed.

'Beg to differ.' The guard took up position on the opposite side of the door, his stance similar.

Kassian slowly placed his hand on the lever, resisting retaliation by biting his tongue. Survival felt more important. Whatever was happening above them was the priority. 'What's the plan, boss?'

'We get out.'

'Don't we need to—'

'We get out.' Logan kept his gaze level. 'Mace is at Iðun, this club's closed, whoever's left in there, they're gone. We get out.'

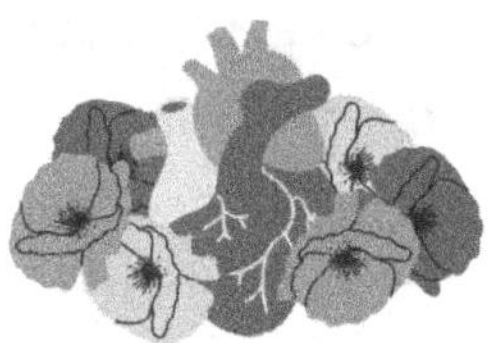

Though the patrons had departed, a few loitered on the pavement. Their drunken steps stumbling toward taxis, with groping hands steering willing bodies. Bored security guards still remained by the doors; judgemental gazes, hands in pockets.

Accustomed to working with each other, Vadim's brigade operated with an efficiency Mace could only aspire to. Hand gestures, silent slides of the eye, an almost imperceptible change in stance, enough to confirm who would approach first. Who would follow. The plan formed, practised until all possible contingencies were accommodated.

With the objective being to capture, to locate soldiers and guards within Septer, none of Vadim's men had drawn a weapon. Their skills in hand-to-hand combat sufficient, a knife if necessary. Their firearms were a last resort, and only if Vadim's life was in jeopardy.

For this incursion, at least.

The convoy had gathered with space to move unhindered, unseen beyond the club's cameras. Split to cover every entrance, every exit, as pre-arranged from the research Nikolai had completed.

In black, stalking toward the entrance, Vadim trusted his team would follow. Nearing the club's guards he signalled for Makari to strike. Vadim understood the importance of both leading and conceding; in allowing others to take the risk.

To clear the route.

Vadim's lips retained their tight smile, watching Makari wrap his arm tightly around a security guard's throat. The chokehold delivered with brutal precision. The other similarly brought down by Pavel.

Propping open the doors, Ilya waited for the men to enter, dragging the guards with them, before drawing it shut. Slow. Quiet. The two men bound by a cloakroom. At the rear of the club, Pyotr mimicked the action; the smaller exit carefully returned to the frame.

Both teams of men working their way to the main floor.

Vadim following, allowing Artem and Makari to defensively lead. His head turning at the click of a door, the noisy footsteps behind. Finding another security guard.

'Who're you?'

'Pakhan—'

His eyes cut Makari off.

Makari nodded then continued as planned.

The man glanced toward the entrance, hearing his colleagues begin to groan. He swiftly reached for the baton at his waist, lunging toward the trio with a wild swing, twisting the barrel. Spikes revealed and whipping through Vadim's upper arm, slicing through fabric to skin. Blood creeping from the wound to soak into the long-sleeved t-shirt and jacket.

Inhaling, Vadim gritted his teeth.

The second strike swept across his abdomen; ripping the jacket and shirt, deeply grazing the skin. It stung. But Vadim retained his stance, his determined posture; protecting his men.

'Who the fuck are you?' The guard panted, exertion beading sweat on his brow; it had been a long night, which he had ended with several beers. The buzz from the alcohol was wearing off, but it compounded his altered perception. His lack of coordination.

'Go join your friends,' Vadim stated.

'Fuck that.' He raised his arm once more.

Vadim was quicker; hand to his belt and шайтан-м[29] thrown.

The security man staggered. Blade forcing blood profusely from his gargling throat. The scream distorted as his knees hit the tiles. Fingers scratching at the skeletonised handle. The steel slick.

Stepping forward, Vadim snatched the knife from the man's neck in an efficient twist; blood spraying his hand. He wiped his weapon on the man's back, then returned it to his belt.

The other men had progressed to the dilapidated main room; sticky and worn flooring, peeling paint, taped over switches. On scuffed tables were abandoned bottles, smeared glasses. The staff tasked with clearing up and securing things moved without any sense of urgency.

Until one of them heard the scream from the entrance.

Their confused shouts questioning what was happening; if this was a police raid, a rival gang, or someone trying to break in and take what had been earned that night.

---

[29] шайтан-м - Russian for 'shaitan-m', a type of throwing knife

Questions becoming whimpers and cries as the first of the men strode through. The braver members of the staff rushing forward to throw punches; a fight the soldiers answered as brigadiers Pavel and Nikolai scanned the scene for members of Septer.

Vadim's entrance a momentary distraction which permitted one of the barmen to escape Ilya's grip. The initial tumble turned sprint forward gaining enough momentum to smash a bottle and drag the edge over Vadim's cheek. The Russian caught the man's wrist, bending it back and forcing him flush to his chest; arm pinned.

'Должен ли я все делать сам[30]?' Vadim's eyes tracked his men and catalogued who was present, who had cuts, who had bruises, who had the remaining staff cowering and static.

'I'm sorry, pakhan,' Ilya said in Russian, lines creasing his brow, and seating his knife in his hand.

Ready.

Vadim kicked the barman forward, heavy pressure on the back of his knees to bring him to the floor.

Arriving before them, Ilya quickly gripped the man's hair and pulled his head back. The soldier met his leader's gaze, seeking permission, before then sliding the blade through the man's arched neck. It breached the flesh with ease.

He dropped with a subdued thud.

Catching movement in the periphery of his vision, Artem instinctively drew his firearm. One of the men they had tied in the entrance surged in their direction, the discarded baton in his hand. The bullet was released with ruthless efficiency, piercing between the security guard's eyes.

The baton spun patterns in the pooling blood.

'Someone needs to revisit their rope technique,' Vadim said, sighing before shaking his head. 'We're better than this. Fuck!'

Retching broke the tense silence; one of the trembling members of staff spilling their stomach.

---

[30] Должен ли я все делать сам? - Russian for 'Must I do everything myself?'

'We should be setting the example.' Vadim began to pace, dark eyes tracking the room, the appearance of the club, the people. He started to fold back the sleeves of his t-shirt; blood dampening fabric. 'Tie them all to the poles.'

In the club's uniform, the people remained confused, unaware. None understood the request Vadim had made, none knew who the men were or what they wanted. Nervous faces betrayed the fear, shaking limbs and hoarse begging evidence of anxiety.

Artem, leaving to collect the bound guard by the cloakroom, fed off the terror in the air. The bitten down tears, choked sobs. It was music to him, and he smiled as he made his way past the two dead guards. His knife making quick work of the rope. His combat boot to the man's back urging the shackled guard forward.

Kicked to the ground before Vadim.

The man groaned, struggling to his knees with wrists raw from the thick rope. He fought the vomit climbing his throat; the bloody remains of his two colleagues imprinted on his eyes even as they closed. Focusing on the staff being tied to the stage's poles brought a glacial sweat to his skin, dragging slowly down his spine.

Maksim leapt from the greasy platform, crossing the dance floor to grip the guard's collar. He glanced to Artem, then Vadim, checking if his instinct was correct; that this man needed to join the others.

The slightest of nods confirming his assumption.

'You either move,' Maksim suggested in English, 'or you never move again.' The tightening of the man's collar persuasive.

Watching his solider encourage the guard, Vadim narrowed his eyes as disappointment gnawed his veins. 'They're not here.'

'We're checking—'

'They'd've made an appearance by now.'

'They're cowards,' Artem reassured him. 'They'll be hiding.'

A low, breathy laugh crept from Vadim's throat. His advisor's words were correct. If this club was being used to house women, to keep them captive, then there would be confirmation in the lower rooms. If this club was being used to recruit them, to take them, then Vadim knew only one route remained. Every employee was complicit.

The objective transforming.

His jaw ticked. The hum of those tied to the sticky poles a discordant whimper, scared pleas muttered amongst prayers. As though Vadim was a god who would provide them with salvation.

'The basement's empty,' Nikolai announced, returning to the activity with Pyotr. 'But someone was down there; they left in a hurry.'

'Any trace of detainment?'

'No, pakhan,' Nikolai confirmed.

'Then we leave.' Vadim turned, knowing his men would follow.

Knowing the last would pour the gasoline and strike the match.

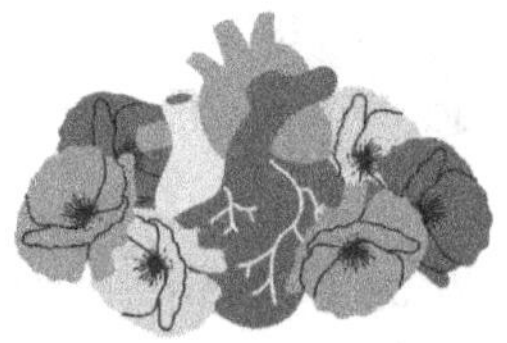

Drawing the ripped t-shirt from his torso, Vadim clenched his teeth; the dried blood pulled. Tacky. Reopening the wounds. He bundled the fabric before placing it in the middle of the rear seat. Turning his left arm, he assessed the damage.

'Do you want me to call the doctor?' Artem asked, critically checking his leader's injuries, as Makari drove back to the estate.

He shook his head. Now the work was done, his thoughts moved to other matters. To chasing down Mace's crew. To hunting for the premises used to hold those they captured. To destroying Septer entirely.

To seeing Anara.

'Is the house secure?' Vadim asked, confident one of his team would provide the answer. He grabbed a replacement shirt, carefully drawing it on and smoothing it over his frame.

'Yes, pakhan,' Nikolai stated after a brief pause; the request made to the surveillance team patrolling and confirmation received.

'Why wouldn't it be?'

Vadim glanced to his advisor.

'Anara.' Artem shook his head, smirking, a chuckle vibrating over his chest. 'Vadya, you need—'

'I need what?' His eyes narrowed.

He waved his hand, gesturing his capitulation.

'No, Tyoma, please enlighten me about what I need?' His tone was precise, venomous. Vadim curled his hands into fists above his thighs, a tightening of his jaw increasing the tension.

'I know you enjoy the pain,' Artem said, after a pause, his head tilting slightly, 'but tonight you were reckless.'

'And?'

'You know so little about this woman—'

'Tyoma—'

'—about her past, this thing with Origins,' Artem continued, ignoring the curt interruption. 'Just fuck her and get her out your system, and out of your house, before you end up dead.'

'Makari, stop the car.'

'Pakhan?'

'Stop the car.' Vadim had not shouted, had no need to. The delivery of the instruction sufficient for the guard to comply.

'Vadya, pakhan—'

'No,' he said firmly, twisting to his advisor. 'Enough.'

'I'm too old to find another vor to take your place,' Artem remarked, a glint in his eye. These arguments never resulted in acrimony for long; he was confident Vadim would mellow.

In time.

'And you won't have to.' Vadim exhaled. Returned his attention to the front of the car. 'Kolya, make sure Artem finds his way home.'

Nikolai did not answer, his hand already opening the door, exiting the vehicle. A series of updates provided via their team communications to explain the change.

'We'll debrief later—'

'We need—'

'We will debrief later,' Vadim repeated.

A sense of calm followed the departure of the two men; a softness in the silence as Makari continued toward the estate. Leaving the other two cars to navigate a new, different, route.

Welcoming the hush, Vadim fell into a trance of image and sound. A marrying of the car's smooth wheels over asphalt, the indicator's click, of breath. The ache of his wounds reminding him of the sting. His mind full of Anara. Of how he could ever possibly reconcile this life with her gentle nature. Even if he had yet to completely understand her.

The arrival at the gate, the farewell to Makari, forgotten the moment the frigid pre-dawn air caressed his face. Though the broken bottle had not cut too deeply, there was enough raw skin to bring a hiss when the breeze swept rain against it.

With such high-levels of security, there was no requirement to lock the front door, and Vadim strode straight through. Shedding his jacket to pass to Sofiya who greeted him in the hallway. Vadim waved away any offer of refreshment, his steps quick to climb the stairs.

Taking them several at time.

He was unsure what was driving his movements, but his heart wept for clarity. For comprehension. Every nerve felt on the verge of breaking, his body clamouring for some kind of affirmation.

Reaching Anara's door, he finally paused. His breath held. Finding it slightly open made the erratic surge of his pulse freeze. One hand went to his belt, feeling for the hilt of his knife. The other tapped lightly on the wood, pushing it further, waiting for an objection.

An attack.

Nothing.

Vadim rushed in, his eyes scouring the room. In the spilled light from the landing, there was enough illumination to confirm the bed was empty. Uncreased. He spun, checking the dressing room, the en-suite.

Running back to the stairs, he gripped the rail. 'Sofiya,' he called.

'Yeah.' She had loitered in the vestibule, curious about his behaviour and how he had diverted from his usual routine. Tilting her face up, she witnessed the anxiety which clung to his. It rolled off him as he rapidly descended, made her own breathing pick up pace.

'Where's Anya?' He frowned. Corrected. 'Anara.'

'I… I don't know.' Sofiya pressed her lips together. 'She, she came down earlier to find something to read, I think.'

Vadim was already walking toward the library, eating the distance in long strides. The glow of the lit fire within cast amber tongues, webbed shadows dancing over the polished hardwood floor. Each of the double doors wide and overhead lights dim.

Relief punched breath from his lungs.

'Fuck,' he mouthed, barely voiced. One hand rubbed over his jaw at the sight of Anara curled, peaceful, on the library's wide window seat. A thick blanket was draped over her lower half, the book splayed and bent on the floor by her sagging arm.

'Do you want me to get one of the—'

'No, thank you, Sofiya.' He did not turn to his housekeeper, aware of every single cell of his body and how his eyes glazed with heat. 'That's all for tonight, I'll take her to bed.'

# Eighteen

He had not slept. Had found no weariness. The usual drop in adrenaline after an operation never came; the exhaustion, the emptiness, replaced with Anara's presence. It felt natural to keep her safe. Protect her. There was always the potential Mace would finally crack and try to enact some form of revenge for the actions he had taken.

The club's fire may become the catalyst which finally brought him to the estate. Futile as such an attack would be. Vadim had confidence in his team, in the soldiers who patrolled the perimeter, those who worked the surveillance room, the gatehouse.

But he preferred to handle what he could himself.

His lips quirked into a smile, knowing that was the cause of many of his scars, his broken bones. His refusal to take the normal pakhan role, and be more involved in every day operations.

Vadim hoped such commitment would be witness to his strength, his suitability to retain control of this group. Despite the likely rumours which would be whispered. He was fully cognisant of how her room remained empty, her bed remained made, that comments would be made about where Anara slept.

The intention had been pure, even as desire coaxed him to deny the steps he took. He had taken her to her room, only to find himself pausing on the threshold. His arms did not wish to relinquish her weight, her body draped across his chest, resting against his abdomen; ignoring how she pressed against the sore wounds.

Instead, he had turned.

Walked away.

Brought her to his bed, laid her amongst his scent, and welcomed how her raven-black hair spread over the crisp white cotton. A paradise in her every breath. He had stood over her, fingers gently stroking her face, watching slumber drag her deeper.

Stooped, his lips ghosted with her exhales.

Almost connecting.

Only to form fists, to shed his weapons and retire to the sofa.

To wait.

Each sigh suggesting dreams he longed to visit, each restless turn of her body under the duvet ones he wished to feel. His eyes tracked her every movement, a pattern he sought to understand. To devour. To find her peace, to corrupt it together. To swallow the screams from her throat and collapse completely into her body, heart, soul.

It took discipline to sit there, his every nerve burning, cock painfully hard, and do nothing. To only listen. To watch. Even as his teeth ground with desperation to bite, to mark, to claim.

As blood pooled in his mouth from the bite of his tongue.

In growing daylight, Anara began to wake. With the same bedding as the room she had been provided, it took a moment for the unfamiliar to register. The way the early-morning sunlight fell differently across the room, how it highlighted art she had not seen, how it glinted on lamps she had never used.

'Good morning, kroshka,' Vadim said, voice rough.

Scrambling to sit up, Anara's eyes widened. Heart loud and mind spiralling. Quickly assessing the bed to determine if she had slept alone, if her fantasies had somehow become real.

If she was dreaming.

'Don't worry,' he continued, 'you're perfectly safe.'

Slow, he stood, limbs aching.

In the soft glow from the window, his body remained partly shadow, preventing definition. Yet, knowing he was close, and being wrapped in his bedding, consumed by his fragrance, only made her body sing. Cry out for him to close the distance and join her. To trace every pore she had the night before.

Anara's cataloguing of her body confirmed his words, her body felt her own, her clothes felt undisturbed. What she had worn to explore the house, to read, the same. But, she remained confused as to why she was in his room.

*Did I just walk in?*

*Did he reject me?*

*Put me to bed then leave?*

'Why wouldn't I be?' Her words were of a similar huskiness to his, a slight slur to them as day eroded night.

Then his words finally broke through her reverie, digesting what they could mean. His muscular frame becoming clearer, seeing the blood on his skin, the cut on his cheek. Her heart lurched. 'What happened?'

He breathed a laugh. 'Bar fight.'

'And that would put me at risk?' She sensed there was more he was hiding, that there was more behind the comment. Something about the way his dark eyes failed to crease, how he was not moving his left arm the way he normally would, how he walked differently.

And not just due to spending a night on the sofa.

'Was it Kassian?' Her question was shrouded in concern.

He shook his head. 'If he tried anything, he'd regret it.'

She swallowed; his assertion carried menace. Threat. Tentative, her tongue rolled over her lips. 'Let me go get my herbs—'

'I don't need—'

'Vadya, I can help.' She stood, unsteady, she reached out, her hand resting on his arm.

He winced.

She frowned. 'There's more, isn't there?'

Vadim shrugged.

'This will only work if you're honest with me.' Anara sighed, knowing she was keeping secrets from him. Yet, at this moment, his stoic nature and his evasive responses felt more necessary to dissect. 'Tell me what happened, and why I'd be at risk.'

'Kroshka, it's fine.' He took a step back, allowing her to dictate their movement, giving her the space she needed. Even though he longed to choreograph their bodies in a different way.

To pin her, worship her, consume her.

'It's not.' She narrowed her eyes. 'I'm going to get my herbs. While I'm gone, you can decide if you want this to continue, or not.'

'Anara, what do you—'

'If you want me to act as your wife, you need to tell me exactly what I'm playing along with.' She kept her head up, her back straight, walking from the room without looking back. She knew if she did, she would have crumbled, would have allowed him to create an excuse, an illusion she would have meekly accepted.

And she had promised herself, years ago, that she would no longer tolerate such things from anyone.

In her absence, Vadim inhaled deeply. Tracing the last remnants of her presence, the peace which lingered even after her request. The plea for answers he could not give. Not everything.

Not yet.

He was still in the same position when she strode back in, closing the door behind her. The click broke through his contemplation. Broke his resolve. If Artem did not like what he was about to do, then he would find another advisor. But this, whatever this was with Anara, meant more than a quick fuck, more than a short-term fling.

Vadim acknowledged there was more he needed to discover about her, especially with the representative from Origins turning up; however, he could not deny the way she had captivated him. From the first time he saw her in Prey, to now, in her pyjamas and robe in his bedroom, Anara Eden was endgame.

And he knew it.

Even if she did not.

'I found you in the library, when I got home,' Vadim stated. 'I never planned on bringing you to my bed, I did go to your room first, but then I just couldn't… I couldn't risk leaving you alone. I can protect you better if you're with me, and I've more weapons in here.'

'Weapons?' Her throat dried, her hands tightening their grip on the tin of herbs and tinctures. A cold sweat began to gather at the base of her spine, creeping higher as her pulse quickened.

'That's what you took from that?' He smiled, eyes darting to the floor then back to her. 'Аня[31], Anara, I… I need you to know that you're not in any danger with me.'

She stepped forward, cautious, placing the tin down on the low table before the sofa. The sprawling room seemed suddenly even bigger, the monochrome colours emphasising the stark nature of his tone. Anara sat, her eyes following him as he moved to perch on the bed.

It was not lost on either of them how they had taken up the furniture the other had used during the night.

'But you have weapons? In here?'

'I have weapons in every room in the house—'

'Every room?'

'Yes.' He paused, his elbows resting on his thighs, hands loose. 'I do own Prey, I own many things, but it's not my main role.'

Anara's mind conjured different images; some of which made her hands move toward the tin. There were deadly herbs in there she could use should she need to. Weapons or not, she had her own.

She was wise enough to know when to use them.

---

[31] Аня - Russian for 'Anya' an affectionate name given to women who have names similar to Anara or Anna

When to stay quiet.

And in this moment, she needed to know if Vadim Morozov should be on her list. If she had made an error trusting his motives, if his hostile takeover of her heart should have been blocked. If the way he continued to feast on her soul should be starved.

'Did Kasdeya tell you who I am?'

'What?'

'Kasdeya used my title, when she came to the house,' he said with no judgement in his inflection, 'and I wondered if she'd mentioned—'

'All she asked was if I was okay.'

He nodded.

'What's your title?' Her voice broke slightly, which infuriated her. She clenched her teeth, her inhale deep.

Unsure what she was bracing herself for.

'Pakhan.'

'Pack what?'

'Pakhan,' he said, 'the head of a cell, in the Bratva.'

The cold sweat spread, tendrils feeding her skin and coiling around her ribs, caging her throat. Her eyes unfocused. Her body no longer her own, but a host for a mass of conflicting energy and sensation.

*He should be on my list*, she thought.

'Kassian is a solider in a rival Norse gang,' he continued, watching her reaction closely. 'Septer is cruel, they're traffickers, and I'm doing all I can to shut them down.'

Her head snapped up, clarity of thought emptying her lungs as she processed his statement. 'Shut them down?'

'I won't stand for that kind of… trade.' His eyes seemed to darken, a viciousness to the set of his jaw and how he emphasised the words. 'I won't allow it.'

Anara believed him. There was truth in his statement, the sentiment carried in what she knew of him. In how he had behaved with her. Slow, the chill began to recede. Heat pooling in her veins.

'Seeing you with him, in my bar… I could've killed him then.' Vadim stood, crossing to sit on the table before her. The pull of the cuts on his abdomen creating a slight flinch.

'Because you thought I was a target for them?' The heat changed to rage; underestimated again. 'I could've handled it.'

'I'm sure you could, kroshka.' He smiled. 'You're strong.'

'Damn right.'

Silence settled, the potential admission caught on his tongue. The truth of why he approached her in Prey, and the initial interest in Erinyes, a confession he could not find the words to voice.

Anara hoped the silence would provide more. Would validate her own desires, that the lust she saw in his eyes was honest, something he would pursue. That his decision to manipulate her was about more than point-scoring with a rival gang.

'I went looking for him last night,' Vadim admitted, 'but, despite the intelligence Kolya obtained, he wasn't there.'

'And that's where you got hurt?'

He nodded. Once.

'May I see?'

Vadim stood, holding out his hand to her. 'Come.'

She hesitated.

'The bathroom has better light,' he added.

Skin touched skin, the heat in her veins becoming a fire. Intense and violent, every part of her pleaded for Vadim. The instant dilation of her pupils a siren to the hunger which pulsed in her core. Swallowed down and denied, she snatched up the tin and kept her eyes on the floor.

'Where do you want me?'

'What?' The sound was more croak than word. Her pale skin furious with warmth, the large mirror above the double-sink and marble counter reflecting her image. Deepening the blush.

'Do you want me to sit down? Stay standing?'

'Sit down, please.' Anara lowered the tin, opening it.

He complied, adjusting himself as he did. The endearing flush to her skin only increased the reaction in his. It had not escaped his attention that in her retrieval of the tin, she had also smoothed over her mussed hair, had brushed her teeth. The considerations she made for him ones he had undertaken as she slept.

Surreptitiously, Anara's gaze flicked to his reflection. Her fingers on the tinctures so thoughtfully provided by Origins Research Group, finding one which would be most effective for the cut to his face.

Vadim's hands were on the hem of his shirt as she turned back. His muscular arms easily drawing it over his head and tossing it to the tiled floor. Her audible intake of breath when the raw flesh was revealed louder than his choked down groan.

'What the fuck happened?'

'Bar fight, like I said.' He laughed.

'Vadya, seriously.' She had moved forward instinctively, her gentle touch moving over the wounds on his arm. Trembling slightly to trace the ones on his abdomen. 'What did this?'

'A spiked baton.'

'But your t-shirt was—'

'I got changed; didn't want to alarm you.'

Anara stepped back, slipping effortlessly into the knowledge which came from years of owning her apothecary. The years of study. Years of caring for those who needed help they could not find anywhere else.

'Artem suggested I get the doctor, but I've had worse.'

She pivoted, eyebrows raised. 'Worse?'

'Perks of the job.' He offered her a smile. Vadim knew, despite his honesty, sharing his title and hinting at what he did may not be enough to keep Anara in his life. She could still run. She could still prove to be too fragile, too tender. This world was not one she may wish to remain in, no matter how he blunted the edges or shielded her.

He knew it would have to be her choice.

And the consequences would be his to bear.

Though, how calm she appeared was promising.

Vadim wondered if he should have explained things more clearly; if his use of unfamiliar terms had changed how she understood. The more complex nature of his organisation withheld.

'This will sting,' Anara stated, moving toward him, a doused cloth in her hand. The aromatic fabric suggested her words were kind.

Astringent and sharp, the reality bit.

'Fuck.' His teeth felt the pressure, forcefully gritted. Each sweep of the wet cloth wicked. He met her gaze. 'You're enjoying this.'

'You shouldn't keep secrets.' Anara pressed more firmly, removing a stubborn smear of dried blood from his abdomen. The hard muscle only increasing the heat in her core, her devotion to his healing causing her to chew on her lip.

Imagine the taste of his flesh on her tongue.

How she could dip into the ragged slices and suck on the pearls of his elixir. Make his body her banquet. Even now, bloodied and bruised, with the aftermath of the fight, she imagined he would be delicious.

The touch of his fingertips on her chin, tipping her head up, brought a catch to her breath. It would be so easy to glide closer, to take the one step into his body, to bend and taste his lips. Her chest heaved with the erratic inhales she forced into her lungs.

'I did it to protect you,' he said sincerely. 'I will always protect you.' It was a risk to make such a proclamation, yet Vadim felt it reverberate in every atom.

She nodded, her brow creasing. The desire refused to die, and the craving continued to demand her attention. Yet, history taught her to be cautious. Anara moved back, returning to rinse the cloth and refresh the herbal blend.

A pattern formed in hushed requests and obeyed words. Her hands wielding the tincture until his skin was clean, the injuries pristine. Leaving them to dry, she paused in her task.

The whispered suggestions in her mind growing louder.

Her arm reaching instinctively to trace the black lines of his tattooed wrist, moving higher. Curving over the prominent veins and solid muscle to follow the ink. She smiled when he shuddered, her fingers light at the nape of his neck, before dropping, brushing the outline of the large piece on his sculpted back.

A skull, surrounded with roses and a winding snake.

Vadim watched her progress in the mirror, his composure slipping with each exploration. The pressure building in his blood, his cock. The urge to spin her around and take her incessant.

Temptation to bind her wrists and kiss her howled.

'Roses?' Anara's voice was more a thought, faintly offered.

'I was incarcerated before I was eighteen,' Vadim explained, twisting slightly to meet her eyes. Their pupils blown obsidian. 'I'll never be held captive or controlled again.'

'Me neither,' she said, almost as softly as the question she asked.

His brow furrowed, another facet to unravel, another piece of her puzzle to decipher. *Kolya needs to work harder*, he thought.

Regretting the vulnerability, Anara removed her hands from his skin, hastily striding over to the sink's countertop to collect a small jar. Amber and clear, the honey's scent wound around the room. The small wand providing her with the distance she needed, even as the craving to gorge on him thudded in her veins.

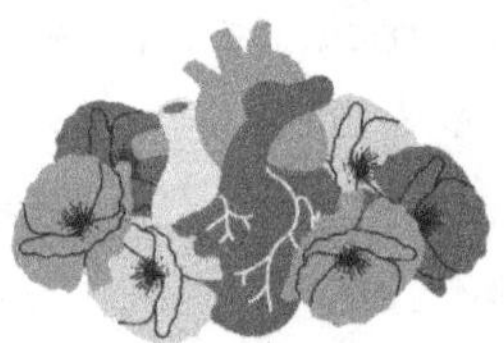

Standing in the mist of the morning, Mace Kersey tried to contain the heated rage in his gut. What had been a relatively successful club was a blazing inferno; thick black smoke and wild tongues spreading up and out from the building. The fire had spread with furious abandon, using gasoline and alcohol to feed the devastation.

Once the fire crews left, only a brittle skeleton would remain.

Ash and bone.

Charred beams and gutted floors.

Rubbing his palm over his beard, he watched the firefighters work, watched them try and douse flames refusing to die. The fluttering barrier tape almost inconsequential considering how vibrant the fire was, how it pushed people away. Even in the lingering chilled air, Mace was not the only spectator who found sweat forming.

The hiss of burning warmth against the cold current creating a low fog, exacerbating the sense of desolation.

Mace had deflected the suggestion this fire had been set to claim on his insurance. Had angrily accused the police officer asking the question of malicious entrapment. But the scent of accelerant and liquor spiralled in the wreckage, in the drifting, musky, smoke.

Which meant only one thing.

This was revenge.

Destruction for destruction.

'Boss?' Aeron Barnes lifted one eyebrow, witnessing Septer's leader seethe underneath falling flakes of ash.

'Morozov,' he spat.

# Nineteen

Relieved to discover Vadim had departed, Anara opted to continue her explorations begun the night before. The house was pristine, a beautiful series of rooms and features which spoke of restrained luxury. Quiet and tempered. The pieces chosen for quality, not the cost. Not the impression they would make.

Each addition was thoughtful, considered.

Practical.

It was so opposed to her home; the discordant colours and choices which she had loved. Lost. Anara gravitated to the icons in the corner of the sprawling main ground floor space.

An ivory candle burning before the range of painted images, the tall wooden Orthodox Cross. Gold frames and delicate lettering; words she did not understand. Saints Anara did not recognise. And religious figures she did.

'Do you wish to light a candle?' Sofiya asked, with reverence, her arrival behind Vadim's guest almost silent. The velvet soles of her shoes barely registering.

Turning, Anara's face darkened with a warm blush. 'No… I… I hope I've not been disrespectful, standing here—'

'No, not at all.' She smiled.

'Sofiya,' Anara began, 'may I ask you some questions?' Paused. 'I don't want you to feel pressured to answer them.'

Her throat dried, but she nodded.

'Why did you come to me, to Erinyes?'

The sigh was deep, her hands lacing then splitting, fingers picking at the opposite hand. Blonde hair falling to shroud her dipping face.

'Did Ilya not—'

'It's not that,' Sofiya said hastily. 'Let me make some tea.'

She followed the younger woman toward the kitchen at the front of the house; the large window overlooking the long driveway, trees hinting at the further arrival of spring. Buds creeping on branches.

'You'll never be alone here,' Sofiya said eyes suggesting more, 'so it's very safe. There are soldiers patrolling the estate, and a surveillance suite which is always manned. And the gatehouse, of course.'

'I understand.' Her mind turned over the comments, the underlying truth, the caution, in what had been delivered.

'Do you?' She placed the kettle on the stove.

'Vadya told me who he is.'

Sofiya's teeth caught her lower lip, her shoulders tensing. 'Then you also know there's a complex code, and… expectations.'

She nodded tentatively. After wrapping Vadim's wounds Anara had retreated to her own room, to shower, to find a needed release. To utilise the encrypted laptop to discover more.

But, she presumed, it would not be the whole truth.

That could only be found in talking with those who lived it.

Those who knew the reality behind the façade.

'We're a devout people,' Sofiya continued. 'And our faith requires us to make certain choices.'

'Of course.' The conversation between them in Erinyes recalled with a greater depth of comprehension. Anara's heart ached. 'I'm glad I could be there for you,' she said, almost a whisper.

Hoping the broken words would be enough.

Would be unheard by others.

Sofiya brushed a tear from her cheek. 'How's your progress with the store?'

'Slow.' She leaned against the marble island, one ankle crossing the other. 'I'm so grateful that Origins is helping, and Vadya's generosity is far beyond anything I could ask—'

'Vadim is a good man.' Sofiya said firmly, efficiently measuring the aromatic leaves, tipping them into the pot.

'Yeah, I think... maybe—'

'No, Anara, he's a good man.' She stretched for a tin of honey cakes and a small plate. 'He takes care of us, all of us; we're loyal because he's fair. He can be strict, but that's to be expected.'

Her heart seemed to heat, to flutter. A kick in Anara's stomach. In her blood. The knowledge he had been honest while she continued to lie eating into her skin, returning the blush to her face.

'And he likes you.' Sofiya grinned.

She shook her head, about to object.

'Just don't wander into places you don't need to be.' Sofiya's smile fell, brow creasing. Hoping she had not said too much.

Or too little.

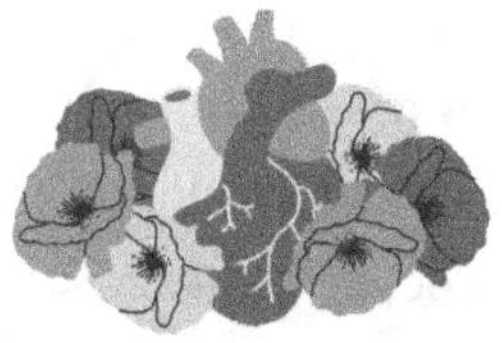

Conscious putting a bullet in their heads would not fix the problem, Mace had resisted the action. Instead, he had permitted Logan and Kassian to sit before him, his narrowed eyes finding only bowed heads. Dodging his stare with humiliation in their rounded shoulders. In how their hands kept fidgeting with their clothes.

Both men consumed with denied embarrassment.

Their sly escape from the club's flames bringing a simmering guilt which they struggled to overcome. Not from their survival at the expense of the staff they left behind, but in the judgement they expected. In the spiked barbs which drifted from their leader.

'What the fuck,' he hissed through clenched teeth, 'do you think was fucking appropriate in your cowardly fucking action?'

Logan's knuckles were almost chalk, his nails digging into the palms of his hands, above his thighs. A slow rivulet of sweat scoring through his spine. His throat dry. Mind hollow. The arguments considered in those moments after they rushed from the building lost in the first plumes of smoke they witnessed.

'You didn't think to fight? To stay? Fuck!' He slammed his fist on his desk; the whiskey in his glass shaking in decreasing ripples. The sides smeared with cocaine dust.

'There were too many—'

'Too many! *Too many*,' he sneered, mimicking a whining voice. His lips sour. Mace pushed up from his chair and began to pace. Anything to prevent drawing the firearm from his holster, from making an example of the men he once relied on.

Men he had selected.

Groomed.

'Kassian is right,' Logan ventured, lifting his brown eyes. 'They took out our systems, our security—'

'And you didn't think to check when the screens went dark?' Mace paused, leaning on the desk and looking from one man to the other; his guard and a soldier. He expected better.

'We knew you were safe,' Kassian stated, dodging the lie.

Though he had not directly seen the screens, he also knew they had not been without power. There had been no alert to suggest the cameras or alarms had been compromised.

Which meant Logan was not being honest.

And Kassian wanted to know why.

'We also knew there was no-one left in the club,' Logan added. 'Only some of the bar staff—'

'Staff we trusted to help us recruit people to trade.' Mace snatched his whiskey, draining the glass and refilling it; liquor spilling over onto the desk. 'You let them burn to death.'

'They were probably dead before then,' he argued.

'It sounded bad,' Kassian said. 'Really bad.'

'Sounded! You cunts didn't even go and check? Fuck!' He shook his head, the exhale heavy. Mace swallowed another mouthful of liquor, the warmth welcome, and levelled his gaze on Kassian. 'This is on you, you destroyed Erinyes, now Vadim fucking Morozov will destroy every single fucking thing we own.'

Kassian's hazel eyes refused to drop, he refused to blink; the sting hot. He kept his head high. Ire rushed through his blood, desperate to retaliate, to leap from the chair and throw a punch. To explain how this was *not* his fault. That Vadim was using Anara as an excuse to escalate the conflict between the Bratva and Septer.

With the slightest of raises of his eyebrows Mace took another long drink. *This soldier has balls*, he thought. 'I'll give you one thing, Kassian, his wife's pussy must be fucking exquisite, if Vadim's prepared to let us slaughter his entire brigade for her.'

# Twenty

The words had echoed. That there were places she should not discover and people always watching, that faith required choices. Devotion. Such thoughts were difficult for Anara to ignore, the luxury of time allowing her the opportunity to dwell on possibilities. On insinuated truths.

Of how the rooms she had been shown, had visited, were not quite aligned to the external dimensions of the property. Of how there must be hidden doors she had not found, locked access points to be revealed.

Though she had been given a tour the first morning, and was given freedom to leave the estate, walk the gardens, Anara had felt no desire to push those boundaries. She had other priorities; administrative tasks and insurance claims, grief to deny and lust to navigate. Such burdens had not departed, they continued to gnaw her bones, but there was now a greater sense of peace.

A different kind of tension.

The screams of her core begging for relief. For her to dig her talons into Vadim and feast. The longer she spent breathing his air the greater the hunger.

It was futile to deny it.

But Anara was not quite ready to admit to these cravings. She had fought too hard to have someone she did not fully understand have such control over her mind. Her body. Her soul. And Vadim threatened to do just that; his entire being radiated danger, power. Learning of his title as pakhan, and what she had then researched online, only emphasised her first impressions.

Feeling as though she was alone, though cognisant there could be others *somewhere*, Anara left her room and began to hunt. Her phone's screen providing her the images of the estate's aerial outline to compare with the internal dimensions.

The discrepancy seemed to be on the ground floor; the sketch she had made and overlaid suggested something was concealed. Outside, the windows only reflected her image. Cupping her hands to the glass did nothing but provide an abyss. And, she considered, maybe whoever was on the other side a close up of her curious gaze.

'Fuck,' Anara muttered, hoping no-one had discovered her attempts to figure out what was being obscured. She hastily pivoted toward the wide front door, rushing inside and closing it behind her.

Counted to ten, calming her breath.

No-one arrived to scold her, to challenge her.

She exhaled.

Confident she had determined where the disguised truth lay, Anara made her way to the library. Aside from the pantry, she rationalised there was nowhere else a door could be hidden.

Unless one was so perfectly placed in the pristine plasterwork of the hallway, which she felt was unlikely.

With her own suite above the front of the house, above whatever rooms she had not been shown, Anara was confused. She had heard no sound to betray anything below her; no voices, no music, no movement of bodies. And if the surveillance area was what had been divided from her, then, surely, there would be something to suggest the presence of people, of technology.

Entering the library brought a surge to her blood; her heart loud as she saw the padded window seat where she had fallen asleep. Where

Vadim had swept her into his arms and carried her to his bed. Chewing on her lower lip she closed her eyes. Dragged her hands through strands of raven hair. Cradled her neck.

*Focus*, she thought.

Dismissing the two external walls, she began to skim the solid wood bookshelves, the books. Leather spines and clothbound. Her pulse beat an erratic pace, reminding her of the possibility someone was watching her. Anara's eyes tracked the panelling, seams where shelves met, and the almost invisible joins between pillars.

Finding nothing.

'This is ridiculous,' she muttered. She considered asking Sofiya why the floor plan did not match the footprint. The exterior windows.

Hearing male voices made her pause. Hands dropping to her sides. Eyes darting around. Being in the library was not a cause for panic, nor chastisement. But something made Anara feel guilty. She reached for the first book she could grab, rushing to an armchair by the unlit fire, and hastily opened it.

'Hello kroshka,' Vadim said, striding through; Artem, Makari, Nikolai, and Pavel behind him, loitering politely in the doorway.

'Vadya.' She was breathless as their eyes met.

'Are you enjoying your book?' He choked down laughter, his dark eyes glinting with mirth. His lips quirking into a smile, which tugged on his healing wound, as he walked closer to stand before her.

'Yes.' Anara did not want to duck from his gaze, even as she felt heat continue to snake over her skin. 'Why?'

Vadim leant forward, gritting his teeth as his abdomen's cuts pulled against the dressing, the tender flesh. His mouth was almost touching the lobe of her ear. 'Because it's in Russian,' he whispered.

The combination of his scent and the warm exhale of his words only brought an intense ache to her quim. Her thighs clenching and breath caught. The shift of his body to rest one hand on the arm of the chair and cage her in making her heart shudder.

'Может быть, нам стоит пойти куда-нибдь ещё[32]?' Artem asked, head slightly tilted. Hoping Vadim would turn, would understand, would realise the importance in not revealing their reality to her.

Vadim retained his gaze on Anara, but pushed back slightly, blood on fire and body desperate. 'It's okay, Tyoma; go through.'

The advisor began to object.

'It's okay.' Vadim sighed, standing, twisting. 'I want to ask her about Origins, but you can go into the study and get settled.'

'Ты подвергают ебаный безрассудный[33].'

'Tyoma,' he warned, eyes narrowing. 'She knows who I am, there's no reason to keep her from my study.'

Artem's jaw ticked with the potential risk of such disclosure. His role was to advise, to guide. And his every suggestion to use this woman for what she could offer then kick her out, to tread with caution, to protect the fraternity, and prevent being seen as weak, was being ignored. He shook his head, but walked forward, aware the brigadiers followed.

Makari waiting in the doorway for Vadim.

With her eyes studying the movement, Anara observed the removal of one of the books from the shelves. Witnessed his fingers press into an innocent knot in the wood. Heard the click of the internal mechanism to release the hidden doorway; the silent swing of the shelving as it peeled open to create a double-width entry into the library.

Her mouth hinged open.

Then slammed shut as she sensed Vadim twist to face her again. A shiver pulsing over her skin when their eyes met.

'Tell me, wife,' he said with a softening to his tone, 'about how you first began working with Origins Research Group, and what you know about them.'

She watched him move to perch on the window seat; tried to figure out his purpose. 'What do you mean?'

---

[32] Может быть, нам стоит пойти куда-нибдь ещё - Russian for 'Perhaps we should go somewhere else?'

[33] Ты подвергают ебаный безрассудный - Russian for 'You are being fucking reckless'

'Did you find them, or did they find you?'

'I got an email, I think,' she said, casting her mind back; it had been so long that they had worked together, it was difficult to recall. 'Kasdeya visited and we talked about what support they could provide.'

'And what exactly is that?' Vadim's focus was trained on her, even as he registered his men in the study. Their drinks poured and seats taken. Artem's folded arms and defensive exhales.

She frowned. An uneasy weight roiled in her stomach; the anxious taste of her lies being detected. *Did he tell me who he was to test if I'd share my own truth*, she thought as her lips pressed together. The lower caught on her teeth and she saw him flinch.

Vadim shifted his position, pressure building. 'I'm curious; I've never heard of them before and they intrigue me, kroshka—'

'I doubt you know every single business,' she retorted, her voice a little strained. Her throat dry. Every nerve ice and fire, alternating fiercely under her flesh.

He laughed, head tilting. 'No, I don't. But if they're helping you, then I want to know who they are and what they do.'

'Why?' Anara's grip of the book increased as she fought regret over how she had reacted. She should have provided more relaxed answers, should have been more casual and open in her acknowledgements. 'It's not a competition Vadya, you've been so generous in allowing me to live here—'

'You're my wife,' he said smoothly.

Her breath caught at the words; that familiar heat spiralling through her entire body. Coursing through her blood. Settling in her core.

'It's my business to know you're safe,' he continued, standing, eating the distance between them in easy, long strides. 'Origins is a new entity to me, and I want to understand so that I can better protect you.'

'I don't need you to protect me,' she argued faintly, eyes on his.

Vadim shook his head. 'I know you don't need me to. But I want to, and to do that I need to have all the information.'

She swallowed; unsure if they were still talking about Origins, or if he was insinuating he wanted to know more of who she was. What she continued to hide.

'Their website looks impressive, but it doesn't tell me much,' Vadim said, turning from her and pacing; he needed the distraction. Staring into her eyes only dilated his until she was all he could think of. 'It doesn't tell me much about what they offer. I know they're helping pay the salaries and assist in the rebuild, but I don't want you to be let down—'

'You're my husband, I'm sure you'd help,' Anara interjected sweetly, forcing herself to move from the chair, 'if it came to it.'

Before the fire, Vadim paused. He rested his hand on the mantle, his eyes closing briefly. *This woman*, he thought. 'You really detest anyone helping you, don't you?'

'That way I don't get let down, do I?' She clutched the book to her chest. 'Your… men are getting restless, I should go.'

As she began to walk toward the hallway, he reached for her arm. A cascade of sparks snaking through them both from the touch, from the instant meeting of their eyes. The air still. Sound drowned. Her breath an erratic shudder, his a coiled ache.

'Pakhan, we do need to discuss progress,' Artem called, in Russian, from the study. His words cutting the tension.

Anara took the opportunity to leave; conscious of Vadim's stare as she did. His slow lick over his lips coupled with the sharp inhale and tick of his jaw, the pulling of his shirt collar away from his neck. The exhale emptying his lungs. His skin heated, he strode into the study and closed the doors, ignoring the smirks from his team.

'You need to be careful,' Artem remarked, continuing in Russian.

'And you need to leave it,' Vadim said through barely opened lips, a narrowing of his eyes. He grabbed the poured vodka and drained it, filled the glass again. 'Pasha, the poisoner?'

'Still no nearer to getting any real clarity, pakhan,' Pavel said. 'The pattern of kills is really sporadic.'

'But always men?'

'Yeah.' He nodded. 'Always men, and always ones who aren't really missed. From what I've found so far it looks like nearly three-quarters of them had police reports filed by the partner—'

'And it's not the partner who's doing it?' Vadim leant forward, using the desk's solid surface to support him. The wounds on his abdomen hot and arm sore. The cut on his cheek tight.

'I doubt it,' Pavel said. He ran his hand through his short hair. 'They aren't sad to see them gone, but I can't see it.'

'Keep on digging,' Vadim instructed. 'I want to know more; find me the types of drugs, and profile the men who are targeted, where they're from, everything. I need to know if they're a risk to us.'

Though Pavel inclined his head, his stomach rebelled. A settling chill which suggested he would fail, that Ksenia would be disappointed, that his progress with this task would only end with his death. He swilled his liquor in the glass before taking a sip.

'Tyoma, product?'

'All okay,' he confirmed. 'We've increased patrols after the fire, in case Mace tries anything, but there's been no indication of trouble. The levels are good, and we're continuing rotation to schedule.'

'And the payments to the communal fund?' Vadim rocked his head from side to side, redistributing pressure.

'All being made as usual.' Artem smiled. 'Vadya, we've got this. But you need to stay focused, especially now. Mace is angry, and your stunt at his club—'

'It was not a stunt,' he said, enunciating the words with precision.

'Okay, not a stunt.' Artem raised both hands. 'I get it, they're fuckers who need to be hunted and removed, and I love a good hunt, but you're making this personal.'

'It's not personal to want to erase traffickers from our territory.'

'I agree.' Artem leaned forward, resting his forearms on his thighs. 'I just want you to consider how this appears.'

'Tell me, Tyoma, how this appears.' Vadim kept his eyes focused on the advisor, the dark irises unflinching, even as his hand inched toward his drawer.

'You're doing this as payback, for Erinyes—'

'Am I?' The drawer opened.

'That's how it looks, pakhan.' He watched his leader, brown eyes on every movement. 'They tried to take Erinyes, Kassian tried to take Anara, and now you've burned down their club.'

'One of their clubs,' Vadim corrected, locating the knife by touch and removing it from the drawer. Placing it on the desk. 'Are you suggesting I am only capable of copying another, inferior, crime group?'

'Of course not!' Artem shook his head. 'I am your advisor, I'm telling you how this may be interpreted.'

'Pasha, Kolya, how do you think this looks?'

Pavel glanced at Nikolai, their eyes meeting briefly. In the corner of the room, Makari folded his arms and stifled a smirk.

'Vadya, pakhan,' Artem said, waving away the comments as both the brigadiers tried to speak, 'all I ask is that you consider what you're doing with this woman. You don't know her, or her history, beyond what small pieces we've found out. Be careful.'

'Kolya, what else have you found out?' Vadim swept up the knife, his fingers curling around the leather hilt, and dug the tip of the blade into a stack of papers. A slow pirouette made as he spoke. 'About Origins and about Anara.'

'Are you sure you want me to say?' Nikolai's eyes met Vadim's, the slight widening conveying his preference to share the information he had discovered alone.

'Origins,' Vadim stated.

'Kasdeya is legit,' Nikolai said. 'And what Anara's suggested, about them supplying herbs and such, is also legit. They're clean. They're not a threat.'

'Then how did they know who I was?' Vadim asked.

'That I can't answer.' He shrugged. 'I've spent hours digging through every piece of code I can get at, ours and theirs, and every single shred of their online presence, and there's nothing.'

'Fuck.' He sighed. 'Something about them being involved in this—'

'With her,' Artem muttered.

'—doesn't feel right.' Vadim readjusted his hold of the knife, pointing the tip toward his advisor. The narrowing of his eyes and set of his jaw emphasising the silent warning. 'They're Russian, but interested in an apothecary here—'

'So were we,' Artem said. Ducked to one side as Vadim's knife was released; sweeping over his shoulder to embed in the wooden panelling behind him. 'Fuck, Vadya!'

'I did warn you.'

Artem shook his head, eyes rolling. 'We engineered this to get our product into Erinyes; the apothecary's gone. Yes, it's being rebuilt, but in the meantime, we can find other avenues. Continuing this is a distraction we, and you, don't need.'

Makari plucked the knife from the wood, fingers smoothing over the rough gouge in the varnished surface. Quietly he requested the repair be completed, as soon as possible, as he returned the knife to Vadim.

'And yet you're always telling me to get laid,' he retorted.

'Laid yes, married no.' Artem kept his gaze on the knife the pakhan turned over in his palm. 'Look, she's stunning—'

'Kolya, stay for a minute,' Vadim interrupted, his knuckles chalk as his grip tightened. 'The rest of you have an operation to finalise.'

The brigadiers were quick to stand, Pavel reaching for his phone to begin the briefing with his team. Nikolai loitering.

'This isn't over.' Artem stood, smoothing down his suit.

'You're right, it isn't.' Vadim remained seated, dark eyes meeting his advisor's. The knife's blade glinting. 'She's my wife, even if it isn't official yet, and you'll treat her with the respect she deserves. Otherwise, next time, I won't aim to miss.'

# Twenty-One

She had been unable to sleep. Мастер и Маргарита[34] goaded her from the nightstand; evidence of how she had made a mistake. Made herself look a fool. The error replaying vividly every time she forced her eyes to close. Coupled with the searing memory of his touch, his gaze, her blood was on fire; a desire which Anara found almost unbearable.

Her attempts to find a release from it unsatisfying.

The precipice kept her caught. Each curl of her fingers failing, each pressured touch insufficient. Her body was rebelling. Anara craved more, so much more. Her established routine no longer delivering the relief she felt ready to submit to. It teased her.

One more twist of her fingers, one more catch in her breath, would unleash the scream which choked her throat. Always one more. Never enough, never permitting her to fall over the edge.

Hearing voices, drifting through the slightly open window, she let out an exasperated sigh. Resigned to frustration, she threw off the duvet and collected her discarded pyjamas from the floor.

Anara momentarily considered ignoring whatever the disturbance was, but continued dressing. Curiosity winning.

---

[34] Мастер и Маргарита - *The Master and Margarita*, a novel by Mikhail Bulgakov; first published in 1966-67 in the original Russian

She was already awake.

Already distracted.

What was one more thing to add to the tumultuous carousel of her life. With an awareness of being potentially seen, she moved toward the edge of the curtains, tipping the fabric slightly away from the wall. Her eyes drank in the scene, grateful for the lights being extinguished in the bedroom, and the illumination of the driveway.

There were three cars; black, sleek, engines running.

Men stood by open doors, their bodies clad in tactical clothing; an easy stance which suggested swift action. Ready to move, to attack, to strike. Their eyes uniformly trained on the small group by the central car, opposite the house's entry. She recognised them from earlier.

Held firmly between Pavel and Nikolai was Kassian, his body cowed and bloody. His clothes were smeared with spilled elixir, dark-grey shirt untucked and ripped. Boots scuffed. The braid he wore above the shorn sides of his head mussed and beginning to unknot.

A rush of chilled electricity reared over Anara's skin, teeth chewing her lower lip as her hand began to slide down her décolletage. Feeling the hardened, sensitive flesh of her nipples as her fingers glanced over thin fabric. The low sigh which escaped her throat stifled with the bite of her tongue when she watched Vadim stride into the light.

The knife at his side shining.

Kassian's head tipped up, bruises already developing on his cheeks, his jaw. Despite the pain, his cracked mouth quirked into a smile.

'As requested,' Artem stated, in Russian. He had swapped his usual suit for combat gear; the belt stocked with weapons. Firearm holstered beside ammunition packs and knives.

Vadim nodded, his own smile more easy than that of their guest. He drew closer, the conflicting lights creating an elongated, split shadow on the paving. Tossing his blade effortlessly from one hand to the other, he assessed Septer's soldier. The fool who had continued to pursue Anara, who had destroyed her business. Her home.

'You know, if you'd sent an invite, I'd've come,' Kassian said, voice raw and tongue tender. The lost teeth had scratched tissue when they had been knocked from his gums, swallowed. Spat.

Vadim remained quiet, his broad frame calm, breath steady.

At the window, Anara braced one hand against the wall as her other continued the descent. Tucking below the waistband to curl lower.

'I never got the chance to attend the wedding,' he added.

The punch landed on Kassian's side, his pained howl coupled with a stumbling collapse; held up by the two brigadiers. Nerves carrying the blunt impact from his liver to chase his system. Intense and brutal. Every attempt to breathe difficult, his blood pressure falling. His knees bending and whole body sagging from the effort.

Vadim stepped back, his focus dropping to his knuckles briefly. The slightest of turns of his head to a muted moan behind him; not enough to betray he had registered it. Enough to confirm his suspicions.

He smiled.

By the wall, Anara's eyes closed, her body lost to her touch. On the wet heat of her skin and volume of her pulse. The erratic shudder of her exhales. The pain of her teeth biting into her tongue.

Her next moan caught before it left her mouth.

'Nice try,' Kassian gasped, his body relying on the men who gripped his upper arms, but breath slowly regulating. 'Tell me, Vadim, do you love how your wife tastes? I know she's delicious—'

The blade to his throat cut off his words, but not his smile.

A small pearl of blood formed at the tip.

'I had so much time in her apartment,' Kassian began, eyes meeting the pakhan, 'her home. No sign of a husband.'

'Vadya,' Artem cautioned, moving to stand closer to his leader.

This time her moan grew more desperate to escape; her syncopated hips and fingers fuelled by the light glinting on his knife, of Vadim's quiet strength. Of how she felt the radiance of his dominance, his control; skills she wished to experience.

'She's intriguing, isn't she,' Kassian said. 'She lost so many beautiful things in that fire—'

'The fire you lit,' Vadim hissed through barely opened lips. The knife a constant pressure to his flesh; no hint of a tremble.

Kassian laughed.

Anara clenched her jaw; hearing the words slowed her movement.

Stalled her climb to the zenith.

'Not before I fully explored her… things.' His smile was crooked. The feeling was returning to his legs, the pain ebbing. 'Those pretty pieces of lace and silk, they wrapped me so well as I fucked them.'

The knife sliced, blood dripping.

'Vadya, not yet.' Artem stepped forward, placing his hand on Vadim's forearm. Met his leader's gaze and shook his head.

Seeing the incision, the way Vadim was ready to destroy Kassian, in her name, made the heat return to her skin. Made the glistening warmth more responsive. Anara's body a mass of moths, slithering and keening for release; the sweet precipice reached and surpassed with a fractured exhale. Her entire frame tense, then weak.

Bringing her to her knees.

'Take him away,' Vadim ordered, hand dropping to his side. Hushed words which he knew he must say. Even as the desire to kill him gnawed in his bones, ate into his blood; the suggestion of how Kassian had spent unknown hours inside Anara's home creating a web of tension in Vadim's system.

*Tasted her, fucked her.*

Vadim knew she had not been there, that she had been with him at the carnival. But, hearing Kassian's taunts and imagining how he had acted only increased the rage.

He knew he should not, but Vadim followed the group steering him to the garage; to the underground tunnel, to the cells.

Peering, unseen, from the window, Anara watched two of the cars fill then leave, toward the gatehouse. Makari drove the last vehicle into the garage, slow to accommodate the remaining men taking Kassian inside the dark shadows of the building.

Anara dropped the heavy curtain, leaning against the wall, her legs stretched out before her. A peace coated her limbs, her mind; her climax lingering and breath finding a calmer pattern.

Even as the realisation of Kassian's actions screamed.

*Him. It had been him who destroyed everything.*

She wondered if that was partly why Vadim had been so intent on hunting him, but dismissed it. Believing it was too conceited to think he would be that concerned about her loss.

But the idea snagged, and she pushed herself up. Crossed the room to grab her robe from the door and set off to find the men. Her steps sure and swift as they left the first floor, left the stairs, the house, and felt the chilled night air on her face. It was welcome. The sting of the breeze cooling the lust and fury which simmered, entwined in every synapse.

The garage had several doors along the facing wall, allowing easy access to the range of vehicles held within. And though the bonnet of the car Makari had parked remained warm, there was no-one in sight. The emptiness made her wrap her arms around her waist, her head twisting to take in the gleaming metal, the organised tools.

With a frown, she retreated. Certain she had not heard them enter the house, nor seen them as she made her way outdoors. Determined, Anara scanned the open space of the ground floor, then made her way to each room, even checking the pantry. Entering the library, the study door was closed. But, aside from wherever the surveillance room was, it was the only option which remained.

Her fingers curled to her palms, her lips rolling over each other, as she contemplated the shelving. Exhaling to steady herself, she found the book the men removed earlier and then the button to release the door.

The click was loud, causing her to glance behind her.

No-one.

Not even Sofiya.

Her heart pounded in her ears, her throat dry. The house should be full of people; of men patrolling, of people working, of him. Vadim. Even when he departed on business she felt his presence. But now, there was only a void. A silence. Uncomfortable and oppressive.

She stepped into the study and immediately felt a sharp edge bite into her neck. The cold pressure smooth, and gone almost as quickly as it had been placed there.

'Kroshka!' Vadim remarked, sliding the knife back into the sheath at his waist. 'I'm… I didn't know it was you.'

'It's okay,' she said breathlessly. Her chest heaving. The ghost of the knife's touch bringing her fingers to her skin. Tracing the ignited fire. Her breath held when his fingers tenderly arrived above hers.

Their eyes meeting.

'Did I hurt you?' His voice was gravel. His gaze devouring her, pupils dilated and drowning in her scent. Her image. The parting of her lips and heat from her flesh. A lingering aroma of her arousal, evidence of how she had played, bringing a painful ache to his soul. He brought his other hand to her lower back, resting it there after a brief hesitation.

She shook her head.

Her mind was fighting; submit or flee.

Fall into this, whatever this was, or run.

Maintain the walls she had built or let him in.

Instinctive and impulsive, she tipped her head higher and dragged her hand lower; hoping he would follow the route Anara mapped, would continue to hold her.

The press of Vadim's palm on her back was creating a branch over her body, a secure web which moved her closer. The distance between them a breath. Her splayed fingers on her chest held with his own, laced and curled, crushed between their bodies.

His eyes dipped to her lips, rose to her eyes, over and again; his silent request, his plea for consent, unspoken. Anara's smile hopeful as her free hand stroked through his hair, cradling the nape of his neck.

Lips connecting with no sense of chaste sweetness. It was hunger, it was bite. He manoeuvred them to the wooden panelling, hand turning to cushion their impact before entwining in her curls. Vadim's tongue licked the seam of her lips, finding her open, and reciprocal; their banquet one of mutual gratification.

Each pressured caress creating a deeper attraction.

Each exploratory touch affirming their connection.

The respite for breath made with foreheads together; sensual eye to sensual eye. Vadim's gentle tracing of her face at odds to the pressured weight of his cock against her body; the slow grind of her hips bringing an anguished closing of his eyes.

'Kroshka,' he sighed.

'What does that mean?' Her voice was as husky, as needy. The hot aftertaste of their kiss on her tongue. Despite all she had coxed from her body, she wanted more. Wanted to feel what he could do.

He shook his head, smiling wryly; brows still together, the movement brushed their noses. The heat between them coiled and heavy. It would be effortless to pick Anara up, to take her to his desk, to consume her. To lay her out and create a feast from her body. Temptation hummed in his blood. Another kiss an offering, a vow. Stubble grating soft skin.

'Vad…,' Artem began, then chuckled. Witnessing the blushing stare Anara offered from behind Vadim's broad shoulders, the pakhan's hasty movement to create a gap. Pulling at clothing.

'I should go,' she muttered, eyes darting between the two men.

'No, please—'

'You've got to deal with… this,' she said, a deep frown creasing her skin. She felt his hand reach for hers, but dodged it; fingertips glancing over each other as she walked out, quickly, without looking back.

They had returned to the café, the trio of women occupying one table and Maksim watching discreetly from another. He had arrived, explaining he was her driver, while she was being served breakfast; Sofiya refused to allow Anara to prepare the meal.

'You look tired,' Bryony stated, stirring the teabag around her mug, a burst of aromatic herbs drifting on the steam. 'Not sleeping?'

'Just a lot on my mind,' Anara replied. Which was not quite true. The majority of her thoughts were tangled up with one man. Vadimir Morozov. Involuntarily her fingers went to her mouth, tracing her lips, the smile a betrayal of the hunger in her heart.

'A lot, right.' Kerezen winked. 'And I suppose that happens to look a *lot* like a certain Russian bar owner?'

Her eyes widened, mouth opening to object, but finding no words. It was futile. These women knew more about her than anyone, and they would figure it out soon enough. 'Maybe.'

'Finally!' Kerezen laughed, leaning forward. 'You deserve happiness, Anara, and he's a good man.'

She swallowed, unsure if she could agree. Vadim had supported her and there had been no pressure, that was certain; however, he was also a killer. But, she reasoned, so was she. There was blood on her hands, just as much as, she supposed, on his.

Perhaps, if anyone was ever to accept her, he would.

'And definitely not a bad sight to wake up to,' Bryony added.

'If I wasn't living with him, it'd be easier,' Anara said, a frown forming then fading. 'I could… fuck him then walk away if it didn't work out. But I can't, can I? And I don't really know that much about him, yet… and, he certainly doesn't know me.'

'You're making it more complicated than it needs to be.' Bryony's eyes flitted to Kerezen then back to Anara. 'I know you're in this whole fake marriage thing,' she said, lowering her voice, 'but that also means it won't be forever. And there's always options, I'm sure Origins would help if you needed out of there. And I've a couch.'

'I know.' She sighed. Took a sip of tea; the lemon and ginger failing to remove the remembered heated taste of his lips, curl of his tongue, pressure of his body against hers. Her eyes lingered on the mug, on her rings, mind spiralling. 'We kissed.'

Bryony and Kerezen exchanged glances, smiles.

She lowered the mug, a slight tremble in her hands, and brought her face level with the women.

'And?' Bryony prompted, leaning forward and eyes wide, coaxing. A request for more detail. 'Anara! And?'

'That's it.' Her tongue lapped her lip, teeth catching.

'That's it?! No,' Kerezen said with a shake of her head, short auburn strands shimmering, 'was it terrible?'

'Not at all.' She covered her face with both hands, feeling the glow of her skin. 'It was… fuck, it was amazing.'

'Then why—'

'We got interrupted,' she explained, slowly removing her hands then propping her chin on upturned palms, fingertips on her cheekbones.

Kerezen glanced surreptitiously around to the assigned guard Anara had arrived with. 'And if you hadn't?'

'I'd have more to tell you.' Anara laughed, hands moving to hide her broad smile. Her eyes creasing with mischief.

'Would you now?' Bryony rocked back in her chair, mirth bringing a glint to her gaze.

Anara exhaled and nodded. 'He's got a very large—'

'Really?'

'—desk.' Her eyes grew larger, shaking her head. 'Kerezen!'

'What?' Kerezen objected. 'Just because I like women, I'm allowed to appreciate the male form.'

'There's a lot to appreciate,' Anara murmured, recalling how every ridge of his hard body had pressed against hers. How desperate she had felt, how necessary it had seemed to explore every inch, to taste him, to devour everything Vadim had to offer.

'Enough to accept a desk?'

'Yes, Bry,' Anara said, words almost a breath. Her eyes closed, the image of his knife against Kassian's throat bringing a kick to her quim, to her heart. How it felt to have the blade against her skin causing an ache to gnaw through her bones. Vadim was a man who promised danger and protection, she was certain of it.

'Just be careful,' Bryony said gently, resting her hand lightly on her friend's forearm. 'This has all happened fast, in difficult circumstances, which could influence how you're feeling.'

'I know.' Anara nodded.

'But that doesn't mean it isn't real.' With a fold of her arms, Kerezen leaned on the cloth-covered table. 'The challenges may be exacerbating what had already taken root between you.'

She nodded again. Chewed on her lip, considering revealing what had happened the night before; how that would change their plans. 'He's more like us than we thought.'

The women looked to each other, slyly toward Maksim, then back to Anara. Noticing the attention shift, his brown eyes lifted from his phone and met Anara's steady gaze. He mouthed the question, checking she was okay, and receiving the soft incline of her head returned to the texts from Yeva.

'What do you mean?' Kerezen whispered.

'He's a powerful man,' she admitted, her voice barely audible, 'with many secrets.'

'What kind of secrets?' A chill ran over Bryony's skin.

'None that we need to worry about, I think,' Anara said with greater confidence than she felt. 'But… last night, at the house, Kassian—'

'That creep.' Bryony's lips soured.

'—he was brought to the house, really badly beaten.'

'So, your man gets jealous?' Kerezen's eyes remained fixed on her friend, gauging if Vadim was a threat, if Anara was too blind to the reality of her situation.

'Yeah, I guess.' She forced a smile; considering revealing the exact nature of Vadim's role was not something to be shared. Her eyes fell to the mug of tea, the mellow colours soothing.

'At least that means we've one less problem,' Kerezen stated.

'Good point.' Bryony nodded, unseen by Anara, as she and Kerezen shared a silent moment; an unvoiced agreement to dissect the situation in private. To determine if an intervention was required before Anara was beyond saving, aware of the history. The potential heartache.

Anara raised her head steadily, eyes sliding to Maksim briefly. 'I'm still perfecting the blend for Logan, but it's almost ready.'

'Logan?' Bryony asked.

'You managed to get a new supplier?' Kerezen spoke at the same time, their questions wrapping together.

'I identified the man,' Anara explained, 'who'd been loitering outside Erinyes. And when Kasdeya visited me, she brought a tin of useful herbs and a replacement grimoire.'

'That's... wow... they're doing so much.' Kerezen's eyes glistened with quickly gathering tears. She hastily swept the moisture away as one drop began to snake down her freckled skin.

'I know.' Anara's face reflected similar emotion; all three women a mass of gratitude. 'I couldn't believe it when she gave me that, especially after all Origins had promised to do.'

'So we can keep working?' Bryony asked, husky. 'Helping?'

'Absolutely.' She paused, contemplating how to explain the source of the next piece of information she intended to share. Even if she still needed to understand how Vadim had known, how Vadim had kept the knowledge from her. The contradiction, cognisant of her own hesitation to share the truth, coaxing her to soften her anger. 'Kassian set the fire, that night, and I think he and Logan know each other.'

'Why would he do that?' The frown cut deep in Kerezen's brow. 'Was he just pissed you refused his advances?'

She shrugged.

'Men,' Kerezen muttered in response, shaking her head. Scoffing as she leaned back, accompanied by a roll of her eyes.

'So, when do we get to Logan?' Bryony's voice was faint, one hand covering her mouth as an additional precaution.

Anara smiled, a renewed venom in her blood.

# Twenty-Two

Staring into the mirror, she tried to convince herself to move. The swiped steam began to creep over the glass once more, rivulets of condensation sliding. The pristine white marble tiles, sparkling chrome, thick towels, a sweet luxury which enabled her to relax. To compose herself before the scrutiny would start.

Soft, a sigh escaped her lips, Anara's fingertips pressing more firmly into the countertop. Her arms taut. She inhaled deeply, exhaled slow. A plea to settle the rampant chase her heart made in her chest, the erratic beat of her pulse.

'Anara?' Sofiya called, beyond the closed en-suite door.

She stood, straightening her spine. 'Yeah.'

'Do you need anything to eat, before you leave?'

'No, I'm okay to wait until the meal.' She stepped closer to the dark wood, tempted to open the door and find some reassurance.

Sofiya's hands turned over before her stomach. 'I just get nervous about things like this, and I find something to eat helps.'

Anara smiled, eyes closing. 'I'm okay, thank you.' She paused. 'I've some tinctures I can take if I need anything.'

'Of course.' Loitering by the door, she picked at her fingernails. 'Just call if you need help getting into your dress, or anything.'

She offered her thanks, returning to the mirror. The distant click of the bedroom door audible enough to know she had been left alone. Her teeth caught on her lower lip, amber eyes lifting to assess pale flesh and lean limbs. A ghost against the marble; raven curls stretched by a shroud of heated water.

'It's just a dinner,' Anara whispered, even though it felt like more. An expectant tension threaded through her breath. Through the air.

She had not seen Vadim since her hasty departure. Whatever work Artem had needed him for had kept him occupied, and allowed her to get out of the house unseen. Anara shook her head at that thought; *there were men everywhere*, Sofiya had said. Patrolling. Watching. It was likely Vadim may even have witnessed her rushed breakfast, Maksim's arrival as her guard. But Vadim had been nowhere in sight.

'You can do this,' she said more forcefully. Rolling her shoulders and reaching for the moisturiser. The beautifully fragranced pots discovered that first morning, the other items she had bought herself.

Every sweep of her fingers over her skin, through her curls as she dried her hair, over the silk she slipped into, felt like foreplay. Her body a tumbling cascade of sparks ready to ignite. The remembered pressure of his lips on hers, the secure embrace and solid muscle of his body, set to devour her entirely.

Years of living alone had perfected Anara's skills in dressing despite complex and awkward outfits. Had honed the methods to style hair with only her own hands.

Even as they trembled.

Anara closed her eyes briefly before opening the door, her breath trapped, her pulse loud. In her left hand, she held the sleek black heels she planned to complement the long dress; the fabric in a matching shade, with a discreet burgundy stitching along the corseted bodice and hem. Bare foot, she padded along the landing, conscious of each step closer to the stairs.

As though tonight held greater importance than it should.

*You're making too much of this*, she thought. *It was just a kiss, and this is just a dinner. This is all fake.*

Reaching the stairs, she held the bannister and descended. The slit in the floor-length dress almost reached her hip. When she first saw it in the dressing room, she had laughed. It was something she doubted she would ever need to wear, and she had intended to leave it in the house when she moved out. Yet, now it wrapped her body to perfection, Anara felt nothing but gratitude for it.

'Моя жена[35],' Vadim breathed, reverent, shaking his head, his whole body reacting to her. Eyes tracking her graceful steps, tongue slow over his lips. 'Ебать, ты красивая[36].'

She frowned, not understanding the words.

But the way it was delivered, the adoring sentiment, instantly made heat pool at the apex of her thighs. Made her skin bloom with colour. Her mouth opening slightly as she accepted his upturned hand; sliding slim fingers into his palm.

Vadim was tempted to spin her around, sweep her into his arms and carry her up the stairs. To worship her body as his altar. Even her sweet perfume, delicately scenting his inhales, promised a taste of divinity. Of sated hunger. However, Vadim was cognisant of his responsibilities and that meant attending this event.

It would be of benefit for them to be seen together. As a couple.

Such a thing would settle some rumours, and perhaps generate new ones. Anara would not impact his dedication to his fraternity. He would never allow it. But, she had impacted him, and, as he provided a chaste kiss on her knuckles, he never wanted that influence to end.

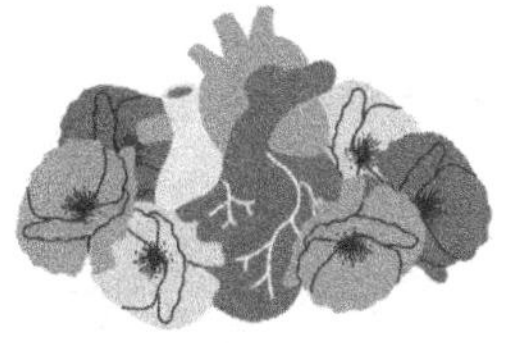

---

35 Моя жена - Russian for 'My wife'
36 Ебать, ты красивая - Russian for 'Fuck, you're beautiful'

The car delivered them to Prey's entrance. With instructions to remain in the vehicle, Anara watched Vadim effortlessly leave; his tailored suit only causing her body to crave him more deeply. The black material of each layer hugged his musculature without being too restrictive. Anara's eyes greedy as they followed his movement.

Her door opened for her, his hand offered once more.

Their eyes met, lingered, before she demurely lowered her gaze and stepped out. The heels he had crouched to slide onto her feet securely supporting her as she felt the cool evening air wrap her exposed arms, the breeze catch her curls.

Vadim tightened his grip on Anara's hand, steering her through the double doors toward the bar. Behind them, Makari followed. Though she did not recognise the staff behind the counter, they acknowledged Vadim and had their drinks already poured.

A glass of vodka.

A verdant muse.

'How…,' she began then stopped herself. His world was an entirely different one to what she was accustomed to. Everything Anara had, all she had lost, had been achieved through sacrifice, through heartache. It had been a challenging fight. This, this was something else.

'Everyone's waiting for you, pakhan,' Makari said softly, leaning in to his leader's side. His own suit as crisp, with the cut allowing easy access to his weapons, should they be required.

'Everyone?' Anara's heavily lined eyes flitted from one man to the other. 'I thought we were just having dinner?'

'We're having dinner,' Vadim replied, 'but there's a few more people who'll be joining us.'

'You could've said,' she muttered. Taking a larger sip of her drink.

'I did.' He began to lead her away from the bar.

'When?' The herbal liqueur was doing little to steady the nervous spike in her blood; Anara recalled Sofiya's suggestion for food and shook her head, cursing her refusal.

'In the car.' He paused, pivoting to face her. With curled fingers, he tipped her chin up so he could look her directly in the eye. 'We can leave if you don't want to do this.'

She slowly traced her lower lip with the tip of her tongue, the verdant muse traces coating the taste buds. This close, she saw how it caused his pupils to dilate; black eating the umber. *Perhaps he did tell me*, Anara thought, *but I was too distracted imagining what was under that damned suit*. 'No, I'm okay,' she managed, husky.

'Shame,' he quipped, smiling, 'I'd've preferred taking you home.'

Anara was about to speak, to agree, when the door opened; a man she vaguely recognised standing ready to usher them through. A similar sunburst design on the tiled floor, leading them to an underground suite of rooms. The space opened up at the base of the curving staircase, the chrome and marble of the bar and restaurant replicated with familiar Art Deco style. Snakes and geometric lines, leather and glass.

It was breathtaking.

There were several different gaming tables, with croupiers ready to work, bar staff carrying trays laden with glasses and bottles. Around the perimeter were booths, each individually lit, with velvet walls and thick fabric swagged to one side. Privacy an available option.

At the far end of the room, the sleek bar's series of leather stools were almost empty. Most of the people stood in small groups, their faces turned to the new arrivals, partly-consumed drinks in their hands. An archway, to the left of the bar, provided a glimpse of laid tables, and the promise of dinner.

'Who are these people?' Anara barely opened her mouth as they continued downward.

'My people.' He stroked his thumb over the back of her hand. 'Don't worry, kroshka, you're perfectly safe.'

Her eyes slid to him, seeing how his jaw had set. How there was a shift in the tension of Vadim's stance. Each step forming further armour around his very soul. The leader reclaiming his crown.

'You didn't say it was *her*,' Yeva hissed, gripping Sofiya's upper arm and pushing her into the dining area. Her eyes were wide, glancing back to Maksim briefly then returning her attention to her friend.

'I—'

'Has she said anything?'

'About what?' Sofiya tried to extricate herself from the woman's firm hold. 'If you mean about the shop, no, she's not really—'

'Not really?' Yeva released her hand, raking it through her short hair and then bringing it to her neck. To take her cross and grip the smooth metal. 'What if she's spoken to Vadim?'

'She wouldn't.'

'Are you sure?' Yeva stepped closer to Sofiya, her words a frantic whisper, urgent and tinged with a choked sob. Her confession, collapsing before Anara Eden in Erinyes, recalled with each shuddering inhale. The consequences of it screaming.

It was a death sentence.

And though she had been prepared to kill Maksim then, to use that as an escape for her children, for her, Anara's refusal had caused her to halt. To think. To consider alternatives.

Not that any had formed. Yet.

'Yeva,' Maksim said, arriving beside the two women, 'come on, you can't hide in here; Vadim's here, with his wife.'

Sofiya's relief at the intervention was poorly concealed, Maksim's brow creasing with brief concern. The sight dismissed with the pressure to be present for his leader. To ensure they presented well. Though he was content to remain a solider, he also knew how important it was to demonstrate loyalty.

This was the ideal opportunity to do that; to be safely amongst those who he worked with every day, the wives who supported them, and the esteemed pakhan who made it all possible.

Vadim drew Anara closer to his side, his tattooed hand providing her with the reassurance he believed she required. His eyes trailed the room to assess who was present, who was not. He knew which soldiers were assigned to protection, who were asked to act as waiters, as attendants, during the event. Observing Maksim, with a clearly distressed Yeva, step from the dining area, brought a slight narrowing to his eyes.

Following his gaze, Anara's breath caught.

'Are you okay?'

'Fine,' she replied, smiling. Another woman she had met; this one had been seeking to murder her husband. Had been seeking a way out of a life she felt destined would lead to their deaths.

The concept flared, spreading voraciously through her mind.

'What do I say if I'm asked about your work?' She hoped that would provide some information she could use, something to ease her anxiety about exactly what she was participating in.

'They won't ask.' He continued to guide her toward the bar, offering guarded greetings to those they passed.

The hushed conversations which paused, then resumed, were being conducted in Russian; Anara was lost. Some faces were familiar, some not. But they all watched her. She fought to keep her breath calm, keep the nervous chill from becoming a hot sweat.

'Ah those early days of marriage,' Artem said in English, more loudly than was required, 'where you don't want to leave the house.'

'Tyoma,' Vadim warned.

'What?' He retorted, reverting to their native Russian, and speaking more quietly. 'I told you to fuck her and kick her out, but you're still playing pretend.'

'I'll slit your throat here, if I have to.'

Beside them, Anara's eyes tracked the interaction; the words meant nothing, but the venom she heard in Vadim's tone sent a kick through her blood. Awakened the carnal hunger which had been overwhelmed by her concerns. 'Vadya, this is a party, isn't it?'

Vadim tightened their entwined hands, nodding but not shifting his focus from his advisor. Jaw ticking.

'Then, perhaps, let's relax and enjoy it.'

'Your *wife* is an intelligent woman,' Artem remarked.

'Anara, it's so great to see you again,' Ksenia Solovyova said with a wide smile. Behind her, Pavel's head inclined in a small nod.

'Ksenia, right?' Anara chewed on her lip for a moment. 'You manage Prey, for Vadim?'

'Correct.' She turned to the bar, waving at Anoushka. 'I believe you prefer a verdant muse? You'll need plenty; I remember when I attended my first event like this, and it was… exhausting.'

She was about to agree, when she saw a man striding toward them, a long beard covering much of his chest. His body clad in a black ryassa and an almost floor length anderi, polished shoes landing firmly on the tiles. Her mouth dried, convinced their ruse was about to shatter.

'Вадимир Львович Морозов[37]!'

'Father Matvey.' Vadim wrapped his arm around her waist, pulling Anara to stand by his side more closely.

'So, you marry without consulting me,' the Father Superior said, 'or following any of our customs.'

Sensing the words were a chastisement, Anara could only smile and hope Vadim would rescue her from it. The religious man was jovial in his appearance, but the delivery of the phrases sounded entirely opposite.

'When you know, you know,' Vadim stated, in English, dipping to kiss the crown of her hair. 'Please, my wife is still learning Russian.'

The touch of his lips sent a surge of electrical heat through her body in an instant. She leaned more heavily into him, relying on his strength to keep her from crumbling to the floor. *You're better than this*, she thought as she gathered her composure.

Anara reminded herself that this was a game.

This was to sell their fake relationship, to ensure people knew she was protected. The kiss in his study was a mistake. His behaviour since only to put her at ease so they would not be exposed as frauds.

---

[37] Вадимир Львович Морозов - Russian for 'Vadimir Lvovich Morozov'

This was purely a theatre, one begun when Kasdeya had visited.

The sooner she accepted that, the better.

She forced a smile. Even as the air around them grew more heated, the words became distorted, the surroundings blurred. Attention fading as they spoke, Russian and English weaving an intoxicating spell.

'Kroshka, follow me,' he said faintly, his fingertips tracing her cheek to tilt her head gracefully toward him.

Complying, Anara laced her fingers with his. Their walk through the guests done with ease; everyone happy to acknowledge them then move out of the way. He never had to say a thing; a look, a nod, a shake of his head, enough to convey intent.

Such power only made Anara fall harder. Not because of his status, but because he had earned it. Whatever he had achieved, she was still unsure, but the title he had been awarded, the way he was respected, it was evidence of his character. These were the things which kept men off her list. These were things which made her want to finally stop fighting and relinquish control.

In every way.

Which was a dangerous thing to feel for someone like her, someone who had only experienced suffering and heartbreak. Someone who had learned to protect herself and remain dominant.

Reaching a door marked for staff, they walked through; the guard on the entry opening it for them as they reached it. Hearing the click as the door shut, Vadim twisted her into the white painted wall and caged her against it, one hand pinning her wrists above her head.

All sense of dominance was being devoured by the proximity of his gaze, his body, his scent. Anara was a swallow away from sliding to her knees. From turning and bowing her back. Anything he asked.

'Anya,' he breathed, resting his forehead on hers. His exhale soft, eyes closing, as Vadim sensed her tremble.

She remained silent. The firm manacle of his hand was a fire which consumed her entire being. Her mind a void. Meeting his eyes, when he opened them, a fuel that would consume her soul. The amber flecks in the umber were barely visible; his pupils blown obsidian. Staring into them, she saw her open mouth, her flushed skin.

She saw devotion.

Such things terrified her. Forced her to blink. 'We'll be missed,' she managed to say, her voice raw, husky.

He released her wrists, fingers trailing down her bare arms, feeling the sway of her body below his touch. The slow lowering of her limbs to allow him to sweep over the curve of her shoulder, her clavicle. Skirting the hem of her dress, the swell of her breasts. He felt the pounding beat of her heart; it was wild, a siren to his blood.

'Do they believe you?' Anara ventured. Her words felt detached, as though she had not spoken them. Not quite present.

He frowned, his eyes on the soft pressure of his knuckles against her snowy décolletage; tattooed skin against unmarked, a few tendrils of raven curls teasing her neck. The glint of his titanium band under bright lighting.

'Do they believe we're married?'

'If they didn't,' he said, voice thick with lust, 'they will now.' Taking her head in his hands, his lips met hers. The initial teasing of his mouth quickly becoming more forceful, more desperate. The seam stroked with his tongue until their caress deepened. Stubble grating.

Her hands reached for his wrists, dragging over fabric, dancing over shoulders; the ridges of something beneath causing her to hesitate for just a moment. Too firm to be the waistcoat. Forgotten with the sigh he made into her mouth, the slide of one hand to her neck, to her waist. To her hip, the tips of his fingers skating over the slit of her dress.

Without thought, Anara hooked her leg around him, drawing him further into her body; feeling how hard he was. Her tongue flicked over his, her hands drifting to rake through his hair.

By the door, voices drifted. Undecipherable. But insistent. Causing Vadim to groan and pull back. His mouth returning to hers, delivering a series of lingering kisses, until he could not ignore his commitments. Her leg returning to the floor, shaking.

'Do you have any idea what you do to me?' Vadim's forehead rested against hers once more, his breath irregular.

'I can guess,' she said, a rough purr to her voice. The slick heat was a pulse which sought more. Sought devouring, sought claiming. Every part of her radiantly craving the man standing before her, her forearms resting on his broad shoulders.

He captured them, pulling her hands to his chest. Holding her palms above his heart for a moment before bringing her right hand up. His eyes on the bridal set she wore, for him. 'I need to get you a better ring.'

'You don't,' she objected. Logic began to erode lust; this was only a game. *This was fake.*

'You are beautiful, kroshka,' he said, willing his body to calm. To find the dignified presentation which would be required. 'You deserve a ring which matches your beauty and importance to me.'

She began to object.

'You. Are. Beautiful.' His gaze fell to her lips; swollen from their kiss, the red lipstick slightly smudged. 'Моя прекрасная жена[38].'

'What does that mean?' Anara could not quite breathe normally. Her chest tight and core screaming; vacillations between desire and reason slow to settle. Hope fluttering in some distant promise.

He smiled, shaking his head.

'I need to take Russian lessons,' she muttered.

'It's time to eat.' He pulled her hand tenderly to his lips to provide another kiss. 'Do you still have that book?'

'Which… oh, that book.' She felt unsteady as she walked, falling into him slightly then recovering to straighten her spine. 'Yes.'

'Read it yet?'

'Clearly not.' Anara glanced to him, the door growing nearer. She did not understand why Vadim had felt the need to suddenly drag her away

---

[38] Моя прекрасная жена - Russian for 'My beautiful wife'

from everyone, but now, about to return, she was glad of the reprieve; it was another act which made her believe that, perhaps, there was more to this fake marriage. 'Maybe you should read it to me.'

'I could,' he said, halting just before the door, 'but, surely, you'd not understand a word; Михаил Булгаков deserves to be understood.'

'Mikhail Bulgakov?' Her eyes glinted. 'Wait, the book is *The Master and Margarita*?'

'Correct.'

'Oh, well, I've already read that. In English.' Anara's confidence was returning, the connection between them deepening.

'So, you don't want me to read it to you?' Vadim asked, his lips a mischievous smile.

'I didn't say that.' She matched his smile. 'When you talk in Russian, it's... I like it.' The flush on her skin was replenished with fresh heat. She placed a playful kiss on his lips, revelling in the way his hand came to the rear of her head. Keeping their bodies close.

The opening door ignored for a little longer.

Part of the contingent left at the estate, Fyodor was using the time well. A slow sway of his head side to side as he studied the man hanging from the chains in the centre of the cell. Still relatively unhurt, the manacles had yet to dig too deeply into the man's flesh. The bruises had yet to fully develop, still a delicate raw merlot waiting to progress to the vibrant hues of aubergine or black.

That would come.

If Vadim decided to allow the man to live that long, or have sufficient skin left for the haematoma to cycle through each stage. For however many hours Fyodor had, he would find suitably varied ways to fill it, while savouring every moment.

Sliding the steel so it sat more comfortably, he readied his hand to strike. The pointed bar creating a sharper punch above his knuckles, his fingers through the holes to keep it in place.

The man's howl when it made contact with his ribs bringing a smile to Fyodor's mouth. He drew back his arm, the second punch landing on top of the first. Not enough to crack bone, but certainly enough to break the skin. To create a heated bloom on the man's chest; a fresh gathering of internal bleeding.

'I thought you Norse men were supposed to be strong,' Fyodor said, his third jab meticulously reinforcing the initial two.

'I'll… tell you… everything,' the man pleaded, stumbling, his feet not quite flat on the floor. The pressure from the steel and the deprivation of sleep, of food, of water, eroding his dignity. His resilience.

'I doubt you've anything useful to say.' Fyodor strode back toward the metal trolley, the trays of weapons neatly arranged. His bowl waiting for whatever morsels he took from the man's body. The decision on what to cut, what to remove, not yet made.

'I can… there's… Iðun—'

'Already know.'

The man swallowed, throat like fire. 'The… drugs—'

'Already know.'

'The… auctions.'

Fyodor paused, his hand on the dermatome. Slow, he licked his lips, hazel eyes flitting to the man. Though Nikolai had uncovered some of the information about how Septer were trafficking women, it would be useful to learn more. With a crooked grin, he picked up the device and checked the blade.

The man's screams welcomed as he collected strips of flesh; mouth watering with hunger as each debrided piece landed in the bowl for him to eat. He would get answers, he was certain.

But, Fyodor had a hunger to satisfy first.

The pulse of his cock urgent, the glint in his eyes bright.

Fyodor's gaze followed the fresh incision; the steel as it dragged the perfect layer from lower tissues. His throat vibrating with the low growl, the swallowed pleas in his blood to accelerate his actions. Discipline his rhythm as he dug lower, harder.

The man's wails desperate.

Almost as feverish as the guard's desire.

Careful, he returned the dermatome. Reverent, he pinched a morsel of skin, draping it over his extended tongue.

The scout retched; mucus and bile coating his chin.

Brushing his thumb tenderly over the sticky moisture from the man's face, Fyodor paced his lust. The knife pulled from his belt grazing across the captive's waist. Slicing deeper. Creating a growing cavity with each trailing pass.

'Tell me,' he whispered, leaning into the scout. The erratic pounding of the man's heart brought a wicked smile; knife discarded. In the cell, it echoed, spun, smearing ichor over stone.

The zip on his combat trousers was lowered, blood slicked along his shaft as Fyodor pressed closer to the trembling scout. Teasing the raw, jagged opening he had carved into his side. Each thrust concentrating his pleasure, his ache, with a slow, sedate, flex of his hips.

His carnal need to be swallowed.

To be enveloped by flesh.

To drown in it.

Fyodor's fractured sigh as he pushed his blunt tip inside, feeling the warm embrace of organs. One hand on the scout's back to hold the man steady; the chains rattling above them.

The cell's air was thick with scent of copper, of arousal. Of Fyodor's twisting entry, his retreat; groans punctuated with the scout's pleas. His whispered beg for freedom.

For death.

Once pressed flesh to flesh, blood soaking into the black fabric of his tactical clothing, Fyodor lifted his hand to dig into one of the man's open wounds. The weeping cut on the scout's chest pulled wider. His cock twitched against bruised muscle, his fingernails brushing chipped bone beneath membranes of sore tissue.

Hot, Fyodor's possessive grip anchored him. His mouth latching on to the man's neck, hips flicking a slow dance. Sweet elixir lapped from torn flesh, feeding the climb toward his expectant release. The sudden rip of thin skin made with teeth, accompanied by an increased tempo. An increased scratch of his nails.

'Tell me,' he repeated, blood staining his tongue, 'everything.'

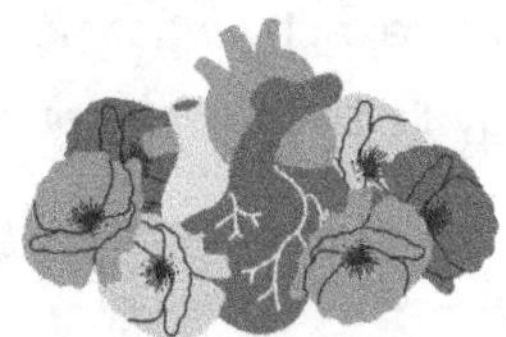

Inhaling deeply, Mace brought the bitter motes of cocaine into his nose before leaning back in his chair. The powder his own product, but not as poorly cut; less benzocaine or starch in the lines which he formed on his desk. He was happy to send out diluted wraps to the street, but he would not compromise on the purity of his own high.

Even if it no longer hit quite the same as it used to.

Waiting for the confidence, the elation, to kick in, he closed his eyes and exhaled. Listening to the steady increase in his pulse, indicating the drug was filtering into his bloodstream.

Mind floating to what the day promised.

The knock brought him upright, his voice calling them through, and eyes opening. Watching Jarah Malinowski arrive before his desk.

'Sit, sit,' he gestured toward the chair. 'You okay?'

'Yeah boss.' The soldier hesitated, dark-brown eyes glancing around the cluttered space before he settled down. His fingers brushed over his trimmed beard, braided and beaded. 'You asked me to drop by.'

'Oh, yeah, I did, yeah.' Mace sniffed. 'Fuck.'

'What can I do for you?' Jarah remained alert; with Kassian missing and reports of him being taken, he was attentive to every possible risk. A skill which had served him well during his time in prison, and which was a trait developed during his school years running product for Septer. His recruitment by Aeron Barnes and integration into the group helped by his record, reputation, and proficient use of technology and firearms.

Things Mace valued.

And why, he assumed, he was here.

'The fucking Bratva got to Kassian,' Mace began, 'and I want every single one of the cunts to pay for it. No-one, no fucker gets to snatch one of my fucking men.'

Jarah nodded; uncertain exactly what he could do. He was already working with Logan, already liaising with scouts to try and discover what had happened.

'Heard the fucker went out drinking,' Mace continued, 'and managed to get himself caught.' He slammed his fist on the desk. The remaining cocaine shivered in the reverberations. Glass of whiskey undulating.

'Logan asked me to—'

'I don't give a fuck what he asked you.' He stood, hands moving to stroke over the tightly braided length of hair above the shorn sides. Mace cradled his neck. 'I want you to lead this, Jarah, as Logan's equal, fuck better than equal, he's slipping.'

'Boss—'

'You're promoted, Jarah.' Mace rounded the desk, leaning his hands on the arms of the chair so he could get directly into the man's face. 'You deserve it.'

'Thanks boss.' A wide grin broke across his umber skin.

'Don't fuck up.' Mace pushed himself back, beginning to pace the length of the office. 'Look, I've got someone who's confirmed Kassian's being held at Vadim's house. So, if he wants to take something of mine, I want us to take something of his. You get me?'

'How reliable is this… someone?'

'Reliable enough.' Mace laughed, checking the time. 'He's due here shortly, so you can ask him yourself.'

'If you trust him, boss, that's sound.' Jarah's fingers drummed lightly on the combat trousers he wore; solid muscle below the fabric.

'Good, now fuck off.' Falling into his chair, he pulled himself closer to the desk, ducking to inhale another line of cocaine. Knowing the source who was coming to visit would soon be on their knees between his.

# Twenty-Three

The very moment they had departed the event, Vadim had been called to a meeting by Fyodor. His trusted men joining him in his study. And even though the doors had been left open, it would have been futile for Anara to stay. None of the words meant anything to her, though it was clear from their tone it was important. Their bodies betraying the weight of every piece of information Fyodor shared.

Instead, the lingering kiss by the stairs had been over too soon.

Resigned to a sweet memory before Vadim wished her goodnight and strode away. To collapse into the high-backed chair behind his desk and listen. Learn. Plan.

The scout Fyodor had interrogated while they ate, while they played blackjack, while they laughed, had provided them with additional options which would change their strategy. They had to trust the confession was not a ruse, not a desperate plea from a dying man. But they were wise enough not to place all their faith in the man's breathless words.

Leaning back in the leather chair, Fyodor placed one ankle on the opposing knee, a steel bowl in his lap. The raw shreds of flesh scenting the room with acrid copper.

'It's a good job we like you, Fedya,' Artem remarked, his eyes sliding to the guard with a shake of his head.

He smiled, pulling a long piece from the bowl and tipping back his head, mouth open and letting it coil onto his tongue. The languid chew a deliberate act, coupled with a low moan from his throat and hazel eyes closing. 'Delicious,' he murmured.

'Fuck.' Artem leaned forward, pouring a liberal measure of vodka.

'What, you didn't bring me anything back.' Fyodor shrugged, his grin creasing his eyes despite the attempt at innocence in his expression. In the way he slightly widened his eyes and slackened his jaw.

'You had enough to keep you entertained here,' Artem said, refilling the glass. He checked the doorway, seeing it empty, he placed the drink on the low table and removed his suit jacket. Emptied his shoulder rig of firearm and magazine.

'Your ideas of entertainment are wildly different to mine,' Pavel said, his tongue loosened by alcohol and his stomach comfortably full from the rich meal. 'I admire your skills, Fedya, but I'm happy to leave such things for you to do.'

Fyodor inclined his head in appreciation, his tongue sliding over his lips to capture any stray juices.

'Is he still alive?' Nikolai asked, rotating his phone on his thigh; a regulated spin, corner to corner.

'Yeah, until the pakhan tells me otherwise.' Fyodor paused, his gaze shifting to the desk.

'Vadya, is this scout to live?' Artem asked, his brow creasing.

Silence.

'Vadim,' Artem repeated.

'I'm listening,' he said, refocusing. His lips still felt Anara's touch, her taste. The way her body fit so beautifully against his.

The way she had conducted herself, even at a disadvantage all evening, testament to her strength, her adaptability. She was perfect. He had known that, from the moment he saw her, she would be the ideal woman for him. And tonight had proven his instinct.

Even if the night had ended sourly.

He should be kneeling at her feet worshipping her, should be dining on her flesh, should be burying himself inside her. Instead, he had new data to process, new strategies to devise. And Anara, despite the craving which rolled off her beautiful skin, which shone in her amber eyes, had graciously allowed him to walk away and deal with business.

'You're not,' Artem stated. 'Too busy thinking about his *wife's*—'

'Be careful how you end that sentence, Tyoma,' he interjected, ice in his voice. Venom dripping through it. His eyes narrowed, reaching for the knife in his desk drawer.

'Debut,' Artem said, his smile crooked.

Vadim shook his head; he knew his advisor too well. Exhaling, and closing the drawer, he shrugged his jacket from his shoulders. Draped it over the back of his chair. 'Yes, the scout stays alive, for now.'

'Anara handled things well tonight,' Nikolai said, light-brown eyes on his leader, then the advisor.

The tension in the study slowly dissipating.

'I never doubted it.'

'Of course, pakhan,' Nikolai said, 'it's just difficult when she doesn't know the language or what it is we do.'

'She knows enough,' he said.

'For now.' Artem balanced his glass lazily, mid-way to his lips. 'But, if she's going to be a more regular guest—'

'She is.'

'Vadya, you don't know her, she's not one of us.' Raising the glass, the welcome contents coated Artem's mouth in warming liquor; slaking his throat.

'No-one is until they are.' He began to fold the sleeves of his shirt to his elbows. 'Ksenia had no idea about this life before she and Pasha began dating, but she's now running one of our establishments, assisting in the laundering of our money.'

'And when Anara discovers our plan for Erinyes?'

Vadim's eyes closed.

The initial hopes for Erinyes remained a raw and grating guilt which he struggled to admit to. Struggled to acknowledge. If Anara knew how they intended to use Erinyes for their product, how some still considered that an option when the apothecary was rebuilt, it could change how she perceived everything he had done.

All he craved.

There was still so much he did not understand about her; Nikolai's research had too many gaps, too many conveniently vague results. Her history almost as curated as that they had forged for themselves.

'Vadya, what about—'

'Fedya, share everything the scout told you about the auctions and Septer's timetable, locations, with Kolya.' Vadim shook his head slightly as he met Artem's eyes.

'Sure.' Fyodor used the last strip of debrided flesh to sweep around the bowl, soaking up any remnants of tissue and blood.

'I need the data cross-referenced,' Vadim continued, 'so we've got a solid target to strike.'

'You think hitting their trafficking will be enough to force them to quit?' Pavel asked, his glass placed on the low table.

'Their product is inferior,' he said, 'so that'll be easier to remove from the streets once we cut off their main funding source. They'll struggle to maintain even the quality they're selling now, and with their men already reduced from our interventions, Septer'll be gone.'

'So, shifting focus to the trafficking?'

'Pasha, we can do more than one thing at once.' Vadim smiled, his eyes creasing. He stood, rocking his neck from side to side.

'I take it we're keeping you from your *wife*,' Artem taunted.

Vadim bit his tongue, letting his icy glare convey his warning.

'It is late,' Nikolai said.

A renewed craving sparked in Vadim's body. The necessary hunger to find her, to see her, to taste her. 'You all need to leave.'

'It's about time.'

'Fuck you Tyoma,' he breathed.

'I think you'd rather fuck her.' Artem held up both hands, watching the pakhan stride to stand defiantly over him. 'Vadya, it's obvious you like her, enjoy yourself, it's been a while.'

'How I spend my time is none of your business.' Vadim clenched his teeth, his jaw ticking with the pressure.

'It is when it begins to impact our work.'

'And when it does begin to impact our work, then and only then will you have the grounds to make such remarks.' He paused. 'Travel safely home.'

Vadim remained rooted to the hardwood floor, watching his curated team of men gather their things and leave. Glasses and half-full bottles left on the low table. His own suit jacket still on the rear of his chair. Slow, he brought his hands to his neck, cradling the skin.

Eyes raised to the ceiling.

Anara's bedroom directly above. Her image cascading over his mind with vibrant clarity; her body astride his. Snowy flesh blooming with lust, his tattooed skin dark where he brought her closer. Consumed her. Took her in his mouth to taste her, devour every inch of her.

He groaned, arms falling to his sides.

Fists formed.

Straightening his shoulders, after adjusting himself, he purposefully walked through the doors; trusting those in the surveillance suite would secure everything. His long, muscular, legs eroding the distance, jogging up the stairs and only slowing when he reached her door.

There was darkness, quiet.

The regular breathing of slumber.

Vadim did not knock. Instead, he carefully depressed the handle and entered with hushed steps. Light spilled softly from the landing, creating shadows. The expansive room ate up the change in illumination greedily as he moved closer to the bed. His eyes ravenous as they tracked how the duvet draped over her, how she appeared so peaceful.

He swallowed laughter, seeing the polar bear on the other pillow.

Willing her to wake, Vadim trailed his fingertips over the fabric of her covering. The touch barely there. Reaching her hip, he closed his eyes and caught his breath.

'Моё сердце и душа, крошка, ты моё сердце и душа[39],' he said, a rough reverence to his whispered tone.

Anara turned, moving from her side to her back; her arm above the duvet, sliding to her stomach. The tips of her fingers almost brushing his as she moved.

He traced her hand, ghosting her arm to her collarbone, delicately pushing her curls from her neck before caressing her face. Bending to kiss her forehead. His eyes closed, Vadim breathed in the pomegranate scent; his hand on the bed's rail curling more tightly.

'Vadya,' she murmured, eyes tentatively opening.

'Hush, now, sleep.' He pulled back a little, smiling, but kept one hand on her face; his heart seizing with the way she fell into his palm.

Anara's focus was slowly forming shapes from the conflicting light, the silhouette steadily becoming more defined. His broad frame, corded forearm so close she could kiss, the black shirt, and the gun. 'So that's what it was,' she said, slurring with sleep.

'What?' He frowned, his voice tender.

'The… sharp edges under your jacket.' The memory of how she had gripped his shoulders as he pinned her to the wall brought heat to her skin. She inhaled, catching her lower lip with her teeth.

Vadim followed her gaze, seeing the firearm he had forgotten he still wore. He inwardly cursed not going to his room to put it away first, then realised she had not reacted badly to it. Though, he reasoned, she was not fully awake. 'Sleep, kroshka.'

'Stay.'

His pulse leapt, body instantly agreeing.

---

[39] Моё сердце и душа, крошка, ты моё сердце и душа - Russian for 'My heart and soul, kroshka, you are my heart and soul'

Mind cautious. 'Not yet.'

Anara's smile fell; her brow creasing. The rejection stung.

'I want to,' Vadim continued, fingers caressing her jaw, moving into her hair. 'God, I want to. But you've a meeting with contractors at Erinyes in five hours, and you need to sleep.'

'Vadya—'

'If I stay, we won't sleep.' He placed another kiss on her forehead, a longer kiss. One Vadim hoped would ease the confusion he sensed, the disappointment he saw in her averted gaze and slumped shoulders.

She was about to argue. To remind him that she had slept in his bed while he watched her. But she swallowed it. If he did not think she was worthy, if he did not think she could be more than just a woman paraded when it suited him, then he was right. Why argue? Anara found his eyes and forced herself to smile. 'Good night, Vadim.'

# Twenty-Four

The contractor was already at the charred ruins of Erinyes when Anara arrived for the ten o'clock meeting; the broken night evident in her eyes. In how she pulled the dark coat more tightly around her frame, the chilled breeze and rain adding to her mood. She had spoken little, her breakfast with Sofiya quiet, and her timely departure made as Yeva walked through the main door of Vadim's house.

'I'll wait outside,' Maksim said, discreetly one pace behind her.

She did not answer, only a weak smile before she stepped into what had been the main store space. The dark grey clouds hung close in the readily visible sky; ceilings gone, beams black, roof missing. The slates splintered on the ruined floor. Wood stained with resins, glittering with melted glass, smashed bottles and fused herbs.

Though Anara had seen photographs, and visited the apothecary several times since the fire, it still hurt. The ache in her chest visceral. A raw knife which dragged through her organs, pirouetted in her mind, the serrated blade forging brutal pathways.

'Anara Morozova,' he said, arm outstretched.

She shook his hand, unsure if she should correct him.

'Your husband expects this to be done in a month,' he continued, 'I hope to meet that target.'

‘A month?’ She blinked. ‘I thought—’

‘It’s all planned,’ he said confidently, ‘here, let me show you.’ With a well-practiced flourish, the contractor opened the tablet and located the store’s rebuild timetable. A detailed spreadsheet of removal, repair, and reinstatement.

Anara was both impressed and furious.

The assumptions he made both kind and inappropriate. She had not fought so hard to build her business to have Vadim make the decisions for how it would be restored.

*Maybe I should’ve put him on my list*, she thought.

She had liaised with Origins about the financing, she had already begun sourcing replacement products, new fittings; the carpenters, the electricians. Everything had been aligned to Origin’s plan, with a detailed agreement to repay the cost via a higher price for their supply.

Vadim should have nothing to do with this.

His interference screamed of further distance, of endings.

‘Will you want the upstairs space as an apartment to rent out?’

‘What?’ She snapped out of the reverie.

‘The apartment,’ he prompted, a frown briefly forming. ‘Do you plan to rent it out, or do you have another use for it?’

She bit her tongue, inhaling deeply through her nose. The lingering scent of herbs and resins branched through, tainted by ash and time. ‘I’ll speak to my husband, and let you know.’

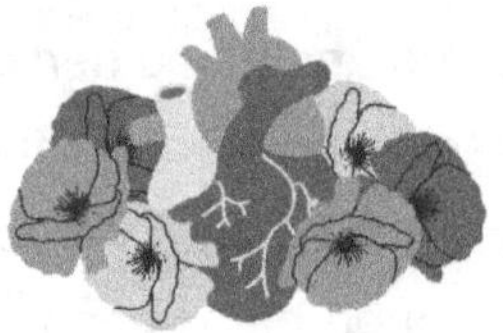

By the time she returned to the house, her fury was simmering, her mind spiralling between gratitude and confrontation. Anara was unsure if she should say anything, if she should just accept this was his way of making sure things got resolved quickly. His way of getting her out of his life in an efficient manner.

The sooner the store was rebuilt, the sooner this fake relationship would be over. His kisses felt real, his body's reactions felt real; Anara knew this. Knew she had some power over him physically. And yet, when she had offered him her bed, he had refused.

Even the relaxed lunch with Kerezen and Bryony had failed to shift the hollow sense of history being repeated. They had not noticed, or had chosen not to comment on, the masked smile she wore. Her responses measured, precise, clinical. Her eyes on the guard who observed in quiet detachment.

Maksim trailed her into the house, senses alert. The additional cars on the driveway were not particularly unusual, but something felt off the moment they walked through the doors.

Reaching the study, Anara's quick steps paused.

Artem, eyes sharp, was pacing behind Vadim's empty desk, Nikolai and Pavel looked pensive. His vacant chair felt ominous. The concern in Anara's stomach growing when the three men turned to face her.

'What did you do?' Artem asked.

She frowned. 'What do you mean?'

'He's sick.' Nikolai's focus moved to her, his hand dragging over the cropped lengths of his hair.

Her body immediately drowned in a nervous chill. A rush of anxious heat chasing the icy bites which nipped under her flesh. Everything felt enhanced and numb all at once.

'The doctor's held up,' Pavel added, conveying the update provided via text. His phone returned to the pocket of his trousers.

'Where is he?' Anara managed to force out. She could argue later, but now, now her mind only sought to heal.

'His room.' Artem paused. 'I'm sure you know the way.'

She gritted her teeth, refraining from sourly retorting, and pivoted on her heel, running back toward the hallway. The stairs. Her coat and curls flicking behind her as she swiftly covered the landing to reach his door. A momentary pause, to exhale. Inhale. Unsure if she should knock.

'Vadya?' Her tone was strained, a cheerful pretence. Her strides into the shadowy suite cautious as she made her way toward the main room, past the closed doors to the bathroom and dressing room.

'Anara? Thank God you're here.' Sofiya stood, meeting Anara in the centre of the expansive space.

'What's wrong?' Anara's eyes were fixed on the bed; drawn curtains made it difficult to decipher. His frame recognisable, certainly, but curled in on himself, on his side with his back to them. Hair mussed.

'He was fine,' Sofiya said hastily, softly, steering Anara back toward the door. Her tone dropping to a whisper when they reached the brighter landing. 'Then he wasn't.'

'What are the symptoms?' Anara felt heat creep over her eyes, her throat. Her brow a series of deep furrows.

'He said he felt really nauseous,' she explained, still faint, 'with really severe stomach pain. Then he was sick, really sick. But when he said he couldn't feel his hands and feet, that's when I called the doctor.'

'Has he had anything different to eat, or drink?' Anara tried to think back; if there was something he may have ingested which could cause such a reaction. Vadim seemed absolutely fine when she saw him during the night. And, accepting they had not known each other long, he always seemed so healthy.

Sofiya's mouth dried, her hands spiralling before her stomach, her eyes darting to the floor.

'Sofiya,' Anara urged, resting her hand on the woman's shoulder. A grip which suggested compassion but required clarity.

'Yeva...'

'Yeah, she arrived as I left.'

'She... she.' Sofiya chewed her lip, her eyes glazed. 'She had some leaves in her bag, but when I asked her what she was doing, she said it was for her to drink because she had a hangover.'

'What kind of leaves?' Anara was already walking away; she needed the tin Origins provided. If Sofiya saw it, if she told Vadim, she no longer cared. She knew if she had the possible medicine to help then it was the least she could do for someone who had done so much for her.

'I… I don't know.'

Anara spun around, her hand on the chrome for her room. 'Nausea, vomiting, abdominal pain, and paresthesia?'

'Yes… and, pares—'

'Numbness.'

Sofiya nodded, walking closer but glancing behind her, to the stairs; hearing voices as Artem brought the other men up.

'Has he got a headache?' Anara depressed the handle.

'Yeah, that's why I closed the curtains.'

'Okay.' She rushed inside, efficiently locating the tin from the drawer in her dressing room. Returning with it in both hands. She met Artem's inquisitive stare before shaking her head and returning to Vadim's suite with a determined set to her jaw.

'Vadya,' she said softly, ignoring the arrival of Sofiya and the men.

He could not feel her hand on his wrist, and his eyes stung when he tried to focus, but Vadim managed to curve his lips a little. His slick skin and the acrid taste in his mouth fought with the spasms of his stomach, the roiling nausea and pounding pressure in his head.

'He has bradycardia,' Anara muttered, releasing his wrist. His pulse betraying the slow heart rate. Unclipping the tin, she searched through the tinctures and remedies.

One already mixed which included all she required.

*How's that possible?*

She refocused; holding the glass bottle up. 'I'm sorry, Vadya, I need more light,' she said, switching on the lamp.

He winced, groaning.

Anara's hand returned, resting on his head, massaging the damp strands of hair. Tender, she stroked down to his neck; skipping over the healing cut, over the rough scuff of stubble. 'Sofiya, can you get some ice, chipped if possible.'

Sofiya nodded, running from the room.

'What's wrong?' Artem folded his arms, eyes hawkish as he watched every move Anara made.

'He's been poisoned.' Anara checked the dilution of the ingredients on the label. Belladonna, ginger, ginseng, lemon, and peppermint. Each designed to address the symptoms she had identified.

'And you know that how?'

'Tyoma, come on,' Nikolai objected, 'she's trying to help.'

'I run, ran, an apothecary; I know how to heal.' She did not add that she also knew how to make men suffer. That would be a conversation for another day.

'And you can heal him?'

'Yes.'

'What are you giving him?' Pavel's curiosity was piqued, moving to get a better look at the open tin, the contents.

'A mix of herbs that will help him produce atropine, norepinephrine, and dopamine.' Anara shook the bottle, ensuring it was blended.

'Herbs can do that?'

'Herbs can do many things.' She held the bottle up to the light once more, eyes narrowing slightly.

'And you're not going to make him more sick?'

'Artem, I know you're concerned, but I can heal him.'

'Without a doctor?'

'What are doctors but modern witches?' She smiled, tilting his head back so she could dispense some of the tincture into his mouth. Focused on Vadim, she met his gaze and saw the relief.

The trust.

She almost believed she saw love.

Anara dragged her gaze away, looking up from where she kneeled at his side. 'I can't be certain, but I think he ingested false hellebore. It produces symptoms Sofiya described, and what he's presenting.'

'Ingested how?'

'That's for you to figure out.'

'Pasha, was this the poisoner?' Artem asked, in Russian, turning his back on Anara.

'I can't understand, you don't need to hide.' Anara followed Sofiya's return to the room, accepting the bowl of ice chips. She selected one and gently swept it over his lips, letting it melt and drip into his mouth.

'What's wrong?' Sofiya hovered, looking down at Vadim then toward the brigadiers, the advisor. She had caught Artem's question and it had almost stopped her entering the room. Almost made her warn Yeva, that Anara had revealed what happened.

'I think he may have ingested some poison,' Anara stated, 'and I've suggested they figure out how.'

Sofiya swallowed, her gaze conveying the gratitude as their eyes met, a tear spilling over her lashes. She brushed it away.

'He'll need more of this tincture,' Anara continued, 'so I'll stay here and make sure he's—'

'That's very convenient.'

'Artem,' she sighed, 'I've been out all morning. Vadya, *my husband*, was fine the last time I saw him.'

'And when was that?' His head cocked to one side.

'That's none of your goddamn business.' Anara almost hissed the words, the rhythmic stroke of the ice across Vadim's mouth stuttering. A coiling ignition of the fury she had arrived home with returned, sparked by the lack of faith they had in her. The doubts. It ate into her heart, into her blood, tempting her to scribe his name onto her list.

# Twenty-Five

There was a calm atmosphere when he woke, a glow from the window shrouded in fabric. He groped for the lamp, adding more illumination to the dull room. Tilting his arm, he squinted to make out the time; he had lost a day. Maybe more.

'Kroshka,' he coaxed, throat dry. Raw.

The coppery sour taste in his mouth making him look around for any possible way to remove it. His half-naked body stiff, stale, in sheets that required laundering. Relieved he could feel his limbs when he flexed his fingers, he tentatively reached for the mass of curls by his side.

His heart ached, seeing her sleep in such a contorted manner. Her body folded, kneeling on the floor, head on the bed, face turned away. It crushed him. Vadim acknowledged he had been unwell, but to refuse to be comfortable while she cared for him, that hurt. He wondered how long she had been there, how long she had tended to him.

'Kroshka,' he repeated, stroking over the curve of her skull.

With a stifled moan, Anara opened her eyes and stretched her spine before straightening. Elongating her arms over her head while bringing her eyes to his. 'Hey, how are you feeling?'

'Better.' Vadim shuffled to sit up, pushing the pillows to provide more support. 'How long have you been here?'

She did not answer, instead took his wrist to check his pulse.

It skipped below her touch.

'Kroshka, how long?'

She stood, turning to pour fresh water from the carafe on the nightstand. Offering it him, she gestured for him to drink. The husky grate of his voice was only making her flustered, and while she needed to allow him time to heal properly, she still intended to speak with him about the apothecary. And what had prompted Yeva to poison him.

'If you won't tell me, I'm sure Sofiya will.'

'I got back around two yesterday afternoon,' she said, pacing, 'and I've been here since, pretty much.' Anara did not elaborate on how she had ordered the others to leave, how she had devoted hours to sliding ice over his flesh, to staring at him as he slept.

Her unvoiced confessions gnawing in time with his breath.

Rain began to strike the window; a swirling breeze lifting the curtains from the frame in an undulating sigh which shifted the air. Made Anara's steps pause.

'Kroshka, sit down, please.'

She moved toward the sofa.

'No,' he said, voice breathy. He rubbed his fingers against his sore throat. 'Please, Anya, please sit with me, here.'

Anara closed her eyes, her body yearning to comply. To rush to the bed and curl against his side and express her relief at his recovery. Her mind was rebellious, suggesting she be wary.

'Please,' Vadim implored. 'I won't beg, not for anyone else.'

'What does that mean?' She remained facing the sofa, refusing to turn and see the truth in his eyes, to witness the lie.

'It means I won't stop, Anya.'

'My name is Anara.' Her voice was barely above a whisper.

He swallowed, one hand raking through mussed hair. 'I know, it's… Anya is… it's like Vadya for Vadim.'

'Oh.' Still she found it hard to turn.

The knowledge of the endearment brought an ache to her heart, an overwhelming tightness to her chest. Her breathing shuddering, her eyes closing. Tears gathering and threatening to fall. Kindness and cruelty in a confusing dance within her mind.

Vadim's eyes narrowed, concern at the curve of her shoulders, the way her arms wrapped around her waist. He wished he was the one to do so; to draw her to him and provide her with the comfort he sensed she craved. That she hesitated to claim.

'Anya, please.' Vadim gripped the edges of the duvet, ready to throw them off and cross the room; weak body and grimy skin ignored. In his dreams, he trusted she would accept him covered in blood, covered in gore, covered in dirt.

Hearing the movement, she inhaled and pivoted. Made her way to his bed, her steps a little unsteady. Her vision tunnelled and hearing a blur of static. Voices from within the house, rain from outdoors.

'I won't bite.' Vadim formed a lopsided smile. 'Unless you want me to.' His eyes glinted. The humour undermined by a pinching reminder of his hunger. The healing cuts from the bar fight.

Judging the available space, she opted to sit where she had laid her head, close enough but with enough distance to feel safe. To guard the carefully constructed defences she had meticulously crafted over many decades of disappointment.

'Tell me what happened.' He reached for the glass of water, taking another sip. Seeing the empty bottle with an Erinyes label prompted him to discover exactly what had caused him to feel so sick.

'You were poisoned,' she explained, 'likely with false hellebore.'

His jaw ticked, a flush of rage whipping through his body. One hand fell to the duvet's edge again, ready to march downstairs and confront his staff.

'I had a tincture that helped with the symptoms,' Anara continued steadily, watching his reaction. 'And I don't think they gave you a lethal dose.'

'I… I could've died?' The heat of anger became a glacial fear; Vadim had always presumed he would die young. Something he now knew he wished to avoid, now he had a reason to live longer. He also assumed an early death would involve far more blood, and more weaponry, than a plant. A herb.

*The poisoner*, he thought. *But I'm not their usual targe*t.

'If they'd given you the root, maybe.' She paused, licked her lips. 'All of the plant is poisonous, but it depends on the dose, and which part of it they used.'

'You know a lot about it,' he muttered.

'I do own an apothecary.' She doubted now was an appropriate time to share the services she offered. 'The tincture I gave you was a blend of herbs, too; effectively I treated a poison with another poison.'

'You tried to kill me?' His eyebrows rose.

*Could she be the poisoner? No.* Vadim dismissed the idea.

'No!' She shifted closer, her hand instinctively moving to rest on the rough stubble of his cheek. Her thumb stroked his cheekbone. Her eyes wildly searching his. 'No, Vadya.'

He leaned into her palm, eyes closing as his heart surged with the sensation of her touch. The gentle rhythm of the rain, the spring breezes, and their breath. It was a lullaby which he believed he could live with for an eternity and never bore of.

'Artem doesn't like me,' she admitted softly.

He opened his eyes, finding her calmer gaze. 'He's just protecting me; he doesn't want me to get hurt.'

'Why would you get hurt?' Anara frowned. 'You're the one who can't wait to kick me out and end this.'

Vadim shook his head, vehement. 'I don't want that.'

'They why rush the contractor? And why put all these plans in place without talking to me…,' her voice trailed off. She tried to stand, only for him to grip her wrist, keep her close. 'No, you're still recovering. We can talk about this later.'

'I'm fine,' he asserted. 'Hungry, pissed off, but fine.'

She resumed her seated position, accepting his hand in hers.

'I wasn't… I didn't instruct the contractor so I could get rid of you,' he said earnestly. 'God, I'd never… I just know how important Erinyes is to you, so I've been working with Kasdeya and Origins to get things done. I wanted to help you have your store, your independence back.'

'Which then means I leave.'

'No!' He shook his head, holding up one hand to apologise for the sharpness in his voice. 'If you want to leave, I'd never stop you. It'd break me, fuck, it'd destroy me, but I'd never stop you. Anya, this is your choice, all of this; I'll protect you no matter what you decide.'

Anara's heart surged, pressing against the barriers of reason. Logic. Her eyes hooked into his and searched for sincerity, for honesty, for any trace of deception.

'I want to stand at your side,' Vadim said, throat thick with emotion and entire body on fire. 'I want you, Anara, Anya, kroshka—'

'You still haven't said what that means,' she said faintly, unsure what else she could say. Her mind was a careening blaze of desire and fear. A craving to believe and an alarm to dismiss his words.

He smiled. 'I'll tell you, one day.'

'One day?'

'One day.' He brought their entwined hands to his lips; flesh cracked from lack of nourishment. Ignoring the sting, he kissed her fingers before twisting to kiss her palm. Her wrist. Her pulse, below his grazing touch, a betrayal of her heart. Vadim kept his eyes on hers, watching the blush spread from her neck to her face. 'God, you're beautiful.'

She shook her head.

'Yes, Anya, you're absolutely divine.' He paused, his exhale heavy. 'I don't deserve you.'

'Vadya—'

'But I'm selfish.' His smile was wicked. 'You're mine, Anya, always will be, whether you stay here or not.'

The return of his mouth to her skin emptied her mind. Brought only feeling, only hunger. A furious wish for him to split her flesh with his teeth and drink her dry, to mark and claim her. Feast on her. To curve his tongue over her body and prove his words.

He nipped the taut skin of her forearm, smile growing as he heard her breath catch. Saw the way her pupils dilated.

The gentle pinch enhanced the heat Anara felt, her body reacting to Vadim's every movement. His every measured caress. The tender stroke of his fingertips up her outstretched arm, the chase of his lips. Eyelashes brushing her skin, his exhale doing little to douse her lust.

'I'd kill for you, Anya,' he said, sincere, his eyes lifting from her arm to meet her gaze. 'I'd do anything to prove you're mine.'

The void of her mind flooded with adoration. Devotion. The sudden urge to fall to her knees and worship him; to provide him with everything he ever wanted. To graze the banquet of his flesh, while allowing him to take all of her. Every single piece.

Her mouth parted, her breath vacillating between shallow and deep as she struggled to form a response.

'Anya, I'm yours.' His voice was gravel, his eyes hot.

'Is this real?' she whispered.

'For me, yes.' He sat back, bringing her hand to his face. Welcoming the way she instinctively drew closer, how her hand began to move into Vadim's hair. The strands unkempt from broken sleep, from the sweat to rid his body of poison. He did not care.

Nor did she. 'Vadya, I… I need to know this is real.'

He picked up her other hand, placed her palm against his chest, his flesh. The beat of his heart his proof, his offering of dedicated protection and enduring adoration. 'You're my wife—'

'Vadya—'

'You're my wife,' he repeated, 'however this began, you're my wife; I will keep you as my wife for as long as you permit me to. And if you're done with me, then I shall remain your husband regardless.'

Her throat was dry, her eyes glazed.

'I love you, Anara Morozova.' His pulse kicked below her hand. 'You are my heart, my soul.'

The tears breached her lashes, dropping over flushed skin. The soft sweep of his thumb over her cheekbone bringing a hitch to her breath.

'I'll wait as long as my heart beats—'

'Vadya,' she interjected, placing one finger on his lips.

He kissed it, then dragged the tip of his tongue from the root. Curled it around the tip. Laughed when she sighed and returned her hand to his hair. Shaking her head.

Part of her wondered if this was the medicine, the poison, the lack of food. If he was delirious. But the rhythm of his heart below her palm, the almost pitch of his eyes, the emotion in his voice, they all conveyed how his words were ready to be confirmed with action.

She could not reciprocate.

It felt too soon, that she still hid too much.

'You need to eat,' she said softly.

'I also need to shower.' He grinned. 'Want to join me?'

Anara laughed, her teeth catching her lower lip as she smiled. 'Not yet; you'd never get clean if I did.'

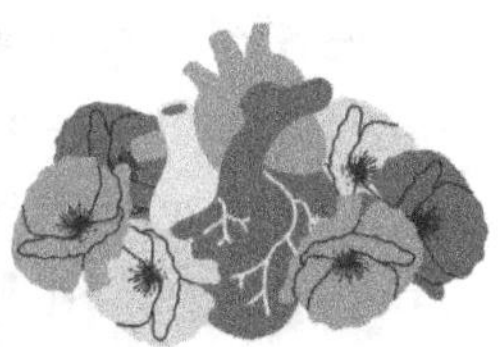

Relieved salutations were expressed the moment Vadim appeared in the hall, Sofiya rushing to offer food. Drink. Preparations done with Makari supervising every move; suspicions slow to melt. Artem, sitting beside Vadim at the kitchen's island, resisted speaking. His brown eyes tracking his leader with critical attention.

Only once Vadim began eating did Sofiya make her way up to his suite to straighten and freshen up the room.

'So, you're alive,' Artem stated.

Vadim, his mouth full of cold soup, hastily swallowed; sighed.

'What, she wouldn't let us stay,' he continued, 'and she told Pasha to cancel the doctor.'

'She's perfectly capable of treating me,' Vadim stated. He tore some bread from the roll, his stomach delicate but appreciative of the fuel.

'I'm sure she is.' Artem chuckled.

'Don't think me so weak,' he said, holding up the utensil, 'I can't stick this spoon through your throat.'

'I don't doubt it.' His smile did not fade.

Striding through from the hall, Nikolai placed the tablet he carried on the counter and spun it to face the pakhan. 'This is the cover story I put out,' he explained.

Vadim turned his focus to the screen, scanning the information. 'Did you also tell Anya about this?' he asked in English.

'Not yet.' Nikolai paused, glancing at Artem. Conscious to follow his leader's language. 'She was... busy.'

'Busy saving your pakhan's life,' Anara said crisply. She trailed her hand over Vadim's shoulders, leaning into him to read the online article Nikolai had manufactured.

The ease with which she moulded to his body caused Vadim to halt mid-chew, his senses alert. The slight tremble in her frame at odds to how confidently she spoke, how effortlessly she then placed a kiss on his crown. He dropped his spoon, catching her hand and pulling her even closer while spinning to face her. 'Did you enjoy your shower?'

'I did,' she replied, 'it was nice to have some time alone.'

Vadim laughed, his hand on the back of her head to bring her lips to his. The kiss languidly heated, a promise of more. An extension of the words he had spoken.

Artem coughed. 'As pleased as I am that your... marriage is in tact, perhaps we could return to the matter of your attempted murder?'

'Tyoma—'

'What? Whatever that was, it could've killed you.'

'Anya said it wasn't a lethal dose.' Vadim released her hand, eyes on her as she crossed to the fridge.

'It wasn't,' she confirmed. 'Whoever did this, they don't know about the correct parts of the plant, nor the correct concentrations.'

'That sounds more like luck,' Makari said. Leaning against one of the cupboards, his arms were folded across his chest; black tactical gear clad his muscular frame.

'There's always an element of luck,' Anara reasoned, 'when using a natural product. Every plant is different, due to their environment.'

'You know a lot about—'

'Tyoma, she owns an apothecary, of course she knows a lot about these things.' Vadim sighed.

'I've asked Maksim and Yeva to come to the house.' Nikolai swept up the tablet and switched the screen. A summary of his research filling the page, with images and recordings added. 'The footage from Prey's event confirmed it didn't happen there.'

With her back to the men, Anara hoped they did not see her flinch at the words. Did not see her hands pause as she prepared a sandwich. A flare of heat chasing over her skin.

'You checked all the cameras?' Vadim asked, scrolling through the information with one hand, the other still lazily chasing the soup around the bowl. Eating slowly to prevent his stomach rebelling.

'Yes, pakhan.' Nikolai's pale skin darkened.

'All the cameras?' Turning from the counter, plate in hand, Anara walked nonchalantly to the island. Taking a seat beside Vadim. Her eyes on his, seeking reassurance. 'How many are there?'

'We have cameras everywhere, kroshka,' Vadim explained. 'There's a catwalk above the casino area, and then we have others installed in discrete locations to ensure we have evidence if anything happens.'

Her throat dried. Her brow creased.

'Don't worry, I'm sure Kolya has deleted anything which isn't of any value to this investigation.' He did not move his gaze from Anara.

'Of course.'

'Are we ruling out the poisoner?' Artem asked, focus pivoting to the flash of light beyond the window; the car's paint reflecting weak spring sunshine.

'Poisoner?' Anara ventured, her bite of the sandwich stalled.

'Someone's going after men,' Vadim said, leaning into her. 'I doubt I'd be a target, considering the profile they're working to.'

'Never say never,' Artem muttered. 'The fact you were the only one to get sick, aside from a few hangovers, from the event, does suggest you were singled out.'

'Which, when we compare something from just as you both arrived to this morning,' Nikolai continued, taking the tablet to locate the data he wished to share, 'gives us a good idea of who did this.'

Anara's entire body was a mass of chilled knives; if Yeva betrayed Erinyes, she would have no choice but to confess. And she did not feel ready to explain what she used her knowledge of herbs for. Did not wish to expose Kerezen and Bryony. The whole operation Anara conducted from Erinyes was done in secret to protect women. The Bratva knowing of their services felt entirely opposed to that.

Even if, she acknowledged, Vadim seemed incredibly considerate to her needs. He had exerted no pressure, even after proclaiming his love for her. He had not expected her to reciprocate.

Taking the tablet, the bowl pushed aside, Vadim's eyes ate through the screen. Sofiya dragged to the dining area by a distraught Yeva. The women talking. Spliced with Yeva's visit to the estate; Sofiya trusting her friend to prepare their tea.

Vadim's hands curled into fists, his jaw tight. Breathing measured.

'I should go,' Anara said, faint and fractured.

He reached out one hand to rest on her forearm. 'Stay.'

The door clicked, Maksim and Yeva entering the hall. Makari striding from the kitchen area to meet them and escort them to Vadim's study. A tension in his shoulders with each step.

Artem and Nikolai following them through.

'Anya,' Vadim said calmly, twisting to face her completely, 'you need to understand who I am.'

'I know—'

'No, you think you know.' He inhaled. Exhaled. 'There are things I've done, and will continue to do, and you need to see it.'

She held his gaze, her heart loud.

'We need to talk more about exactly what I do,' he continued, 'and I hadn't planned on starting with something like this, but… Anya, what she did, it's a death sentence.'

She swallowed.

'I don't expect my men to do anything I wouldn't do myself.' Vadim slid his hand down, entwining with hers. Inwardly relieved she accepted his touch, did not shake him away.

'You're pakhan for a reason,' Anara acknowledged.

'Please, Anya, don't hate me for what I must do.'

'I don't think that's possible,' she said, hoping he would not hate her when he learned the truth. Her smile tugged at the corners of her mouth, her eyes heated.

Vadim released her hand, taking her face in both before running his fingers through her curls. He stood, leaning slightly to place a tender kiss on her lips. His tongue tracing the seam before he deepened the caress of their connection. The peace at war with desire; Vadim needed to feel this union before things changed.

Needed to remember how she felt before their world shifted.

'I love you, Anya,' he whispered against her lips. Another kiss gently placed on her mouth before Vadim stepped back. Hands trailing until he could only wait, arm outstretched, for her to join him.

'Vadya,' she said, standing but not walking, 'before you go in—'

'There's nothing you need to tell me I don't already know.'

Her body flushed with anxious heat, chasing chills. Teeth dragging below her skin and teasing her pulse with vicious, creeping, fear.

Slow, she began to move. To allow him to draw her close to his side and guide her steps; their hands tight, his thumb stroking over. She could sense the tension in his body, the way he fought to remain calm. Eyes alert, jaw set. His strides precise and sharp, muscles taut; anticipation increasing his heartbeat.

And yet, there was composure, resignation.

A resolute acceptance of what would happen once they walked into the wood panelled room. Even if only one of them felt certain about what they intended to achieve now the culprit had been established.

Crossing the threshold, Anara hesitated.

The room empty.

Vadim gestured to follow, directing her to the cupboard door in the corner; full-height, oak, amongst the panelling. He opened it to reveal a spiral wrought-iron staircase.

The thrum of Anara's heart grew louder, her eyes suffocating with what may lay ahead. Her chest constricted. Mind repeating his words; *I love you… there's nothing you need to tell me I don't already know.* The confident adoration in Vadim's tone suggested he did not. He did not know the extent of her skills, the truth of her nature.

Was this merely a way to isolate her, to harm her?

Had she fallen for his words?

Anara forced herself to place one foot after another, encouraged by Vadim to descend into the spacious lobby. The basement's shadows and ambient air accompanied by pristine surfaces and targeted lighting.

'I'll give you the tour another time,' he said, reclaiming her hand and bringing it to his lips. His eyes intensely boring into hers. Concern in his gaze, a mild frown creasing his brow. 'Are you okay?'

She swallowed.

'You don't need to be nervous,' he continued. 'I've got you. I'll never let anything bad happen to you.'

She nodded; surreptitiously checking for exits.

'We're in here,' Makari announced.

It was only one of a couple of open doors along the wall; a bank of metal entrances complemented with supplies, with switches, with scuffed flooring and a delicate scent of chemicals. Cleaning products competing with an undercurrent of blood, of musk. Death.

Her eyes glazed with moisture, heat fighting with ice under her skin as her stomach roiled. Anara gripped his hand more firmly, even as she forced her chin up and shoulders back. Kept his pace.

'Unchain her,' Vadim instructed, eyes scanning the room and where each of the occupants were.

Efficiently, Makari and Nikolai unlocked the shackles holding Yeva's quivering wrists. Her breath stuttering through her chest, eyes streaked with tears, skin flushed crimson. Clutching and rubbing his arms, Maksim could only watch; he knew better than to intervene. Whatever his wife had done, he had their children to consider.

Artem closed the door behind them, the weight of it creating an echo which made Anara flinch.

'Why did you do it, Yeva?' Vadim kept a measured tone, his body almost frozen. Barely a shift in his torso. His head fixed, eyes focused. A slow blink the only real evidence he was alive.

Looking first to her husband, Yeva's lips parted. Her pale blue dress was soaked in sweat, the fabric cloying and revealing the panic she tried to hide. Her hands massaging sore wrists. She stepped forward, only to be restrained by Makari and Nikolai; a light touch on her upper arms.

But persuasive.

'Why am I here? What do you think I've done?' Her broken words were fractured with heavy sobs. Her fingers going to her cross.

'Did you wish to kill me?'

'Why… what,' she said. Paused. Eyes closed. 'You and your… wife were at the coast—'

'You and I both know that isn't true.' Vadim began to fold back the sleeves of his shirt; deliberate and without dropping his gaze. 'It's only because I have such an amazing wife that I'm alive.'

Maksim's eyes lifted from the stone. 'What happened?'

'The pakhan was poisoned,' Artem explained.

'Maybe you just got a rogue dose of our product—'

'When have I ever used drugs?' Vadim turned to the soldier. 'I will never, and have never, used our product, or anything else.'

'No, pakhan.' His head dropped to the floor once more; he began to piece together what may have taken place, and Yeva's role in it. Leaving after Anara reached the study, Maksim had been unaware.

'You sell drugs?' Anara was unsure if she voiced the question, her thoughts consumed by possibilities, by memory. The hints Kassian had made about using Erinyes slowly recalled.

'We run a business,' Artem stated. He folded his arms, eyes flitting between the woman and his leader. 'Just as you do.'

'I sell herbs—'

'And what, you think that makes you innocent?' Artem scoffed. 'It's still a poison, it's still a drug; it's herbs which nearly killed him.'

'Mine are natural,' she said.

'As are ours,' he retorted. 'We use the purest forms, that we blend to create the very best product—'

'Этого достаточно[40],' Vadim hissed.

'You denied to help me.' Yeva, looking directly at Anara, struggled weakly against her captors. 'It's because of him, isn't it? You knew, even then, and sided with him, even knowing it'd be my death!'

Anara's teeth, already tight, felt about to splinter. The pressure, the willpower, the threads of her composure; on the periphery of her vision a darkness continued to swell. *This is it*, she thought.

'We know you went to Erinyes,' Vadim said.

*Fuck*, Anara's mind screamed, *I'm about to die*.

'We know you lied about it,' he continued, noting Anara's snowy skin pale further, 'and said you were at home with your children, your children Yeva!' Vadim exhaled heavily.

---

[40] Этого достаточно - Russian for 'That's enough'

He wondered if this was too much. If, in his pursuit of being honest, he had shared too much, too soon. That this was more than Anara could tolerate. More than she would accept. That this would be the part of him she could never love. Vadim was acutely aware she had yet to say those words, but lived in the hope she would. But now, seeing how unsettled she appeared, he was concerned he had broken that chance.

'I did this *for* my children,' Yeva spat.

'Did you even think about the consequences?' Artem strode toward Maksim, seeing the soldier sway.

The realisation had struck.

Slowly, Maksim fell to his knees. Vomit emptying his stomach and burning his throat. Though neither of them had seen the video, Yeva's words were enough to damn her. Maybe them both. Maksim's wail was a heated cry, evidence of the turmoil he could no longer contain.

Artem rested his hand on the soldier's neck, feeling the slick warmth of nervous sweat. Sliding lower, patting his back. Crouching down to tip up his chin and look directly into his eyes. 'Did you know?'

Maksim shook his head. Breathing panicked.

'He had nothing to do with this.' Yeva's tears flowed, silent syrup to her lips. Dripping onto her stained dress. A wicked tug to her mouth as she turned her eyes to Vadim. 'And your *wife* refused to help me.'

The sneer in her tone made his jaw tick.

Made Anara's eyes close.

'Did you intend to kill me,' Vadim said with cold precision, 'just to get back at my wife? Because she wouldn't give you what you wanted?' He was unsure exactly what Anara could have provided, though, it was not a difficult conclusion to ascertain Yeva was seeking herbs.

Lethal herbs.

And Anara had principles, had refused. Pride glowed in his chest, an electrical warmth in how she had acted, how she continued to show how beautiful, how peaceful, she was.

Unaware of the truth.

And how Anara felt as though the stone was sand, that she was in a vortex, every cell in her body steadily being consumed. Falling. Drowning under the potential ramifications of Yeva's words. Of potential culpability should knowledge be obtained.

'Not at first.' Yeva had straightened up, grown quiet. The tears drying and breathing more steady. 'But then I saw you together and… I wanted to take what I knew I'd lose, eventually.'

Vadim's knuckles were chalk; glimpsed through ink. The curl of his fingers, the tightness of his fists, creating a web of veins and pressure. A fury which he prepared to unleash.

Diplomacy, reason, only went so far.

Though this did not require a gathering to determine what sentence to pass, Vadim still wished to provide Yeva the opportunity to plead her case. To provide some kind of evidence which could spare him having to take her life.

'There's other ways to get herbs,' Yeva stated, her brown eyes firmly fixed on Anara. 'And I got what I needed.'

'Not enough,' she muttered, 'nor the right parts.'

'You still suffered though,' she argued, 'didn't you? You still had to sit and weep, hoping your beloved husband wouldn't die.'

Striding to the metal cart near the doorway, Vadim met Artem's gaze and gave the slightest of nods. His advisor turning to whisper carefully in Maksim's ear; the inevitable fate sealed. Maksim's refusal of the offer to leave a credit to the soldier. Even if his wife had acted so recklessly.

The glint of the blade in the overhead lighting brought heat; Anara's body alert to the knife. To how Vadim handled it. To how he looked with it in his palm. Her mind alight with how he could use it on her. Slicing her neck, her veins. Bringing fevered blood to her skin. Her lips parted, the kick in her pulse and slick warmth in her quim, betraying desire.

*At least I'll die aroused*, she thought.

Noting how Anara's pupils had dilated, Vadim purposefully stroked one finger along the edge of the blade. Watching how she licked her full lips in response. He crossed to her side, his free hand reaching for her face. The slight flinch in her response making him reconsider. Dismissing the hesitation with how she then melted into his touch.

His kiss welcomed.

'You'll realise,' Yeva warned, her voice strained, 'you'll realise every time he's late home or there's a bullet to dig out of his body. You'll never get out of this alive, not together.'

'And what, you thought you'd hasten that by poisoning me?'

'It was the quickest way to your heart,' she retorted, staring at Vadim as he moved away from Anara, 'through your stomach—'

'I prefer going directly through the chest.' Vadim stepped closer, the knife repositioned and ready. He paused, one final assessment made of Yeva Zaitseva before he raised his arm.

Plunged the tip into her neck and dragged.

Hot blood quick to spill, to dye her dress in burgundy, to spray over Vadim's face, his arm. To drip over Makari and Nikolai who continued to hold her upright. Body sagging as her life wound toward the stone. Every repressed sob from Maksim matched with a fresh crimson tear landing, creating ripples across the reflective surface.

Vadim did not turn back, entirely devoted to the task. The knife slid from her neck without leaving her body. Twisting to open a deep wound in her sternum. Hand out to accept the retractor from Artem, he widened the access. The knife reclaimed from her liver to slice her heart from the cavity with brutal precision.

The organ held and carried, placed in a bowl on the cart, while Yeva was lowered to the ground. Maksim scrambling to lean over her, to kiss her rapidly cooling skin, salty water joining thick ichor.

Trusting his men to deal with the body, the heart, Vadim meticulously wiped his hands. His forearms. Pulled his shirt from the waistband of his trousers and shrugged it from his torso. He tossed it onto the cart, critical of the remaining clothes and where any blood remained.

He did not care if he trailed it through the house.

But he cared how he appeared to Anara.

Inhaling deeply, he let the detached professionalism fade, allowed the killer to shrink back a little. Such skills never truly disappeared. He had worked incredibly hard to achieve all he had, and those sacrifices were ones he was proud of. Ones he would never apologise for.

'Vadya,' Anara said gently, resting her hand on his shoulder, fingers brushing his collar bone.

He reached up, placing his hand over hers. Eyes closing.

The relief she felt was duelling with sorrow. She had not known Yeva well, but the way the woman had begged in Erinyes, the way the woman had opted to strike Vadim, ate into her mind. Maksim's keening figure an added ache. The images danced with the noise of the blade, the smell of blood, the way Vadim had moved so gracefully.

Anara was confused and conflicted.

If he had asked the others to leave, she would have gladly dropped to her knees, pleaded with him to fuck her in Yeva's blood. Her body was feverish, crawling with the hot beat of her pulse.

The ache to confess. To be understood.

'We should talk,' he said, turning to face her. The periphery of his vision confirming how the other men tended to required tasks. 'I'm sure you have questions, and I'm happy to answer them.'

# Twenty-Six

Beyond the windows, amber lights illuminated the pathways, the budding gardens. They had talked for hours. They had walked every room in the estate; Vadim explaining what everything was, how everything worked. It was a deluge of information, but Anara welcomed it.

He had taken time to shower before his discourse began; his divine scent one which had threatened to ruin her concentration. Her body too alert and eyes too readily drawn to Vadim's frame, his face, the way he easily commanded every space they entered.

By the time they had settled into the comfortable leather sofas in the lounge area, with coffee, Anara's mind was a tumultuous web. Each new piece of information a layered revelation which brought her confession closer to her tongue. His honesty ripping open old barriers, proving she was worthy of knowledge, of trust.

The scars bleeding through her veins.

Her heart crying to confirm her adoration.

Her head still suggesting she be cautious. The fear he was revealing this only to have leverage, that he would utilise this as an excuse to draw a knife through her own throat. She shuddered at the thought; her core hot, her quim slick, her thighs clenched.

Her teeth playing with her lower lip, eyes instinctively on him.

On his mouth as he spoke, on the way his chest rose, fell. How he exuded power, danger, strength, and safety.

Anara could not deny she had always felt safe.

'We should go to bed,' he said, voice raw from talking. From the way the poison had burned through his body, the time he had needed to heal; weary aches and hunger gnawing at his limbs.

'We should.' Anara was unsure what he meant. Did he expect her to crawl into his bed? Did he expect the truth he divulged to result in sex? A bargain of body for words.

Access for honesty.

His head tilted, seeing her frown, her hands moving to twine in her curls while her eyes darted down. 'Separately.'

'Oh.' The instruction was a punch to her chest.

'I've told you a lot,' he continued, shoulders rounding as he leaned on his thighs, his eyes still on her. 'I've been truthful, and you've seen a side of me not many others do.'

She licked her lips slowly, her breath quickening. Her hand dropping to her lap. 'I need to tell you—'

'No, Anya,' Vadim soothed, 'take the time to decide if you can accept this, and if you can accept me. There's never any obligation; how I feel should never change how you do.'

Nodding, the heat crawling over her skin continued to prick at her nerves. The touch of his fingertips on her chin to lift her head bringing a surge of electricity through her body. Her mind. Her lips parting and eyes glazed as they met his.

'Are you okay?' He took her hand in his other, assisting her to stand and drawing her into his arms. Firm but tender, he ran his hand down her spine, stroking back up and under the long curls. Gripping her neck with splayed fingers.

'Yes.' She was. Exhausted, but okay. Vadim had yet to fail where his words and actions met; he had never broken a promise he made, never made her feel forced to act.

Even his decision to intervene with Erinyes had been made with her in mind. Not to derail her plans but enhance them. To utilise his influence and wealth for her benefit. And while she would have preferred for him to speak with her first, the result was the same. He offered to help, and she was learning that it was okay to accept it.

Tilting her head a little higher, she kissed him; familiar taste, familiar sensation. The touch igniting a desire she continued to feed. Fingers dancing over the nape of his neck, welcoming the shiver which travelled his spine; reverberating through her body. Their reactions confirming the words had broken nothing.

This was a pause.

Time to digest his confession; hers withheld.

Repeated collisions of lips, of tongues, of teeth, a slow departure as they threaded hands and ascended to the first floor. Lingering at the top of the stairs. Arms stretching before connection fell.

And loneliness was their only embrace.

Her mind turning over the emptiness of her limbs, her frame; fabric ghosting her in his absence. The temptation to turn and cross the landing and slide into Vadim's bed one which fought for acceptance. The action dismissed with a sigh, her back against her closed door, before Anara forced herself to curl into the chair, open her laptop.

The encryption ticking, permitting her to open the chat.

No fear in being traced, nor read.

Even with the security in the estate she was now cognisant of.

A: How did you know I'd need that specific tincture?

It was probably not the most professional of ways to begin the thread, but she and Kasdeya had spoken so many times, Anara felt they were on good terms. Friends more than colleagues.

Though she had welcomed the presence of the blend in her kit, and been caught up with treating Vadim without opportunity to reach out until now, it had been a thorn.

A question she needed to comprehend.

K: Was it useful?

She shook her head, a breathy laugh leaving her throat. Kasdeya thrived on riddles. Anara was typing out a reply when her phone began to vibrate. An international number displayed.

'Anara, I'm sorry you needed to use that tincture,' Kasdeya said, her voice smooth. A thick and heavy beat, muted, drifted below her words, a rhythmic thud of bass, lilting melody. Music and breath.

Fading as she closed the door.

'I haven't even said which one yet—'

'Does that matter?' She paused. 'Did it work?'

'Yes.' Her frown had returned, digging deeply across her brow. The tightness bringing her fingertips to her temple, massaging aching skin.

'Good.' Kasdeya exhaled, the pre-dawn sky above a myriad stars, infinite galaxies stretching. The isolated location hidden underground did not tarnish the unblemished natural space. 'And he's okay?'

Anara hesitated. 'Yes. How did you—'

'It's always a man, isn't it.' She laughed, husky. 'Do you have all you require to continue your work?'

'I do, yes,' she confirmed. 'I have a problem I'm working on.' Anara's eyes shifted to the on-screen file which continued to process.

'But nothing that requires immediate assistance?'

'I'm safe.' Anara leaned back, letting the chair support her. 'Vadya told me you're working with him, on the rebuild.'

'We are, yes.'

'You didn't tell me.'

'And ruin the surprise?' Kasdeya's tone was playful. 'Your *husband* only wished to take some of the pressure from you; he's a good man.'

'Is he?' Her head tilted, eyes closing as her neck arched. She hoped he was. His job was demanding, certainly, and his business was rooted in products and tasks that some may determine were illicit, illegal.

But, in many ways, she was no less guilty.

His drugs were chemical, his family wealth isolated from the funds which were laundered through his bars, his casinos, his online activity focused on crime. Yet, he never actually participated in these; as pakhan he oversaw it all, made decisions, gave orders. Vadim was protected by his brigadiers, his soldiers, his men.

His incarceration as a teenager was for intent to supply cocaine, the record sealed. The contract killings the Bratva had asked of him after he was released remained unsubstantiated. Vadim had admitted them to her, had explained his past, but never once asked for forgiveness.

Only understanding.

Time.

And trust.

'Vadimir Lvovich Morozov has his faults, as does any man,' Kasdeya said, her pace measured. 'But he loves you, Anara, whether he tells you that or not, he does.'

Her throat dried, her eyes opening. The shadows from the lamp, the spacious room's furniture, creating a series of spikes across the crisply painted white ceiling. 'He's told me.'

'Has he?' She smiled, laughter lacing through her reply. 'What did you say?'

'Nothing.' Anara tipped herself back upright. 'I'm… I, Kas, it's been so long since I felt I could trust anyone, or love anyone, and he's—'

'Intense?'

'Yeah.' She paused. 'In a good way, but I'm not used to being so well cared for or thought of.'

'And you're scared if you submit, it'll all go away.'

It was not a question, merely a statement of comprehension.

'You may be surprised,' Kasdeya continued. 'Vadim may be the very man who will understand you, all of you.'

She chewed on her lip, her eyes closing once more. 'I hope so,' she admitted, 'I hope so.'

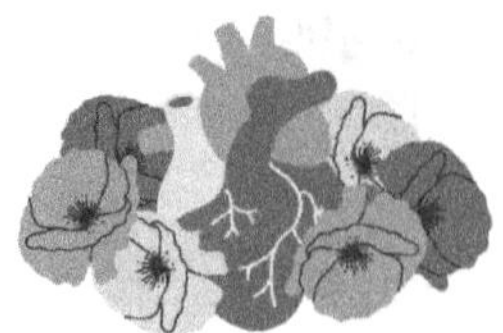

With a deeper cognition of how the estate worked, comfort eased the uncertainty Anara had arrived with. Those earlier days and nights, fragile breath and cautious steps, slowly replaced with routine. Honesty brought less rigidity; black-clad men in tactical gear more readily visible, hushed conversations no longer as soft.

Anara finally felt at home.

The thought of losing this was an ache in her soul.

Drifting, on her back, she watched rain land on the glass roof of the pool house. The warm waters surrounding her lapped her limbs, lulling her mind. Cloudy darkness rolled overhead, a rough growl of thunder an ominous reminder of what she had planned for later that day.

She did not hear the click of the door, so absorbed in thought, in the shifting clouds. Did not hear Vadim's choked sigh, his hesitation, before he slipped smoothly into the pool, the water rippling.

Rocking her with gentle undulations.

'Vadya,' she breathed, twisting to tread water.

Tracking his strokes toward her.

His hands on her shoulders and lips on hers, steering her toward the marbled tiles, the shallower water. The hunger in his embrace matched in her own; each feeding from the other while providing sustenance.

Hot, demanding, eager.

Her fingers clawing through his hair to pull him closer. Legs wrapped his hips. Tongues caressing, exploring, as fingers dropped over skin. Wet with beaded water, heated with craving.

Until he pushed himself back.

Creating a distance between them, his eyes closing.

Foreheads resting together.

His exhale pained.

'Vadya.' Anara brought one hand to his cut cheek, coaxing him to look up and meet her gaze. The swollen flush of her open lips bleeding into the blush on snowy flesh, framed with slicked curls.

Dilated pupils.

'I promised you time,' he said, hoarse, shaking his head. 'This isn't keeping that promise.'

'I don't need time,' Anara stated.

The marble provided her a surface to propel her return to him, to feel the warmth which radiated. The overlapping desire. The solid muscle of his torso, the thud of his heart, the sensitive hardness of his arousal.

She welcomed it all.

Wished to soak into his skin, to be consumed by him.

'Anya, I—'

'I love you.' She kept her eyes locked on his as she spoke, the force of her words echoing in the emptiness of the building.

Witnessing his smile only increased hers.

He swallowed, fingers stroking over her face, his tongue licking over his lips slowly. His heart a frantic beat, threatening to escape his ribs and claim hers. Vadim pulled her closer, both hands gripping her face as their kiss confirmed their appetite; teeth nipping at flesh.

Breathless kisses burning through their veins.

'God,' Vadim said, exhaling the word, 'I've dreamed of hearing you say that.' He lingered on another kiss, the touch of her body against his a cascade of electricity.

The surface of her eyes were brittle with emotion. Her admission had opened up the potential for heartbreak; Anara knew this. She had known it but still allowed the reckless truth to spill from her mouth. They were not words she could reclaim, nor did she wish to. But she hoped he would remember this moment when she shared her own history.

How much blood was on her hands.

'I'm taking you to dinner, tonight,' he said, knuckles tenderly moving down her face, curling to then cradle the back of her neck. Drawing her back for another kiss. Her taste relished, his tongue sweeping over the seam of her lips and delving inside.

'Tonight?' Their proximity screamed of urgency; her body begging for his with each pressured connection. The feel of his erection against her body creating a yearning she wished to satisfy.

One she thought he would also wish to pursue.

The rock of her hips chasing his touch.

'Patience, kroshka,' he teased. Fingertips descending her spine and rounding her hip. Skirting the hem of her bathing suit. 'You deserve to be worshipped, properly.'

She chewed on her lip, hearing him groan at the act.

'Fuck,' he breathed, leaning his forehead against hers. 'We'll explore every inch of this estate, wife, but not now.'

'Not now? What if I don't want to wait until tonight?' Anara's breath was a tremble in her chest, pebbled nipples brushing his flesh sending a hot ache through her body. Every touch increasing the intensity of her craving. Her fingertips spiralled on his arms, careful to avoid the healing slices, eyes fixed on his.

The sky lit up; a flash of iridescent violet and white.

Neither reacted.

Their focus purely the other. Each of them willing the other to break, willing the other to change their mind. To prove their vows were carved irrevocably into their blood.

'You'll wait,' he murmured against her lips, claiming them over and again while he spoke. 'Until then, Anya, I love you; you are my heart and my soul, my heart and my soul.'

# Twenty-Seven

Standing, listening to the rain thrum against the umbrella's arc, Anara's mind was consumed by the memory of the pool. Absently, her fingertips traced her lips. The ghost of Vadim's kiss. The absence when he swam away and hauled himself from the water. She had closed her eyes, the image of his body vivid, and cursed herself for her vulnerability.

For her heart overriding her head.

Despite the fear, she smiled. Her heart a mass of moths, and body a tightly wound wire. Anticipation an incessant scratch over her flesh and inside her veins.

Vadim had been as reluctant to leave the water as she had been to allow him depart. The disciplined restraint slipping with each minute they had remained entwined. Water providing a gentle continuation of every stroke they made over fevered flesh. Teeth teasing lips, tongues curling in coy worship.

Their bodies proclaiming commitment.

Even if they had yet to consummate it.

Hearing the slam of a car door, Anara blinked; forcing herself to find the concentration she required. The hand in her pocket retrieving the vial she had prepared the night before.

Reassurance in the glass against her fingertips.

He did not glance her way, nor cast his eyes over the wealth of wild flowers fighting against the deluge. Yellows, purples, and whites seeking those first warmer days of spring, dancing and breaking under the rain. A bold display in troughs either side of the small coffee shop's doorway to complement the aroma of their produce.

Collar up and head down, Logan shook the water from the braided hair which crowned his scalp; shorn sides more easily slaking moisture to his neck. His broad shoulders relaxing now he was indoors. His head rocking side to side as he strode to the counter.

Dismissing how empty the shop was.

Thunder rolled overhead.

It was dusk at noon.

Logan had only just shed his coat, made himself comfortable, when she decided to walk in. Her focus his table, but a brief exchange of silent understanding shared with the shop's owner. The umbrella at her side, a soft smile on her lips. One which she kept as his brown eyes narrowed and met hers, watching her slide into a chair opposite.

'You,' he muttered, a confused frown creasing damp skin.

Anara kept herself small; her body meek, eyes doe-like. Her coat open enough to reveal the snowy skin of her neck, hinting at more. Slow, her tongue moved over her lips.

He furtively checked the shop's window, before returning his focus to her. The steady drip of her umbrella and his jacket discordant amongst the steam and classical music. Calculating, he assessed her and tried to determine why she would have asked to meet.

'What do you—'

'I know where Kassian is.'

Logan folded his arms, leaning on the table, his mug nudged by his elbow. Frame rigid and mind pursuing the validity of her statement. 'We know where Kassian is.'

She remained silent, hoping it would loosen his tongue.

'Why are you here, Anara?' His eyes were shrewd.

Skeptical, he felt he should be alert, wary.

Yet, there was no sign of Vadim, no sign of any of Vadim's men.

If there had been, Logan would already be dead.

They both knew that.

'To help.' *Not a lie*, she thought.

'With what? We know Kassian's at your *husband's* estate.' Logan's lips sneered the title, eyes watching for her to dispute it. His hand went to his pocket, digging for his phone. 'I'm more interested about why you asked to meet me.'

'I wanted to tell you—'

'We know where he fucking is.' He sighed, eyes dropping to unlock the phone. Looking up when he heard a heavy sigh.

'You're not understanding,' she began. 'Kassian… he's… I'd like to think you'd prefer he got the girl.'

'For fuck's sake,' he hissed, barely audible.

The phone placed on the table; face down. Logan's hands rubbed over his hair, resting on his neck. The last thing he needed was attention or the suggestion he was making a deal with Vadim Morozov. The shop's emptiness registering for the first time; their voices too easily audible, the server's eyes too keen.

Locating the vial in her coat pocket, slender fingers began to ease it open. The movement slight, efficient. Her hand operating with controlled stealth as she brought it to the table; hidden in her fist.

'Why do you think that?' Logan's timbre dropped low.

A loud crash sounded from the counter; the drop of a tray. His head pivoted. Using the distraction, Anara tipped the contents of the vial into his coffee. The container returned to the safe cage of her palm until she could return it to her pocket.

'I'm the girl,' she prompted.

Logan's mind sparked; confirmation flooding. 'He was right,' he said with a shake of his head, eyes on the ceiling, laughing. 'The bastard was right; you're not married.'

Anara blinked, placing her hands below the table.

Into her pockets.

Eyes lowered with mock innocence.

'So, sweetheart,' Logan said, reaching for his mug, 'what've you got for me that'll get you love birds your happy ending?'

The liquid snaked down Logan's throat; the honeyed poison masked by the bitterness of the drink. An irritated cough grating over his tongue with the unusual burn.

'You asked me here to help, right?' His voice was rough, hand going to his mouth as he coughed again. The thickness heavy and refusing to dislodge. His forced clearing only creating a bark.

'I don't need *your* help,' she explained, sitting up tall, 'I only needed your compliance.'

'My what?' Logan's mouth felt tender, his lips tingling. Rubbing his neck, he swept up the mug and drained it; the coffee slipping over raw flesh and plunging to his stomach.

Ingredients seeping through his blood.

She smiled. 'I know what you do, Logan Pottinger. But you clearly didn't research me well enough.'

He struggled to push back from the table; his body clumsy, slow to respond to his commands. His once natural action more challenging. A slackening to his jaw indicated the beginnings of respiratory dysfunction with each laboured inhale.

'You… you're just a… woman—'

'I'm a woman, yes,' Anara said, calm. Her eyes had not shifted from his body; watching his pupils dilate, his hands clutch his stomach. 'But I also own an apothecary, and I know how to make men suffer.'

'Don't they all,' he muttered, then winced as sharp nausea spun. He screwed his eyes shut, vision tricked with swirling colours and strange shapes. The overhead lights too bright, his face crimson, and breathing jerking through his chest.

Fingers cold and head dizzy.

If he could have walked, his gait would have been impaired.

A staggering and weak fall to the wet floor.

'But, for you, I've used my personal blend,' she continued, 'it works fast.' Anara paused. 'Aconite, antimony, belladonna, hellebore, opium, in highly concentrated forms, with a few other herbs.'

He could not focus. Pulse intermittent. His heart contracting painfully with each abnormal beat. Logan could hardly breathe as fire branched through his nervous system, through his lungs.

She studied him closely. 'I give you another ten seconds.'

Seizure created asystole. Collapse.

His body slumping forward; knocking the mug to the tiles.

Shattering.

Remaining seated, she gracefully ducked to collect her umbrella, a smile as she stood. Anara strode to the counter, pulling a thick envelope from her inner pocket. The woman's gratitude, and the agreed payment, permitting Anara access to the rear exit, and freedom.

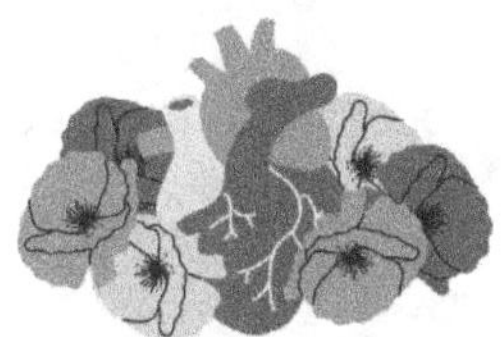

The brush of his hand against hers, seated together in the car, made her shiver; her eyes drawn to him. Finding Vadim already devouring her with his gaze. Amber flecks in the umber barely visible. Lacing his fingers into hers, he brought her hand to his lips. Eyes locked, he tenderly kissed the palm.

'You look divine, kroshka,' he murmured, returning their hands to the leather. His thumb stroked over her skin, relishing how soft she felt below his touch.

She smiled, her teeth catching her lower lip. Anara struggled to find the words to express how greatly she appreciated his appearance; the healing cut faded sufficiently to blend into the trimmed stubble. In a black suit, immaculately tailored, he looked delicious.

Makari drew the car to a halt outside Prey; the evening trade filling each table, with patrons waiting to be seated. With others utilising drinks from the bar to relax with friends. To flirt with potential lovers. Celebrate with family. The music and conversation a blur to Anara as Vadim left the car to open her door, to lead her to the entrance.

To the guarded basement casino.

Once through the doorway, the commotion faded. Lighting was soft, subdued. Music sultry. Pausing at the top of the stairs, Vadim watched Anara soak everything in. The emptiness, the shadows, the fragrant heat which drifted from the main floor below them.

Candlelight indicating where they were headed.

Her throat was dry, her eyes glazed.

Her heart thudded in her chest, threatening to choke her. She turned to him, lips parting, as her mind tried to locate any way to convey the emotion she felt.

'Is this okay, Anya?' Vadim's eyes narrowed, believing he had done something wrong.

'This is… you've done too much.' The heat in her eyes threatened to break, to betray how his actions, extravagant as they were, had further destroyed her defences.

'I've barely even begun.' He ran his knuckles down her cheek, his smile creasing his gaze. Despite the ache of the healing wounds, Vadim swept one arm below her thighs, the other behind her back, to bring her into his chest.

Carrying her down the stairs, her wrists crossed behind his neck. A delicately breathy laugh creating an exhale over his skin as Anara drew even closer, placing a kiss on his jaw.

He strode across the gaming floor, the tables empty, toward one of the booths on the perimeter. The thick fabric curtain swagged open, the lamp within turned low. Candles, at the end of the table, flickering with their movement. With his careful placement of her on the velvet seat; a material which also covered the booth's walls.

'Comfortable?' He asked, taking her right hand.

She nodded, shuddering as his lips met her wrist.

His kiss delivered with his eyes hooked into hers, flesh carrying the erratic skip of her pulse. He smiled, turning her hand over and continuing to kiss toward her fingers, her rings. He took the emerald cut diamonds in his teeth and pulled, teasing.

His tongue sliding over the sleek titanium.

Anara's chest heaved, her breath catching.

'I still need to buy you a better ring,' he said before sliding the tip of his tongue along the digit, sucking it into his mouth.

She swallowed. Her body a mass of need, of desire. Her core wept with lust. Anara was certain he could sense it, how desperate she was, how aroused. The silk between her legs drenched, her limbs trembling with anticipation.

The bite of his teeth against her manicured nail made her moan.

'Do that again, Anya, and we won't make it through this meal.' His body was as tense as hers. Crouching before her, it would be effortless to push her back, pick her up, take her until she screamed with bliss. His imagination had delivered her body to him over and again.

But Vadim wanted to ensure this was more than a physical collision, more than convenience, more than her feeling obligated to offer herself because of what had brought them to this point.

She chewed on her lower lip. 'Maybe I'm not hungry.'

'Oh, you need to eat.' Vadim forced himself to stand, sliding into the booth opposite her. Reclaiming her hands. 'We're doing this properly, so we're having dinner.'

Anara's eyes glinted in the candlelight; the obsidian of the smoky make-up accentuating her amber eyes, her pale skin. The lush red of her full lips. It was mirrored in the raven silk of her dress, in delicate maroon stitching around the hem. 'Vadya, we live in the same house.'

'And this is my restaurant.'

'I mean,' she explained, 'you didn't have to do all this—'

'I didn't have to, no.' He paused. 'I wanted to, for you.'

Anara began to object.

'No, kroshka, you deserve this,' Vadim's eyes confirmed the strength of his sentiment. 'You deserve so much more.'

Somewhere in the depths of her soul, his words felt real. But Anara found it difficult to accept they were true, that they would be manifested with supporting action. She had too many fractured promises, too many broken memories, to trust that connection was more than control. Anara wanted to give this a chance, wanted to believe this could be more than just lust, but she also knew sugar hid venom.

'Anya,' he soothed, gripping her hands more tightly as he saw the anguished frown crease her brow, 'I don't know who fucked up to mean you're here, with me, now, but I'm glad they did.'

Her frown deepened.

'If they still had you,' he said, jaw ticking at the thought, 'their days'd be very limited. You and I belong together, I knew that from the moment I first saw you, but I was prepared to wait.'

'You walked up to the bar and told Kassian I was your wife.' Anara's frown began to fade, bemused by his passion. His desire; it rolled off him in thick pulses. A proclamation there was honesty in his statements, that, maybe, she could finally allow herself to be happy.

'That wasn't the first time I saw you.' He smirked, eyes shining with mirth. He was about to describe the exact moment, when a crisp chime sounded from the kitchen.

The arrival of Ilya carrying a tray of food and drinks creating a pause in their conversation. A releasing of hands to allow for the plates to be carefully arranged, the glasses provided. The bottle of wine placed on the table, with confirmation other options could be delivered.

He left as quietly as he arrived.

'You didn't think to ask what I wanted?'

'Perhaps I'm better at reading you than you think.' Vadim studied the way her skin paled, her eyes darting away. Nikolai's research continued to offer little about Anara Eden, but her nervousness when he suggested there was more to her than she presented was consistent. 'But, kroshka, I'm open to being proved wrong.'

'Vadimir Lvovich Morozov, wrong?' Her eyebrows raised.

'I said I was open to it,' he retorted, playful, 'not that it'd happen.'

Anara bit back laughter; the lightness in her body unusual. Cautious, she welcomed it. So accustomed to having to make all the decisions, all the work, it was strange to have someone else step in. But every time he did, it was never with arrogance, or with an expectation of repayment. At least not yet; she remained guarded should that change.

Especially with so much of what she had yet to share.

'Do you want me to get you something else?' Vadim asked.

Her throat dried. 'No, this is… perfect.'

The smile revealed his teeth, a wry tilt to his head.

*He's going to be insufferable*, she thought.

The sticky honey and chilli sauce, saltiness of halloumi, peppery hit of the rocket, and lemon-roasted sugar-snap peas provided an enticing melody of aromas, of flavours. Anara's fork hovered over the dish as she debated where to start. The chewy texture, below the lightly caramelised surface of the halloumi, melting slightly as she drew the fork's tines from her mouth. Eyes closing as the different layers coated her tongue.

'Aren't you eating?' Anara asked, pausing.

Concerned he was still not recovered from the poison.

'Oh, I could watch you eat all night.' His jaw rested on his upturned palm, fingertips on his cheekbone.

'Just replay the camera feed,' she said, loading more food onto her fork and sliding it between her lips, seeing him forcibly swallow.

'The cameras are off, kroshka.' His body was urging him to swipe the plates to the floor. Envious of the utensils in Anara's hands, in how they so easily invaded her tempting mouth. How her tongue wrapped over them and she sucked on the metal. 'It's just us.'

'And the staff.'

‘I can tell them to leave.’ His eyes were on hers, watching her inner struggle. Still fighting, still resisting. ‘It’s up to you.’

‘You should eat.’ Anara slowly licked her lips, the warmth of the chilli on her skin. ‘You’ll need your energy.’

His smile turned wicked.

Focusing on her plate, she inhaled deeply.

Trying to calm the vibrating ache of her heart. The reckless heat that raced through her blood. A breathlessness which tightened her chest; the bodice of her dress constrictive. Stomach tense and thighs clenched as wet arousal pulsed. Her hips shifting on the velvet chair.

She was unsure how she managed to clear her plate.

How he devoured his.

Offered bites shared from dripping forks.

The next course delivered as efficiently as the first.

‘Don’t you eat meat?’ Her eyes flitted to his.

‘Not tonight.’ Vadim replenished their wine. The Cadão rich and her preference; a choice Anara had never voiced, but he had noticed. Had acted on. ‘During Lent we don’t eat meat, well, some of us don’t. There are other things we should abstain from too, but I bend the rules a little.’

She nodded.

‘Tell me, kroshka,’ Vadim began, ‘are there any rules I need to know when it comes to you?’

Momentarily, her eyes closed. Her chest rising. Gaze dragging to meet his as her lips parted. The words died on her tongue. There was so much she could say, so many things she could ask for, so many things she could plead for. But that would admit weakness, would prove she was vulnerable. And she had promised herself never to be put in such a position again. ‘No.’

‘No rules at all?’ His eyes narrowed. ‘I can do anything?’

‘That’s not what I meant.’

He reached across the table, tipping her chin up so he could meet her eyes once more. ‘Kroshka, I’d never hurt you.’

The touch of his skin against hers burned, fire sparking directly to her core. Bringing heat to her eyes. The vehement tone to his voice, the softness undercut with fierce adoration and devotion, was evident in his stare. In how his body tensed. Jaw tight. Anara's inhale shuddered, her nod made tentatively.

'I mean it,' he said gently, 'I love you.'

Her eyes closed.

'You may think I said that too easily,' Vadim continued, 'or maybe too quickly, for how long we've known each other, but I knew from the very first moment that you were it for me. You are everything.'

Anara felt a tear slip. She hastily moved to wipe it away only for his fingers to curl around her wrist, preventing her from reaching it. Instead, he tenderly brushed his thumb over her cheek.

'If you let yourself feel this,' Vadim said, 'if you let yourself collapse into me, I promise, you'll never have to fight alone again.'

Her heart thudded, a pulse which demanded Anara fall. Demanded she accept his words. His proposal. That all they had experienced was only a taste of what they could have together in the future.

'Kroshka,' he soothed. 'Do I have to kneel? Because I don't kneel for anyone—'

'We'll see.' She opened her eyes, finding his concerned attention on her; relief sweeping over his features at her smile. She laced her fingers into his other hand. Debating sharing a morsel of truth; confessing some of her heart. 'I think I loved you from the moment I woke up in your bed; I just wasn't quite as ready to admit it.'

He waited, sensing she had more to say; twisting their hands to his lips, he placed a soft kiss on her skin.

'Then I saw you with Kassian,' Anara said, 'even though you were injured, you looked so… so fucking strong. And the knife, fuck—'

'I heard you.'

'You… you heard me?' Her brow creased, eyes widening.

'That breathy moan was divine.'

Her face flushed. Flesh already simmering became an inferno. She tried to duck away from his scrutiny, but he kept her chin up.

'Don't be ashamed of your desires, kroshka.'

She exhaled. 'If Artem hadn't turned up when he did, your desk was looking very serviceable,' she admitted coyly.

There was a time for the full truth to be divulged, she knew this. And though Anara did not feel prepared to explain the past, or the reality of her work in Erinyes, she felt their connection was developed enough for some of her character to be released. For the barriers to drop.

As her friends had said, she could always reach out to them, or to Origins, if she needed to escape Vadim's house.

'Fuck,' he breathed. 'One moment.'

# Twenty-Eight

A swift chill sliced down Anara's spine as he withdrew from her, fingers untangled and body leaning back. His phone pulled from his suit pocket and a text sent; jacket discarded and methodically folding back the black sleeves of his shirt.

Ilya appeared soon after, the brittle silence broken only by crockery and utensils. The coiling fragrance of extinguished candle smoke, before they were also stacked on the tray. His quick footsteps and the kitchen's swing door. Vadim's tense poise and deep inhales.

The jagged breathing she tried to disguise.

She kept her eyes averted, her mind consumed with chastising and confirmation of her error. She had said too much. Revealed too much. A mistake she knew every time she relived it. Anara felt the familiar sting of regret begin to prick at her gaze, the claws digging through her flesh, a gnawing ache in her limbs.

The touch of his fingers on her jaw caused her to blink.

'Anya,' he said, more raw exhale than word.

'I shouldn't have—'

'Don't.' He removed his hand, coming to sit beside her. Tucking one leg below him, Vadim reclaimed her face, her lips.

The kiss devouring her breath.

Firm, heated, delving.

'Anya, I love you,' he affirmed, 'and if I've to remind you every damn day that you're a fucking goddess, then I will.'

Their foreheads rested together, eyes blown black. The mellow glow from the booth's lamp softening their features, deepening the fabric that draped their skin. Melted the sharpness of his tattooed flesh, warmed the snow of hers. Her lips swollen, the colour blurred.

'I… Vadya, I always fall too fast,' she whispered, 'and I've tried not to, because I can't… be hurt again. Please… tell me this is real.'

'This is real,' he vowed. He took her wrist, placing her palm on his chest. 'I want to spend my life with you, Anya.'

She felt the kick of his heart, heard the break in his voice. Her hard descent into this relationship had the potential to shatter her, she knew that, but she also knew he had yet to fail her.

Knew she should have faith, should let this consume her.

Vadim tightened his grip on her wrist, shifting his body and hers so she was on his lap. Her thighs falling either side of him, she instinctively drew closer; the curved edge of the table lightly against her back. The hard pulse of his arousal bringing a stifled moan from her throat before her hips rocked. His fingers tangled in her hair, lips exploring, tongues running along seams.

Teeth nipping at sensitive skin.

Sighs swallowed.

'It's just us,' he said, between kisses, 'and I want to hear the echo of your screams.'

His fingers splayed as they dragged down her neck to her chest, pushing her away. Her body arching against the table. The hot tip of his tongue tracing her skin, teeth playing, as he moved lower. Fingers on the bodice of her dress, skimming her curves.

'You have my devotion,' he murmured against her décolletage, eyes lifting to meet hers. Tongue tasting the swell of her breast as her breath shuddered; his stubble brushing over her flesh. 'Always.'

He wished to make her his altar, to feast from her body, her soul. To drown in her blood and discover if his name was scratched in her bones. In the cathedral chambers of her heart. He wished to split open her ribs and curl into the cavity of her chest, to find the peace he knew she could offer, to thread into her veins and find home.

To be swallowed by her whole.

His Eden, his wife.

Both hands on her waist, he lifted her to sit on the table. Trailing his hands down her legs, ducking to retrieve his knife. Her eyes widening at the glint of the blade and breath catching.

'I can buy you another dress,' he said, his smile lopsided.

'And I'm capable of unfastening this one.' Anara was uncertain, the tremor in her hands made her touch unsteady, her body not quite her own. It took her three attempts to catch the zip and lower it.

The blade resting on the table.

'Ты ей вдоль, а она поперёк[41],' he teased, watching her loosen the silk from her frame with rapt attention. Body aching to surrender, to claim her, to love her. To convince her being stubborn was futile. That he would always be the shield, the protector, the champion.

That she could finally rest.

The heat of his exhale against her breast, the sweep of his tongue over her nipple, entwined with his words, made her moan. Brought her fingers back to his hair, raking through it with affection. The onyx of the strands melting into the obsidian of her nails.

Slack fabric permitting his lips to suck on her, to bite into the darker flesh. The sharp intake of her breath the precursor to the cry; his eyes on hers when she lowered them. A narrowing as she tightened her grip in his hair and pulled. Fisting the strands and dragging his head back, even as the surprised wail became a moan.

A desperate absence which craved his return.

---

[41] Ты ей вдоль, а она поперёк - a Russian idiom which means 'Every woman is a rebel, and usually in wild revolt against herself'

She met his lips with savage force, tongue caressing with fury, and teeth seeking to draw blood. Anara's body pressing, seeking the solid muscle of his torso, to grind her quim, her legs wrapping him tightly and drawing him closer still.

Her own hunger needed satiating.

Smiling against her mouth, Vadim allowed her to believe she had taken control. Permitted the tender devouring. One hand grazing her hip before curling around the knife. Bringing the chilled metal to her fevered skin, ghosting the flesh in a snaking path from elbow to shoulder, down her clavicle, her sternum.

'Vadya,' she breathed, chest heaving.

There was no blood, not yet. He had not bitten, had not slipped the sharpened edge below her skin. Head bowed, he latched his teeth into the top of her breast and laved it with his tongue, the blade flat beside his jaw. Knuckles almost bone with temptation.

The cautious arrival of her hand around his, wrapping the leather of the hilt, brought a pause. A tense stare. The potential drifting around their bodies in unspoken exhales.

'Not here,' he finally managed to say. Throwing the knife to the floor beyond the swagged fabric; the booth still open to the empty room. The oscillating weapon threw shards of light, splintering over dark marble and wood, over voids. 'And only when you're ready.'

She leant back a little. 'What part of this suggests I'm not?'

Vadim's exhale was laced with laughter. 'Oh, kroshka, you're divine, perfect for me, in every possible way.' Arms dropping, fingers clutching her smooth calves, sliding up below the silk of her dress.

The intrusive reminder of her truth ripped through her mind, a cruel confession ready on her lips. Stolen when his hands reached her hips, a firm pull to tilt her back. Their eyes conveying longing, their lips parted, their thudding hearts screaming for more.

Her arching neck and released moan the reward for the delicate trail of his fingertips along lace. Anara's hips shifting to try and direct his movement, to put him where she wanted him, even as he kept his gaze fixed on her reactions. On how her entire body was alert, alive, electric. A vibrant tremble sparking every sense.

'Anara, Anya,' he said softly, pausing. Waiting for her hooded eyes to meet his. 'Do you want this?'

She fought to steady her breath, to focus. Her hand reaching for his neck, stroking over heated skin. Feeling his shiver as the tip of her nail caught his lobe. 'Yes, absolutely and always.'

Hooking his fingers, he coaxed the fabric lower, bringing her thighs together, until it slid over her feet. Reverent, he delivered slow kisses from her ankles to her knees, from her knees to her thighs, a velvet touch of mouth and tongue.

Venerating her flesh.

A paced return to her hips, to her heat. The glide of his tongue, the nip of his teeth, the measured exhales of his breath. Restrained bites love notes of intent; his desire to consume her held back, caged in his throat. His chest. His soul. The image of the knife, her body; plunging himself into the secure home she offered.

Each moment increased the hope, the desperation. Anara's mind and body ready to fall, deep, before he even reached the apex of her thighs. His exquisite torture tightening her chest, bringing bumps over her skin, an increasing series of moans from her throat.

When his tongue finally swept languidly over her sex, Anara almost cried with relief. Only for Vadim to move back, to look up. To meet her anguished eyes, her parted lips, and smile.

'God, I could dine on you forever,' he stated, voice gravel.

'And leave me hungry?' The words were fractured, raw. Her body was being eaten by lust. By anticipation gorging on her veins with every laboured breath. Her need for control battling with the persuasion to lose it; to allow him to be her sanctuary, her escape.

'I'll feed you,' he promised, 'as much as you desire.' The incessant pulse of his cock underlined the pledge with how painfully hard it was; an ache he used to drive her pleasure. His hold on her thighs stronger, his head ducking back to taste her. The stroke over slick flesh with the flat surface of his tongue bringing a guttural moan from her throat.

Made her hips oscilate.

The repeated flicks, twists, and sucks he delivered bringing a louder and more frantic response. Her coy moans becoming wilder, her words pleading, her back bowing, flesh craving more.

Pausing, he brought one hand to her shoulder, drawing her to him; a fevered kiss allowing her to discover what he feasted on. The curl of her tongue over his lips, their eyes open and fixed on each other, brought an anguished groan from his chest.

Timed with the pinch of her clit, the lowering of his palm, firm glide of two fingers; a delicious burn. A tight welcome. The pulsing digits causing sparks to flare, the release of her pressured breath forcing her head to fall back. His knuckles coated in nectar; slick, hot. Her body liquid and bones fluid, her mind lost to the pattern he orchestrated.

The descending kisses peppering her chest.

The deeper stretch of his fingers, spiral of his thumb.

The nip of flesh.

Anara was about to break.

His attentive touch designed to ruin her. To stretch every nerve until she snapped, until her body found the paradise she deserved. That she had denied. Vadim's dilated pupils trained on delivering worship, to bring her to the precipice of surrender.

'I've got you, kroshka,' he confirmed.

The return of his mouth to her clit brought a scream. Every limb taut as the electric heat shuddered from her core; spreading within her to the beckoning beat of his fingers. His lips unrelenting as they sucked, forcing her to surrender to the sensations he savoured.

A banquet. A chalice which Vadim sought to empty of every sour memory, every scrap of hurt poisoning her soul. To fill her with bliss, with ecstasy, with the pleasure she deserved.

A lingering bite made, marking the top of her thigh with his teeth.

His conquering almost breaking the skin.

Breathless, Anara's body sunk to the table. Her hands draped over the gap, eyes closed and skin flushed with fiery dissipation. The leisurely kisses Vadim continued to place on her trembling thighs as he dressed her, barely registering; only the sense of being loved.

Of being cared for.

Warm tears gathering in her eyes.

Taking her gently, Vadim drew her down into his lap, hands moving to re-zip the dress and stroke the stray curls from her face. His gaze on her smile, on the silent escape of water from the corner of her smeared eyes. He brought his thumb to her cheek, catching it.

'Anya?'

She blinked, placing her palms on his chest.

'Are you okay?' Vadim could feel every shiver as she nestled into his body. 'Did I hurt you?'

Shaking her head, she tried to find words. Her tongue licking over her lips to find moisture. 'No, it was… it… you… fuck.'

The lamp at the end of the booth flickered; three times.

Vadim tensed, but ignored it, his focus on her.

'I should've made you stay in the pool,' she finally managed to say. A frown briefly forming at the repeated darkness and light. She wondered if her brain had lost all function.

He laughed, fingers splayed behind her head to bring her forward, to tuck her against his neck.

'Give me a minute, and then… you can do that again.' Anara's lips ghosted his neck, her eyelashes grazing his earlobe. 'And maybe after… I should—'

'You don't have to do anything,' he said, leaning in to tenderly kiss her crown, her hair. 'Tonight was all for you; I can wait.'

The light died and brightened another three times.

'Fuck,' he muttered.

She leaned back. *I didn't imagine it*, she thought.

'Take your time, kroshka,' Vadim said, jaw tight, 'I must go deal with something.' Seeing the fleeting disappointment in her eyes, even as she complied and moved from his lap, almost broke his obsidian heart.

# Twenty-Nine

Vadim took the steps down to the basement with haste, the diversion in the bar one which he would return to later. The interruption unnecessary and something he intended to address after resuming his evening. Anara deserved his full attention, and an apology.

He should have treated her with far more devotion.

More reverence.

Should have taken her home, to his bed. Their bed.

The dark silence of the empty space felt flawed as he approached the base of the stairs. One lone light barely visible, the swagged curtain dropped and almost covering the booth they had occupied.

Though he considered Anara may have sought some privacy, the quiet suggested otherwise. He ducked to his boot, then remembered he had thrown the knife onto the floor. Narrowing his gaze, he found it and swept it into his palm as he neared the shadowy illumination.

'Anya?' He paused to the side of the upholstery of the neighbouring booth; the velvet soft against his frame.

Nothing.

He closed his eyes; every sense alert. Simmering.

Knife secure, Vadim strode forward, dragging the heavy fabric open to reveal what he feared. She was gone.

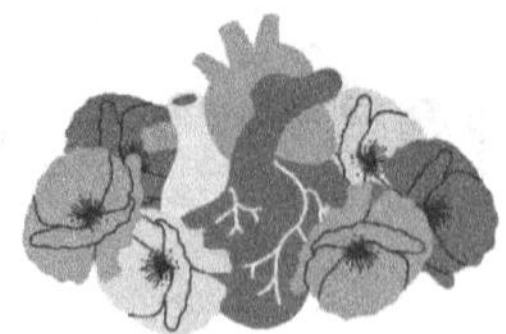

She knew something was wrong when they stepped out into the chilled night; the van's blacked out windows and running engine ominous. The vehicle's lights off, and parked just beyond the reach of Prey's lamps and, they had assumed incorrectly, their security cameras. The grating drag of the sliding door confirmed her disquiet when the partly-shaven head and blond braid came into view.

*Septer.*

Anara's heart cracked, her body frozen. Alert. Eyes rapidly scouring the surroundings for any means of escape. She knew the man who had steered her from the booth, along the dimly lit corridors to the exit, was one of Vadim's men. Recognition, coupled with Vadim's urgent departure and her mellow satisfaction, had left her vulnerable.

She clenched her teeth, curled her hands into fists.

About to turn and run back toward the door.

'Don't even think about it, sweetheart,' Aeron Barnes stated, his smile leering from the shadows; watching Yakov grip her upper arm and push her toward the waiting van.

'He'll kill you, every single fucking one of you.' She tried to shake off the man's hold, her eyes narrowing as she looked directly ahead. Chin up and spine straight. The night's breeze coiled around her bare legs as her heels hit the asphalt. 'If I don't kill you first.'

It was a risk, delivering those last words. But if they knew she had poisoned Logan, then she guessed she would already be dead. It made more sense for her to be taken to coax Vadimir Morozov to retaliate. Her for Kassian, her for every one of Septer's scouts Vadim's men had killed; Anara was, publicly, his wife, a prize worth capturing.

Worth using to destroy the Bratva's control.

A shiver sliced down her back; unless they meant to sell her.

Use her in other ways.

Her chest heaved, a forceful swallow made as she stumbled.

'I think we can handle you.' Aeron's hand slid down her back, forcing her into the rear of the van. His touch lingering. Feeling her tense below his fingertips as they skimmed her silk-covered skin. Her hip.

Anara almost hissed, her head twisting to him with vengeful eyes. A curl in her lips, teeth glinting in the amber glow of the van's interior light as she collapsed into the seat. The fabric gritty, rough against her limbs, and there was an acrid, cloying scent of tobacco.

'I need to get back,' Yakov said, eyes shifting toward Prey.

'Sure.' Aeron hoped Vadim would rush from the doorway so he could put a bullet in the man who had caused Septer so many issues. Even if he knew such a privilege should be reserved for someone else. 'Yasha[42], he'll be expecting you.'

He nodded. 'Tell him I'll be there as soon as I can.'

Aeron clambered in, taking the seat beside Anara; vehicle rocking with the change in weight as he slammed the door shut.

Pressing closer to the window, Anara closed her eyes. She refused to crumble. Vadim would come for her. He had to.

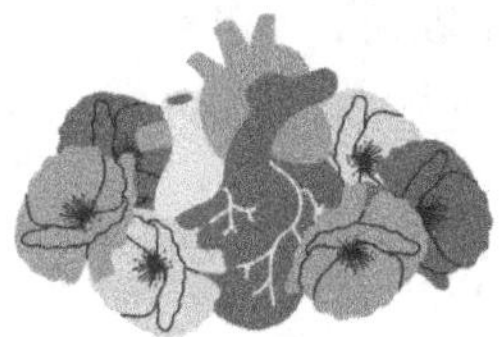

He regretted leaving his firearm at home. After realising Anara had felt the rig below his jacket, he had opted to bring only a knife. Which was very unlike him. But Vadim had trusted his men would protect them, had trusted that a knife would be enough.

Tonight was a date.

A moment away from business.

Away from deals.

From plans.

---

[42] Yasha - the diminutive form of the name Yakov

A moment just for them.

Instead, he found himself alone.

The darkness of the gaming room only emphasising the hollow shell without her presence. Her fragrance an echo of the way she had filled his every breath.

His heart.

Vadim released a fractured roar; his fists curled and nails cutting into his palms. His strides becoming a run as he traversed the corridors and empty rooms, lights flicked on and confirming his solitude. The basement was a void, a reminder of how brittle this life could be. He had lost family, had lost friends, but this, this had ripped out his soul.

Lungs ragged, limbs sharp, pulse erratic.

Returning to the booth, he found Artem waiting; his advisor's face a grim warning. Vadim knew he was poorly masking his emotions, the raw ache a tattoo in his cold gaze, his tight jaw. The effort he was making to suppress the fury which snaked through his blood desperate to splinter his measured inhales.

'It's Septer,' Artem said through clenched teeth.

The connection of Vadim's fist with the table was a fierce crack. His knuckles splitting with the force; blood smearing the wood.

'We were betrayed.' Artem stepped closer, his hand cautious to rest on his leader's shoulder and find his eyes.

Slow, Vadim twisted to meet the stare. 'Who?'

'Yasha.'

Vadim's jaw ticked. His teeth pressed hard, grinding. The pressure radiated in his cheekbones, his temples; increased the headache which had descended the moment he had discovered Anara's absence. He swept his hands up, over his face, fingertips massaging his scalp briefly before cradling his neck. Warm blood ignored as it seeped over cracked skin. 'How?'

'We don't know how they persuaded her,' Artem explained, 'but they had a van parked out back.'

'And no-one thought to tell me?' Vadim's head tilted toward the false ceiling, eyes closing with a heavy exhale. The cameras hidden in the catwalk off; no way to know what they did to her, what they said, before forcing her to leave.

He was utilising every scrap of discipline to remain calm.

But it was unravelling; gnawing through the restraint.

'We didn't know, our focus was elsewhere.' His brow creased as he spoke, his tone curt. 'It was almost time to close the bar, and things were busy already with the scouts—'

'I don't want fucking excuses.' Vadim lowered his arms, rocking his head side to side. 'I want Yakov in my cells.'

'He doesn't have the power to organise something like—'

'I. Want. Yakov. In. My. Fucking. Cells.'

'Yes, pakhan.' Artem nodded, moving back. Pivoted on his heel, his hand already dragging his phone from his pocket to relay the order.

They had the probationary man cornered; Makari had grabbed him the moment the camera footage had been reviewed. Yakov was tied to a chair in one of the offices. Pavel stood watch, his firearm trained on the man's bowed head. Finger itching to fall to the trigger.

'Who made the request I leave her alone?' His voice was soft, the words travelling easily to reach Artem as he began to tread the stairs.

'The intel was legit,' Artem said, hand on the rail. He turned his torso toward his leader. 'Logan Pottinger was found dead, and Mace sent his soldiers onto our territory to antagonise us.'

'That didn't require my attention.' Vadim's body vibrated with rage. A barely contained thrum with each restrained step; deliberate placement of his booted feet. His eyes cold, intense. 'Any of our brigadiers could've managed a few of Septer's scouts.'

'True.' Artem stood his ground, relieved to see the strength rolling off the pakhan. After the poisoning and with how Vadim was behaving with Anara, he had been concerned Morozov was compromised. 'But Ksenia panicked when she saw them outside Prey.'

'And she didn't trust her husband to deal with them?'

'There were more than a few, pakhan.'

'Eight, there were eight,' he pressed, reaching the advisor. Taking a few steps to ensure he was level.

'We had a full bar, it was best to handle—'

'That was for me to decide.'

'Which is why we called you.' Artem's hand tightened on the rail, his tattooed skin betraying the tension in his grip.

Vadim knew his advisor was correct; the knowledge sour, creating a numb emptiness. Throat grating with the sigh he choked. His shoulders sagging as the culpability sunk into his blood.

He should never have left her alone.

He should have taken her with him.

He should have ignored the request.

But it had been protocol, it had been their procedure.

They had rules and contingencies.

Protect the women.

Protect their business.

If they were to continue to thrive, then their actions must be above suspicion, or at least appear to be. Payments made, deals struck. Any disruption to that would have caused significant damage; a gun fight in Prey would have been devastating. Not just to their business, but to the communal fund and those who depended on it.

Vadim had obligations, he had families who relied on the stability he provided, the income he generated, the safety he offered. To have lost all that purely because he wanted to prolong time with Anara would have been the end of his life.

And he had so much more life he wanted to live, now.

But not alone.

Not now he had tasted what life could be like.

He straightened his spine, locked his eyes on Artem.

'Find her,' he said, rough and fractured. 'Bring her home.'

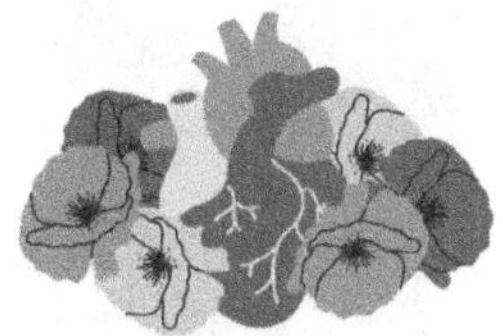

Anara thought she would have heard a car. Would have seen the rapid strobe of lights. Anything, something. Evidence of Vadim chasing after her to prove this was more than fake. That the words were substantiated by action. That her dreams would be supported by his vow.

But there was only the radio.

Their voices; jubilant self-congratulations and lewd remarks. Calls to whoever was in charge and urgently issued commands. Instructions. The texts causing a shrug, a chuckle. A menacing glare.

She shrank into the rough seat, kept her sore eyes on the roads. A raw ache in the determined refusal to cry. To allow her already smeared make-up to become more dishevelled. Observing the buildings thin and countryside drift by, watching night's inky shroud succumb to dawn's pale glow, Anara felt her hope fade.

The humiliating drop of heated, salted water which escaped closed eyes swiped from her cheek with fury. He was not coming.

She was alone.

Again.

# Thirty

Sensing the change in speed, in sound, Anara's eyes blinked open. The heavy gunmetal clouds revealed little about how long she had managed to sleep. Her neck screaming from the awkward position. Her limbs stiff and complaining from being cramped. Tense. Defensive. A sliding gaze assessing, trying to make out a time. Failing.

The van's dashboard smeared with dusty prints, a creased photo of a naked woman tacked over the display. The driver navigated the gravel driveway poorly, struggling to miss large holes; the original driver now in the passenger seat. Beside her, Aeron appeared unaffected by the rough jostling. His snores rhythmic, off beat to the low music.

Turning her focus to the looming building ahead, Anara's melancholy dug deeper talons into her mind. Her soul. The render was peeling from the brick, rust stained and stark against the thick sky; sunlight chained by cloud. Though the trees were beginning to bud, the place felt desolate.

She shuddered.

Wrapping her arms around herself, she slowly rubbed her skin; the van was not cold, but it was not warm. The prolonged requirement to be static, the dress she wore, was not enough to prevent a covering of bumps as Anara shivered. She had not planned on being outside, nor being prevented from returning home.

*Home*, she thought, scoffed. Her eyes drifting to the marked ceiling of the van as fresh moisture gathered. The maroon streaks, dirty and coppery, on the lighter fabric dried her throat.

*He'll come for me*, Anara repeated over and again in her mind. Her reliance on logic momentarily ignored in favour of aspirational desire, in faith. Vadim was a man of action, yes, but also of planning. Of restraint. He would need to ensure everything was in place, and would trust she could survive until he arrived.

The brakes of the van squeaked as they came to a halt. The double doors at the top of stone stairs opened in readiness, a man appearing in the entrance. Arms folded. Sub-machine gun cradled to his chest.

'Boss,' the driver stated, loud.

Grunting, Aeron sniffed then stretched. In the dull light, the bandage around his hand was more grey than white, the tape holding it beginning to peel at the edges. Lint sticking to the adhesive. 'Cheer up, sweetheart, you're perfectly safe here.'

The look in his eyes conveyed something different, but Anara stayed silent. Cataloguing surroundings, deciphering options, forging possible routes of escape. The gravel had taken some time to traverse, but now they were parked, she believed the private drive was not entirely without access.

The building looked more institution than residence.

Skeletal trees permitted glimpses of fields, which ruled out running, at least until she could figure out where exactly they were. A nearby farm or home may provide a friendly reception, even if she had to walk for a few miles. Anara's heels would be awkward but not impossible, and she could always utilise the stiletto points to fight with.

Anara settled her heart, tipped up her chin, as she stepped unaided from the van's side door. She took a moment to stand and look around, a chorus of aches begging her to stretch. Refusing to appear weak, such internal knots and clicks were ignored.

'Come on,' Aeron said, shoving her forward.

Behind them, the remaining two occupants swapped seats, with the van's engine firing up. The revving and kick of gravel breaking the quiet as they returned to the main road.

Stepping back, the guard waited for them to enter the hallway before pushing the doors closed; the lock turned. Dim, heavily patterned paper covered each wall, a nicotine-stained ceiling stretched toward stairs at the end of the corridor. Several doors were resolutely shut, white paint flaking. The floor felt sticky below her feet.

'I don't want to hurt you, sweetheart,' Aeron began, paused. 'No, I do want to hurt you. I want to drag you down and fuck every hole you've got until you're in too much pain to resist anymore.'

A glacial shiver sliced through her every nerve. The tight hold Anara kept of her frame, the curl of her fingers against her ribs, prevented her from shaking with the image his words delivered.

'But, I also know you're worth much more without my… attention.' A lingering pass of his eyes over her body made his smile twist. Her lack of reaction, the detached glaze to her eyes, almost made him lash out. His fingers keen to strike.

To claim.

'Don't be fucking stupid, Aeron,' Mace snapped, jogging down the stairs to meet them. His unbuttoned suit jacket flared with the movement, revealing the firearm tucked to one side, ammunition on the other.

Anara's eyes followed his descent and approach, forcing her breath to remain steady, to continue to stand tall. Composed. Rigid. Her tongue rolling over her lips. She recognised Mace Kersey, but was unaware he had other property outside the city. Her research had not got that far into Septer and their operation.

'Anara Eden… sorry *Morozova*,' Mace said, holding out his hand in futile expectation, 'I'm so pleased you could come.'

'I wasn't aware I'd been given a choice.'

Mace's hand dropped, his eyes slow to flick over to Aeron then back to Anara. 'If you'd like to freshen up, there's a bathroom there.'

She followed the sharp gesture he offered, his head jerking to one side. The obscured glass of the door revealing likely sterile white fixtures and scratched mirrors. Anara nodded, wary, her movements cautious as she kept her eyes on the three men in the corridor.

The man in tactical gear guarding the main doors.

Aeron and his lecherous stares.

Mace's false salutations.

There was no lock on the door. And the glass made her conscious of her actions; no time to waste on leaning against the wall, the door, to feel any sense of calm. She hurried through what she needed to do, trying to make herself feel a little more human. Refreshed. Ducking under the tap, the cool water was welcome in her mouth. On her tongue.

Last night's dinner tasted bitter.

The memory of all they did, all they laughed about, all they bonded over, soured. In a room full of shades of white, Anara's dark hair formed a veil around her pale skin, the remnants of her make-up scrubbed from her flesh; blotchy and irritated by the furious pressure.

The dark silk of her dress restrictive.

Her steps too loud.

Her eyes too hot; mascara stubborn and stained.

The reflection blurred as more water gathered in her eyes.

'Fuck this,' she muttered, 'and fuck him.'

Her jaw ticked with the pressure of her teeth. Her knuckles tight with the curl of her hands on the sink. Back bowed as she leant her body on the smooth porcelain. Her eyes closing as she inhaled deeply. Exhaled to a slow count. Coaxing her pulse to become more sedate, her blood to be less warm.

There was always a chance she would be caught; her work made it a risk. She just never expected it to be like this. Anara had assumed the police would be who imprisoned her, not a group of men who believed they could outmanoeuvre the Bratva.

*Men*, she thought, *just men*.

She had faced men and survived.

She would survive again.

Anara straightened up, her final inhale swelling her chest against the constrictive stitches of her dress. She smoothed the fabric over her body and listened to the growl of hunger which coiled low.

'You okay in there sweetheart?'

She did not answer him, instead strode to the door; heels punching out a swift rhythm on the tiles. The handle depressed and forcing Aeron's stocky presence back to allow her through.

'Mace's waiting for you, upstairs.'

The serenity she had forged in her heart stuttered.

'In his office.' Aeron sneered; lips a smug smile, blue eyes raking her body once more. He nudged her shoulder, steering her toward the stairs, following just behind.

'I'm capable of walking unaided,' she said, glancing to him when his hand landed on her lower back.

He did not remove it. Instead, Aeron pushed more firmly, driving her to walk more quickly. The rock of her hips bringing greater depth to the reddish tint to his cheeks. His neck. The intrusive chime of his phone in his suit pocket ignored; Aeron's fingertips pressing sharply to force her to comply. To move her toward the open door of his leader.

Mace had his ankles crossed, feet propped on the table, a steeple of his hands, elbows resting on the arms of the chair. He watched the pair arrive, his brown eyes slightly pinched.

The repeated intrusion of the phone a distraction.

'You should answer that,' Anara remarked, twisting to face him.

With a heavy exhale, Aeron cursed and dug for his phone. Incessant noise silenced by the hasty slide of his finger across the screen. A shake of his head as he stalked back out to the corridor.

Door open.

His voice fading as he put distance between them.

'Can I get you anything?' Mace was yet to move.

'A car, a phone, a change of clothes, food, and opium.' She kept her gaze level, her voice steady. Though Aeron had shoved her toward one of the chairs, she stayed standing.

'No to all of those,' he replied, feet dropping to the floor and tipping his body upright. 'But I admire your fortitude.'

Anara's shoulders remained back, her neck at risk of betraying the strain in her posture, her mind. The tension in her muscles forcing a loud thrum in her blood to roar, to heat her skin, her vision. A fixed stare which relied on the periphery to digest the features of the room; one door, one large barred window, sparse furniture.

'You'll be treated fairly,' Mace continued, leaning on the desk. 'Just as, I'm sure, your *husband* is caring for Kassian.'

She swallowed; jaw clenched and throat thick.

'Your *husband* made it easy for us, Anara.' Mace pushed himself up, palms flat to the wood. 'Turning off the cameras while he tried to prove himself worthy of you, despite his lies.'

'Lies?' Anara cursed herself inwardly at the response.

Mace smirked. 'All in good time.'

'I'm surprised you've left Kassian with us so long,' she said, her tone brittle, forced, 'especially considering how valuable an asset he is to you, and what information he's providing.'

'We needed time to get you, love.' Mace circled her, his hand trailing her shoulders, her neck, drifting over her clavicle then up to her chin. His breath falling over her skin.

Her eyes resolutely fixed on the fields beyond the window.

'And now we have you, we can trade.' Mace curled her hair into his fist, dragging her head back until she had no option but to sway.

Almost stumbling.

'He won't—'

'He will.' Mace pulled harder, winding the strands tighter. His smile growing as her eyes glistened, her mouth opening. Releasing her with a swift kick to her shin.

Anara bit her tongue. She refused to give him the satisfaction of a response, even as pain surged through her body. Rushing back to her feet, she resumed her mask; emotions proficiently hidden behind a cold smile. It was a familiar shroud, a void, a cruel embrace she fell into with detached weariness.

Walls rebuilt with efficient resignation.

# Thirty-One

Vadim leapt from the car before Makari braked, before the engine was cut. His strides eating the driveway and slamming through the door with determined fury. The stairs taken several at a time to his suite, a range of blades and a fully loaded firearm taken from his personal arsenal, before returning down to the hallway.

All before Artem and Makari had gathered by the closed doors.

'Vadya—'

'Have you found her?' He did not stop, resolute in his progress to his study and the spiral staircase to the cells.

Trusted they would follow.

'Kolya is tracking—'

'He needs to work faster.' His feet echoed on the stairs, his focus on the open cell door. The groans which resonated from wet impact of fist against split skin; Pavel working over the man who betrayed them.

Betrayed him.

Vadim's jaw pulsed with the pressure of his teeth; an inferno gnawed through his blood, strangled his heart. The ache of her absence fuelling necessary vengeance. If his mood could have brought her back, it would have razed the earth until only they stood in the ashes. The loss bitter, a cascade of shards spitting from him with each step.

His breath was ragged when he reached the threshold.

Below the bright light, Yakov was prone; stripped naked and wrists bound in iron shackles hanging from the ceiling. Arms at the limit of their joints and limbs turned to ensure the pain did not abate. His neck lolled, eye already swelling from the cut cheekbone, the fracture webbing below the mottled skin. His feet were curled, legs weak.

It was not enough.

Vadim withdrew the Grach from his holster; pistol aimed with swift precision, bullet released. The crack loud in the enclosed space. Yakov's scream a satisfying break in his laboured breathing as it tore through the flesh and bone of his knee.

Splintering the cap and shredding tissue.

The additional weight shifting to one leg resulting in one stretched shoulder dislodging from the socket. The scream becoming a wail. A sob which shuddered through his beaten chest and brought mucus from his nose, spittle from his lips. Saliva syrupy drool over his bloodied chin.

Firing again, the second bullet struck Yakov's other knee.

Yakov's bladder emptying with the fresh pain.

To one side of the prisoner, Pavel flexed his fingers; the bruised and cracked skin of his knuckles of no consequence. The spiked steel bar lay in his pocket, ready to be slid back on and another round of punches to be thrown. He watched his leader carefully, waiting for the signal.

'Why, Yasha, why?' Vadim barely opened his lips, his eyes pinched and thumb hovering on the trigger. It would be so easy to open the man's chest, to release another bullet, to empty the entire magazine, into his cavity.

Force Yakov to feel even a minute sense of what Vadim felt.

His body vibrated with anger, with sorrow, with guilt. The weight sour on his tongue, his heart sticky with pyrolysis. Anara's divine sweetness from earlier that evening an addiction Vadim craved; desperate to bring her back, for him to crawl into her.

Body and soul.

And this man, this probationary apprentice, had dared to collude and steal her away. Vadim wanted to rip Yakov's arms from his body, to tear the flesh layer by layer until there was only bone.

Only a shell; emptiness and anguish.

Yakov's head remained lowered, his breath rasping over sore tissue, lungs aching with fractured ribs.

Plunging the tip of his knife into Yakov's hip, Vadim twisted.

Simultaneously, Pavel grabbed a fistful of the man's hair, dragging his head up. Yakov's mouth opened with another plea, a broken cry for a halt in the assault.

'Why did you do this, Yasha?'

He shook his head.

'Your silence is admirable,' Vadim said, spun the blade again. 'It's a shame it's for the wrong reasons. You'd've made a valuable member of my team.' He stepped back, pulling the knife with him, the curved edge forging a deep crevice through the man's skin.

Blood gushing down his thigh to the deformed knee.

Vadim glanced to the door, seeing Makari arrive with a clear bag of white crystalline powder. There was no smile, only a weary, sharp nod which conveyed appreciation. The guard opened the seal, pouring it over the slick blade, a bowl beneath to catch the motes of dimethyltryptamine as it fell.

'Who should I send your heart to, Yasha?' Vadim asked, his back to the captured man. The pivot slow as he lunged forward, burying the knife in Yakov's abdomen; letting the drug soak into the blood.

He howled. The blade's hilt pressing into the trembling skin of his stomach, searing and hot as it oscillated. Vadim's body close, the spiral of his wrist increasing the inflicted damage. Still he refused to talk, his mind a mass of pain, of a longing for it to end, for the attack to cease.

The drug spiking his heart rate, distorting perception.

'Would Mace want it?' Vadim said, almost a whisper, leaning into the man's ear. His teeth grazing the shell.

The slightest flinch was all the evidence they needed.

'Fuck!' Vadim whipped the other blade from his waist, plunging it into the man's neck. The carotid spilled, hot and fresh, over his hand. Ripping downward, Vadim tore through the man's chest, carving deep.

Pavel's hasty steps and rattle of metal confirming the retrieval of a retractor, offered without words.

The heart sliced from Yakov's chest without ceremony.

In Vadim's bloodied hand, it almost appeared innocent. The organ smeared with ichor, lined with arteries, with creamy muscle. Hot from the man's body, elixir draining. The limp apprentice broken, chained.

Pocketing his phone, Artem stepped into the room and assessed the scene for a moment. His eyebrows raised in satisfied commendation of what he assumed had taken place. 'Mace is missing.'

Vadim flung the heart to the floor. 'What do you mean?'

'We guessed Septer had her—'

'And?'

'He's not at Iðun, or his other clubs,' Artem continued, his attention on the pakhan, even as Pavel stooped to retrieve the thrown organ and begin to tidy up. 'I've asked Kolya to search for other locations.'

Vadim cradled his neck, head tilting to the ceiling; eyes closed and a heavy exhale released through his nose. Tension screamed through his body, a sense of failure eating into his bones. He had Yakov's heart, had his confirmation of the connection to Mace, but nothing more.

Anara was still missing.

Gritting his teeth, Vadim lowered his hands and took a measured breath, retrieving the knife from Yakov's liver.

'Where are you going?' Artem asked, eyes narrowed.

'Kassian.' Vadim stalked from the cell, knife nestled in his palm.

Watching Anara straighten up, Mace tilted his head to one side, teeth on his lower lip and eyes narrowing. He had broken defiant women before and he would do so again; Anara Eden was no exception. Leisurely, he paced the worn floorboards of the temporary office. This location usually utilised for their auctions, not any day to day operations, which meant the building was cold.

Dirty.

The next sale was imminent, and the preparations would begin later that day. Those men who came to bid on the women did not particularly care how presentable the rooms were, how clean. Only that the women were compliant, complacent, naked.

This woman could be made to behave, he was certain of it.

'Tell me, Anara,' he said, pausing before the window; corroded iron bars lay horizontally at intervals across the glass. Still serviceable, still a deterrent. 'Is it Eden or Morozova?'

She inhaled deeply, her eyes refusing to drop. Her arms folded over her chest; studying him for any signs of weakness, assessing how she could escape the situation. With nothing in her possession, she had only her words, her body, her clothes. Shredding the silk of her dress began to look promising; to wrap it around his neck, hold it, and kick him down the stairs. The point of her heel in his chest.

Anara smiled.

The image vibrantly playing out before her eyes.

'Boss,' Aeron said tentatively, reappearing in the room. There was a slight shake in his hands, a tremor in his voice. His eyes anywhere but the leader of Septer. He nodded to the doorway in suggestion Mace join him outside.

'Fuck's sake, Barnes, just say what you have to fucking say.' Mace tensed; hands going to his hips, flicking out his jacket. A chilled dread in his stomach as the pause dragged.

Slow, Aeron licked his tongue over his lips. 'They've got Yasha.'

Anara's smile broadened. *That's my man*, she thought.

Mace clenched his teeth, eyes closing.

The heavy punch of his advisor's words ricocheting violently through his blood. Mace's hands forming fists to prevent the shake being seen, a tightening of his jaw to choke the emotion. His face paling as weakness seeped over his limbs, below the skin. Every single thought suggesting he crumble, despite the people in the room.

Despite how he had only seen Yakov as a body.

A decent fuck, a man he could manipulate to get information.

Someone who was easily dispensable in this game.

Yet, the loss cut deep; more than Mace had anticipated.

*He's going to come for me, I just need to survive this, I just need to buy him time.* Anara's mind worked through what may be happening, the things Vadim would need to do. Question Yakov and Kassian. Determine where she had been taken. Gather his men and get here.

Unfurling his fingers, Mace walked stiffly toward the desk. His hands gripping the back of the chair and raising his eyes to her; grieving could wait. 'It seems your husband wants to make this personal.'

'You made it personal by taking me,' she retorted.

He shook his head; burying the sting of loss. 'He really wants what you've got to offer, very fucking badly.'

She chewed on her lip, unsure what Mace was inferring.

'Has he told you?' Mace's voice was all restrained fury; cold, barbed, and precise. 'Has he told you the truth?'

'I know exactly who Vadim is.'

'Your *husband*,' he sneered, 'correct, Anara *Morozova*.'

Anara's teeth ground firmly, the ache thrumming through her body as she retained her eyes on Septer's leader.

'Your husband has considerable wealth—'

'I know,' she muttered.

'—family wealth, and business wealth,' Mace continued. 'There was no reason to take Yasha, no fucking reason.' He shifted from behind the chair, both palms slamming onto the desk. 'No. Fucking. Reason.'

Anara flinched at the sound.

Behind her, Aeron smirked at her reaction.

'He's got Kassian,' Mace said, 'there was no reason to take—'

'Yasha betrayed him,' Anara interjected, 'there's your reason.'

'So, love, betrayal is worth death?' Mace leant heavily on the wood, his shoulders strained, neck marked with protruding veins. They may not have Yakov's heart, yet, but it would come. He was certain of it.

'We all die eventually.' Anara refused to bow to their pressure; but Aeron's proximity and Mace's tone, coupled with growing hunger, was steadily eroding the adrenaline; her spark to fight fading. Anara's initial resolution to persevere duelling in a constant oscillation. Dignified attack or meek retreat. Painful wounds reopened.

Old fears teased, hissed.

'He won't want you to die, love,' he confirmed. 'You're too valuable right now; I'm counting on him coming for you.'

She bit down a sigh.

'But I'm not sure you'll want him to.'

'Why?' Anara watched him pace toward her.

'Because, love, if betrayal is worth death, you're going to want to kill him.' Mace spat the words, venom on his tongue, the wrath in his body evident in his face.

She swallowed, feeling the hot flecks hit her skin.

'Do you know why he married you?' Mace circled her, studying her muscles as they tensed, as her eyes glazed, her breath shuddered. 'Why he pretended to marry you.'

Her eyes closed.

'We know it's fake, love.' He trailed a finger over her shoulders, her neck, drawing her curls away from her skin. Smiling as the shiver bit down her spine from his touch. 'It was all for Erinyes.'

Anara's head twisted, seeking his eyes, needing to know what Mace was trying to say. Her brow a series of deep lines, her eyes pinched with a trepidation she willed to abate.

'We both wanted it,' Mace said, 'your cute little shop.'

Her throat dried. The cries of doubt were swallowing the whispers of Vadim's love, his pledge it was real.

'Kassian fucked up by burning the place down.' He dropped her hair, stepping back before the urge to throttle Anara overtook him; revenge for Yakov's capture. Likely torture. Expected death. 'But we still hoped we'd get the chance to work with you and rebuild.'

The pieces were tantalisingly close to clicking, but she did not want them to reveal the truth. Warmth gathered in her eyes and clawed at her throat, her heart erratic and loud.

'Vadim was smart, I'll give the fucker that,' Mace said curtly. 'Getting us to believe you're his wife… smart move.'

'What… what did you plan to do?' Her voice was faint, hollow. 'With Erinyes?'

'Sell our product.' He returned to the desk, ducking down to open one of the drawers. A small bag of white powder flung onto the surface with no finesse. 'Get you to grow some product, too.'

'I'd never—'

'Vadim believed you would.' He stared at her, daring her to cry or to avert her eyes.

'He only began this… for Erinyes?' She walked uneasily toward the chair, collapsing into it. 'He wanted me to grow and sell… what?'

Mace merely grinned, more grimace than smile. He tossed another small bag over to Aeron; the advisor swiftly unsealing it to dip a damp finger inside, rubbing the cocaine into his gums.

Sauntering back out to seek updates.

*Everything had been a lie.*

Anara had been consumed by his promises, had believed Vadim's words. Believed that the actions were conducted from a place of love, of trust, of devotion. She had given herself entirely. Had chosen to embrace the craving, the hunger. And now, now all she had was lack.

Emptiness.

Starvation.

'He won't come for me,' she admitted, raw and broken. 'None of this is real; it's fake, it's all fake.' Anara was uncertain if she was confirming Mace's words, or making herself believe the reality of her situation.

Vadim had got what he wanted from her.

Anara had relinquished control.

She had allowed him to seduce her, had been able to manipulate her into contractors for Erinyes, had reassured her with lies. What was one night to him? Anara shook her head; *he had me for dessert, that's all I was worth, price paid. A body to use, before he used my shop.*

Vadim may have said he loved her, but Anara knew people had said that in the past. It was never enough. For all the effort, all the time, all the sacrifices she made, Anara continued to have nothing. She was never someone's first choice, never the one to be fought for, never the one who would be saved. She could only save herself.

'He fucked up,' Mace said, proficiently cutting the cocaine, 'with the ring, that's how I knew for sure.'

Blinking, Anara looked up to him.

'Considering his wealth, and his status, the ring's pathetic.' Leaning to inhale a line, then rubbing his nose as he sat back in the chair, ready for the kick in his heart, the boost in his mood.

Instinctively, her fingertips moved to the titanium, spinning the trio of rings. They felt cold. Heavy. *It's all my fault*, she thought. She had been the one to move them to her right hand, she had given Vadim the perfect excuse to make a move and claim her.

Drag her into this in a more intimate way.

Anara would always have refused to work with them, regardless of a connection. She had her own underground operation to manage.

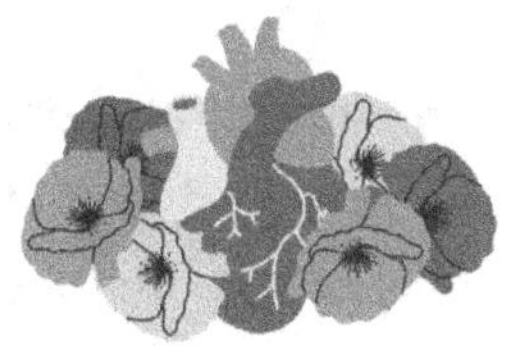

The anger refused to leave; his blood ran hot in his veins, his heart a furious thrum demanding retribution. Every slice of his blade, every split of flesh, every punch which landed, failed to satisfy the appetite; Vadim's healing wounds reopened with the pull of his abdomen, the swing of his arm. His body used to express the pain.

Pulling the lever for the overhead shower did little to cool him; ichor curling into the drain only a reminder of how helpless he felt. How scared Anara likely was, how isolated. The potential for harm tightened every muscle, even as he shook the water from his hair.

Strode from Kassian's cell.

'Kolya's got something for you,' Artem said, handing fresh clothes to him without breaking step. The two men only pausing once they reached the stairs. Artem acknowledging the pakhan's gesture to go up, allowing Vadim to quickly change from drenched clothes.

Arriving in the study, conversation halted.

Eyes turning to Vadim with something close to pity.

It only fed his ruthless fury.

His gaze narrowing and strides forceful as he crossed to his desk.

With Makari and Fyodor returning to the adjoining surveillance suite, and Pavel down in the cells to continue supervising conversations and cleaning, only Nikolai and Artem remained in the room. Any soldier not patrolling the estate had been sent out, leveraging information from any source they could; searching for Septer's scouts.

Capturing men and depositing them in their cells.

'How well did you know Anara?' Nikolai asked, breaking the silence after several moments. The tablet in his hands remained loose, a laptop on Vadim's desk remained closed.

'She's my wife—'

'Vadya—'

'She. Is. My. Wife.' Vadim's lips barely opened.

'Pakhan,' Artem continued, one hand up to Nikolai, 'we understand that's what you want, and that you care about her, but—'

'Do you?' He leant forward, resting his head in bloodied hands; his knuckles stained with crimson, tattoos smeared. 'Do you think I *care*? I love her, Tyoma, I love her. She's… everything. I need her back.'

'And we're doing all we can to get her back,' Artem said, calm, body open as he approached his leader, his friend. He perched on the edge of the desk, nudging the laptop closer. 'But, Vadya, I don't think we know who she is.'

He looked from Artem to Nikolai before focusing his attention on the laptop. It appeared new. And expensive. He knew he had not bought her it; he would have, if she had asked. But, this was not something he even recalled her mentioning. Not that he expected her to. Vadim lifted it open, the screen quick to brighten.

'It's encrypted,' Nikolai explained, 'and very sophisticated; I've only just begun to dig into it.' He rounded the large desk, placing his tablet down, and indicated the folder for Vadim to click into.

Vadim's head tilted slightly, eyes quick to devour the information as it populated. His brigadier was correct. This was an elaborate operating system with a great deal of sensitive data hidden on it. Images and text, surveillance and locations. Online searches and orders. The names he saw familiar; though Vadim could not quite place them.

Until he saw Logan Pottinger's name.

'There's a folder for each of the men who've been poisoned,' Nikolai said, watching his pakhan navigate the screen.

He was unsure if he was impressed or wary by what the laptop was suggesting. *Anara was a killer?*

*She had poisoned these men?*

*Or did she have a different kind of interest in their deaths; a macabre need to investigate and understand how each man lived and died, and what herbal poisons had been used?*

'We think she was given the laptop by Origins,' Artem stated, a quick nod to Nikolai to bring up the security feed on the tablet.

Evidence of the potential assistance Anara was provided.

Vadim remained silent, his eyes pulled from the laptop to the smaller screen. The search of Kasdeya's bag. The herbs and tinctures. A thick book. No sign of a laptop, but there may have been a hidden layer, when viewed from the side and compared against what was removed. Maksim distracted; attention drawn to the woman.

The coppery wash of blood filled his mouth; Vadim's teeth bit hard into his tongue. Comprehending exactly what he was seeing surged, vital and raw. *Was this why Anara accepted my truth so easily?*

*Because she's like me?*

*Did she intend to target me?*

'Ilya… there's a folder for Ilya.'

That brought his attention back with haste, his contemplation swiftly cauterised. 'What?'

'It doesn't look like Anara did any more than create the file,' Nikolai continued. 'There's only a few pieces of information, just basic things.'

'What are you trying to tell me, Kolya?' Vadim's hand curled tightly on his thigh, fingernails digging into the softer skin of his palm. His dark eyes raised to meet his brigadier's cautious gaze.

'That, maybe, Anara… perhaps we've considered these poisonings all wrong,' he said tentatively. 'All this time Pasha's been searching for a man or a drug connection, but it's been her.'

'Logan died the same day as… as she was taken.' Vadim's voice was fractured, his throat dry and thick. He swallowed forcefully. 'But she had a guard with her, all day.'

Artem folded his arms. 'Vadya, this is pretty damning—'

'I'm not saying she's not capable of this,' Vadim retorted, shifting his focus to his advisor. 'Fuck, if she has done all this, alone, fuck… she's an asset, she's even more perfect than I thought. I just want to understand how she could escape one of our guards.'

'I'll ask,' Nikolai confirmed, swiping over to the relevant information on the tablet and a message dispatched.

'Damning or not, we don't know anything for certain—'

'Vadya,' Artem interjected with a sigh, 'this is not usual property for the owner of an apothecary, and you've got to admit she's got the right knowledge for creating potions; hell, she healed you.'

'Yeah, healed.' Vadim took a breath. 'If Anya is a killer, then my wife is even more of a fucking goddess than I first thought. And if she's not a killer then she's got the skills to help us in other ways. Until I can ask her in person, I'm not making an assumption.'

'You've got the laptop—'

'It's a laptop.' He stood, leaning, palms down on the table. 'Maybe she's prepping the information and sending it to Origins; we know hardly anything about how they operate. If Kasdeya came here especially to hand over this equipment, then it must mean something. Kolya, once you've got hold of the guard, do more research on exactly what Origins do, any historic information in a forensic investigation.'

'I've already exhausted—'

'Kolya, do more.' Vadim slammed the laptop shut, his eyes lingering on it for a beat, fingers drumming on the lid. Breath steady. Heart crying for solace, for the woman he loved; killer or not. The desire to consume her, to embrace her shadow and light, piercing his veins.

# Thirty-Two

They arrived together, both women unsure why they had been asked to come to the tall imposing gates. Security cameras turning, following their steps. Bryony had reached out to the intercom, the smaller pedestrian entrance sliding open with a barely audible hum to allow them through before she had touched the button.

She glanced to Kerezen, seeing a similar disquiet.

It had not been Anara to invite them over; instead they both received an almost formal request via personalised courier that morning. A sleekly presented message on thick card, in an Art Deco style, which provided instructions. The moment Kerezen had handled it, cold dread coiled in her stomach; something bad waited.

She was sure of it.

The guard led them up the driveway; their steady walk made in near silence, eyes roving the early signs of spring, evident in the immaculate, sprawling gardens. The towering branches slowly budding with life, early flowers shyly unfurling petals in the hope of warmth.

Reaching the house, the women paused.

Kerezen's hand extended to rest on Bryony's forearm. Their eyes wide, absorbing the pristine exterior, the timely opening of the main door and a recognisable woman waiting for them.

'I've made tea,' Sofiya said, ushering them through into the hallway after closing the door. The guard returning to the gatehouse, and the soft shake of her head suggesting any past connection be ignored. 'Vadim'll be with you shortly.'

'Where's Anara?' Kerezen asked, her arms folding; the late morning light filtering through the large windows added fire to her auburn hair. Her hazel eyes drifting around the spacious room. There was nothing here to suggest their boss, their friend, even lived in this house; monochrome and sleek, without any of the touches Anara had curated in her home.

Sofiya froze as she approached the lounge area, the tray shaking in her hands. Her body seemed to shrink. Eyes blurring as water gathered along her lashes.

'That's what I want to know,' Vadim said, striding through from the hallway; his dark hair slicked wet from the shower. All traces of blood had been scrubbed from his skin, but additional growth of his usual stubble betrayed the haste in which he had changed.

Every minute she was missing, every minute he was not searching for her, felt too long. Too precious to squander. If he had not invited these two women to talk, he would have continued to interrogate the scouts in his cells, would have bathed in their blood all day, all night, until he could bring Anara home.

His tension ate through the guests; both women reaching for each other, heads turning and eyes meeting as hands connected. Sofiya's soft placement of the tray on the low table unreasonably loud amongst the charged hush which settled.

Thick and fragile.

Her retreat from the trio made while surreptitiously wiping the single thread of salted water from her cheek.

'Did you speak to her yesterday?' Vadim asked, composure taut and stretched. His words precise. His body moving with restrained intent as he sat in the leather armchair and propped one ankle on his knee.

Neither woman answered.

Both aware of Anara's plans for Logan the day before, the decision to enact her preparations at their usual café. Both receiving the agreed text to confirm it was done; coded and innocuous. And both arranging to meet and review the plans for Erinyes within a few more days.

There had been no hint of trouble.

But now, the fear Kerezen felt when receiving the invitation grew, hot and insistent. The consequences of Anara's illicit actions were always a possibility, they each knew that. Perhaps their underground operations had reached a conclusion beyond their control. Their pursuit of justice for women no longer safe, no longer a crusade they could feed. Confession clawed her throat, her tongue, her lips parting.

'Yes, we did,' Bryony said, a small crack in her voice.

'Only by text,' Kerezen added.

'When?' He tightened his grip on his shin, the split knuckles pearling and fingertips pressing; a distraction for mental catastrophising.

Bryony twisted, digging into her bag.

Vadim's hand slid to his boot, only to pause when she withdrew her phone. He was too on edge. *I should've left this to Artem*, he thought, as his breath shuddered through his chest. The strain in his jaw creating a heavy pulse to his neck, his shoulders.

'It was around four,' she confirmed, lifting her eyes to his; creases in her brow deepening when Bryony saw his haunted gaze. 'Why?'

He forced a swallow.

'Vadim, why?' Kerezen's already pale skin was becoming more and more translucent as ice crawled over her spine.

'She was taken.' He paused, debating how much to share, debating if this was due to her relationship to him, or if she really was the target in this. If Septer believed she had killed Logan Pottinger. 'We've figured out who, but I've not been able to find her.'

'Her phone—'

'Here.' He inclined his head in apology for interrupting Bryony. 'We went out to dinner, and she left it here.'

'So, she was with you and then she wasn't?' Bryony had laced her fingers into Kerezen's, needing something to anchor her.

'Yes.' Leaning forward, he collected the mug of tea and brought it to his lips; the heat welcome on his raw throat. 'I was called away, and one of my men betrayed us; she was gone when I returned.'

'Have you called the police?'

Vadim's eyes flashed, meeting Kerezen with a wry smile. Eyebrows raised. 'We don't deal with such people.'

Her gaze fell to her lap; a warm flush of colour spreading below her freckles. She focused on her breath, on the way her wedding ring shone in the sunlight.

'Would Anya have done anything to make... someone want to take her?' Vadim asked, purposefully phrasing the question, with a deliberate pace. His hands clung to the mug, unsure what answer he wanted.

If they were aware of Anara's potential skills.

If they would defend her.

If they would lie.

Bryony squeezed Kerezen's hand; a silent confirmation of unity. Her eyes locked on Vadim, she firmly said, 'No.'

'I know about the laptop.'

'Laptop?' Kerezen looked up.

'The one Kasdeya delivered after the fire,' Vadim explained.

Both women remained quiet.

Vadim was well-trained in silence. He could wait, usually. Patience a tool he was as adept at wielding as a blade. Now it was drowning him in doubts, in nightmares of what Anara may be being forced to endure. The risk she was in, the potential harm being caused.

And he was in his home, drinking tea.

Cursing, he flung the mug to the floor; it shattered.

The women jumped.

He ran a hand over his mouth, his jaw. Eyes apologetic as his frown dug deeply across his forehead.

Makari appeared, firearm drawn. Hastily sliding it back into the waist holster before the two women turned and saw him. Hesitant, he waited for a direct order to leave; body clad in black tactical gear, queries voiced in his ear as colleagues checked in.

As new intelligence was confirmed.

He pushed back his shoulders, his head lifting. The smallest gesture to convey the positive development when his eyes met Vadim's.

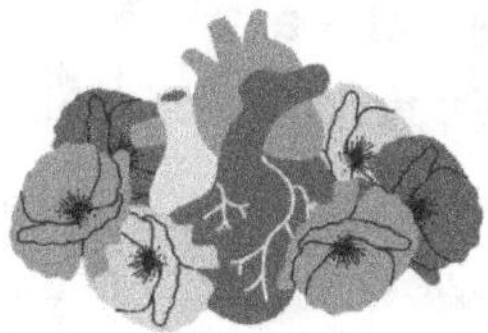

Anara was ravenous. The growl in her stomach a sour reminder of how empty she felt, how lost. Familiar aches which snaked through her blood and whispered in her mind; taunting her with confirmation of inadequacy and abandonment. Memories rooting with every breath, cloaking her cold limbs with loneliness, with ridicule.

The solitude of the past hours had provided too much time to dwell on the words Mace had delivered. His hazy statements of the future he planned, the way he intended to use Anara, to use Erinyes.

It was clear he did not know she had killed Logan.

Or any of the other men he had lost via similar methods.

That provided solace. Even as the desolation spread; there were too many reminders of Vadim's touch, his words. The promises poisoned by all that had happened after. Anara's body still wished to unfurl for him; to open her ribs and allow him into her heart.

To surrender herself and allow him to claim every inch.

To devour him, and be devoured by him.

Yet, her mind fought against the desire for his taste. It displayed for her image after image of why such hopes were futile, why she had been a fool. Why she had martyred herself for nothing.

Anara's faith in Vadim Morozov proving to be worthless.

His behaviour an act.

His vows a performance.

And she had fallen. Hard, fast, deep. An overwhelming craving, fuel to every beat of her heart as she swallowed his poison-soaked words. A venomous touch which had rotted through to her blood. Had created an addiction she felt unable to recover from.

What should have been her place of safety had become a prison.

Had become a shell, something brittle and dangerous. Had led her to this place; a barren room with a stained mattress. A guard who stood with lecherous eyes on her; no door, only him. Feet wide, back straight, and sub-machine gun cradled in his arms. His only movement to raise a cigarette to his lips, then lower it toward his thigh.

His eyes never dropped.

'Could you at least turn around?' Anara's voice was rough; the lack of food was making her weary. The slanted sink, almost ripped from the partially-tiled wall, her only source of water. 'The window's boarded up, I can't go anywhere.'

He did not reply.

Did not move.

Sighing, she clenched her teeth and crossed to the sink. The pipes screamed when she turned the tap. Anara laughed; relieved something could express the anguish, even if she felt numb. Cupping her hands below the cool flow, she brought the water to her lips and drank.

With nowhere to dry her hands, she wiped them over the dress. She paced, mind a pirouette. Vadim had orchestrated everything, had used her, manoeuvred her; a doll to be manipulated. She had been vulnerable for nothing. Had shared more with him than she had planned, believed he would understand her pain.

Believed they had a future together.

Anara studied her rings. *These fucking rings*, she thought. Turning them, she contemplated ripping them from her hand. They had allowed him to claim her. *Perhaps he only wanted to buy me a better ring so he could prove it's real to Septer*, she considered.

'I should've put him on my fucking list,' she muttered.

'A list?' Mace said, leaning against the doorframe.

Pivoting on her heel, Anara swung to face him, hands falling to her sides. She cursed her lack of attention, cursed missing his approaching steps, cursed her naïvety.

Cursed Vadimir Lvovich Morozov.

'I need you to look a little more presentable, love.' He tossed over a small bag of toiletries.

They landed on the floor, skidding over the worn surface.

Ignored as she kept her eyes on him.

'We've got guests arriving,' he stated, 'and you can either be on my arm, or in a cage.' Mace took a step forward, entering the room. Silently, the guard returned to the doorway.

*Cage or arm, they sound the same.*

Anara did not move; the urge to attack duelling with logical instinct to obey. She knew he would be armed. Knew the guard could simply pull the trigger.

Vadim would not be coming for her; this was fake.

Had always been fake.

Which made her expendable.

*Perhaps*, she thought, *a cage is all I'm good for*.

'Anara, love, I need you to make an effort,' he continued, taking hold of her shoulders; the tension under his hands evidence of how tightly she was trying to hide her trembling. 'Whether you end up being part of the sale, or enjoy my company while we run it, is up to you. But, either way, love, I need you to look better than you do right now.'

'Sale?' His touch was a brand; it ate through the thin straps of silk, through her flesh.

'If you're my guest, then you can keep this dress on.' Mace ran his hands over her arms. 'If you're part of the sale, then I'll tear every single thing you've got off this pretty little body of yours, and see just what that husband of yours thought was his.'

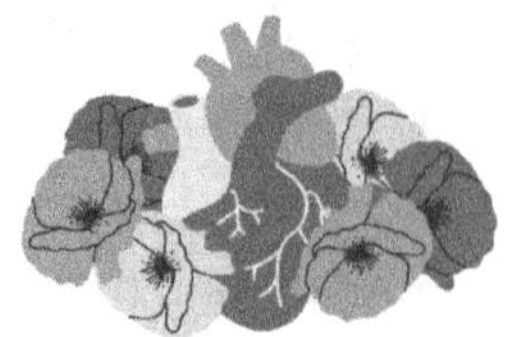

Parked a short distance from the location, the men clambered from their vehicles and gathered in a tight group. Every single one dressed in black from head to toe; tactical gear with weapons stored and ready. Firearms and ammunition. Knives and rope. Batons at their hip. Under the silvered glow of the moon, they were shadows.

Only Vadim was less armed. His body, still healing from the last fight they undertook, covered by a tailored suit; silk waistcoat neatly buttoned below the black jacket, over his shirt. He had taken time to prepare, now he knew where Anara likely was.

And he knew he needed to blend in with the other buyers.

The thought brought a tick to his jaw.

'Anara is the priority,' he stated, teeth gritted. 'But, if you can, free as many of the women as possible; provide them refuge.'

The men nodded, verbalised their agreement. Nikolai swept over the screens on his tablet to confirm the layout, again, after the brigadiers had hastily formed a plan. Blueprints pulled from online archives, strategies crafted. The team worked well together; they knew each other, knew how to protect each other. A different location was merely a challenge they sought to overcome.

'Here,' Artem said, handing over a mask. He had been dispatched to obtain the final pieces required to gain entry; travelling separately and last to arrive.

With one raised eyebrow, he held it before him, assessing it; black metal with an elasticated band. The piece was a half volto in style, with the lower sides flaring to allow access to the mouth. Vadim turned it over, exhaling heavily.

'I've added you to the guest list,' Nikolai said, glancing up from the tablet, 'because their security is fucking pathetic.'

'Usual alias?' Vadim was already striding back to his car.

'Yeah.'

He threw the mask onto the passenger seat, driving away, trusting the others would follow. The looming building a beacon.

Every window illuminated, and the low thud of bass pulsing over the midnight fields. Other men were already present, wandering the building to view the offerings displayed; masks on, drinks in hand.

The only man not to wear any covering was Mace. He strode around the rooms with pride, arm around Anara's waist, steering her through the guests. Her body swaying slightly with fatigue, with hunger, with the rage she fought to contain as she witnessed more and more suffering.

Each room within the lower floors had been transformed. The entry tiles had been overlaid with a roll of carpet, the walls draped in billowing cloth, the windows likewise; lights on the sill to confirm the event was on to those who parked outside. In the centre of each enticing room was a large metal cage, a spotlight above.

There was nowhere for those being sold to hide.

But an abundance of shadow for those who sought to buy.

Entering each space brought further nausea to Anara's stomach, ire to her blood. The sickening sounds of men ordering the naked women to turn, to bend, to move. To follow commands. Those who delayed found themselves beaten, whipped. A man in each cage, fully masked, ready to punish any woman who resisted.

Any woman who appeared upset.

Who allowed a tear to fall over gaudily made-up faces.

'You see, love,' Mace whispered, leaning firmly into her, 'you made the right choice.'

She did not answer, did not trust herself to answer.

'Boss,' Jarah said as he approached, 'there's reports of trouble.'

'Trouble?' Mace narrowed his eyes and scanned the room; guests laughing, guests stroking hands over the trembling captive women, and guests wandering to dark corners to slyly masturbate.

The air was thick with lust, with greed.

*Everything is as it should be*, he thought.

The men circulating the rooms with trays of liquor, with drugs, with sealed boxes for bids. The buyers loitering in the right places. The music and lighting balanced to keep the drinks flowing. Though the upper floors remained empty, they were guarded.

*No, everything's fine*, he repeated to himself.

Jarah slid his eyes to Anara then back to Mace, the roll suggesting she was the cause of the problem. That her presence was attracting the wrong kind of attention. 'Scouts say Vadim's sent men.'

Anara felt hope smoulder in her blood.

Hiding the thickening of his throat with a mouthful of whiskey, Mace gestured for the promoted man to continue.

'They've seen some cars, a convoy,' Jarah explained, 'too many to be guests.'

'Lock the place down,' Mace instructed. His grip on Anara tightened, moving them toward the hallway. 'And check all the guests—'

'How the fuck can I?'

'Jarah,' he said, sighing, 'be discreet, but get them to unmask.' Mace resisted the urge to admonish the new guard. Working as a leader not a follower took time, took skills. 'Get it done.'

He nodded, retreating to begin the process.

'You see anyone you know, love?' Mace waved over one of his men, glass deposited on the tray. His fingertip dipped into the dish of cocaine before rubbing it into his gum. Tongue curling around his teeth.

She shook her head.

Which was when she saw him; Vadim. Her eyes widened, her lips parted, breath caught. *It could be him*, she considered. The right height, the right build, the right clothes. His jaw familiar and the slightest hint of the wound on his cheek visible below the mask. His stance suggested he had seen her, the hesitation in his approach causing her to blink.

To lower her gaze.

*I'm not good enough.*

Mace, sensing her react, had considered challenging the man who loitered in the room, watching them.

But, the man stalked away, moving through the closest doorway.

'Come, love,' Mace said, tugging firmly at her waist, 'let's not let your *husband* spoil a successful night.'

'He's not my husband,' Anara hissed, reaching for the rings. Deftly, with heated moisture in her eyes, she ripped them from her finger and flung them to the floor.

Bouncing from the carpet to the tile.

The chime of their contact shuddered over Vadim's spine; overriding the thrum of his heart, the incessant beat of the music. Vadim closed his eyes, teeth clenched, curled his hands into fists. Every cell of his being begged him to turn, to run to Anara and damn the consequences. No matter how outnumbered he was, no matter the risk.

Normally, he would.

And he was unsure why he had walked away.

Perhaps it was his new desire to live, to forge a life with her, to not be as impulsive. Knowing his injuries would make him less effective, less able to protect her. Yet, in doing so, Vadim had permitted his very reason for survival to be taken.

Again.

Hearing the recognisable crack of gunfire forced his shoulders back, his body lithe as he ducked to pull the knife from his boot. To drag the mask from his face. He ran, heading back toward where he had seen her and Septer's leader. Feet sure and pulse wild.

Eyes tracking his men as they dealt with Mace's crew.

As they began to open cages.

Vadim dodged a punch thrown by one Mace's soldiers, wincing with the pull on his healing abdomen. Cursed when a hand clutched for his arm, catching still sore wounds. He gripped his knife more firmly, ready to wield it if anyone tried to prevent him reaching her.

The empty hallway creating a gnawing foreboding to eat through his blood, his veins on fire with wrath. With unwelcome fear. Unfamiliar and unwanted. She had been here, he had seen her.

Groans and cries, weeping and gunfire, orders and pleas.

The building was alive with activity, but the one person he needed to find, to hold, was nowhere. Vadim raced to the doors, still thrown open from his team's entrance, and out into the night. The glimpse of Anara's body being thrown into the back of a dark sedan, engine revving near the gates, brought a pained scream from his throat.

# Thirty-Three

He had not slept since discovering Anara was taken. And though it was now approaching over thirty-six hours, Vadim fought the signals his body gave. He refused to allow himself the peace of slumber; after failing to bring her back, he did not deserve it.

Wondered if he still deserved her.

What kind of man would permit his wife's suffering?

Vadim chastised himself; she had thrown the rings away, had seen him turn his back. His hopes of a future were fading. Despite this, he was comforted by the presence of her clothes in his dressing room when he collected more knives. His suit jacket dropped onto the leather couch before striding back to the landing, turning a blade over in his hand as he descended the stairs.

'Vadim,' Sofiya called, her arms hugging her waist.

He pivoted quickly, coming to a halt, facing her.

'You need to eat, please.' Her brow was deeply creased, the tension which permeated the whole estate at home in her. The hours she had spent transferring Anara's belongings to Vadim's suite only increased the sense of attachment to the woman, and the sense of loss. 'You'll be no good to anyone if—'

'Sofiya, I'm okay.' He would not rest, could not rest.

Not until he had Anara back where she belonged.

Back by his side. In their bed.

If she would accept him after such a dereliction of his vow.

'You're not,' she countered, with greater confidence than she felt. A warm blush creeping over her skin.

'She's right,' Artem said, placing one hand on his leader's shoulder as he arrived behind him. The strain below his touch radiated. Knowing Vadim, and knowing he would not quit, he changed his approach. 'You'll only get yourself killed if you're not sharp; if you get yourself killed, she's never coming back.'

Vadim spun to his advisor, knife to his throat.

The man did not flinch. The cool pressure of the blade shifting with his calm swallow; Artem met his friend's gaze. The anguish he witnessed ate through to his heart.

'I'm not weak,' Vadim stated, precise and venomous.

'Never said you were,' Artem said. He stepped back slightly. 'Strong men know when to refuel and rest, that's all.'

'Fuck you,' he muttered. Lowering the knife, he shook his head and stalked toward the kitchen.

Sofiya met Artem's eyes and mouthed silent thanks before placing the steaming food before them, and two mugs of coffee. She remained quiet; the scrape of their cutlery the only sound as both men devoured the meal. Their mugs drained and plates pushed back.

'Now, may I go interrogate the fucker who thinks it's okay to keep my wife captive?' Vadim asked, one eyebrow raised.

Artem smiled, head inclining slightly and arm outstretched. 'Lead the way, pakhan.'

With guards and soldiers busy replenishing weaponry, stored in one of the basement's secure rooms, and the extensive research Nikolai was undertaking, every door was open. The library, the study, the entrance to the spiral stairs. A couple of the cells were also ajar. Sobbing screams grew louder the closer the men got.

'She's already given up a couple of different locations,' Pavel said, exiting the cell while wiping blood from his hands. 'Kolya's begun looking into them.'

Vadim nodded, stepping inside the small room.

'Please... please...,' Melora whimpered. Salted streaks ran through the heavy layers of her make-up, revealing discoloured skin beneath. An array of bruises in various stages of healing. Her dress was drenched with sweat, with blood; the golden fabric barely covered her fake-tanned flesh, with a high hem and low neckline.

'Pasha,' Vadim asked in Russian, 'which of these cuts are yours?'

'Pakhan?' He returned to the cell.

'Did you deliver all these cuts on her arms?' With her wrists held in the ceiling chains, open wounds fed a river of crimson to her torso.

'Yes... was that not—'

'The bruises on her face?'

'Already there.' Pavel ran a hand over his brown hair.

'I thought as much.' He studied her for a moment, unsure if he felt anything but rage, anything but disgust. Her eyes displayed how ignorant she was of their discussion. 'Bleed her.'

Pavel nodded, dismissing the wail which erupted when he picked up the knife one more time.

Leaving, Vadim met Artem's satisfied stare before they walked to the adjoining cell. There, naked, his arms stretched wide, was Aeron.

The bandage wrapping his damaged hand dirty, the twist to his shoulders creating an uncomfortable ache. Standing to one side, Fyodor appeared nonchalant.

'Your *wife* will die for this,' Aeron spat.

Vadim inhaled deeply. Though he would not admit it, the quick meal had helped. But the pause had also allowed his healing injuries to offer complaints which refused to subside. Believing he deserved to suffer, he took another step forward, welcoming the sore thrum in his abdomen, his arm, his hands, and lodged his knife in Aeron's thigh.

Septer's advisor swore, gritted his teeth.

'And your wife is dying as we speak,' Vadim whispered, leaning into the prone man. His cool breath fell over Aeron's heated skin, feeling the tremble he tried to hide.

'Mel!' Aeron yelled, pulling against the manacles.

Her sobs the only reply.

'She doesn't deserve this,' Aeron said, his breath quick. The words fading as Vadim twisted the blade inside his flesh; pointed tip grating on bone. His howl met with increased sobs from the neighbouring cell.

'Only you're allowed to harm her, yes?' Vadim stepped back, leaving the knife embedded.

The blood sticky as it seeped down the man's leg.

Aeron narrowed his eyes, nausea climbing higher, with intense pain rushing through his body. His usually ruddy skin ashen, heart loud with anxious beats. Though being snatched had sobered him quickly, alcohol continued to percolate in his stomach. Cocaine continued to drift through his veins.

'Yet she's fully cognisant of your actions,' Vadim continued, tattoos on his forearms stained burgundy, ichor soaking into his shirt's folded back sleeves, 'which makes her as culpable as you.'

'She's a woman,' Aeron argued, sniffing.

'And we should protect them.' He remained calm, studying how the man had tensed, how Aeron tried to prevent any movement which would aggravate the injuries inflicted. The quiver from the effort bringing a soft melodic chime from the chains binding his wrists.

'Yes.'

'Then why do you drug them, strip them, fuck them, place them in cages, and sell them?' Vadim kept his eyes on him.

'That's different.' Aeron's breath was thready, his chest shuddering with the inhales, the exhales. He shifted slightly, resulting in an instant flare of pain as the blade caught a nerve. 'Fuck,' he hissed.

Stepping forward, Vadim twisted the knife one more time.

The anguished scream was beautiful.

As it faded, Vadim rolled his head, massaged his neck; digging the tips of his fingers firmly. The pull in his muscles doing little to ease his tension; the lack of updates from Nikolai were concerning. He needed a destination and a plan.

Without them, he felt hopeless.

'Where's Anara?' He asked, dragging the blade up to Aeron's hip in a languid, meandering, arc. The movement smooth, skilled; avoiding the vital conduits of blood and preventing Aeron bleeding to death.

At least, for now.

The pressure in Aeron's jaw from his clenched teeth failed to remove the sting of the knife, the continued tightness from how his shoulders had been manipulated and caught. His face contorted.

Vadim glanced to Fyodor. 'Dimitri.'

The guard nodded, pushing himself from the wall and moving to the trolly. The crystalline powder already prepared in a syringe; pulled from a drawer and offered with well-practiced efficiency.

Aeron's eyes widened; his heart kicking. 'No, please.'

'Tell me where Anara is,' Vadim stated. He had yet to take the drug from Fyodor, he hoped Septer's advisor would be too concerned with the mix of others already taken to risk this.

'I don't fucking know,' he panted, 'not for sure.'

He gave a small gesture; Fyodor obeyed and stepped closer.

'No… please,' he begged, 'I… it's probably Iðun—'

'She's not there.' Vadim reclaimed the handle of his knife, twisting it over the pelvic bone toward the man's groin. Prone and pliable; it would take only one slice to exsanguinate.

'Fuck.' Aeron's breath was frantic. He could not get enough oxygen in or out; his chest tight as anxiety and panic set every nerve on fire. 'He won't… he…, fuck, please.'

Turning to his guard, Vadim provided the instruction; a locked gaze and disciplined incline of his head. The return of his focus bringing fresh spirals of his blade. 'Fedya will feast on your wife, but tell me, who do I send Melora's heart to once you're dead?'

He swallowed the hot bile in his throat, eyes glazed; pain dilating Aeron's pupils. The swift scratch of the syringe, when Fyodor injected the dimethyltryptamine, barely registering. Head bowed, breath shallow.

'Normally I like to deal with my guests personally,' he continued, 'but with so many of Septer's members enjoying my hospitality, I've had to be more selective.' He paused, increasing the pressure of the knife. 'Where do I send your wife's heart, Aeron?'

The man spat, mucus trailing from his lips. 'Fuck. You.'

'Where is Anara?' Vadim turned the knife, bringing it lower.

'Your… wife,' he sneered, taking as much strength as he could from the spite in his system, 'has such soft skin.'

Vadim's vision tunnelled; his desire for violence elevating his pulse and quickening his breath. Muscles taut with the determined restraint to prolong this, to not kill too soon, to not destroy the chance of obtaining the information they needed.

He needed.

Slow, he withdrew his knife from Aeron's pelvis.

With great effort, he stepped back, crossing the cell to the chain's control mechanism. The slackening of the manacles bringing a mewling whine from Aeron as blood rushed through stretched joints.

Fresh suffering merging with the beginnings of hallucinations.

Of distorted colours and sounds.

'Get him on the floor,' Vadim ordered, through clenched teeth. Paces measured, he plucked an axe from the trolley, and returned. Crouching over him, Vadim clutched the chains in one hand, drawing Aeron's wrists together and plunged the axe down.

The crack of bone softened by flesh.

Aeron's scream followed by vomit. His hands on the floor as Fyodor dragged his body back upright; the manacles casting shadows as they spun an empty pirouette.

The guard's grip on Aeron's upper arms holding the man still.

'Is there any other part of you that touched her?' Vadim asked, the axe held loosely, blood dripping to the stone.

Pulsing from the raw edges of Aeron's wrists.

He shook his head. Eyes wide in disbelief.

'This is the very last time I'll ask you,' Vadim warned, repositioning his grip of the axe. 'Where's Anara?'

Aeron's sobs grew more splintered; agony a cacophony poisoning his senses. His body no longer feeling his own, while simultaneously experiencing every single ache, every single moment of torture, over and again. His heart a staccato dance, his mind fuelled by horror. The room was blurring, distorting, mixed with the scent of iron. 'I don't… I…, maybe the… Mill.'

Behind him, Artem turned to leave; comparison with the information obtained from Septer's scouts and soldiers, and Melora, required. His quick steps resounded in the corridor as he headed back to Nikolai in the study above.

'That wasn't so hard, was it?' Vadim struck the man's face, palm open and firm as it tapped flesh.

The contact driving Aeron's head back, bringing a renewed keening cry. Broken with the cleaving of his heart as Vadim plunged the axe deep into the man's chest.

# Thirty-Four

There were no guards to command. No men loitering to defend the small bar Mace had retreated to; only Jarah remained by his side. Closed for the day, the two men had rushed in and steered Anara to the rear of the building, leaving the public space in relative darkness. Small windows, blinds drawn, and main lights off, created a void between the entrance and the office the trio inhabited.

It had been a reckless decision.

The office may have been where Mace could collect cash and make calls, but it was also without escape. Only one point of access. Only one path they could take.

'What's the plan, boss?' Jarah asked, wiping his hand over his face, down his beard. The rip in his sleeve providing a glimpse of the dragon tattoo which wound from his wrist. His waist holster was empty; the gun thrown when the ammunition had been exhausted.

'There's nowhere you can go.' Anara had quickly calculated options the moment they arrived. The opportunities for her to overpower the two men slim, but the potential for revenge already forming.

'I've plenty of places for us to go, love.' Mace turned his head, body crouched before the open safe. Fingers curled over the edge; cold metal hard against soft flesh.

‘Not where you’ll be safe,’ she countered.

‘Your husband—’

‘He’s not my husband.’

‘—won’t find us.’ Mace chuckled, despite the apprehension.

Despite the enormity of Septer’s loss; the men Vadim’s soldiers had slaughtered, tortured, and captured.

‘Perhaps it’s not him you need to worry about,’ she muttered; tongue licking over her lips. Her throat was dry, voice rough. Though permitted to have a meal, the service station food had been insufficient to satiate the hunger. Her body weary, mind tired.

‘What, sweetheart, you think you can hurt us?’ Jarah scoffed, a wide smile breaking across his face. The grazes on his cheek ignored as the sting branched through raw skin; dried blood was already turning russet on his shirt. Bruises beginning to form, tender within the cuts.

Anara opted not to answer, her arms folding, leaning back into the uncomfortable desk chair. The fabric stained, the padding uneven, and a layer of smeared powder across the plastic arms.

The splintering of glass brought her upright.

‘Fuck!’ Mace stood quickly, reaching for the pistol at his side; drawn from the leather shoulder rig and readied. He tossed a knife to Jarah with an apologetic grimace. ‘Not now.’

‘It’s okay, boss.’ He clenched his teeth; he had hoped for more time before they were discovered. Had hoped for more time in the role he had been promoted into. But he could recognise the impending end; the life dreamed dissipating, eaten away with each breath.

The silence was thick.

Taut.

Mace grabbed Anara’s arm, dragging her up and placing her in front of him, flush to his chest. His ragged inhales pressing grimy cotton to her flesh. He backed up to the external wall, pulling her with him. Her feet stumbling over the carpet tiles.

Her every sense straining to determine what may happen next.

The lack of anything but breathing was disconcerting.

'Maybe it's just some fucker messing with us,' Jarah whispered, with a terse clip to his tone. His grip on the knife tight. 'You know what they're like when they want a fix.'

The scuff of noise from the corridor brought renewed attention; veins in their necks pulsing with expectation, with anxiety. Each man cognisant of death, even as they quietly prepared to fight.

Anara gambled on Mace not killing her, not firing his weapon; she was still a valuable asset. Still someone they could bargain with. Until the very last negotiation failed, they would hesitate. She used this change in focus, and assumption of her safety, to act; the sharp heel of her stiletto brought down on Mace's ankle while simultaneously forcing her elbows into his ribs.

His surprised cry loosening his fingers and enabling her to duck, to slide away from him and run. The room small enough to cross quickly. A rip of black silk from Jarah's knife barely registering. The blade caught her skin, but only made her hiss with the momentary slice of pain.

Mace's clawing fingers dodged as she reached for the handle.

'Here!' she yelled.

Throwing open the door, she found Artem and Makari, eyes a blaze of concentrated fury, firearms poised. The narrow corridor crowded with black-clad men, some she recognised.

Some she did not.

'Are you okay?' Artem asked, shifting to move her behind him; one arm cradling her while his other kept the pistol aimed at Mace's head.

Makari's gun remained trained on Jarah, watching as both cowed men reluctantly threw down their weapons and raised their hands.

She did not answer.

There was only one man Anara wanted to see, despite everything, and she could not see him. A hollow melancholy settled in her bones, a cruel ache in her heart. Every word Mace had uttered, every revelation he had delivered, echoed violently through her mind.

*I'm not good enough.*

*I'm not worthy of love, unless it's fake.*

*This was all only for Erinyes.*

Heat consumed her amber eyes as she chastised herself for such weakness. Such vulnerability. The past familiar in the present, her desire found to be nothing but poisoned crumbs, insufficient to keep his pledge alive and yet too weak to kill it. Anara's heart shattering in absence, in an affirmation of her beliefs; Vadim never meant a word he said.

And she would never be worth loving.

Pressing her back toward the wall, Artem shielded her to allow Ilya and Pyotr to move in and detain the final Septer members; digging ties from their trouser pockets.

'He's outside,' Artem said softly, not shifting his gaze from the room's activity, arm still raised and safety off.

Anara swallowed.

Her jaw tight. She closed her eyes, trying not to allow hope to break the walls she was trying to rebuild. Trying to ward off the embers already warming her blood.

'I refused to allow him in,' he continued, 'so if you're angry, be angry with me.' The arrival of Pavel acknowledged with a nod.

The brigadier retreating once confirmation was gained.

'He listened to you?' She laughed, but the deep creases of her brow suggested the breathy sound was more nerves than humour.

'He's been insufferable since you've been gone.' Artem's lips quirked into a smile. 'That man is besotted with you. The last thing I needed was a lovesick fool fucking up my operation.'

'Anya!' Vadim shouted, striding through from the bar; with Mace and Jarah restrained, the crowd had thinned. His pace increasing the closer he got until he could sweep her into his arms. 'Слава Богу[43]!'

His breath curled over her skin. His arms secure, wrapping her to his chest in efforts to absorb her body in his, to bring her closer still.

---

[43] Слава Богу - Russian for 'Thank God'

Tender, Vadim placed kisses on her crown, peppering them through her hair as his hands roamed, finding the rear of her head, her lower back, to prove he really had her.

That she was real.

The hitch in her breath, the fractured sob, causing her to stiffen. To try to pull away. Anara's emotions too fragile, her mind too splintered; his touch too restrictive, too confusing.

There was much to reconcile to simply accept a quick reunion, to merely melt into his world once more and act the dutiful wife.

To allow him to pretend everything was fine.

When it was not.

'Anya?' Vadim relaxed his hold, his hand sliding to cup her face and drift his thumb over her cheekbone to wipe the smear of salt water. His careful study of her gaze made with concern.

'I'm fine,' she said, 'I'm fine.'

'You're not.' He shifted position, scanning lower, noticing the crimson threading down her leg. 'You're bleeding. Who did that to you?'

She shook her head. 'It doesn't matter.'

Vadim's head tilted back, umber eyes on the ceiling, his deep exhale prolonged. The return stare intense. 'Who did this to you?'

'I can deal with it myself—'

'That I don't doubt, kroshka,' he said, more gently, his fingers curling her hair behind her ear, 'but let me.'

Anara could not resist falling into his palm, resting her head, closing her eyes. The conflict within too exhausted to argue. She needed to get home, showered, fed. Sleep. The touch of his lips on her brow brought an audible sigh from her throat. 'Jarah.'

He placed his other hand on her face, turning her head so he could kiss her mouth; a soft brush of his lips over hers. The instinctual trace of his tongue over the seam met with no resistance, only welcome. Only memory; the slow surrender of barriers. He could have stayed in such an isolated moment forever.

The noise of the corridor, of men talking, fading to static.

Drawing back, he placed one more kiss before stepping away. Hand tucking into his jacket to pull the Grach from the holster. Two shots sent in quick succession; Mace and Jarah slumping to the floor with breached skulls. Blood pooling around their fallen bodies.

Sofiya had insisted they eat, had forced them to sit at the kitchen island while she finalised preparing a meal. The brittle silence punctuated with the guards returning to their usual roles, hushed conversations of men leaving until their next shift. The placing of the dish, and vodka, on the marble countertop.

'Leave the plates, and I'll sort it later,' she instructed, her azure eyes moving from one to the other with a smile. Her retreat to her own rooms filled with relief; gratitude for the woman who provided kindness, a way to escape a difficult situation, and admiration for the man who had finally chosen to embrace the opportunity for happiness.

Vadim waited until he heard the click of the door, his gaze fixed on the woman beside him. On how she avoided his scrutiny, on how bruises were developing on her skin. On how her change of clothes failed to hide all her injuries.

Some, he knew he had delivered.

Others, he had not.

Her reluctant disappearance into the bathrooms at Mace's bar, after a bag was delivered by Maksim, allowing her time to freshen up, even as Vadim paced outside the doors.

He had her back, and would never lose her again.

'Anya, I need to know what happened to you.'

'That's sweet of you to ask,' she replied, eyes on the food.

'You're my wife, of course—'

'Am I?' Anara bit her tongue, the grip on the cutlery tightening.

'Yes!' Vadim's heart kicked, his brow creased deeply; blood hot with conviction. 'I love you, Anya, but—'

'But what?' She turned to him. 'You've realised I'm not good enough, not suitable, or loveable enough?'

He took her chin, holding her still to prevent her looking away. 'Anya, I love you; I've meant it every time I said it. I mean it now. I'll mean it for the rest of my life.'

She swallowed, her eyes blurring.

'When you threw your rings away, it damn near broke me,' he said, umber eyes chasing hers.

'How do you think it felt seeing you turn your back on me?' Anara hated how the admission made her appear fragile. There was venom laced in her almost whispered tones, anger in her gaze. The snow of her skin blossoming with rage.

And yet, her amber eyes were glazed with tears.

The dichotomy of it ate into her mind.

'I knew my men were on their way in,' Vadim explained, 'I thought I'd more time to get to you.' He laced his other hand in hers, relieved Anara did not shrug the touch away.

The pressure of her teeth radiated through her jaw.

Her body begged with her to submit, to curl into him and allow him to protect her, to trust he would never destroy the sanctuary they were forging. But her thoughts continued to provide logic, to provide evidence of where things had fractured.

'Now I can give you a better one,' he said, offering a smile; the truth of his words, the desire to make their union official softening his gaze. A slow stroke of his thumb over her skin delivering a hypnotic lullaby. The confirmation she was really here.

'What, so you can prove to the world that you own me?' She inhaled a shuddering breath; the accusation reforming the walls defending her heart. 'That you've got the monopoly on my store?'

He dropped his hand from her face, lips parting. Sharp heat wound over his flesh, under his bones. The realisation of what may have been shared, why she was so uncertain, hurting, biting deep.

'Mace told me, Vadim,' she said coldly. The memory ingrained, the way he took such pleasure in breaking her with his words, before then lashing out with his fists. 'That you only wanted me to sell drugs through my apothecary.'

'I never—'

'How can I believe you? How can I believe anything you say?' She angrily swiped at the tear which escaped her lashes.

He curled his fingers to his palm, his other clinging to the one in her lap and trying to convey his integrity, his loyalty. 'When I first saw you, I'd no idea who you were. You came to Prey, with Bryony and Kerezen, for a meal. I saw you on the surveillance footage—'

'And then you figured out how to use me,' she muttered. 'How utterly chivalrous of you, my love.'

'На языке мед, а не сердце лёд[44],' he exhaled, exasperated and keen to make her understand. 'When I found out about your connection to Erinyes, I shut that avenue down; I can show you—'

'But you had been thinking of it? You'd thought about using my store for your drugs?' She narrowed her eyes; the consequences of the Bratva utilising her apothecary had plagued her since Mace revealed it. She had nurtured a safe refuge for women who needed help, and a fraternity did not belong in such a space.

'It was an option, yes.' He saw no value in pretending otherwise. He wanted to destroy any lingering secrets between them. 'My job requires me to provide for many people and families. I have to keep my business running, any way I can.' Vadim paused. 'They depend on me, and I can't walk away from that.'

Her breath caught in her chest.

---

[44] На языке мед, а не сердце лёд - Russian idiom, which translates as 'on the tongue there's honey, but on the heart there's ice', and means 'a honey tongue, a heart of gall'

The touch of his hand burning through her blood; sliding through her body with every moment the connection remained. His words devouring any threads of resistance she clung to.

'But I would, Anya,' Vadim continued, eyes hooked in hers and voice like gravel. 'This job, this title… I'd walk away if you ask me to.'

'I'd never ask you to do that,' she said, husky. Her throat hot, thick with the weight of her history, with the honesty she saw in his gaze. With every truth she had witnessed in their time together.

'This time without you… I've never felt so fucking helpless.' Vadim stroked his thumb over her cheek. 'I've never suffered as much.'

'Suffered!' Her eyes widened, leaning away from him. Her emotions rapidly oscillating as affection became incredulity, empathy became rage, the thread between them pulling tighter and at risk of snapping. Anara shook her head. '*You* suffered?!'

'I—'

'I was taken and held against my will, threatened with being sold at some kind of auction, beaten,' Anara said with clipped anger, 'and all while being denied food, or even fresh fucking clothes.'

'You should never have been—'

'Never been what?' She dragged her hand from his, folding her arms across her chest; her stare fixed and eyes pinched.

'I shouldn't have left you without a guard,' he said, the emptiness of his palm cold. Concerning. The changeable atmosphere corrupting his intent, his desire to confirm how much she meant to him. How much he was prepared to sacrifice.

The consequences of his actions had taken her from him. The feud with Septer, the choice to turn off the cameras, leaving her alone due to his obligations. Such things were the roots of his pain, the crumbs which had destroyed what they were creating. Their foundation too weak after only a short time together, despite how he felt they belonged in this lifetime, and every lifetime before and after.

Vadim inhaled deeply. 'I should've implanted a tracker.'

'I'm. Not. Property!' Anara lowered one arm, preparing to get up from the stool, to use the marble to steady her, only to find him grab it. The cage of his fingers sending an instant thrum through her blood. Directly to her core, to where she had already carved him a home.

Anara could not pretend; this man, infuriating at times, possessive at others, had etched his name into every single beat of her heart. Had lit a fire in her veins she thought she had extinguished.

Thought she had successfully protected herself from.

Thought she had successfully buried to conform.

'I know, I know.' He closed his eyes, sliding his hand down; fingers entwining. 'It was… I was trying to make you smile.'

Her eyes rolled, her jaw tightening. 'You want me to smile?'

*He's dangerously close to being put on my list*, she thought.

'You're misunderstanding me,' he soothed.

'I understand perfectly.'

*I'll add every fucking one of them*, she reconsidered.

'I only want to make you happy,' he said gently, 'I hate seeing you hurt, I don't like that I wasn't there, I detest that I wasn't strong enough to rescue you. With my injuries, which isn't an excuse, I didn't want to risk making things worse, or causing you more pain by fucking things up with any attempt at getting you back.' Vadim paused. 'But that didn't mean I wasn't fighting for you, for us.'

She studied him closely, witnessing the anguish in Vadim's eyes, the fracture in his voice. Anara knew, of all the disappointments, of all those who had promised and failed, Vadim had been the only one to deliver on his words. And, from the overheard discussions between his team, she knew he had devastated Septer in her absence.

Which had to count for something.

'I know you may find it hard to trust me right now,' Vadim said, lifting their hands to his lips. 'And if you want to fight me, then we can channel that in other ways. I love seeing your fire… I love you. I'll always protect you, Anya, and I'll always be there—'

'But you weren't,' she whispered, her eyes blurring.

'And I'll always hate myself for that.' He stood, his jaw ticking. 'If you want me to beg, Anya, I will. You are the only person I will ever kneel for, but I will. From now on, nothing will keep me from you; even if you reject me, reject this, you come first. I'll always be there to protect you.'

There was power in his tone, in how he delivered his vow; confident and earnest. The amber flecks of his eyes barely visible as the obsidian spread, his chest heaving with each devout breath.

'I can think of better reasons to kneel.' Anara left the chair, pressing her body to his, her free hand gripping his neck, fingers curling into the short hair at the nape. The contact sending a loud surge of hunger to her quim. 'But I like the idea of me always coming first.'

Vadim smiled, dipping to kiss her. The touch hard, penitent, but hot with promise. With the silent decision each made to devote themselves entirely to the possibility this could be real. His slow retreat made despite how loud lust whispered in his pulse.

The return to his seat at odds to the insistent reactions of Vadim's body to hers; how he wished to swipe the plates from the counter. To grab Anara's waist, lay her on the marble and feast. To free his aching cock and discover the salvation she would provide when he surrendered to his carnal appetite for her.

Pushing the empty plates to the floor and taking her on the kitchen island could be a diversion for another day. No, Anara should be loved, should be worshipped.

Should be enfolded in his skin, his bones, his heart.

Taking a forkful of their meal he offered it to her. 'You should eat.'

'So should you,' she retorted.

His smile formed crooked, wicked.

The tines of the fork at her full lips. She parted them, welcoming it onto her tongue, sucking the contents from the steel.

The exhale he made broken with a groan; a further unraveling of his patience. His desire.

Swallowing, Anara slowly ran her tongue over her lips, catching the lower with her teeth. Her breath quickening. The prospect of what they had begun in Prey being continued carving through her every thought; an urgency which tugged at the knowledge she had yet to be entirely honest with him.

'Anya, are you okay?' He saw the ghost of something drag over her face, saw the smallest of curls in her shoulders.

Deciding now was not the time, she straightened up and stabbed a sugar-snap pea; crystals of sea salt on the pod. Holding the fork, she drew the tip into her mouth and swirled it with her tongue. A resolute lock of her eyes on his as she bit.

His patience almost broke. 'Promise me,' Vadim said, 'that if we ever argue again, we use that anger to fuck instead.'

# Thirty-Five

Vadim insisted on carrying her up the stairs; arms securely bracing her to his body, her head against his shoulder. The peace of the house at odds to the thrum of his heart, of the screams in his blood; he relied on honed discipline, on restraint, to keep his pace steady. To keep his memories of Prey, of her taste, from overruling his self-control.

From dictating possession, not veneration.

She deserved more, and he intended to deliver.

Reaching the top of the stairs, he turned toward his suite.

'My things are—'

'In our room,' he interjected, placing a kiss on her hair.

'Our room?' Her eyebrows lifted, head twisting to find his eyes.

'While you were gone, I had your things moved.' He manoeuvred his grip, enabling him to depress the handle and bring them inside.

'You went through my things?' Anara's heart surged; her laptop, her tinctures, her grimoire. The potential for discovery, for the truth, causing her to try and extricate from his hold.

*Perhaps I need to tell him first*, she thought.

'You're my wife, Anara Morozova, even if not officially… yet.' He held her more firmly to his chest. 'I'm never letting you sleep alone again.' The glint in his eyes suggested they would not sleep, either.

His words sweetened the concern, flooding her body with heat. Her body aching for confirmation, for consummation. For surrender. All sense of weariness had deserted her, every synapse alive. Alert. Weeping for his every touch, his every breath.

Vadim brought them into the suite's bathroom; white marble pristine, chrome glinting. He crouched, ignoring the pull of his abdomen's injuries, and placed her feet onto the floor.

Her reflection brought a heavy sigh.

He took her chin with thumb and forefinger, tipping her face up. 'You are beautiful, Anya, don't ever think otherwise.' Ignoring her shaking head, he placed a tender kiss on her brow, then stepped away. Crossed the room to turn on the shower, a responsive and forceful stream falling from the large head onto the inlaid tiles; no screen, no wall.

His boots and socks pulled off.

She followed his return to her, eyes hungry, body desperate. It had been so long since she had given herself so entirely, so completely, and the emotion brought a shudder to her breath. The fear of drowning under such depths she had succumbed to, the fear of being broken beyond all she could fix, creating caution.

Creating a hasty swallow, wrapping her arms around herself.

If she allowed this, if she offered her heart, Anara also had to trust it would be kept safe. Secure. Cherished.

'I can leave, if you'd rather—'

'No.' Anara's voice was raw. Devout. The plea made with vulnerable instinct, spoken from the chambers of her heart. Her soul. Her hope. She had sliced into her veins, she had found only him, only them. Intrinsically bound. The desire to crawl inside his bones, to curl into his ribs, to feast on every part of him overwhelming the hesitation.

Drawing Vadim closer, her fingers on his neck, lips fierce when they collided. Her tongue caressing his with tender pressure, her teeth sinking into his lower lip, her hips oscillating; a sigh shared with the hard pulse of his cock against her body.

‘You’re mine, Anya,’ he breathed, ‘always and forever.’ His lips roved her neck, tongue sliding over flesh, hands dropping to the hem of her top with slow exploration. Lingering touches on her curves, playful sweeping of her skin, fingers digging under fabric.

She raked her hands through his thick, dark hair, as she relished his exhales in the hollow of her neck. The pressure of his bite, the honey of his tongue. The rough scruff of his stubble. Alternating between pain and pleasure before the reluctant parting to draw the top over her head.

Her movements quick to push her trousers to the floor.

Hands gliding lightly over her skin, Vadim circled her; lips parted and adoration blowing his pupils black. Fury at the bruises on her flesh, at the cut on her leg, bringing ire to his blood.

The evidence of his own bruised bites increasing his lust.

She turned, catching his hand and meeting his eyes.

‘You can trust me, Anya,’ he said tenderly.

‘I do.’ Her breathing was shallow, tongue tracing her lips. Trembling limbs eager to touch, to erase the distance.

‘You want to stop, you say so.’ He welcomed her hands on the shirt buttons, how she skipped over them hastily. ‘No safe words.’

She laughed. ‘You think you’d need one?’

Vadim groaned as her answer broke through the haze in his mind; a feast of dissipation, an altar of his devotion. The addictive fever of all he planned to do. ‘Fuck, you’re perfect.’

Dragging his shirt from his waistband, then his torso, Anara shook her head; she would have preferred to prepare herself more luxuriously than the quick routine she had completed earlier. She reached for his belt, only to find his hands grip her wrists.

Her brow creased. ‘Vadya—’

‘You come first, remember.’ He slid his hands up her arms, pushing the straps of her bra from her shoulders. Flowing over, his fingers quickly worked the clasp. His mouth on her skin as he peeled silk from her body, tongue tip circling her nipples with reverence.

With gentle bites.

Fingers gliding lower, ripping the last item of clothing from her.

Anara slowly licked her lips.

Naked, Anara's body was on fire; stomach a mass of snakes, her every sense heightened. Her heart erratically threatening to break from the ivory cage of her ribs and claim him. Her core cried for his touch; wet and hot. She needed him inside her, needed him to devour her, needed his taste in her mouth.

Needed to swallow him whole.

To satiate her hunger while feeding her appetite.

Walking her to the shower, the water was a shroud. A welcome heat on her aching muscles, her sore flesh. The expansive space one she drank in eagerly, her arms stretching overhead, back arching. Knowing exactly how he would watch.

Hoping he would conquer.

Vadim was aware if he had permitted her to remove any more of his clothes, his already fragile compliance would have shattered. He needed the barrier before he crossed it.

Restraint was an art form he had mastered.

And losing control a craving he finally understood.

Tender, he massaged her scalp, poured oils over her skin. Her sighs a melody he orchestrated with his fingertips; a siren call which burrowed into every cell of his heart. Tattooed into his bones.

Eyes closed, Anara bit her lip and willed his hand to stray to where she needed the pressure. His teasing glances, skirting her hip, caressing her stomach, too near and too far all at once. She needed him to crawl in and travel every artery, every vein.

The ghost of his mouth on her thigh was not enough.

She opened her eyes, seeing him below her; beads of water on his torso, suit trousers stuck to his muscular legs. Broad shoulders taut with how he balanced, how he remained so focused on her limbs. The dark ink of his tattoos smudged with soap.

Raising one foot, Anara pushed him onto his back, dropping herself down onto his narrow waist. Her palms on his chest and a curve to her spine, she smiled. Water dripped from her sodden curls, kicked up from the tiles as the shower's fall continued; steam a miasma.

'Anya—'

She placed her finger on his mouth, only for him to draw it inside. A firm suck followed by a sharp bite. Her hips rocking in response, finding the friction she sought.

He could have pushed her off, easily. Could have pinned her to the wall, thrown her onto her knees. But this Anara, this goddess above him only made Vadim wish to relinquish power. Maintaining contact with her hooded gaze, he slowly spread his arms wide, allowing her full access to his body. One eyebrow raised in challenge.

Hooking her feet over his calves, she slid lower; her body flattening to his and claimed his mouth. The kiss firm, her tongue delving, her nails scratching over his scalp. On her lower back the rivulets fell, pouring from her hips, meandering over her legs. Her writhing frame bringing a low growl from his throat.

She breathed it in, welcomed his exhale and consumed it. Coaxed it to nestle in her chest, to ruin her. Opening her eyes, she began to move lower; hands tracing his arms and watching him flinch slightly when she caught the wounds. Shifting, she kissed them.

Dined on his skin with each lingering kiss she placed, navigating to his chest. To bite his hard nipples and suck on his flesh. Her body always in contact with his, using his thigh to deliver the pressure to her clit. Eyes locked on his and seeing how pained his were.

How his control was about to splinter.

Reaching the deeper injuries on his abdomen, Anara's tender kisses caused his muscles to contract. They were more sensitive, more raw. A bruise still bloomed below the surface; she probed it with her fingers, her tongue. Her teeth on the seam of fresh skin knitting the wound. Tempted to rip it open, to drink the blood she could locate.

To fold herself inside his skin.

'Anya,' he groaned.

She propped herself up, hips still moving, and met his eyes. 'Do you want me to stop?'

'No.' Vadim began sitting up, only to find her hand on his chest.

Pushing him back down.

'I want to take you to our bed,' he stated, breathless, 'and fuck you like the divine creature you are.'

Her body begged for his words, for how confidently she was sure he would fulfil every syllable. Pressing her quim more forcefully against his leg, her hands found his belt. The buckle unfastened while keeping eye contact, the black leather drawn slowly from each loop; his hips lifting from the tiles.

'Good boy,' she praised, leaning forward to kiss him.

'Fuck, Anya.' He gripped her head, holding her still and deepening the kiss. His leg raising to try and direct her shifting hips, to offer her the release she hungered for. 'Ты мне сейчас нужен[45].'

She moaned; his low voice, lust fuelled and dangerous, coupled with the slide of his hand down her spine, evidence of his adulation. Her body wound so tight it could snap. But Anara wanted more. Needed more. Her hand tucked between them to locate the zip of his trousers.

The brush of her fingertips over his clothed cock bringing a yearning exhale from his throat. Water drowned the grating metal, the release of the button, the plea from his lips when she slid lower.

Her kisses languid, tongue curling, following the ink, then defined lines of muscle. Hands shrugging his clothes from his hips; feet dragging fabric from his legs. The size of him making her hunger scream for haste even as she paced her descent.

Vadim forced himself to be still.

To allow her this, even as the urge to conquer her chewed eagerly through every synapse. His resolve slipping with every kiss she placed

---

[45] Ты мне сейчас нужен - Russian for 'I need you now'

and each nip of her teeth against his skin. When her tongue tip licked the crown of his cock he hissed. And when Anara's mouth sank around him, devouring every thick inch she could manage, he swore.

She smiled, jaw aching as she tasted, as she consumed, swallowing him to the back of her mouth. Forcing her throat to relax. Hand curled at the root, she hummed over his cock; relishing how Vadim tensed below her. She sucked; the stretch of her lips an ache which fed her craving. A blissful moan as his taste ate into her blood.

Her tongue a ribbon, her fingers a cage, his cock her banquet.

The tears and her ragged breath ignored as she focused on him; on how he felt, how he trusted, how his anguish threaded through his every animalistic groan. His hips bucking slightly, before her nails dug into his thighs. Vadim's immediate obedience rewarded with her lowering further and tightening her throat around the head of his cock.

'Ебать[46],' he roared, hands fisting her hair, unable to hold back; his submission salted nectar she swallowed. 'Anya… fuck.'

She licked his shaft, root to tip, with her tongue flat, broadly coiling to capture every remaining drop. The velvet of his flesh hot. His body flinching as electricity danced through his body.

'You broke the rules,' he said, hoarse.

Anara stilled, the shower warm as it coated her skin even as a chill ate into her bones. His dilated gaze and shuddering chest full of threat and menace; it only tightened her anticipation.

She knew was safe.

Yet, she allowed the potential for fear to dance through her blood.

'You're supposed to come first,' he elaborated, raising his legs to tip her forward as he gripped her waist, flattening his feet to the tile to push them both up.

Her back slamming into the wall.

Instinctive, Anara hooked her arms and legs around him. His body hard and teeth sharp; his bite of her clavicle forcing her to arch closer. A

---

[46] Ебать - Russian for 'Fuck'

fractured cry even as she ground her hips against him. As she raked her nails down his back.

Vadim's head tilting to meet her ravenous gaze.

'I was hungry,' she retorted, 'and you're delicious.'

He shook his head, eyes closing; laughter throaty as he efficiently silenced the shower. Gripping her rear, he carried her, placing her on the countertop. Vadim's stubble-framed lips delivering rough kisses along her jaw, her neck, before reaching for a towel to drape around her.

'You think this'll make me dry?' Anara's teeth caught his earlobe, a nip offered playfully as he attempted to soak up the moisture. Open legs drawing him into her, a coy smile conveying her desire.

The slick heat of her arousal glistening on her flesh.

He dropped his hand, gliding it up her leg to the apex of her thighs, while keeping his eyes on her. The torturously slow stroke ending with a more pressured spiral on Anara's clit.

Removed when her hips chased the touch.

Needing to recapture the sensation.

'Are you denying me, now?' Her eyes narrowed. 'Is that your idea of punishment? Because I'll just fix it myself.'

His smile was wicked; the image of Anara pleasuring herself as he watched an immediate burst of hot lust. An image he considered would be delectable. 'That's almost worth denying myself,' he said, raspy, 'but I'm not done with you yet.'

'So, I don't get punished?' She licked the tip of her tongue over her full lips, her eyes wide; pupils an abyss of obsidian.

'No punishment today.' He paused. 'But after I take you to our bed, wife, you'll never want me to be anywhere but inside you.'

His vow surged through every cell; his body preparing to deliver the truth of his words. His light touch whispering surrender. A command she was powerless to refuse. Nestling against him when he swept her off the marble to carry her through to the bedroom.

Their bedroom.

Seeing her, naked, on his bed, Vadim's heart kicked. This is where she belonged, this is where his pilgrimage ended; she was his altar, his goddess, his home. A desire to rip open Anara's flesh, to crack open her ribs, to curl into her body and feel how her lungs offered slumber, how her pulse marked time, was a fire in his blood.

Her taste was already a delicacy he wished to dine on for eternity.

Her mouth had already proven she was divine.

Vadim needed to find the restraint he had lost; the persuasive licks she delivered had ruined him. Anara was the ultimate sin. One he would never seek absolution for; she was and would always be the owner of his heart. His body. His soul. Kneeling at her feet, he swallowed.

He had imagined this moment, craved it.

'Vadya?' She began to sit up, only for him to drag her by the ankles to lay before him; an open offering.

'I don't know how I got so lucky,' he said, voice gravel, 'to have such an exquisite wife.' He had fought so hard to find such raging peace; mind and body finally unified in their worship of this woman.

Every part of her was trembling with need. With a yearning ache for him to claim her entirely. This cruel waiting was pins under her flesh.

His hands slid, slow, up her legs; the tips barely making contact. He kept his dark eyes on hers, relishing how her lips parted, how her breath caught. How her body quivered under his teasing reverence. His thumbs dipping toward her quim bringing a sigh, fingers bracing her hips.

Sweeping higher, leaving her sigh to become a mewl.

Desperately keening for more.

Her hands on his muscular arms slipping to his wrists; hoping to use gentle direction to get him where she needed him. Only for him to shake her off and grip both hands together. Vadim rocked back onto his heels and shook his head, settling his hold of her more securely.

'Please,' she whispered, all sense of resistance, all sense of caution, devoured by desire. By the need to have him consume her, for her to consume him; for their relationship to transform.

An ouroboros of flesh, devoted and unified.

No hiding, a reciprocal vulnerability, of holy and unholy love.

'I'd never deny you, kroshka.' Retaining hold of her wrists, he bent to trail his other hand over the curve of her waist. Fingers then lips a caress on the swell of her breasts, the peaks of her nipples. Tongue then teeth, he measured control.

The erratic beat of her heart loud against his jaw.

His breath hot in the hollow of her throat.

Her shuddering breath a prayer.

The union expectant in their blood.

Their bodies pressed; her arms dragged above her head, his body a weight she tried to digest. Each sway of her hips chasing friction, each arc of her spine teasing the pulse of his hard cock.

'Do you want me to stop?' Vadim's exhales ghosted her skin.

'Never,' she panted, grinding her hips. Every synapse alive, begging for him to gorge himself. 'I need you; Vadya, I need you inside me.'

He rested his forehead on hers, eyes closing, fingers grazing her skin to dip to her clit; the heat making him groan as he pinched it, sliding in two fingers and curling them. His rhythm immoral, a beat she clung to with every writhing limb, with her back bowing from the bed.

Pupils dilated, breath fluttering, her control lost with each certain touch he delivered. The worship sacred, the shrine of safety enhancing her pleasure. Until he saw her body still.

Taut. Wet. Intense.

Her head tilting back with a moaning scream.

The pressured electricity he coaxed from her body wild fire.

Searing pleasure intensifying her hunger.

'Vadya,' she panted, 'please… please…'

'Please what, kroshka?' He was barely holding himself together; a thread stretched and ready to tear. His discipline being eaten by lust, by the carnal need to find the salvation in her flesh.

'Fuck me,' she breathed. 'Vadya… husband, fuck me.'

His heart almost broke through his ribs. The ivory fracturing wide for Anara to slice into the organ and wander every chamber. It was entirely hers. Hers for the rest of his life, perhaps even before they ever met, and until time ended.

Removing his fingers, Vadim stroked her arousal over his cock; the final thread mere smoke. Control he so proudly maintained lost. The bite of his teeth in her neck breaking her skin as he buried his cock deep.

Deeper.

The hiss against his ear causing him to pause, to study her face and ensure Anara was okay. That she was adjusting to his size. Shifting his hand to stroke then hold her damp curls, cupping her head, delivering a gentle kiss on her brow.

'I need you to move,' she begged.

The thrum of his cock and the ache of her cunt, almost made Anara unravel, again. Before he had even begun to discover the sensations he could fuck from her, before Vadim had even begun to play the honey of her quim, to sink into the heat of her skin.

'As you wish.' His voice was as raw, as devout.

The feel of her body surrounding him, below him, was an enchanting narcotic; Anara's flesh all he wished to ruin, all he wished to save. Her tight pressure a chalice he worshipped with every retreat, every return.

Discipline reclaimed with determined lust.

With desire to deliver satisfaction.

Anara's eyes were glazed, her mind empty of anything but him; the way he filled her, the way her body wailed for his brutal tempo, brutal touch, the way she craved to swallow him entirely. For him to claim her body and blood, bones and soul. Her surrender offered willingly as she curved into his frame, wrapped her legs around his hips.

Moved with him as they used entwined limbs, as they explored the limits of their flesh. Vadim's abdominal wounds opening, dripping blood she licked from greedy fingers; shared in his mouth. The mutual pursuit of dissipated screams savoured with bites, with scratches.

With love.

With fists in their hair for leverage, finding new depths of sin.

His hand caging her throat as they stared eye to eye.

Breath to breath.

The roll of her hips, the matched flex of his, feeding their satisfied cries; their bed wrecked, their throats sore, their suite echoing with heavy exhales and sweet pleas. With Vadim's breathy growl against her arched neck as he emptied himself into her while she crumbled.

Lying broken together, a tangle of bruised flesh.

Blood smeared on tattoos and snow.

On the sheets.

He drew her to his side; her every cell trembling, tears snaking over her flushed cheeks. His fingers stroked gently over her arm, twisting to run knuckles back up, allowing them this moment.

The heaving of their chests, the ragged breath filling silence.

An accepted peace.

'You've destroyed me,' she said huskily.

He tilted his head down, brow creasing. Eyes roaming the bites on her thighs, the scratched welts on his arms, their combined release on their flesh. The shadow fractured with her every inhale, exhale, from one of the inverted lamps; the nightstand's top in disarray.

She raised her eyes to meet his concerned gaze; adoration carved through her veins. 'Vadya, how did this happen?'

'What do you mean?' His heart cracked with her words, fear coiling in his stomach. Vadim pulled her closer, his other arm shifting to draw her onto his body entirely. That she willingly permitted it relieved him; the heat of her skin welcome.

'I… I never thought I'd meet someone who'd… understand.' Anara's mind struggled to find the words, to explain how he had unlocked a part of her she had hidden. 'But you, you just knew.'

'Knew what, kroshka?' He curled strands of her hair in his fist, his eyes hooked on hers.

She was glad of her warmth, that any embarrassment in voicing her passion would not add to the heat radiating from her skin. Lacing fingers with his, Anara smiled. 'I needed fucked, not loved. I needed a man who wouldn't treat me like a fragile doll, but as a woman who could draw blood. I needed a man who'd devour me.'

Vadim released her hair, his hand snaking down her back to rest on the curve of her rear. Fingers spiralling.

'You fucked me, Vadya,' she said, 'because you see me. I've never loved anyone more than I love you.'

His hand lifted, coming to the back of her head to push her forward, lips fierce as they connected. Savage and devoted. 'Fuck, Anya, you're absolutely perfect; you're my heart, my soul; I love you.'

She caught his lip with her teeth, drawing back to be able to see him more clearly. The swipe of his thumb over her cheek removing the salted tears, before he sucked it into his mouth.

'Stay there, kroshka,' he said softly, gently sliding her to the bed.

Anara watched his strides; curling onto her side, admiring his frame and the ink which decorated his skin. The musculature Vadim had used to bring her pleasure beyond anything she had imagined, anything she believed she would find.

The man who she believed would permit her to explore every one of her fantasies. Her desires.

Returning with a soaked cloth, Vadim gestured for her lean back; his tender movements cleaning her thighs. His kiss on her clit bringing a soft moan. The traces of blood on her stomach, her hips, wiped. Glancing down at his abdomen, Vadim smoothed the white fabric over his opened cuts; crimson blooming into thread. Throwing it aside, he drew her into his arms with every intent to watch her sleep.

# Thirty-Six

Anara had not woken so sore in years. She relished the pain, the ache in her joints, in her skin. A delicious poison she would readily swallow time and time again. There was beauty in the rawness of her throat, the grip of his hand on her hip; bodies pressed close.

Close enough to open up flesh and restitch it as one body.

She rocked slightly, teasing his hard cock; smiling at his groan. The creeping of Vadim's fingertips to her breast, to drift his thumb over her nipple; a confirmation he was awake. A lingering kiss on her shoulder warm with his exhale, rough with his stubble.

His head falling forward, inhaling her scent, pulling her closer.

Quick to circle her wrist when she slid her hand to his waist. Head shaking, even as he longed to feed his addiction; to bury himself inside her and play with her pulse.

'Vadya,' she said, voice still thick with slumber.

With desire.

'You should rest, wife.' He placed another kiss on her shoulder. 'I've plans for us, for later.'

'What if I have plans for us now?' Anara oscillated her hips, feeling her arousal between her thighs, and on the tip of his cock; hard and hot against her back.

'Your plans for now should be focused on relaxing,' Vadim said, 'and letting me soothe those raw marks.' In the dim light, filtering through the drawn curtains, the reddened welts and evidence of his teeth, were dark on her pale skin. His own flesh as claimed by her touch.

She collapsed deeper into his embrace, allowing him to stroke over her arm, her stomach. The bristle of his jaw nestled in her neck, his lips ghosting her earlobe with gentle kisses.

The room hushed with only their breath.

'I could stay here forever,' she murmured.

'If only we could, kroshka.' Vadim's eyes closed; the aftermath of the raid on Septer, the almost entire destruction of their rivals, work he could not avoid, if he was to monopolise on their success. The clock had been knocked from the nightstand, but the creeping light and distant sound of activity suggested they needed to leave their bed.

The growl of her stomach underlining his words.

He smiled. These moments were the ones he had longed for, ones he had fought for, and now he had them, he refused to relinquish them. A renewed determination to protect her, them, eating through his veins. 'I was careless, kroshka, last night—'

'What do you mean?' She twisted, trying to face him; his hold on her only tightened. 'Careless how?'

'I'm too selfish to share you,' he continued, trying to formulate the unfamiliar trepidation, the realisation the morning had delivered. 'I never asked, but I should've, before we slept together.'

Anara's brows knitted, she was failing to make the connection in his statements, in the night they had spent. 'Never asked what?'

Vadim loosened his grip, gently turning her so he could look into her eyes. 'I'm serious about spending my life with you, Anya, and, in time, I'd love to grow our family, if you want to. But, I never checked, last night, and I want more time with just you, just us.'

She smiled, catching her lower lip with her teeth. 'It's okay,' Anara said, 'I trust you—'

‘And I trust you,’ he said earnestly, cupping her face. A kiss offered devoutly to her crown. ‘I’d’ve never done what we did if I thought you’d be at any… risk from me.’

‘And I’d’ve never allowed it to happen, either.’ She pressed into his palm, eyes hooked into his. A slow lick of her lips as she contemplated her next words. ‘Vadya, I know herbs, I know how to take care of myself. If they ever fail, I’d tell you.’ She paused. ‘But know I’ll decide based on our circumstances, not your faith.’

His chest heaved with his breath, the understanding of her defiance, her autonomy, only reinforcing his love. He grabbed her thigh, hooking it over his, her body pressing with forceful hunger. His lips claimed hers, fingers sliding to trail over her clit; his groan eaten by her throat.

‘I thought your plans were for later.’ She said between kisses.

He nodded, resting his forehead against hers and withdrawing his hand to rest on her hip. ‘They are, kroshka.’

‘Now could be later.’ Anara nipped his lip, her leg pulling him closer once more. The teasing tone to her voice matched by her actions.

‘We need to eat,’ he argued, pushing her onto her back. Vadim propped himself above her, eyes greedy. ‘Fuck, you’re breathtaking, but I’ve no idea what time it is, and if we stay here any longer we’ll end up with company. None of my men deserve to see you like this.’

She reached out to him, hands aiming for his shoulders, his waist, only for him to leave. To drag himself from their bed.

‘I do have something for you, though,’ Vadim called, from within the dressing room. In the large mirror, he glanced over his body; the marks she had inflicted and the wounds which had re-opened, proof of how she had wrecked him.

And how he would allow her to do it forever.

She waited, snakes in her stomach, for him to explain. Anara’s eyes on the mess of the room; cushions thrown, bedding tangled, the toy polar bear buried under blankets. The knowledge Sofiya would see it, that her screams would have been heard, brought fresh warmth to her skin.

Even as she drew the covers higher.

'Septer are done,' he said, walking back into the main part of their suite; trousers low on his hips, t-shirt in his hand. He passed her a set of pyjamas, willing his body to calm as he drank her in; how she gracefully stood. 'But I saved Kassian for you.'

'Saved him?'

'He's in the cells.' He raked a hand through his hair, striding to the bathroom. 'I thought you'd like to decide what to do with him.'

'I want to kill him.' There was no hesitation in her response.

But her words made Vadim halt in the doorway. His lips quirking into a smile, head tiling as what he knew about her began connecting.

*That's my girl*, he thought, *and she's a fucking goddess*.

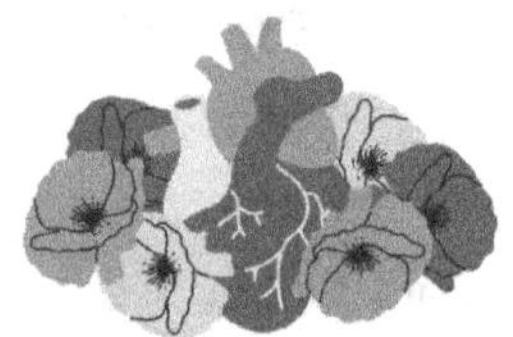

He had convinced Artem to delay arriving until later; his mind keen to explore who Anara truly was. To understand the woman he loved. The confidence in her assertion to murder Kassian had renewed suspicions he had ignored; his focus on proving his devotion. Proving his contrition after failing to keep her safe.

Vadim's phone retrieved and messages skimmed, the instruction to his advisor sent, before they made their way downstairs; arriving to calm silence. The hum of appliances. The melodic harmony of birds. Sunlight broke over the dark floors, long and lean.

All evidence of their meal the night before, gone.

'What can I make you?' Vadim asked, releasing her hand to cross to the stove. He tested the kettle, removing it to top up the water.

'Get out of my kitchen,' Sofiya called, walking quickly toward them.

He smiled, a breath of laughter escaping his lips as he acquiesced to his housekeeper's jovial request, stepping around the marble island to sit beside Anara; lacing his fingers in hers.

'Does this mean there's something you *can't* do?' Anara teased, her shoulder nudging his. 'I'm disappointed.'

'I can cook,' he objected.

Her eyebrows rose.

'I can!' He took a deep breath, feigning hurt.

'To be fair,' Sofiya said, leaning against the counter, 'he can; I just prefer things to be where I left them.'

Vadim's smile was almost smug.

'You pay her,' Anara said, 'she has to say nice things.'

His smile twisted, leaning into her. 'Careful, wife,' he whispered, 'I'll have to punish you.'

She licked her tongue over her lips; his words ate straight through to her quim. The thin fabric of her pyjamas did little to hide how her nipples peaked, how her chest bloomed with colour, despite her robe; her thighs pressing together to try and relieve the ache. 'I thought I was supposed to be resting until later.'

Catching her chin with his thumb and forefinger, he offered a kiss, a slow slide of his tongue along the seam. Deepening the touch, a caress of lips, of muscle, of flesh. His body as alive as hers.

The deliberately loud placement of their meal causing them to part with haste; Anara's eyes averted and Vadim discreetly rearranging how he was sitting. Their thanks mumbled as aromas drifted from the plates and the steaming mugs of coffee.

'I'll be back,' Sofiya announced, bemused by their behaviour.

Anara's hand rushed to stop her, catching her wrist. 'If you're going upstairs, you don't need to, I'll—'

'Kroshka, it's okay' he said. 'Go ahead, Sofiya.'

Her fingers uncurled. 'But, Vadya—'

'You don't need to be embarrassed,' Vadim soothed.

She tried to catalogue how to express how things had changed; how her privacy was, and would always be, important, how everyone would know what they had done.

How everyone would have heard her loss of control.

Stroking one hand over her curls, he kept contact with her eyes. 'It's okay, Anya, the room's soundproofed, and Sofiya's dealt with worse.'

Her heart chilled with the thought of what Sofiya would have seen after he had entertained other women in that room.

In that bed.

Anara's eyes glazed with heat, her throat thick.

Her head dipping.

She knew it was irrational; they both had history.

'I only mean she's had to deal with the aftermath of my work, things like bloodied clothes,' Vadim explained, his brow creasing. His attempt to reassure her unintentionally causing distress. 'You are the only woman who's ever been invited to this house, and the only woman to be in my bed. *Our* bed.'

A tear dropped. She tilted her head to the ceiling, willing the emotion to settle; frustration in how weak she appeared gnawing in her veins. Yet she did not fight when he gently steered her face back to his.

'Anara, you don't ever have to worry,' he said, placing a kiss on her forehead. 'You're mine, I'm yours; now and in the future. Hell, maybe the past too, because I never understood love until now.'

# Thirty-Seven

It had taken a little while to locate her herbs, but Anara emerged from the dressing room with an appropriate tincture; a drug to bring suffering. To deliver death. Her spine straight and mind focused.

Waiting on the tidied sofa, Vadim tracked her steps to him. Strength radiated from her. With every reduction of the distance, his heart grew in admiration, in adoration, in devotion. This Anara who stood before him was every inch the goddess he believed her to be.

If it was not for the pressing need to deal with Kassian, Vadim would have knelt before her with sacred love.

'Take me to him,' she said, voice low.

Eyes locked on him.

He stood, gripping her face in both hands; fingertips on the nape of her neck, thumbs brushing her cheeks. His kiss primal. Devouring; trying to impart the force of his love, his trust.

His fidelity.

Their hands entwined, they strode side by side from the suite; a nod provided to Fyodor, who followed them from the landing. The descent to the cells made in silence. A hush which only increased in the emptiness of the basement. The aroma of copper and musk infused with citrus and bleach.

'What do you need, kroshka,' Vadim asked, pausing outside the only cell with a closed door. After the great purge of Septer, there was a lull in threat, a pause in their necessary terror.

'For you to tell me what that means.'

His lips formed a lopsided smile. 'Later.'

'Always later,' she muttered, eyes rolling.

'Careful—'

'What, you think I won't punish you?' Anara matched his smile, her lips ghosting his neck before nipping the lobe of his ear.

Fyodor bit back a chuckle, unlocking the cell.

'I've every *crumb* I need,' she confirmed, smirking

Vadim nodded, his eyes on her as she strode into the room; her use of the word crumb suggesting she knew exactly what he had called her since they met.

Even if she continued to ask for him to explain it.

Standing in the centre, supported by the ceiling's chains, Kassian swayed. His body bruised, sliced, naked. The dragon tattoo snaking from his arm to his chest blurred with swathes of blood.

Pacing around him, Anara's gaze flicked over his body. Each step an assessment of the brutality Vadim, or his men, had delivered since his capture. The torture inflicted to obtain information. Her heart pounded in time with the pulse of her desire; pupils dilating when she met Vadim's affectionate stare. Her teeth catching her lower lip.

*Can I do this? Will he still love me once he* really *sees me?* Anara's body flushed with heat as she considered if she could pull the tincture from her pocket. If she could murder with an audience.

This was different to luring men to a café.

This was different to how she helped women in Erinyes.

Here, there was the potential to lose everything she had finally been able to obtain; the love she never believed she would feel.

The loyalty she doubted she would be shown.

Confirming her reality may destroy everything.

'You… came for… me… sweetheart,' Kassian rasped. Weak, weary, his body rebelled against the effort to raise his head. His swollen eyes all he could use to follow her movement.

Anara paused, turning back to him. 'I'd've arrived sooner, but your leader had other plans.'

In the doorway, Vadim folded his muscular arms. Though confident in how robust the chains were, and the proximity of weapons, he had no intention of leaving her alone with him.

'How… is Mace?' His throat was raw, his tongue sticky. Nourishment had been provided, albeit less than he would have preferred and never when he wanted it; only sufficient to keep him breathing.

'No longer burdened with running a business,' Anara stated.

Kassian swallowed, with difficulty. His mouth opening and closing to try and find some moisture. Fatigue making it challenging to completely understand what Anara was saying.

'You're the only member of Septer left alive,' she continued, seeing the confusion in his eyes. 'For now.'

The chains rattled with his shiver. Though uncertain if he preferred to die or be detained, Kassian still clung to the possibility of rescue.

Of escape.

She considered how likely it was that Vadim had already determined who she really was. While she was held, he had sufficient opportunity to search through her belongings, to investigate her history, to pick apart her friends. He had an effective team, he had resources, and yet he had not said anything since her return.

Anara exhaled, digging into her pocket for the vial.

It looked so innocuous; a slender glass jar, with a sealed cork lid, full of granular white powder. The wax around the top was a deep violet and blue, tonally marbled.

Unfolding his arms, Vadim stood straighter.

Keeping her focus on the captive, Anara gently inverted the vial; her wrist tipping it over and over. 'I only need one drop, *sweetheart*.'

Vadim's jaw ticked.

He took a step forward.

Anara held up her hand at the sound.

He stopped immediately.

'Lower his chains,' she requested, 'I need him to kneel.' Slowly, she twisted the cork free of the wax. The flakes cracking and drifting toward the ichor-slick floor.

Vadim gestured to Fyodor to slacken the tension.

The relief from the pressure sent a flood of painful sensation through Kassian's limbs. His wail fractured as he stumbled to his knees; the loud collision of bone on stone causing another whimper.

She took the opportunity to grip his hair; the braid further unravelling above the undercut, the dark-brown strands greasy and matted.

Kassian gritted his teeth.

'Open up, *sweetheart*,' she crooned, dragging his head back.

He tried to twist away, feeling the sharp scratch of Anara's nails on his scalp, the pull in his neck. Cognisant of potential, fear was a glacial snake slithering through his blood.

Ducking to his boot, Vadim swept his knife from the sheath.

'It's okay, Vadya,' she said, 'he thinks if he plays hard to get, I'll still be interested in the game.' Anara's eyes raked over Kassian, deliberate and slow. 'But now I've seen what's on offer, well, I'm glad I have such a magnificent husband.'

'Cunt,' Kassian hissed, 'like you're even worth it.'

She gripped his jaw. Tipped the vial's contents onto his tongue and slammed his mouth shut before he could spit. Pinching Kassian's nose, the vial splintered as it smashed by his bloodied knees.

Satisfied he had swallowed, Anara released him and stepped back with a glance to Fyodor. The switch thrown to drag Kassian back onto his feet; chains tightening to the ceiling once more.

Vadim licked his tongue over his lips, admiration and awe duelling with lust as he watched her. The calm expression on her face, the speed she had delivered the drug, only endeared her to him more. Knife still in his hand, he whipped her to him and claimed her mouth with a hungry kiss; fingers splayed on her lower back to push her close.

Her arms by her sides and hands in fists.

'I love you,' he breathed, resting his forehead on hers.

'Which is why I need to scrub my hands.' She extricated herself from him; sensing him follow as she poured soap onto her skin, drenched the lather with water. Smiling as he did the same.

'The fuck… it's… sugar,' Kassian panted.

'It is,' she agreed, rinsing her hands then turning back. 'I wanted to sweeten the dose.'

'What did you give him?' Vadim inclined his head; a confirmation of Fyodor's suggestion to rinse down the area, the bottle fragments.

'Sugar,' she explained, 'and aconite.'

'Aconite?' Vadim's heart kicked; pride and caution.

'Wolfsbane.'

The chains shook, a muscle spasm causing Kassian to jerk. The hot burn in his throat creating a rush of saliva he tried to swallow, to spit. His already weakened state increasing the impact of the drug. The room was a blur of sound, of shape, of colour; he struggled to find any focus, which only exacerbated the nausea chaffing his stomach.

'Every part of the plant is poisonous,' Anara continued, ignoring the plight of the captive man, 'but I was careful, so we should be fine.'

'Should?'

'We'll be fine,' she said, smiling. Her kiss delivered to reassure him, her fingers stroking down his jaw, his neck.

Vadim did not resist her touch.

Relieved in his trust in her, Anara exhaled.

Behind them, Kassian's breath grew increasingly ragged; a dogged pant with trailing mucus from his mouth. The seizures forcing a melody in the chains, his limbs grating further against the manacles. His heartbeat fracturing, an abnormal rhythm which courted death.

'Tell me, wife,' he said tenderly, cupping her face, 'how long you've been the poisoner we've been hunting?'

'Hunting?' She paled.

'Unsuccessfully, clearly,' he added. 'We thought it was a man trying to get into our drug trade.'

'But the profile of the targets threw us,' Fyodor said, his eyes on the suffering victim in the centre of the cell.

Anara's smile broadened. 'I'm very particular about who I help.'

'Remind me never to ask for your help.' Fyodor chuckled, folding his arms and leaning against the wall; one boot raised on the stone.

Kassian retched, fresh mucus and bile smearing over open cuts and bloodied skin. His inhales sharp and broken.

'Did you kill Logan Pottinger?' Vadim asked.

She nodded. 'Not like this; I usually do things more gently.'

'How did you evade Ilya?'

Chewing her lip, she considered how much more she had to explain, how much of her life, her business, she would need to divulge. That was something for later; the thought amused her. *Always later.* 'I managed to slip out the back of my appointment.'

Vadim shook his head, a wry smile hiding laughter. 'I'll have to keep you chained up, to keep you from getting into any trouble.'

'It's only trouble if I get caught,' she retorted.

'Anya, I adore you.' Vadim pulled her into his body, hands on Anara's lower back and neck, and kissed her brow.

The gasping breaths from Kassian, punctuated with spasms of muscles and limbs, were becoming further stilted. His heart slipping into a brutal asystole. His anguished cries barely audible.

Tipping her chin up, Vadim delivered a deep kiss, loaded with the promise of all they intended to pursue, to achieve. Sharing how they had their taste embedded into every atom, every cell, every breath.

How she would be his faith, his goddess, his wife.

How he would be her relentless protector, standing by her side.

They were lost in their feast; the sound of their hearts loud, the ache of their pulse torturous. Anara's fingers on his shirt creasing the fabric to prevent her hastily unbuttoning it. His hands on her warm face to prevent pinning her against the wall. It would be so effortless to succumb to the desire gnawing through their veins.

'Seems I missed all the fun,' Artem stated, arriving in the doorway.

Kassian's last breaths stuttering through his chest.

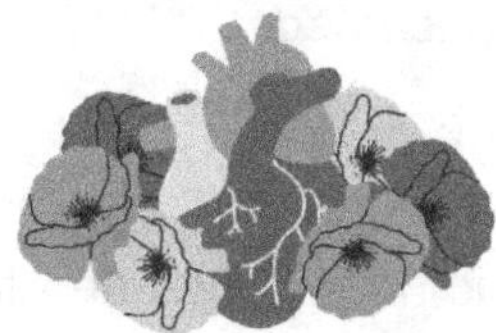

Artem watched their interactions with a bemused smile. Leaning back in the armchair, he had his ankle propped on the opposite leg, one hand curled over his shin. In midday sunlight cascading through the full-height doors, his peppered hair seemed lighter, his brown eyes softer. His black suit darker.

Though reassured by Vadim's comments, Anara still blushed when Sofiya handed her the mug. Her gaze averted and teeth catching her lip at the thought of what the housekeeper had seen.

'So, how long've you been a killer, Anara?'

'Tyoma!' Vadim shook his head, reaching for her hand and lacing his fingers in hers before bringing it to his mouth.

His kiss tender.

The advisor chuckled.

'It's okay,' she said. 'I just do what needs to be done, when it needs to be done.' Anara hoped her answer would be sufficient, the information enough to avoid further scrutiny. She intended to keep protecting Bryony and Kerezen, to keep protecting the women who sought her support.

'And what exactly is that?' Artem shifted, leaning forward. 'Ilya was a target, yes? What did you plan to do to him?'

*Fuck*. Though, Anara considered, it was unlikely Artem would ever have been satisfied with her vague answer. She refused to betray Sofiya, and how she had come to her for assistance; the file created for Vadim's soldier before greater understanding had been reached.

'The file was empty,' Vadim said.

'Almost empty,' he retorted.

'It was research,' she said, calm. Her words close enough to truth to be believed; her tone convincing, body still. She was proficient in how to conduct herself, how to ensure she was perceived appropriately where her less legal skills were concerned.

'But you created the file.'

'Tyoma, leave it.' Vadim's jaw ticked. The presence of a folder for one of his men was a topic he still intended to discuss privately. 'She's told you what you need to know.'

Artem's eyes narrowed, swiping his mug from the table to take a sip of the tea; amber liquid hot on his tongue.

She welcomed the rhythmic stroke of his thumb over her skin, falling into Vadim as he drew her closer. The soft kiss on her crown making her close her eyes, smile. His solid warmth a soothing presence she curled into, a comfort she had quickly learned was as necessary for him. That he was never ashamed to be with her, never denied the opportunity to prove his attachment, reinforced her sense of being loved.

Of this love being one she could drown in without dying.

Feast without starving, without nausea.

'The pakhan manages to find a poisoner for a wife,' Artem muttered with low laughter. 'Would you ever have told us, Anara?'

'Yes.' She was certain. 'I've no reason to hide who I am.'

'But you didn't tell us, at first.'

'Tyoma,' Vadim sighed. 'She was working out what was real, and if she could trust us; you'd've kept such a thing secret too.'

He inclined his head in acknowledgement.

'You kept things from me,' Anara stated, twisting to meet Artem's keen observance. 'I know you'd planned to use Erinyes for distribution and possibly even for me to grow—'

‘Plans change.’

‘They do.’ She nodded. ‘And I’m glad you saw sense. I’ll never allow you to use Erinyes, never. That place is…,’ she paused, softly biting her tongue, cautious to share too much. ‘I’ve obligations to my staff and my customers; I won’t compromise that.’

‘A killer with principles.’ Artem’s smile grew, a tattooed hand rubbing over his neck; eyes creasing when he saw Vadim’s warning stare. ‘What are your plans for the apartment?’

‘Above Erinyes?’

He slowly nodded, gesturing with the mug for her to continue.

‘I thought about keeping it for myself.’ Anara felt Vadim tense beside her at the words; she tightened her hold of his hand to reassure him. The split skin of his knuckles raw. ‘But I’ve decided to convert it into a refuge, for women who need somewhere safe to go.’

Vadim took her chin between his thumb and forefinger, tilting her up to face him, his heart surging with admiration. ‘I’ll do anything you need me to, Anya; I know this is your fight—’

She began to object.

‘—I don’t ask you to tell me why you need to do this, but I can piece things together based on who has been poisoned.’ He kept his gaze on her, watching for her reaction. ‘But, the world is a better place with you in it, kroshka, and I know you’re capable, so fucking capable. If you ever can’t do what needs to be done, you tell me. I’ll stand by your side. You don’t have to deal with this alone.’

She swallowed, her throat thick and eyes raw. Blurred. She blinked, feeling the moisture on her lashes. Her exhale shuddered through her chest. The lightest graze of Vadim’s lips on hers a welcome distraction to the overwhelming onslaught of emotion.

The vibration of her phone pulling them apart.

‘I need to take this,’ she rasped, glancing at the screen. ‘Kas.’

He released her, watching her stroll away. Her silhouette curving in the sunlight; a shadow he remembered with a smile, an ache. Their time of forced separation something he never wanted to experience again. A bond forged he intended to keep, to nurture, to feed.

'So you took my advice.'

Slow, Vadim turned his focus back to his advisor.

'You finally fucked her—'

'Tyoma,' he warned; his smile falling.

'—but I've changed my opinion. Your wife is—'

'Fuck,' he hissed, eyes closing and fists curling.

'—a very worthy addition to our family.' Artem grinned, the restrained laughter vibrating gently in his chest. 'Don't fuck this up Vadimir Lvovich Morozov; she's the best thing that's happened to you in years.'

The truth of his friend's words cut deep. His jaw flexed with the tight clench of his teeth, his skin chased with ice at the sincerity he saw in the man's eyes, the warmth in his tone. 'I've no intention to.'

'Good.' He took a mouthful of tea. 'You've worked hard, despite your losses, and I'm glad you've finally found the happiness you deserve. Just don't allow her to distract you, you've responsibilities—'

'I'm aware of exactly what my role entails, Tyoma.' He spoke without venom; accustomed to the taciturn nature of his advisor, accustomed to how Artem needed to fulfil his own duties.

The advice he provided appropriate and effective.

'You need to marry her,' Artem stated, 'for real, before she comes to her senses and leaves.'

# Thirty-Eight

She had to double-back, turning away from the room she had made her own and toward the room they were carving into theirs. The conversation with Sofiya one which reassured them both; secrets safe and friendship sealed in hushed whispers. The carnal knowledge of what the night may hold hastening the discussion.

A growing tension writhing in her blood.

The click of the door's closure blurred by desire.

'Wife,' he said, a low growl. His body shadow, seated on the leather sofa, and shirt unbuttoned. In the soft glow of the lamps, his tattoos were an obscured pattern over the defined muscle of his abdomen, his chest, his hands. The steady folding of his sleeves made as he keenly watched her cross the room.

The glint of the knife beside him only seen as she drew closer. An immediate pulse in her quim and catch in her throat. Halting by his open legs, she tried to silence the snakes sliding through her stomach.

'You're wearing too many clothes.' He raked one hand through his dark hair; even eclipsing the lights, he could see the blush bloom on her skin. He rolled his tongue over his lips.

'So are you,' she retorted, breathy.

'I can't have my dessert until you're naked, Anya.'

She swallowed. A tremble in her hands causing her to slip on the zip of her trousers, the hem of her top. Her snowy skin marked by their past collision; bruises she had studied in the shower.

Had considered scribing into her flesh to confirm she was his.

The tight pressure of his cock against the constriction of his clothes almost made him reach out to rip the lace from her frame.

Almost.

His discipline, his resolve, keeping his hands on his thighs. He slid lower, off the sofa to sit on the floor. Beckoning her to step closer with a curl of his fingers. 'Good girl,' Vadim muttered in response to her instant compliance.

Her naked body shuddered with the hot touch of his exhale on her skin, the slow spiral of his fingertips on her ankle. Painfully sedate as he dragged his touch higher, a kiss on her inner thigh almost making her crumble. A bite nipping her flesh followed by the stroke of his tongue. His firm grip on her rear pushing her toward his mouth.

The broad lick over her quim brought her hands to his shoulders to prevent herself falling. His hand steering one leg to the sofa behind him, her arched foot assisting in her balance, even as her head spun. The flick of his tongue, the pinch of his teeth, and taps of his fingers, coaxing a raw moan from her throat.

'Vadya,' she sighed, threading her fingers in his hair.

He hummed in response; her taste dripping over his tongue. Into his mouth. The pads of his fingers roaming the swell of her rear, her hip, to claim the entrance of her cunt. Two guided to the knuckle and forcing a moan from her lungs with the wicked pulse he commanded.

Anara's spine curved, her breath ragged. Standing over him, every part of her quivered; legs shaking, core electric, eyes hooded. Strands of her black hair shrouded him, cloaking them both in sweet pomegranate scent, entwined with evidence of her arousal.

A combination Vadim found addictive.

Her delicious fractured mewl arching her head back.

Body tense.

Her collapsing frame caught in secure hands; Vadim drawing her to his lap. Arms sliding to cradle her to his chest, delicately sweeping curls from her face, while she licked her taste from his lips. Eyes closing.

Breath regulating, Anara reached for his belt, her nails scoring down his abdomen; skipping over sore wounds. The buckle unlatched, button undone, zip unfastened. Her hand wrapped his cock, sliding the pearled moisture from the tip down to the root, then back. Wrist twisting.

'Kneel up, kroshka,' he requested.

She shifted to straddle him; holding his gaze as he lifted his hips to push the clothes off. Her hands on his face, she chewed her lip as she sank onto him. Her sigh matched by his groan. The pressure of her body against his intensifying as Anara remained seated and still; relishing the pulse of his cock, the stretch of her quim.

Their lips pouring every ounce of their love between them.

'How does it feel, Vadya?' Slow, her hips oscillated; a lemniscate fall and rise. 'How does it feel to be inside me?'

He rested his forehead against hers, fingers splayed, sliding down between their chests, hand inverting to circle her clit. 'Like paradise, like I want you to take me even deeper and swallow me whole.'

Anara closed her dark eyes, the gentle pace she set allowing her to conquer him. Accepting how he surrendered to her movement. Grateful for this moment of calm; even as her body shattered. Nerves on fire and desperate as he manipulated them.

Her conquest becoming capitulation.

'I would,' she breathed, 'if I could; swallow you entirely.'

The rhythmic spiral on her skin faltered; a pause to his ministrations as Vadim considered her words with a mischievous smile. 'You do.'

She ground against his hips, meeting his gaze as Anara remained in his lap. 'More than that; I wish I could bring you into my skin, to consume you, so I'll never be without you.'

Vadim tipped her chin back to him as her eyes darted away.

Her blush partially hidden by her arousal, by the shadows.

'Fuck, Anya.' He kissed her, hard; trying to convey the perfection he saw in her every cell. 'You'll never be without me.'

He brushed a tear from her cheek before kissing the warm flesh. His knees bending, arms on the sofa, hands cupping the backs of her thighs, he stood. Her legs wrapped around his waist; bodies entwined.

The changed angle hitting different places for them both.

Anara looped her arms around his neck as pleasure sparked. The security of his embrace retained even as he slammed her into the wall; her back curving against it. Body an arc with the cry from her lungs. His hips increasing the tempo, Vadim fucked her with primal appetite, with fevered lust.

With devoted love.

Her hands clawed at his shoulders, his neck, his hair; greedy for all he could deliver. The depths he could reach, the force he could inflict. A powerful drive of his body into hers.

'Eyes open, kroshka,' he said, voice rough, feeling the tension in her body, the catch in her breath. 'I want to see you.'

Lips parted, Anara blinked and tried to focus on his gaze; his pupils blown black, her own an abyss which drowned him. Saved him. Spine bowing, she felt her body unravel.

Felt his release spill.

She was relieved he held her so tightly; her limbs boneless. If he had released her body, she would have fallen. Instead, he tucked her to his chest, brought her to their bed. Ensured her head found the pillow before dragging his fingers over her heated flesh. Pads dancing from the hollow of Anara's throat to the arch of her foot.

'We're not done, kroshka,' he said, striding to his discarded clothes to whip the belt from them. The shirt shrugged from his torso, dropped amongst the layers of black by the sofa. 'I know you've at least one more orgasm in you before we sleep.'

Anara smiled; *this man can try*, she thought.

Her eyes widening when she saw him grab the knife. Watched him arrive back at the foot of the bed. His body glistening with exertion, even as his chest rose and fell with measured ease. As he crawled over her with soft kisses, the leather of the belt trailing over her skin, the knife by her foot.

'Grab the railings.' It was not a request.

She licked her lower lip. 'If I don't?'

'Grab. The. Railings.' He wrapped one hand around her throat, firm but with the suggestion it could be made unbearable. With his legs either side of hers, he leant back on his heels and waited, the belt twisting over her abdomen. Each pass created a shudder.

Stretching her arms over her head, Anara curled her fingers around the metal bars of the bed. Her eyes locked on his. The thud of her heart roared in her blood, her nipples aching, her body alive. Anticipation ate through her veins, feasting on her imagination.

Her desire.

Releasing her throat, Vadim took the belt in both hands; pulling it taut with a snap. The sound reverberated, fracturing her breath. His body dominating hers as he wound the leather over her wrists, through metal, to secure her hands. The graze of his fingers on her skin cascading their connection through their bodies, their minds.

'Do you trust me, kroshka?' Vadim placed tender kisses on the inner part of her arm, moving to her clavicle, her chest. His tongue laving her breasts, teeth pinching flesh. The suck creating evidence of his victory over her body. Her soul.

A willing submission.

'Yes.' The answer was more a sigh. A breath. The soft bend of her spine as his tongue slid down the centre of her torso confirmation.

Vadim continued his descent, sliding past her quim to kiss one thigh then the other, to bite the warm flesh. Every mark a claim, a declaration of his hunger, his desire to feed.

The caress of his tongue broken by the bite of his teeth.

Captive, Anara's entire body was alert. The pressure of his limbs on hers, the way the bed shifted, highlighting every move. In the heavy quiet their breath indicated the anticipation, the thrum of her pulse counted the divine possibilities.

'You want me to stop, say so,' he instructed, voice gravel. Adoration in his dilated gaze. The knife gripped with certainty, with skill, with intent as he looked over her prone body.

A cornucopia he could feast on for eternity and never be sated.

She licked her tongue over her lips, forcing a swallow. The glacial tip of the knife on her ankle causing an involuntary flinch. A shiver which ran under her skin. Brought a soft moan from her throat.

Brought a fresh urgency to the pulse of his cock.

With a lopsided smile, Vadim raised his eyes from where the steel rested on her flesh. 'You like that?'

Anara did not trust herself to answer; from the moment she saw him wield the knife against Kassian, from the moment she felt it against her neck, the craving to experience it herself had consumed her.

Carefully, Vadim dragged the knife toward her knee; a light pressure which did not break the skin. Did not draw blood. A long scratch over each raised bump, each trembling cell. Her body responsive, leaning in to the gentle contact. Reaching the apex of her thighs, Vadim pressed a little harder, a pearl of blood gathering where the sharp edge pierced hot, sensitive flesh.

Keeping his eyes on hers, Vadim lowered, sucking then licking the wound. The knife held firmly against her hip, blade angled away. His tongue drank in her taste, their combined climax; his breath bringing a tilt to her hips to chase his attention.

'Vadya, please,' she rasped.

'Patience, kroshka.' Satisfied the cut would knit, he resumed his path. The knife turned, the curved blade sweeping over her undulating stomach, heaving breasts. When he drew the tip around her nipple she held her breath.

Exhaled when he nicked a slender opening above her heart.

Moaned when he bit around the wound to draw out more blood; his thirst for her drenching his every thought. If he could crawl into the sliced flesh, he would be willingly dyed with her elixir, would claw his way into the vaulted chambers of heart. Would relish how her pulse would provide him with a lullaby.

'Vadya,' she pleaded.

Trailing his tongue from the wound over the curve of her breast, he met Anara's frustrated gaze. Felt the grind of her hips against his as she sought friction. Sought his cock.

He moved; the knife placed on her throat.

She pushed into the blade, daring him to keep it steady. Daring him to bring a crimson line to her neck. Her body desperate. Breath hard.

One twist of the knife was all she required.

The climax teasing her body without Vadim returning to her aching quim; her every muscle on edge. Ready to succumb.

'Fuck, Anya,' he sighed, throwing the knife away. 'I won't—'

'Untie me.' Anara forced herself to remain calm despite the need for release. 'I need to punish you.'

His eyebrows rose; resting on his heels, he curled his hands around her ankles. 'Punish me?'

'I'm not going to break, Vadya.' She pulled against the restraint. 'You think a woman is afraid of a little blood?'

He smiled, leaning over her. One hand on her quim, one around her throat; tightening his grip while sliding two fingers inside her. His mouth on hers to swallow what little breath she had caught. The wet heat of her body clinging to him as he moved from knuckle to pad, while his thumb played with her clit.

'You still want to punish me, wife?' Vadim asked, a softer kiss placed on her jaw. The shudder in her chest as she tried to breathe delivering a smile to his lips.

'I—'

He removed his fingers, slamming his cock inside and cutting off her reply. The hand around her neck still firmly in place. She cried out from the pressure, the fullness, the pleasure. Her body wrapping around him even as Vadim drove into her harder, their bed an embrace she sank into with every forceful connection. The leather around her wrists digging in as her body shook.

As her lungs emptied of breath.

Her heart screaming with heated lust, with desire, with every pledge she intended to keep. A vow to commit. Now she had found someone who could both challenge and defend, she intended to keep him; Anara refused to be starved of such worship ever again.

# Thirty-Nine

Whatever deals Vadimir Morozov had negotiated, and whatever support Origins had provided, Erinyes was almost ready to re-open, well ahead of schedule. The main construction was complete, though the conversion planned for Anara's apartment was not; there was more to do to ensure the refuge met her aspirations.

Now she understood what it meant to feel safe, Anara did not wish to compromise on building that for others. She intended to go beyond all she had done before; the tinctures and poisons would continue, certainly, but there was more she could do.

With assistance from Kasdeya, and Vadim.

She may not ever be a part of the Bratva, and she had no desire to be, but knowing she had such strong allies had eased her mind. It gave her a greater confidence to track her targets and plan her interventions knowing that, should something go wrong, she had a lover who would decimate the world in her honour. There was relief in knowing if she had to fight, she had Vadim by her side.

There was security in knowing she had such a fierce protector.

Vadim may have thrown the knife away the night before, but the threat in how he wielded it proved who he was. There was danger in his every cell, his every bone.

But there was also control.

He had the power to destroy her, to use his advantage to cause her pain, to kill her. And he chose not to. He chose to prevent damage.

He chose to show her love, not hurt.

And that was dangerous for Anara's heart; there would never be any other person who could ever satisfy her, love her, the way Vadim did. He had absolutely broken her. She was his.

Absolutely and irrevocably his.

It terrified her and excited her in equal measure.

'Where'd you go?' Bryony asked, nudging her friend with her hip as she placed the mug on the polished new counter.

Anara frowned, blinking.

'You were in your head; wherever you were, it must've been good because you're blushing and smiling.' Her own smile was suggestive, a glimmer of the humour in her tone.

With her teeth catching her lower lip, Anara's eyes closed.

'I imagine she's wherever she was to get those marks.' Kerezen's gaze shifted to the raw skin on her friend's wrists.

Heat brought Anara's hands to her opposite elbows, dragging down the sleeves of her top. Her attention drawn to open packages, the array of herbs and tinctures waiting to be added to new shelving.

'Anara,' Bryony soothed, 'it's a good thing. You deserve this.'

'If it's consensual—'

'He'd not hurt me,' she interrupted with soft words.

'Unless you ask him to?' Kerezen continued with a wink; low, throaty laughter echoing through the store. She watched the younger woman's flesh grow an even deeper shade of crimson.

'It's… I,' she said, stumbling over how she could explain the freedom she had found; a frown creating deep lines on her brow, 'it's—'

'As long as you're happy,' Bryony said, placing her hand on Anara's forearm, 'which you obviously are, we don't need to know anything more than what you'd like to share.'

'Exactly.' Kerezen collected her tea, both hands wrapping the mug as she leaned against the counter. Her hazel eyes roaming the gleaming shelves, the neatly placed items, the remaining stock. 'We're delighted you've finally let someone take care of you.'

'However that is.' Bryony's laughter broke through the smile.

Anara shook her head; her eyes warming with emotion. The friends she had made in the apothecary bringing a glow to her heart, her soul. A sense of belonging she had never dreamed would be possible, until the trio had formed.

Until Vadim had proved what devotion could be like.

'What if it doesn't work out,' she whispered.

'Why shouldn't it?' Kerezen lowered the mug from her lips. 'He loves you, Anara. He was distraught when you were taken; that man would've burned the world to find you.'

'He adores you,' Bryony agreed. 'Does he know?'

'Know what?'

'The situation with—'

Anara shook her head, curtailing Bryony's words.

'Perhaps you should tell him.' There was persuasion in her tone, in how she met her friend's eyes and offered quiet encouragement.

'Maybe.' Anara exhaled. 'I just worry he'll—'

'You really shouldn't.' Kerezen took a sip of tea. 'You've told him the truth, about what we do here—'

'What I do.' She was determined to keep the women distanced from exactly how she plotted and executed her work. 'It's not fair to let you get embroiled in that.'

'Okay, what *you* do,' Kerezen said, humouring her. She had long ago decided that should their underground activity be discovered, she would take the blame. She had less to lose. 'He accepted it.'

'And he's not exactly a saint, himself, is he.'

'Bry!' Anara's eyes widened.

'What? The man's clearly into some shady shit.'

'He does live in a massive gated estate with guards,' Kerezen added cautiously. 'And he certainly sped up the rebuilding of Erinyes.'

'That doesn't mean—'

'Anara, honey, we're not saying it's a bad thing.' Sliding up, Bryony settled on the counter, propped on straight arms. 'He's perfect.'

In the afternoon light, Kerezen's auburn hair was fiery. 'You needed someone who'd be your equal in every way; he seems ideal.'

'And if he can convince you to be tied up,' Bryony said playfully, 'he must be incredibly persuasive… with his tongue.'

'You know, I can find new staff,' she muttered. Clutching her mug, a fresh burst of heat feasted on her skin. The mischievously shared words were a balm, a connection Anara enjoyed, despite the potential impact of discovery, of being understood.

'The grass may be greener without us,' Kerezen remarked.

'But only because of the buried bodies.'

'That's it,' Anara stated, unable to hide her bemused smile. 'Both of you are getting one of my special blends.'

The women had missed this; the routine which came from company, from the bond they had nurtured inside the walls of the store. While the paint may be new, the fixtures pristine, there was familiar purpose. An ease which had languished, waiting for them to gather.

Anara ran her hand over the granite, her eyes studying the work which remained before they could re-open Erinyes. Even as her mind calculated, she felt the change. Her body sensing his arrival before he even opened the door.

Raw anticipation coiling in her stomach, snakes tumbling over her skin, breath shuddering and lips parting.

The chime of the door a siren.

'Ladies, I need to borrow my wife,' Vadim stated. His eyes locked on her, the two other women in the periphery.

'Vadya—'

'I'll bring her back, but we need to go shopping.'

Kerezen glanced to Bryony. Both women accustomed to how Vadim spoke of Anara now, yet hearing him say wife still brought a smile. The term reinforced their faith in how this relationship would last, that Anara had finally found a person who could be relied on.

'I've still work to complete here, perhaps later?' Her body rebelled; the intensity of his gaze burrowing straight into her and undermining her weak objection.

'Anya, we need to go.' He strode closer, eating the distance between them. Both hands cupping her face, his lips ghosting her brow. 'We can't use the belt all the time.'

Her eyes widened, heat rapidly blooming over her body, bringing a slick warmth to the apex of her thighs. 'Vadya!'

'A belt?' Bryony's eyebrows raised. Curiosity piqued, and the marks on Anara's wrists bringing a suggestion of what the shopping trip may entail. 'Yeah, you should go. We've got this.'

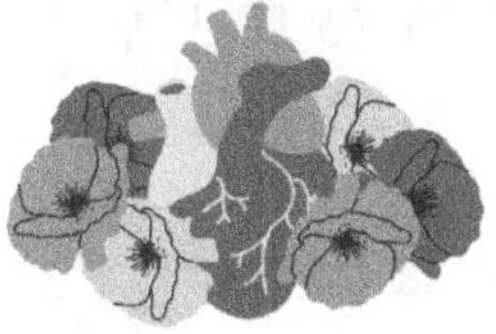

She had not laughed so hard in many years. Shopping with Vadim was both exasperating and enlightening. He had such a disregard for cost; if Anara wanted it, they bought it. If he wanted it, they bought it. Exploring their tastes had only confirmed how compatible their appetites were.

The shopping bags a promise of future endeavours.

Of how they intended to pursue pleasure, together.

Which made her friends' words from earlier more potent. The need to share why she was so cautious, why Anara had such recurring fears about this attachment crumbling, a truth she could not ignore.

Grateful of the return to Erinyes, and the way she could consider the way forward, Anara had sent the other women home. Silence permitting her the time, the space, to think. A determined resolution formed; a vow to be honest.

If her admission broke their commitment, then better now.

She would rather leave before it was too late.

Even if such an outcome would destroy her.

The thoughts remained prominent as they ate; the food delicious but barely noticed. Each bite, each chew, a mechanical instinct.

'Anya, what's wrong?'

The words did not register. The spiral of her spoon around the bowl a hypnotic pattern which trapped her gaze.

'Anya,' he repeated, 'what's wrong? Should I have stayed away from the store today?'

Her head snapped up, his tone, his question, shattering her muted contemplation. 'No, you're... not at all.'

'Then what's wrong?' Vadim twisted her hand into his, eyes chasing her face, her tense shoulders, her tight jaw. 'Talk to me, please.'

She inhaled, eyes closing for a moment as the loud thud of her heart thrummed in her blood. 'Yeah, we should.'

'We should what?'

'Talk.'

A chill scraped under his skin. That one crisp word hooked into his mind and tore at every imagined future he had been crafting. 'Anya, you can always talk to me.'

She nodded.

He purposefully placed his cutlery down, not releasing her hand. His movements precise, disciplined, as he steered her from the table toward the sofas. No hesitation in how Vadim took the seat beside her, intent on remaining as close as possible. Intent on allowing her control.

Even as the quiet clawed at his senses.

Vadim hoped she felt safe enough to share, comfortable enough to trust he would repair any damage she had endured.

Would exhaust every possible resource to ensure her survival.

'When I was taken, I hoped you'd come for me,' Anara began, voice tentative, grating over her throat. 'But you didn't.'

He bit his tongue; copper in his mouth.

'And that hurt,' she continued. 'I understand you were fighting to find me, and there were circumstances which made things… difficult.' Deep creases created grooves in her brow.

Vadim ran the pads of his fingers over the lines, relieved she did not flinch away from his touch.

'The reason I threw the rings away,' Anara croaked, then paused. A swallow forced through her throat.

'Let me get you a drink.' He waited for her to agree before he strode to the cabinet, grabbing a bottle of vodka and two glasses. Beside her again before pouring.

Her glass emptied; the burn fuelling her faith in him.

In them.

His eyebrow raised as he refilled the spirit. His own barely touched; a sip sufficient to steady the anxious gnawing in his mind.

'I've never been anyone's first choice,' Anara admitted, her voice an almost impossible whisper. The glistening moisture in her eyes falling in a silent rivulet to her jaw. Being this vulnerable, and willingly lowering the walls which she defended intensely, was blurring her vision.

'Anya, you will always be my first—'

'But you didn't come for me.' She closed her eyes, inhaled. 'I know why, I do, but when you didn't, when you turned your back on me, it just reinforced everything I've heard my whole life.'

His chest tightened, his hand curling into a fist out of sight, the skin flush to the leather. Now Vadim drained his vodka, replenished it. The heat a fire which sparked a new mission.

A desire to ruin, to kill, anyone who had made Anara feel anything less than the goddess he saw.

The goddess he loved.

'You were the only person who could come for me,' she said, eyes resolutely shut. 'I've no-one else.'

Vadim waited, his dark eyes locked on her.

‘When I needed help, no-one was there for me.’ The frown returned with the knitting of her eyebrows. ‘No-one believed me, and when I set boundaries they only tried to manipulate me and undermine me.’

His fingernails were almost breaking his skin.

‘I put in so much effort, every single time,’ Anara continued. ‘I gave myself, I tried… but, but I got nothing.’ She angrily swiped at the tears on her cheek. ‘Every promise they made was broken; they told me they’d keep me safe, then hurt me. They made me believe that if I followed their rules, I’d be loved. But it was just sugar-coated poison.’

‘Anya,’ he breathed, lacing his fingers into hers. The anguish in her voice, in her face, breaking his heart.

Reaffirming his rage.

‘I was always excluded,’ she explained, ‘told nothing but punished for not knowing.’ She swallowed insistent memories. ‘It makes it hard to trust anyone now, and it makes it hard to believe I’m worthy of all this you’re offering.’

He brought her hand to his lips, placing a gentle kiss. Vadim hoped she could feel how much he valued her, how much he needed her. She was his heart and his soul, and always would be. There was so much he could do to support her, if she would only allow him to.

‘So, I fought to get away.’ Anara opened her eyes, but avoided his gaze. ‘I put my energy into where I could make a difference, and where I could support others.’

‘And you have, Anya.’

She shook her head, sobs persistent in her chest.

‘You have.’ He spoke with tenderness, with adoration. ‘I don’t know who fucked things up for you, but when you feel ready, we can find them and make them pay.’

Anara twisted her focus, meeting his eyes.

There was truth in his statement.

And it was delicious; her body clawing for the calm he offered in the fury he promised. Her lips curved into a tentative smile.

He unwound his fist, moving to wipe the tears from her face before placing a kiss below each eye. 'Tell me when, kroshka, and I'll hunt them down and deliver everyone who's ever hurt you.'

Slow, she licked her lips; unsure if she could voice it.

'I'm going nowhere, Anya,' he said firmly. 'I love you.' He paused, his hand sliding to cradle her neck.

'I'll think about it,' she said, hoarse. The emotion heavy on her throat and her mind. Their names tempting on her tongue. But she did not wish to sour the air with their presence. 'Thank you.'

Vadim tipped his head forward, resting his brow against hers. 'You don't need to thank me, kroshka.'

She shrugged; old habits were hard to break. And the gratitude she felt for this man, the love she felt, finally felt peaceful. There was finally trust, reliable and devout, which she believed would endure.

Their kiss slow, a meeting of demons, a taste of divinity; their union one which saved them both. Vadim's losses, Anara's pain, a grief which could become a faded memory. A forgettable wound healed with their feral surrender to each other.

'Come.' He stood, hand outstretched to pull her up. To lead her to his study; the door opened. Closed behind them.

She waited, watching him dig through the drawer of his desk. The steady thud of her heart a slightly off-beat tempo as moths began to turn in her stomach. Concern quick to eat into her resolve.

Caution lingering and needing more time to settle.

Vadim sat in the leather chair, patting his thigh for her to come sit with him. His arm circling her waist as she got comfortable. 'I've added you to everything, Anya,' he stated, gesturing to the paperwork he had arranged before them, 'what's mine is yours.'

'No… you don't—'

'I do; I want to provide for you.' He tipped her chin up, capturing her gaze, her lips. 'But don't think if anything happens to me, that you get to date anyone else, or fuck anyone else; I'll haunt you, and kill them.'

'You'd be dead,' she reasoned.

'Not an obstacle, kroshka.' He grinned.

Her breathy laugh became stronger as she considered all he had done for her. All he had engineered. The documents she glanced at were legal, which meant he had been planning this for some time. This was not a whim, this was evidence which supported his words.

But her attraction to him was never about money.

This was about his desire to provide security.

Her heart had never felt so full.

So light.

Vadim was relieved to see her smile, pulling her closer.

'So,' she said, eyes roaming the shadowy room, 'if you're dead, how do I entertain myself in this estate?'

'That's your question?' His eyebrows quirked up. 'You're not going to mourn me, or…?'

'I wonder what fucking myself with your rib would feel like.' Anara could not prevent the thought from spilling from her lips. 'After all, women are supposed to come from a man's rib, right?'

'You are fucking amazing,' he said in an exhale; both hands drawing her face to his, lips on hers with a fierce hunger. Leaning back to allow Anara to shift and straddle his hips, his fingers sliding to her head, her neck. 'My perfect goddess.'

She rested her forehead against his, catching her breath.

'You are my Eden… for now,' he said, winking. The memory of how being buried inside her had provided paradise. The intent to change her surname creating a calculating smile. 'And you are no weak cast off from a man; you're my heart and soul. Don't you ever forget that, Anya. I'm yours, and you're mine.'

'I love you.' Anara's body screamed with desire, with emotion. Every demon from her past slain with the conviction of his loyalty, his pledge to be by her side. She could use the hurt, the fury, in other ways. Ways she intended to claw from his skin.

To claim his body with hers.

To bite into his flesh.

To bleed her past from her veins. Her nails gripped his hair, pulling Vadim's head to one side, her tongue tip stroking along the stubble of his jaw, his neck, teeth nipping at his throat.

The rough gravel of his groan bringing heat to her quim.

Her fingers on the buttons of his shirt hasty, even as he clutched her waist and lay her down. The papers below her back, his kisses on her chest. Her arm stretching for the knife she had seen on the desk; seating it against her palm.

Her body arching up against his mouth as he descended, the heated touch of his tongue, his teeth, nipping at her skin. The tender exploration of his hand below her clothes.

Vadim felt for the button hidden on the desk's wooden leg; the door to the surveillance room sealed, the cameras off.

No-one but he would ever see Anara this way.

Only he would ever ruin her, rebuild her.

Just as Vadim was hers to use. The tip of the blade glancing over his shoulder creating a shuddering exhale against her stomach. A groan from his throat which made her tighten her thighs around his waist. Her fingers in his hair steering his mouth lower, her hips tilting up to welcome the curl of his tongue.

The flesh she offered his surrender to the divine; Vadim would fall to his knees and worship Anara for the remainder of his life. And for every life he got to spend with her after that.

# Forty

Returning home, Anara sensed change. Spring had unfurled leaves, had coaxed petals to open, had brightened the skies. Warmer days hinted at impending summer. With Erinyes reopened, business was thriving, which resulted in long hours. Her steps were marked by the soft amber glow of the driveway's many lanterns; twilight blanketing her.

On the periphery, she could see dark shadows; the black-clad men guarding the estate. Patrolling the gardens as occasional chatter of their communications broke through the evening hush.

Anticipation bloomed in her every inhale.

She was unsure why, but everything felt finely balanced. It increased her pace to the door, the heels of her boots striking the paving and dress flaring in her elongated stride. The arrival at the steps found Sofiya in the entrance, with a broad smile and a glint in her eyes.

The closure of the door made deftly.

'Vadim asked me to tell you to meet him in the library.' Sofiya's arms were outstretched, ready to take the woman's bag, her coat. 'I'd suggest you freshen up first.' She winked.

Anara's eyes narrowed, but she passed over her things. A detour to their suite made with almost no focus; her mind whirling through why Sofiya would behave in such a way.

Why Vadim had summoned her.

Navigating to the library, Anara was coiled tight. It would take only one glancing touch to shatter her, to splinter the sweet apprehension in her blood.

For whatever waited, she felt certain it would be delightful.

Every game they played, every conversation they held, all spoke of another thrill. Another twist of their pleasure. Their passion. An ouroboros of dominance and submission in how they entertained each other. Gone was fear, the poison of dread, replaced by the confidence Vadim would not cause her any harm.

Aside from any she asked for.

Or he requested her to deliver.

The emptiness of the library, with the hearth cold and hidden door to Vadim's study closed, the shutters drawn across the window, forced her to pause. To swallow as Anara refocused on the darkness; her shadow long from the hallway's light.

Smothered by his silhouette.

His breath against her neck bringing a shiver.

'Anya,' he whispered, his fingers running up each arm. Body close but not touching; a gap he longed to cross. His reflexes quick to grip her upper arms when she tried to turn. A soft kiss placed on her crown.

'What—'

'Patience, kroshka.' He smiled, drawing his hands slowly down to enfold both her wrists in one. His other locating the length of black silk from his trouser pocket, shaking it loose.

She shuddered an exhale at the movement.

'Are you happy for me to blindfold you?'

'Yes.' Her confirmation was a breath.

Her vision was further hindered; the tender wrap of fabric secured across her eyes, knotted above her long curls. Her body spun and a kiss welcomed. Vadim's lips gentle, his tongue tracing the seam for entry and a deepening of their caress.

Their hands lacing together so Vadim could steer her where they needed to be; the house silent. Their steps echoing on the hardwood floors, through the hall, the spacious living area, and to doors Sofiya had opened in readiness. The evening air greeting them, the path followed to the summer house.

Under the growing greys of twilight, the glass was a beacon. Warm and fragrant. The click of the door sealing the pair inside. Soft music was sufficient to drown the sound of the pool's ripples, the flowers which filled the space plentiful.

Anara had tried to determine where they were headed, had counted the steps, but her senses were overwhelmed. The anticipation and the aroma a blend which caused confusion. The slide of the knot, the slip of the silk, bringing a blink. A parting of her lips and sharp intake of breath as her eyes widened.

The entire room was a mass of tiny lights on the foliage, with lamps hanging from the roof. A small table was set with glassware and candles. And around the perimeter of the pool and the building's external walls were plants. Lush and covered with flowers; a cascade of reds.

'Vadya,' Anara sighed; eyes glazed.

He observed her reactions. Seeing how her palm flattened on her chest, how bumps crept over her skin, how her breath changed. She was revelling in the space, in the proximity of his body to hers, in the peace of the moment.

In the beauty of nature's display.

'This is… it's…,' she began, unsure how to even voice the adoration and awe which feasted on her mind. Anara turned to him, hand reaching to cup his face. The creases on her brow ones of emotional conflict; the restraints of vulnerability fighting for attention, even as love eroded every painful memory.

'All for you, Anya,' Vadim said, curling his hand around her neck, his intense gaze an abyss for her to find a home in. 'I love you.'

'I love you.' Her tone was husky.

He smiled, taking her hand to lead her to the table. She trailed her fingers over scarlet flowers; funnel-shaped and bright amongst glossy leaves. Their shape recognisable, her head shaking.

'Pomegranate flowers,' she remarked, eyebrows raised.

'What, you think you're the only one who can research a name?' His laughter held a nervous tension; Vadim's heart an erratic thrum, fuelled with rehearsed words.

'But, they're not in season yet,' she muttered.

'I know.' He pulled out one of the chairs, gesturing for her to sit. The candles guttered slightly at their movement; an amber flicker enhancing the red of her lips, snow of her skin. 'I'd've arranged this sooner,' Vadim continued, 'but it took a while to get them shipped.'

'You couldn't wait a few more months for them to bloom?'

His jaw ticked; the time spent organising and preparing had felt too long, even with the resources he had available. Waiting until further into summer was impossible.

Anara kept her eyes on him, watching him pour their wine; the dark Cadão adding to the rich fragrances. Yet, his scent consumed her. The pronounced swallow he made drew her gaze.

'This was where you first told me you loved me,' Vadim said, gravel in his voice. One hand digging into his pocket.

She nodded, her throat dry. Her body almost still, if not for the loud thud of her pulse and tumultuous breath moving her chest. The warmth in her eyes which simmered as he moved to stand before her.

Drop to one knee by her feet.

The box pulled forward, opened, bringing a quivering inhale and a fractured sob from her throat. Her teeth caught her lower lip. The flames and amber lights sparkling on the stones, the metal.

'Anara Eden,' he began, his eyes locked on her, 'you are my heart and my soul, and a life without you is a life I refuse to live. I crave to give you everything you could ever desire, I want the privilege of being the man you come home to, I would kill for you and with you.'

'Vadya—'

'I vow to worship you every day, to ensure you're safe, and hold you as you sleep. It'd be my honour to care for you every day for the rest of our lives. Anya, will you marry me?' His veins beat a visible dance, the slight tremble in his hands an unfamiliar sensation.

He had never been so terrified in his life.

'Yes,' Anara whispered, tears dropping over her dark lashes as she slid from the chair and threw her arms around his neck. 'Yes.'

Vadim released a stuttering breath.

'Absolutely yes!' There had been no hesitation. Her hand went to her mouth, laughter and tears mixing in a euphoric haze as she attempted to process what had happened.

Vadim gripped her waist, picking her back up and placing her on the chair. He had continued to wear the titanium band from the beginning of their fake arrangement; a new one with her name inscribed inside it was waiting for the day they married.

Until then, the velvet box housed two rings, both for her.

Still prone below her, he tilted his head up and gently took Anara's right hand. Eyes locked on hers, he kissed her fingers, his unrestrained smile creasing his gaze.

Anara was unsure if she was still in the room; her eyes were salted with happiness, her stomach vibrating with nervous joy. Her limbs did not quite feel her own. When Vadim twisted to pull her ring from the box and glide it down, toward her palm, she focused on breathing.

On the way the ring reflected the light.

'It's beautiful, Vadya… I… this must've cost—'

He placed a finger on her lips, shaking his head. 'You're worth more than everything I own, many times over.'

She brought her right hand closer to her face. The titanium band, in an Art Deco style, fit perfectly. The large Asscher cut garnet, surrounded by black diamonds provided shimmering depths of colour; wide step cuts on the clip-cornered stones were precise.

The touch of his hand on her left brought her focus back to him, a soft frown denting her brow as she watched him slide a thinner titanium band, inset with black diamonds, onto her ring finger. 'What—?'

'I may be Russian, but you're not.' He gripped both her hands. 'This way, my commitment to you is absolutely evident.'

She laughed, her teeth capturing her lower lip.

'Usually, betrothal ceremonies are more formal,' Vadya said, pushing up to stand before her; relief in his gaze.

Even as his pupils dilated with devotion.

Anara dragged her eyes from the rings, getting to her feet. Her lips on his and hands on his face, his neck, his hair. She wanted to be closer, to be under his skin. To express how these rings changed nothing. Their dedication to each other being formalised was delightful, but her love for him had not altered.

She needed him to understand her gratitude was not due to a grand gesture or jewellery. That her agreement to this union was forged from love; fast, deep, and all-consuming love.

No more games, no more pretence, all entirely real.

'Usually, we get approval to ask, from family—'

Anara stiffened in his arms. 'You… you contacted—?'

'No, Anya.' Vadim leaned back, stroking her curls. 'Your digital skills rival Kolya's; it was damn near impossible to find anything out about you when we looked.'

She smiled at the compliment, slowly exhaling.

Curious, Vadim studied her, witnessing the proof of his suspicions. A past she had shielded so vehemently, which had left such scars, one he intended to rectify, to avenge. But, there was time for that.

Now, now was time to celebrate their future.

'You researched me?' Anara's head tilted coyly. 'Was that before or after we met?'

'I like to know who I'm going to spend my life with.' He placed kisses on her brow, her cheeks, her lips. His arms tightening around her.

‘How are we going to explain this to the Priest… Father?’

Vadim rested his forehead against hers. ‘I’ll handle that.’

‘But—’

‘Tonight, I want to worship you,’ he interjected tenderly, steering her back to the chair. He followed her descent, returning to his knees before her, his hands on her calves. Roaming higher, feeling the shiver in her flesh below his touch. Her heated arousal bringing the tip of his tongue to roll over his lips.

Brought the silk from his pocket to bind her wrists.

Brought his mouth to her skin; teeth scribing love notes.

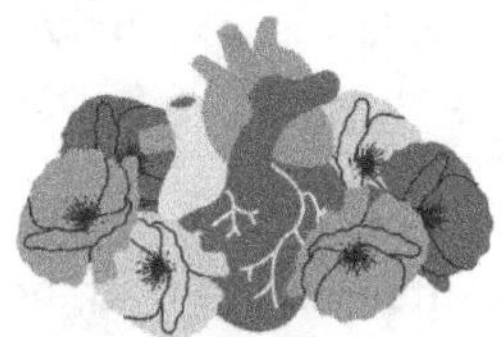

Beyond the one-way glass, skies were clear; hardly a cloud amongst the pale blue. A creamy sun offering warmth. The estate’s gardens a thriving blend of greens, of pastels, of whites; the cusp of summer. Though the shadows of the perimeter continued to be patrolled, there was a more relaxed gathering nearer the house.

Laughter and conversation which permeated the air.

Vadim rocked his head from side to side, stretching muscle; his eyes still focused on the screen before him. The voices muted behind closed doors, even as he watched people arrive unseen.

The click of the hidden door being opened shifted his attention, hand pausing, the reflex to grab his weapon cauterised. His smile creasing his eyes, watching her walk through. Vadim contemplated closing the laptop to prevent her reading what he had found; however, he had vowed not to hide anything from her.

‘You know this gathering is for us, yes?’ Anara kept the large desk between them, leaning her palms on the surface while keeping her eyes on his. In the diffused midday light, the garnet and diamonds of her rings shone gently.

'I do.' His head tilted slightly, body relaxing into the chair.

'And you know Fedya is cooking human organs?'

'I do.' Vadim nodded.

'I'm concerned Bryony's kids may—'

'He's far too protective of his food to allow anyone else to eat it; and he knows I'd kill him if he fucked up.' Vadim bit back laughter.

'Please tell me,' she said, 'he won't have any say in the menu when we get married.' Anara pushed herself up, folding her arms. The date for their ceremony was set, but work ate into their planning time.

Septer may be gone, but there was still product to distribute. Still the obligations to the fraternity. Still the extensive businesses Vadim owned to manage. He shared every detail with her, hoping it would confirm his trust, hoping it would never leave Anara wondering about the depth of his devotion. His commitment. Just as she had, finally, shared every detail of her work with him; his admiration and understanding a source of greater attachment.

'Absolutely not.' He had many ideas for the feasts which would mark their union; none of them included any trace of Fyodor's preferences.

'Good.' Anara dropped her arms, walking around the desk.

He tipped forward and pushed the laptop closed.

Her progress halted, a question in her gaze.

'I'm working on a gift for you,' Vadim said. The intelligence he and Nikolai had gathered remained spoken of in hushed terms; he intended to leave this development as a surprise.

'I don't need any—'

'I'll deliver the world to your feet, kroshka.' Vadim remained seated, chair pushed back. The black layers of his clothing complementary to the leather.

She exhaled, shaking her head. Anara knew better than to argue on this matter. She would find out, one way or another. There were tricks she could employ to convince him to talk. 'Later. We've company; you can't spend all your time in here.'

‘You weren’t complaining this morning,’ he retorted, ‘when I bent you over the desk.’ Vadim had crept from their bed to work, knowing most of the day would be consumed by their guests. The arrival of Anara, with coffee, had been a welcome distraction.

For them both.

One his memory had turned to over the course of the day.

The blush sweeping over her skin spoke of a similar remembrance for her. The pronounced swallow evidence of how her body craved his.

‘We’ll claim every inch of this house,’ Vadim said.

‘Once our guests have gone.’ She held out her hand, relishing the way he met it, twisted it to bring her knuckles to his lips. The kiss offered with gentle eye contact as Vadim stood and brought their entwined hands to his heart.

Their kiss leisurely, even as their pulses quickened.

‘Do you need fed, kroshka?’ he murmured against her lips.

‘I’m starving,’ she responded huskily.

‘Then, let’s eat.’ He stepped back, confident the contents left on the desk would remain undisturbed, and began to stride toward the door.

‘That’s not what I meant,’ she objected, but followed.

The study’s door sealed shut behind them.

The garden’s voices growing louder as they sauntered through the house. With the folding doors open at the rear of the property, the aromas blended; food, flowers, perfumes. Fresh sun-soaked air drifted with conversation and laughter. With Sofiya’s footsteps as she navigated the guests and coordinated the other servers.

Under a web of unlit lights, ready for the evening, the paving housed multiple chairs and tables. The lawn around it, and between the summer house and main building, had more. Two large grills supplemented food produced in the kitchen; Fyodor diligently refusing to serve anyone but himself from his small grill.

They managed to get to the temporary bar without interruption; the provision of vodka and a verdant muse efficiently offered. Anara’s thanks voiced with sincerity to Anoushka. She needed the cool liquor, needed to settle the hunger in her blood.

'We were beginning to think you got lost,' Kerezen said, smiling; her wife by her side. There was mischief in her eyes, in how she looked from Anara to Vadim with teasing happiness.

Bryony's gaze was fixed on her twins, her husband. She had been uncertain about bringing them, despite the invitation, only to find Maksim and his two children by the gatehouse when they arrived. 'It's a beautiful house, but it's huge.'

'And still needs a bit more of your influence.' She ignored the nudge Willow made to her side. Their last visit had been after Anara had been taken; this was much more preferable, and after several glasses of wine she felt more emboldened.

'Kerezen!'

'She's right,' Vadim said, nodding; his glass held in one hand while retaining his other laced with hers. 'This is our home, Anya, you should make any changes you like.'

'Vadimir Lvovich,' Father Matvey called, striding across the paving in his black ryassa and almost floor-length matching anderi. His long beard caught by the purposeful movement.

'Does *he* know you invited a witch?' Kerezen whispered, one hand to her mouth to disguise her words. 'And her wife?'

'Or our work?' Bryony added with a frown.

'It's okay,' she reassured them. Anara's rings had made it impossible to avoid confirmation of the engagement when she arrived at Erinyes the day after the proposal. And the speed of it had not fazed her friends at all; they were delighted for her.

For them.

But Anara did not, and could not, tell them just how suited she and Vadim were for each other. Just as she shielded them in her work to rid troublesome men from the lives of women, so she would protect them from the reality of Vadim's world.

At some point, perhaps, they would learn the truth.

But not yet.

'Anara, I look forward to conducting your marriage ceremony.' The Father Superior's kindly smile was warm; he had known Vadim since his birth, had helped him through the loss of his parents. Seeing him happy was something to celebrate.

Even if Vadim had initially deceived him.

That long confession had been made and forgiven.

With Anara's innocence established at Vadim's expense.

Something Anara had taken great pleasure in punishing him for; her gratitude for their soundproofed bedroom used to her advantage as she pursued Vadim's limits. The sharp blade drawn over his skin, his body bound and teased until he begged for her to provide salvation.

Her own passion sated.

There was freedom in finding security; now Anara knew she had his support, she finally felt able to rest. To fully embrace her desires, to fully submit to him, knowing he did the same. His dominance needed just as much safety as she did.

She watched him as he spoke, even as her own conversations drew her away from his side. His men respectful; their hushed words and clear instructions delivered with tact. Ksenia's intervention to check on timings made with discretion.

'I don't think he's going anywhere,' Bryony said, smirking.

'Yeah, you don't give someone rings like *that* and run.' There was a similarly playful smile on Kerezen's lips. 'Though some of the food smells like I want to leave.'

Anara bit her tongue; knowing exactly what her friend referenced and just what Fyodor was guarding.

'I hope you convince him to improve his tastes,' she added, resting her hand lightly on her friend's forearm, 'in food, I mean; he clearly has great taste seeing as how he's marrying you.'

The copper in her mouth increased as she bit more firmly.

Anara's mind searing with the remembered bites which mapped her inner thighs, the brush of his tongue over her skin. How Vadim relished dining on her body, how he lapped at her until she screamed.

She was relieved when Willow steered her wife away, to get food to soak up some of the wine. Bryony winked before following, gathering her family with her to ensure they all ate together.

'Wife,' Vadim said, his lips almost touching her ear. His arms coiling around her stomach to pull her to his chest.

'Not yet.'

'You'll never be anything but mine,' he argued. 'Always have been, always will.' He placed a kiss on her temple, inhaling her scent.

Anara twisted in the loop of his arms. Her eyes glistening with mirth as the pupils dilated; the amber of her gaze shrinking into the obsidian of lust. 'Until I have to resort to your rib to entertain myself.'

His groan was low, reverberating in his throat.

The splayed hands on her lower back tightening, pulling her closer to his frame. Their lips parted slightly, each drinking the other in, until no one else mattered; until the noise, the sun, the surroundings, were only a blur of static.

'My apologies, pakhan,' Artem stated, 'but you're both needed.' The advisor, vodka in hand, gestured toward the main table.

In the centre was the specially baked bread; something Sofiya had explained to Anara the day before. Something she and Vadim had made under the young housekeeper's supervision. The loaf was domed and in the centre, a small ramekin of salt had been placed.

'That's also not what I meant when I said I needed feeding,' Anara whispered, leaning into him and nipping his ear. The slide of her lips to kiss the stubble on his jaw covering up the bite; her eyes open, revelling in his discomfort.

Vadim's inhale was a hiss, the desire to drag her from view, to drag her below him, around him, a strong ache. This woman truly tested his patience in every way.

And yet, he would not want it to change.

Trusting that his guards continued to keep the estate safe, Vadim kept his attention on Anara, their guests a kaleidoscope of movement, of sound. Their joint tearing of the bread, the dipping of it into salt, made with their focus devouring the other.

Arms entwining to feed each other the torn offering.

The applause and increase in music barely noticed as Vadim tipped her back in his arms; their kiss only increasing their hunger.

# Forty-One

She tried to follow the words, her eyes drawn increasingly to the sculpted muscle of his abdomen, the veins on his forearms instead of the text. It was a distraction only enhanced by his voice. The book open for them both to read; Cyrillic softened under the bedside lamp's glow.

Her hand trailed his stomach; the small incisions she had inflicted with her knife the night before tender. Faint scars remained visible from the injuries he sustained dealing with Septer.

'I thought you wanted me to read to you,' he teased, tilting the book so it rested on his chest.

'I do.' She raised her eyes to his, her touch spiralling.

'If your hand gets any lower, this lesson will change considerably.'

She caught her lip with her teeth, the descent of her fingers toward the defined iliac furrows camouflaged by the duvet. Sensation delivered with a whispered glance as her heart kicked; his hard cock brushed by her fingertips.

'You are insatiable,' Vadim muttered, leaning away to put the book on the bedside table; marker in place.

His swift return dragging Anara lower; his arms braced either side of her, legs trapping her.

'And?' She smiled, rearing up to kiss him.

'It's not a complaint, kroshka.' He groaned with the slide of her hand around his shaft, the stroke of her thumb over the head. His hips flexed into her grip, his back arching to deliver kisses to her face.

Her neck.

Sliding down, and out of her reach, his tongue traced her clavicle. A slow pressure of his teeth, his mouth, as he gripped her waist. Laving her nipple made to the same rhythm as his fingers on her clit, as Vadim sunk one inside. Curling to pulse within her heat.

'Твое чтение для меня,' Anara breathed, digging her fingers into his hair, 'это почти мое любимое занятие[47].'

He paused, eyes finding hers. 'You've been cheating.'

'No, just doing homework.' Kasdeya's tutoring effective. She slowly rolled her tongue over her lips while pushing harder against his palm. A fractured cry in her throat when he pinched her clit.

Bit her breast before soothing it with his tongue.

'Ты моя любимая вещь[48],' he said, adding another finger, another kiss on the swell of her flesh.

'I'm not a thing.' Her hips oscillated, her feet running over his legs, hands trailing to his neck. His breathy laughter delivered a shudder; her stomach dipping with the path of his tongue.

Her moan low when his mouth met her clit. The shift of his hand to hold her hips steady and prevent her from moving increased Anara's soft mewls to a plea. A merciless pace and skilled pressure creating fists of her hands, the bed's fabric shrouding the cut of her nails.

Each flick of his tongue and drag of his fingers feeding his desire, his eternal need. Her taste honey dripping over Vadim's mouth, down his throat; she was his banquet.

A feast he would partake in at every opportunity she permitted.

Her satisfied screams ones he would dine on with pleasure.

'Vadya,' she begged, 'I need you. I need more.'

---

[47] Твое чтение для меня — это почти мое любимое занятие - Russian for 'You reading to me is almost my favourite thing'

[48] Ты моя любимая вещь - Russian for 'You are my favourite thing'

He smiled, but did not halt. Coaxing her to crumble.

'Please.' Anara's breath caught; her body a tense mass of electrical overwhelm. The ebbing reach of dissipation eating through her senses as he continued to savour her ruin beyond her climax.

Slow, Vadim rotated his hand, removing his fingers. Caging her with his elbows at her waist, his eyes locked on hers. One by one, he licked from his palm to pad, tongue relishing every morsel of her release.

Leaning into the raking of her hand through his hair.

'Please,' she whispered huskily.

Vadim raised one eyebrow, body roaming higher; the blunt head of his cock against her hot quim. Tempting her while testing the limits of his resistance. The threads of his restraint in tatters; Vadim may have finally found the woman who held his heart, his soul, but Anara also knew how to play every part of him.

And he would have it no other way.

'Пожалуйста[49],' she said, raw. Her hands drifting down to the base of his spine, the curve of his rear. Her hips trying to force him to provide the relief she needed. 'Vadya.'

Every time she welcomed him in, he wished to go deeper. To find a way to collapse entirely into her. To soak into her body and find the point where they merged. Their body and spirit aligned in divine, unbreakable union. The moans she made, stretching around him, a sound he longed to hear for eternity.

Placing his hand on her throat, she curved up into it. The fracture of her breath broken with a deep sigh; her body full. Her mind euphoric. A fall into this connection renewed every time they explored the limits of their bodies. The boundaries they could splinter.

There was freedom in knowing she would always be safe.

No matter how hard, how brutal, their games became, Anara knew she was safe with him. And such knowledge healed every sharp edge of her heart.

---

[49] Пожалуйста - Russian for 'Please'

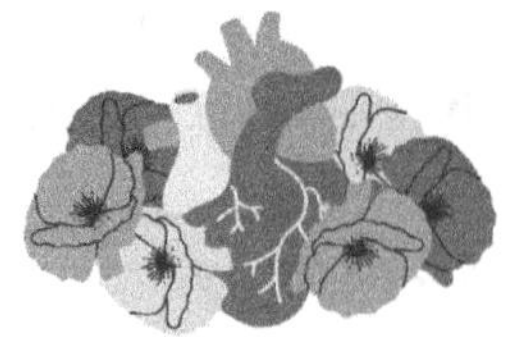

The text arrived as they were walking down for breakfast; the vibration bringing the device from his pocket. His glance at the screen confirming the activity they observed on the driveway. Several vans arriving, pulling into the open garage.

'Your wedding gift is here,' he said, 'but first, we eat.'

'My what?' She had stopped in the hall, tracking the convoy as they disappeared into the shadows. Cognisant of the estate's layout, she now understood they would be continuing underground, to the cells.

'Your wedding gift.' Vadim continued to lead them to the kitchen, a gentle stroke of his thumb over her hand.

'We're not getting married for another month—'

'This may take that long.' He smiled, settling onto the bar stool; his thanks offered to Sofiya when the coffee appeared before them.

Anara frowned, her acknowledgement to the housekeeper distracted as thoughts gnawed through her mind. Though she had spoken honestly with Vadim about her work, all parts of it, she had not shared her list. Nor had she seen any interference on her laptop; she trusted him, but habit meant she still did routine checks.

'Anya,' he said gently, 'I promised I'd find who hurt you.'

She swallowed; her body instantly glacial. Numb.

'Now, now it's up to you what happens to them.'

Her eyes had smeared, the moisture hot and her throat thick. 'All of them?' The words were almost inaudible.

'All of them,' he asserted; his thumb running over her lips.

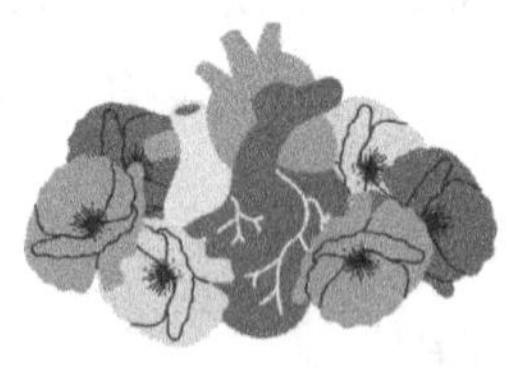

With so many options available, Anara had chosen to work. The hours at Erinyes spent debating the order, the methods, the consequences. If she did this, if she removed their influence to only a memory, then her future would be truly her own to forge.

She knew, in time, they would have arrived at the estate.

The first comments had been made online when their fake marriage had been made public. And though she had the support of Origins and Kasdeya then to deflect the enquiries, Anara was confident her wedding would have been interrupted.

Was certain they would expect her to help them.

And she refused to do so. She had fought too hard, had worked too hard, to allow them to destroy everything good she had established. Her friends, her business, her relationship.

By the time she locked up Erinyes and returned home, she had a list and she had a plan. Those who had found it too hard to know the truth, who told her that the past was the past, would be first. Those who had wanted to preserve perception, to maintain appearances no matter the cost, would be next. And the ones who inflicted the most damage, they would be the ones waiting to face her wrath.

They could listen to all the others die.

Vadim was correct; this could take weeks. If she did things properly with the herbs she had decided to use.

'You are the most incredible partner a woman could ask for,' Anara stated, entering the study. Her bag and coat dropped to the leather chair as she strode closer; his push back from the desk permitting her to easily straddle him. To place a fierce kiss on his lips.

'I love you too.' He smiled against her mouth, hands on her waist.

'We start tomorrow,' she said. 'I'll prepare the tinctures tonight.' She cupped his face, her fingertips playing with his jaw; rough stubble below her softer skin. 'If my calculations are right, we'll be done with them all in three weeks.'

'Three weeks,' he mused. 'I'll have to find you more victims.'

Her head tilted, a puzzled frown creasing her brow.

'You'll have a week to fill, before the wedding.'

'I'm sure I can find something to do,' Anara said, one hand dropping over his neck to rest on his chest while her hips rolled slightly.

'Do that again and you won't be leaving our room all night.' Vadim's eyes conveyed the intensity of his words; the depth of black swelling, the pressure in his cock increasing. The weight of her body an immediate fire to their craving to consume.

She tucked her finger beneath the shirt's placket, her nail smooth on his chest. The twist of her hips bringing a groan from his throat.

'I will chain you to the fucking bed,' he began.

Interrupted by the loud scuff of a boot against the floor.

In the open doorway, holding a stainless steel bowl of smoked lung, Fyodor gave an apologetic smile. 'Sorry, pakhan.'

'Later,' she whispered, kissing his cheek before standing, hand on his shoulder to keep her balance. 'Do you ever eat anything… else?'

He chuckled, collecting another strip of meat between his pinched fingers. 'Yeah. But there's something about human organs that really do it for me; the harvesting, the cooking, the eating.'

Anara nodded tentatively.

'You asked the question, kroshka,' Vadim said, his tone playful even as he drew his body under the desk to hide his arousal. The disruption one which was likely necessary; his staff knew better than to disturb him for anything else.

Fyodor would have walked away the moment he saw them, had the news not been important. 'Tyoma's on his way,' the guard explained.

Vadim waited, assuming there was more to relay.

'Kolya and Pasha, too.' He took another bite. 'There's been a strike on one of the warehouses; there's a new player in town.'

His palms lifted from his desk, fingers tucking in to form fists. With a measured inhale, Vadim gritted his teeth. The possibilities for retaliation mapping swiftly in his mind.

The destruction of Septer had only created the ingredients for a new group to form. That was the way this game worked. The trick was to play it better than anyone else, and Vadimir Morozov intended to win. He now had a future worth winning for.

'I'll let you boys figure things out,' she said, bending to kiss Vadim's brow. The tension below her touch evidence of the long night ahead; her only hope that he would return to their bed.

That he would continue to be the man she could rely on.

He was her sustenance; Anara had been starved of such love, such devotion, such worship for too long to allow it to be taken. Now she had his taste, she refused to be famished again. He was the poison, the cure, the very blood in her veins. And if he was threatened, she was ready to stand by his side.

Or deliver venomous revenge.

An author curated playlist to accompany
**Vore** is available on Spotify

1. Hurt Me Harder - Zolita
2. Aftertaste - LORYANN
3. Cinnamon Sun - Daisy Gray
4. HONEY - LUNA AURA
5. I WANNA BE YOUR SLAVE - Måneskin
6. EAT - Zoe Ko
7. Poison - BUNNY
8. i like the way you kiss me - Artemas
9. Red Velvet - Jutes, Ari Abdul
10. Caviar - Two Feet
11. if i didn't know better - Mack Lorén
12. Thirst - Nyline
13. Sugar - Sleep Token
14. CAROUSEL - Echos
15. Beside Myself - Hesta Prynn
16. KANDY - Kami Kehoe
17. Medicine - Cameron Hayes
18. Sinner - DEZI
19. bite - Ellise
20. Taste - Ari Abdul
21. Crave - Tove Lo
22. Heartburn - Wafia
23. Wicked Little Monster - Veda
24. POISON - Arankai
25. Martyr - KiNG MALA
26. Cannibal - Xoe Wise
27. Desire - MEG MYERS
28. Vore - Sleep Token

**Vore** Content Warnings:

Abortion
Alcohol
Cannibalism
Drug use / Drugging
Explicit content
Kidnapping
Knives / knife play
Manipulation
Murder
Physical abuse / assault
Rape
Sexual abuse / assault
Smoking
Torture
Trafficking
Violence
Vorarephilia
Weapons

Please read with care

Every effort has been taken to cover key areas where sensitivity may be required; however, should any enhancements to this non-exhaustive list be appropriate, please let Ariadne know.

**The Elemental Pentology**

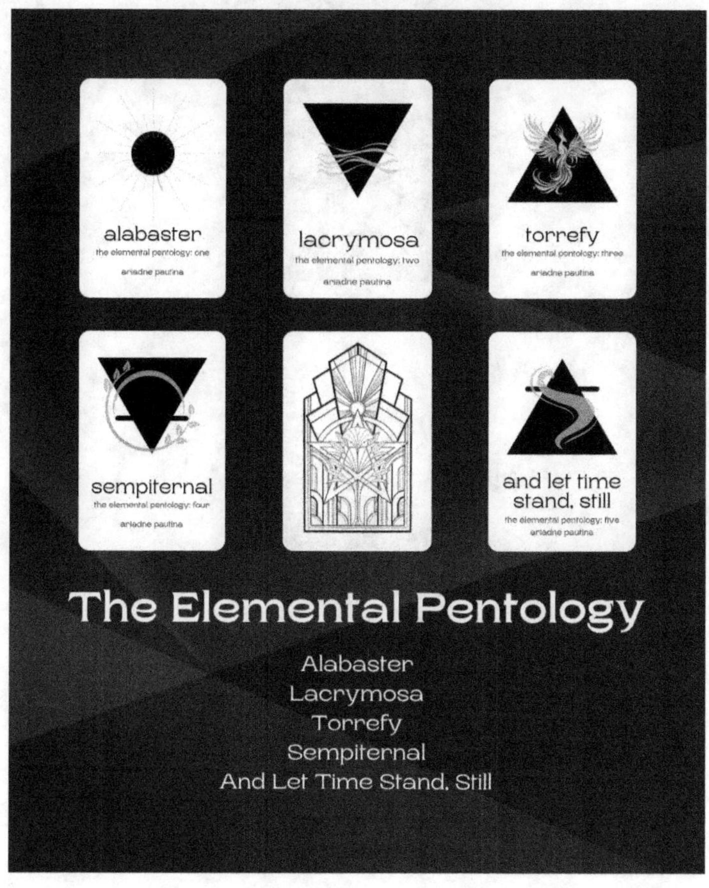


Available as e-book and paperback

**The Menagerie**

Available as e-book and paperback

**Path To The Dark Moon**

Available as e-book and paperback

SolarMoonBooks

www.ingramcontent.com/pod-product-compliance
Lightning Source LLC
LaVergne TN
LVHW020648110826
845149LV00012B/1947

* 9 7 8 1 0 6 8 7 0 5 1 4 4 *